Praise for L.A. Witt's
Out of Focus

"I devoured this book... It's BDSM, done right! It's hot m/m/m action. It's TWO Dominants. It's people with real lives!"
~ *Dear Author*

"An intense D/s threesome that wowed me... I think *Out of Focus* will really move you if you like stories about threesomes. Highly recommended."
~ *Reviews by Jessewave*

"Hang on for the wild ride of three men learning there is more to love than two. L.A. Witt conveys emotions to the reader and enables a true understanding of love and submission."
~ *Coffee Time Romance & More*

Look for these titles by L.A. Witt

Now Available:

Nine-tenths of the Law
The Distance Between Us
A.J.'s Angel
Out of Focus
The Closer You Get

Tooth and Claw
The Given and the Taken

Out of Focus

L.A. Witt

SAMHAIN
PUBLISHING

Samhain Publishing, Ltd.
11821 Mason Montgomery Road, 4B
Cincinnati, OH 45249
www.samhainpublishing.com

Out of Focus
Copyright © 2011 by L.A. Witt
Print ISBN: 978-1-60928-619-4
Digital ISBN: 978-1-60928-507-4

Editing by Linda Ingmanson
Cover by Angela Waters

First Samhain Publishing, Ltd. electronic publication: August 2011
First Samhain Publishing, Ltd. print publication: July 2012

Dedication

To Lia.
I hope it's everything you wanted it to be.
— L. A.

Chapter One

"Hey, Dante." Phoebe's voice was tinny over my Bluetooth headset. "Ryan and I are leaving now with the bride and groom. The guests are clearing out and heading your way. How close are you to the reception?"

"About three blocks." I drummed my fingers on the wheel as I waited for a red light to change. "What's your ETA?"

Phoebe said something I couldn't hear. From the background came a lower voice, that of Angel—Ryan to everyone else—my partner in both senses of the word. Distance and static muffled their brief conversation, but a moment later, Phoebe came back on the line.

"They want to do a few shots down by the marina and a quick one at a park about a mile from the reception. So, probably thirty to forty-five minutes."

"We'll be waiting." I hung up just as the light turned green and started across the intersection.

In the passenger seat beside me, my assistant, Troy, rubbed his ankle and cursed under his breath.

"Feet bothering you?" I asked.

"It's these damned shoes," he said. "They were fine when I put them on, but Jesus, they're killing me now."

"I told you not to go cheap on shoes, didn't I?" I shot him a pointed look.

He sat back, fussing with his bow tie. "If I could afford two-hundred-dollar shoes, I'd get them."

"Trust me, Troy," I said, putting on my signal to turn into the country club parking lot, "if you're going to shoot weddings, comfortable shoes are worth the money, even if it means living off ramen and tap water for a month to pay for them."

"Well, if my boss gave me a raise—"

"Don't push it." I pulled up in front of the stairs leading into the lavish club. "I will, however, be nice and not make you walk across the parking lot this time."

"*Thank* you." He grabbed his coat and camera off the backseat, then got out so I could go park the car. He limped toward the stairs, and I chuckled to myself as I drove to the other side of the mostly empty lot. One of the earliest and most painful lessons of being a wedding photographer was that comfortable shoes were worth twice their weight in platinum, and the only thing worse than dealing with a bridezilla was shooting a wedding while one's feet were on fire. Angel and I had both learned that lesson the same way Troy learned it now: the hard way.

After I'd parked, I got out and put my tuxedo coat back on. I clipped my battery pack to my belt, put the camera strap over my head, and joined Troy inside the club. We had, I guessed, about ten minutes before the guests started arriving, so we split up to get shots of the various decorations, wedding favors, and of course, the towering cake.

About the time I'd finished playing pastry paparazzi, the double doors opened. Blinding natural light spilled across the dance floor and dining area, and I squinted against the brightness. Two silhouettes entered the room, and when the doors fell shut behind them, severing the light, I blinked a few times until my eyes adjusted.

When they had adjusted and the pair of newcomers was no longer backlit, my pulse went haywire, because the bride's brothers had arrived.

The younger of the two was obviously the type who'd rather be in torn jeans and a punk band T-shirt than a tuxedo, at least if the piercings and long hair were anything to go by. He had the "fine, I'll trim it just this once" goatee and insisted on wearing his wallet on a chain even when he was dressed to the nines. In spite of his bad-boy-wannabe appearance, he was friendly and polite, just like his siblings. And he was cute, I'd give him that, but nothing to write home about.

The elder brother, though. Jesus Christ. Clean-cut, fit as hell, with a smile that had damn near made me drop my camera when he'd walked his sister down the aisle. He was older than both of his siblings by quite a few years, I assumed. Probably mid- to late-thirties, so close to my age.

They kept walking, carrying a couple of boxes to the head table, completely oblivious to the photographer checking out the way that jacket fit the elder brother's shoulders. I wondered if Angel had noticed him. Hell, of course he had. This guy was totally Angel's type, *and* he was wearing a tux. Tuxedos made hot men hotter. It was an undisputed fact, written into the laws of physics and thermodynamics.

I shook my head and went back to making sure every last ribbon and petal had been documented for posterity. About ten minutes later, my cell phone vibrated. I pulled it off my belt, and Angel's name came up on the caller ID.

Keeping my voice low, I said, "Hey."

"We're pulling off the freeway right now," he said. "This limo driver thinks he's Mario-fucking-Andretti, so we'll be there shortly."

"Can you keep up with him?"

Angel clicked his tongue. "Can I keep up with him? Please."

"Just don't kill anyone, would you?" I said with a laugh.

"No promises."

Typical Angel. Rolling my eyes, I said, "See you when you get here."

"Be there in a few."

I clipped my phone back to my belt and flagged Troy down. With him limping behind me, I went outside to wait for the limo.

By this point, most of the guests had gone outside as well, and the air was alive with chatter and dress shoes clicking on pavement. I snapped a few shots of everyone waiting for the bride and groom to arrive, all the while keeping an eye out for the limousine.

And, of course, scanning the crowd for a glimpse of *him*.

It didn't take long to find him. His mood had changed considerably, though. While he'd appeared relaxed and pleasant with his younger brother earlier, he wasn't happy now. Another guy stood close enough to imply they shared more than just platonic intimacy. And, by the expression on the gorgeous brother's face, just close enough to be irritating. They both spoke in hushed voices, punctuating their terse conversation with sharp gestures and icy glares.

Then the second guy put his hand on the brother's waist. The brother's expression darkened a little more and his posture stiffened, but he didn't pull away or brush off his companion's hand. They had that air about them of a squabbling old married couple, and the sexy one looked like he was a clenched jaw away from abandoning any hesitation to make a scene. Or kick the guy's ass.

Just our fucking luck. He was gay but taken, even if he wasn't too thrilled with his current circumstances.

It certainly wasn't my place to get involved, but this guy was supposed to be enjoying his sister's wedding, and wedding photographers had tricks up our sleeves for subtly defusing situations before they erupted into bigger problems. It was up to him if he wanted to take the bait.

Approaching like I was completely oblivious to their heated conversation, I said, "You're Jennifer's brother, right?"

He blinked in surprise. Then he cleared his throat and shifted his weight. "Uh, yeah, yeah, I am." He extended a hand. "Jordan Steele."

I shook it. "Dante James." I gestured over my shoulder. "Listen, any chance I could get you to rope a few people into keeping everyone back a little when the bride and groom get out of the car? I don't like to make a huge deal out of it, but sometimes guests get a little overexcited and crowd them."

Jordan shrugged. "Yeah, sure."

"Why don't you talk to the ushers about it?" his companion said through gritted teeth, narrowing his eyes at me.

Jordan put a hand up. "It's fine." They exchanged icy glares, and he added, "We'll finish this later, okay?"

"Fine," came the terse reply, and the companion stormed off. I couldn't help noticing the relieved breath Jordan released.

He rolled his shoulders and tilted his head sharply to one side as if to ease some tension. To me, he said, "Sorry about all of that."

"It's all right." I smiled. "Sorry I interrupted your conversation."

He gave a quiet laugh, and his eyes darted in the direction the other had gone, then back to me. "Don't worry about it." Our eyes met briefly, and I thought there was something else on the tip of his tongue, but he dropped his gaze and nodded

ut of Focus*

toward the group of guests. "So, what was it you needed me to do again?"

"What? Oh, right." I gestured in the same direction. "Just, you know, keep everyone from mobbing your sister when she gets out of the car."

"Hey, what else is a big brother for?" He looked around. "And if I can find my baby brother, he can help too."

I nodded past him. "I think he's chatting up a couple of bridesmaids."

Jordan glanced in the direction I'd indicated, then chuckled. "Why am I not surprised? I'll go grab him."

"Good, thanks. Sounds like the bride and groom should be here shortly."

We exchanged smiles. God Almighty, his smile was as sexy as it was shy. If there'd been more confidence behind it just then, I might have needed medical attention.

Then he left to pry his younger brother away from the bridesmaids.

Moments later, Angel's car turned into the parking lot. The limo was behind him, but didn't turn. Probably circling the block to give Angel time to get out of the car and get his camera pointed in the right direction. Considerate driver. There needed to be more of those in this business.

Angel took off his sunglasses as he stepped out of his car, and my pulse was once again all over the place. I couldn't count how many weddings we'd done over the years—well into the triple digits, I was sure—and my heart still fluttered whenever I saw that man in a tux. It was no wonder we always had scorching-hot sex after shooting a wedding, even when we were exhausted.

Oh, wasn't I the very picture of professionalism today? Ogling the bride's brother and my own boyfriend to the point of distraction. Such was an occupational hazard when my job required me to be around beautiful men in tuxedos, I supposed.

God, I love this job.

Jacket draped over his arm, he joined me on the curb. "Mind holding this for me?" He held his camera out.

"No problem." I took the camera so he could straighten his cummerbund and pull his jacket around his shoulders.

He shrugged a few times and fussed with the lapels, then tugged the ends of his hair out from under his collar. Once he was apparently satisfied, he put his arms out and thrust his shoulders back. "How do I look?" How did he look indeed. His dyed black hair was almost darker than his jacket, emphasizing his fair skin and blue eyes, and he was, as always, gorgeous.

I grinned and spoke just loud enough for him to hear me. "You look like it's going to be a long night tonight."

Angel winked and took the camera back. "Good. Then all is working according to plan." He searched the crowd of guests. "Where the hell did Phoebe go?"

"Over there. Probably wants to get some shots of the limo arriving."

"Ah, that's my girl." He beamed. "Creative kid. I'm getting spoiled having an assistant like that."

"We could always trade."

He snorted. "Yeah, I don't think so."

"Come on, Troy's good."

"Yeah." He nodded toward Phoebe. "But he's not *that* good."

A flash of sun on glass turned both our heads and stopped our playful banter as the limo pulled in. In seconds, we were back to the usual chaos and craziness of wedding photography. Dodging people, trying to get every shot as the bride and groom got out of the car and went inside. Then it was receiving lines and the deejay announcing every member of the wedding party and at least half a dozen guests who insisted we needed to get shots of their children in their adorable suits and dresses. Eventually, everyone was herded toward the buffet line, and things died down once again.

"How are you doing on batteries?" Angel checked his own battery pack.

I pulled my jacket back enough to look at my pack. "This one's getting low, but I still have two fully charged."

He nodded. "What about Troy?"

"He changed his out when we got here."

"What about memory?"

"Still have six untouched four-gig cards." I put a hand on his arm, resisting the urge to make a reassuring gesture into an affectionate one. "Relax. We're good."

Angel started to speak again, but Jennifer appeared and grabbed us both by the elbows. "Come on, you two. Take a break. Eat." Before either of us could protest, she shook her head. "Don't argue. I paid for all four of you to have plates, and you're damn well going to use them."

Angel laughed. "Well, I'm certainly not going to argue with that."

She showed us to a table that had been reserved for the four of us. Phoebe, Angel and I left Troy to babysit our cameras while he rested his sore feet, and we went to get food. Brides like Jennifer were the best. Saints, really. They understood the need for people—even lowly beings such as wedding photographers—to eat. As it was, we had the advantage of enough manpower for any one of us to take a break if needed, a luxury solo photographers didn't have. Still, there were plenty of clients who made sure they got their money's worth, running all of us ragged until the reception finally ended at some ungodly hour and we drove off in search of the nearest fast-food joint.

Jennifer had been sweet and gracious from the beginning, though. "Anything you guys need, just say so," she'd said when we arrived this morning. "Water, someone to help you out, anything."

How about your brother's phone number?

Right. Like that would happen.

With a plate for me and one for Troy, I returned to the table. Angel and Phoebe joined us, and we spent a little while eating and relaxing, just shooting the breeze. No discussion of the rest of the reception or where we all needed to be for the cake cutting or bouquet toss, or Angel's obsessive need to make sure everyone had enough batteries and memory cards. The two of us may have been workaholics, but even we could turn it off long enough to inhale some food.

Angel laid his napkin beside his empty plate and sat back, drink in hand. He gestured around the room with his glass and said to our assistants, "Time for you two to earn your keep. Guests, candids, people doing what people do at weddings. Off you go."

Phoebe sighed and picked up her camera. "No rest for the wicked?"

"No rest for the assistants," I said.

Troy pushed his chair back and stood gingerly. "I suppose saying I have three blisters on my left foot won't get me out of it?"

Angel set his drink down. "If anything, it'll make me send you outside to run laps around the parking lot so you never, *ever* forget to wear comfortable shoes to a wedding."

Troy looked at Phoebe. "How do you put up with him?"

She shrugged. "I wear comfortable shoes, he stays off my ass."

Troy muttered something as he put his camera strap over his head. Then the two of them wandered off to do our bidding.

Once we were alone, I slid my hand onto Angel's knee under the table. As he often did, he'd been tapping his foot against the chair leg, but he stilled beneath my hand.

"You get a look at the brother of the bride?" I asked.

He whistled, sliding his hand over mine. "Oh God, yes. I got several looks at him."

"You and me both." I shook my head. "That man is liquid distraction."

"No shit." He ran his thumb back and forth along my wrist. "Imagine how I felt, trying to focus on the bride when I had *that* standing there being all gorgeous and entirely too dressed."

"Too dressed?" I glanced in Jordan's direction, then turned back to Angel. "He's in a tux."

"I know." He shrugged. "He should be naked in our bed."

I chuckled. "Pity he's already got someone."

"Seriously?" Angel released a sharp huff of breath. "The good ones always do, don't they? It's a crime, I'm telling you." He clicked his tongue. "And his other half probably doesn't share, either."

"I don't know; I didn't ask. He was pissed enough that I interrupted their little lover's quarrel."

He blinked. "You did?"

"Well, I didn't have much choice." I turned my hand over under his. "I needed Jordan's help with something."

"Yeah," he said, lacing our fingers together, "I'll just bet you did."

"Okay, so I didn't." I shrugged. "But things were getting a little heated between them, so..."

"Eh, I'd have done the same."

That much was true. We had our subtle ways of separating people when tensions got too close to a breaking point. Situations like that, particularly with the way alcohol and grudges made frequent appearances at weddings, could too easily erupt into a screaming match or a fistfight. So, we'd long ago devised ways to casually intervene. Moderately intrusive? Yeah, probably. But if it kept a wedding from turning into a brawl—and that had been known to happen—then it was worth a little social faux pas.

The bride and groom were making the rounds, saying hello to guests while Troy's and Phoebe's cameras flashed. Normally I wouldn't leave assistants to cover anything without at least one of us shooting as well, but these two kids were damned good. They were going to be some serious competition for us when they were out on their own. Assuming Troy ever got a decent pair of shoes, anyway.

So, we didn't worry about them while they trailed the newlyweds and we took a break. Ah, it was good to be the boss.

As dinner wound down, the cake cutting and such were coming up. Almost time to get back to work. While I did a quick battery check and changed out my memory card, fabric rustled behind me.

"Enjoying yourselves?" Jennifer asked.

"Absolutely." I started to turn around. "This food is—" The words stopped in my throat. That wasn't the groom standing next to her.

She gestured at him, as if I hadn't noticed his presence. "This is my brother, Jordan."

I smiled. "Oh yes, we've met."

"We haven't." Angel stood and extended his hand. "Ryan Morgan."

Jordan shook his hand. "I—it's..." He paused, moistening his lips as a hint of pink appeared on his cheeks. "It's nice to meet you."

To her brother, Jennifer said, "I need to go pretend to like my in-laws, so I'll leave you alone with them."

He chuckled. "Okay, thanks." She picked up her skirt and headed back toward some of the other tables. After she'd gone, Jordan said, "I, uh, my sister said you guys do pretty much any kind of photography?"

I'm dreaming. I'm totally dreaming. Oh God, please tell me he wants—

I cleared my throat. "What did you have in mind?"

"I breed and train horses," he said. "And I'm campaigning a couple of stallions this year. I need a few more up-to-date photos for my website and some ads." He raised his eyebrows. "Is that something you guys would be interested in doing?"

"Well, we're always happy to help someone flaunt a stud," Angel deadpanned.

Jordan blushed even more, dropping his gaze as he muffled a cough of laughter. "Right. Well. I haven't had great luck with my last couple of photographers, so I'm very much in the market for someone new." He paused, the color in his cheeks deepening slightly. "A new photographer, I mean."

"Can you handle two?" Angel asked.

If the poor man's cheeks got any redder...

"I'm sure we can help." I shot Angel a glare, and he widened his eyes as if to say "What?" I rolled mine and looked at Jordan again. "We haven't done any equestrian work in a few years, but show us some examples of what you have in mind and we should be able to give you what you want."

A shy smile played at his lips. "Good. Then—"

His teeth snapped together as his significant other materialized and put a hand on his shoulder. Jordan's hackles went up, his eyes narrowed, and judging by the way his cheek rippled, he must have been tightly clenching his jaw. The two men exchanged the coldest glare I'd seen at a wedding since the last time we put divorced parents into one picture, and the hand on his shoulder lifted away.

Then Jordan shook himself back to life and made a sharp gesture his companion. "Sorry, I'm being rude. This is Eli. My—"

"Just Eli is fine." He didn't offer a handshake or any other greeting, and neither of us made any attempt to do so either. Awkward silence descended, and I had a feeling Jordan was once again seconds away from lashing out at his...just Eli.

"Anyway, you were saying?" I asked Jordan. "About your photos?"

"Right." Jordan cleared his throat. "Anyway, I'd like to sit down and discuss what I'm pricing, scheduling, all of that."

"When would be a good time?" I asked. "If you'd like, you can come by the studio, and we'll sort out the specifics."

He nodded. "I can do that. During the week would be best. My weekends are usually shot."

Angel pointed at his camera. "So are ours."

Jordan laughed. "Yeah, I guess they would be."

"Would Monday be good for you?" I turned to Angel. "We're there all day this Monday, aren't we?"

He nodded. "All in-studio shoots that day. Last one's at four thirty, and we're usually there until six or seven."

"Why don't I swing in around five, then?" Jordan asked.

"Five works," I said.

Angel pulled out his wallet and took out a card. "That's the address. Just give us a call if anything changes." Jordan took the card, but jumped like Angel had shocked him. Knowing Angel, he'd made sure their fingers brushed, and Jordan's blood pressure was probably all over the place now.

Jordan recovered quickly though, sliding the card in his back pocket as he said, "Will do."

Eli shifted beside him. "Good, now why don't we go grab a couple of drinks?"

"Okay, okay." Jordan exhaled and added a muttered, "Like you need another fucking drink."

"Hmm?" Eli asked.

"Nothing." Jordan looked at us. "I'll see you guys on Monday. Thanks."

"Not a problem," I said. "See you then."

We watched the happy couple wander toward the bar with a good arm's length of frosty distance between them.

"You know," Angel said, "I take back what I said earlier about it being a crime that a man like that is taken."

"Oh?"

"Yeah." He turned back toward the table and picked up his glass. "It's a crime a man like that is taken by a douche bag like *that*."

Chapter Two

Dante and Ryan's studio was a forty-five minute drive from my farm. I couldn't decide if the constant barrage of cell phone calls on the way made the time fly by or slow right down. Either way, between the traffic and the calls, my blood pressure was through the roof when I pulled into the parking lot.

Laura, my barn manager, called twice about farrier and vet appointments. The other trainer, Noreen, needed to borrow my saddle because a new client's horse was too high in the withers for hers, oh and by the way, Bravado kicked two more boards off the fence in his paddock.

Such was life in this business, of course.

I parked in front of the studio, and just when I'd kicked off the engine, my phone rang again. I closed my eyes and groaned. Not because it was yet another fucking call, but because that specific ringtone always made my teeth grind.

Sighing, I picked up the phone and clicked it on so the call would go to my headset.

"Hey, sexy." Eli actually sounded like he was in a good mood. That was promising enough for me to ignore his irritating attempt to be flirty.

"What's up?" I asked.

"Just wanted to let you know the interview went well. She seemed pretty impressed, and she'll be calling tomorrow if they want to have me back for a second interview."

Oh, thank God. "That's great. Well, good luck."

"The pay's better than I thought too."

Please get this job. "How is it compared to what you were getting before?"

"Almost four dollars an hour more."

"Holy shit. That's awesome." *Please get this job. Please get this job. Please get this job.*

"I know, it's great." He paused. "So, they're—"

"Listen, I gotta go." I took the key out of the ignition and unbuckled my seat belt. "We can talk about it more when I get home."

"What time will you be home?"

I rolled my eyes, even though he couldn't see me. "I don't know for sure. I told you, I'm in town to meet with those photographers we met at Jenny's wedding."

"Oh, right," he muttered. "Them. Well, I'll see you when you get home, then. But before you go, I—"

"Eli, my battery's dying." Fidgeting in the driver's seat, I glanced at the studio doors. "I have to go."

"Don't you ever charge that thing?"

"Yes, but I use it almost constantly. I'll see you when I get home."

"See you in a few."

After we'd hung up—without a forced "I love you" this time, thank God—I swore under my breath. I changed my phone to vibrate, pretending not to notice the battery indicator, which showed three-quarters full. I could have sworn there was a time when we actually liked talking to each other. Oh well, those days were long gone, and the only thing I wanted to hear from him now was, "I've got a job, I've got an apartment, and I'll be out of your house by the end of the month." That day just couldn't get here fast enough.

I got out of the car, shoved the phone and keys into my pocket, and went into the studio.

The lobby was small, but they'd certainly used the space well. Toward the back, two desks flanked another desk where a brunette receptionist currently spoke on the phone. The front half of the lobby had a few chairs and a coffee table on which someone had fanned several leather-bound portfolios.

Framed portraits of everyone from brides to athletes lined the left and back walls. Along the right, landscapes, abstract images and various print ads that prominently featured sharp, colorful photos of different products.

The brunette receptionist hung up the phone. "Sorry about that. Can I help you?"

"Yeah, I had an appointment with Dante and Ryan." I paused. "Name's Jordan Steele."

She checked something on the spiral-bound book on her desk, then nodded. "I'll let them know you're here. They're still in their last shoot for the day."

"No rush." I shrugged. "I'm early."

Pushing her chair back, she smiled. "I'll be right back. Have a seat."

I sat in one of the chairs while she disappeared through a side door. While she was gone, I kept looking around the room, trying not to drum my fingers on the armrest. It wasn't that I was nervous about consulting with photographers. I'd done this a million times, and it didn't make me bat an eye.

It was *them*.

Ever since my sister's wedding, I hadn't been able to stop thinking about them. Either of them. It had been bad enough trying to maintain some semblance of dignity around Ryan all morning long while he'd photographed my family and the wedding party. When the ceremony started, I'd just about gotten the hang of breathing with him around, but I hadn't expected Dante. I'd damn near tripped over my own feet when I walked Jenny down the aisle; he'd momentarily lowered his camera right when I'd glanced in his direction, and...damn. Just...*damn*.

They were sexy as hell, each in his own way. Similar in some respects, polar opposite in others. Both had sharp, angular features, though Dante's were a little smoother. Both had blue eyes. Dante's were a more vivid blue, but Ryan's were intense, the kind that could see right through someone. Dante's platinum blond hair was short and meticulously spiked. Ryan's was ink black, though I couldn't decide if it was natural or dyed, and dipped just past his collar. I curled my fingers around the end of the armrest, fantasizing for the millionth time about running my fingers through his hair.

The receptionist came back in, startling me back into the present. "They probably won't be more than fifteen minutes."

"I can wait."

She smiled and took her seat behind her desk again. Her fingers clattered across the keyboard, and my thoughts drifted back to the two men in the other room.

It didn't help that Jenny had told me she was almost certain they were not only gay but together. Didn't it just figure the sexiest two men I'd encountered in a long time were both taken? By each other? Bastards.

To pacify my mind and give myself something else to think about, I leaned forward and looked at the portfolios on the table. Each was a different color and labeled according to content. *Bridal. Landscape. Commercial. Senior Portrait.*

I picked up the one marked *Landscape.* Flipping through it, I could definitely see how these guys made their living with their cameras. Besides being visually stunning, there were several notations that this or that photo had won prestigious-sounding awards. A few images were marked *National Geographic.*

Ryan and Dante were also obviously quite well traveled. I couldn't identify all the exotic monuments, landforms and cities, but I recognized shots of Easter Island, St. Basil's Cathedral, and in the background of a photo of a little boy hand-feeding a camel, the pyramids of Giza.

I wonder if they went to all those places together.

I shivered. I couldn't imagine them ever leaving their hotel rooms if they did.

The side door opened, and my head snapped up just in time to—

Madre de Dios. Even in jeans and a grey sweatshirt, trading Saturday's formality for Monday's laidback and comfortable, Ryan was gorgeous.

He glanced at me as he went back to one of the two desks behind the receptionist. "Hey, Jordan. Sorry we're running behind here."

"Fine by me."

"We should be wrapping this up soon. I just need..." He furrowed his brow, rifling through papers and shuffling folders around. "How the hell does he... Where is... Christ, how does he find anything?" He gestured sharply at the desk. "He calls this organized chaos. I see the chaos, but I'm not finding the organized. Where the—" He released an exasperated sigh and craned his neck toward the door through which he'd come. "Dante, I don't see it."

"It's right by the monitor," came the reply.

"So are three dozen file folders and a bunch of other crap."

Footsteps approached, and a second later, Dante appeared, cranking my heart rate up another notch or twelve. Like Ryan, Dante had traded formal for casual. Khakis and a polo, in his case, and it was no surprise he looked damned good in them.

"Oh, hey, Jordan." He shot me a quick smile, then reached for something on the desk. When he held it up—a memory card, I guessed—Ryan scowled and plucked it from between Dante's fingers. Dante laughed and disappeared back into the other room.

Ryan glanced at his watch and said to the receptionist, "You're clocking out soon, aren't you?"

"Few more minutes," she said. "I'm just about through with those bids you asked for." She gestured at a stack of file folders. "Where do you want them when I'm done?"

"Just leave them on my desk. I want to go over them before I take off tonight."

"Will do."

"Thanks, Kendra." With that, Ryan disappeared into the back.

I exhaled. Being that attractive around someone who was this sexually frustrated had to be in the Geneva Convention somewhere. It had to be.

To distract myself again, I mentally ran through my list of things to do when I got home. Bring in the horses that were still turned out. Make sure every horse who needed to be was blanketed for the night. If there was still daylight, see how badly Bravado had damaged the fence again. Find the kimberwicke bit for Noreen before tomorrow's lessons. Talk to Eli.

Eli.

Fuck.

Now that was a mental bucket of cold water. I sighed, staring up at the ceiling. There was nothing quite so miserable as living with an ex-boyfriend, particularly one who didn't like the "ex" part of the equation. I rubbed my eyes. I just had to deal with it until he got a job. And an apartment. Both of which assumed he could find an employer and landlord who were willing to overlook his shitty credit and a résumé that may as well have listed "professional freeloader" as his job for the last three years.

I suppressed a groan.

Before I could spend too much time wallowing in fantasies of evicting Eli into a cardboard box, the door opened again. Dante came back into the room, and all the thoughts my irritating ex had scrubbed from my brain came flooding right back.

I was honestly starting to wonder if Ryan and Dante were both constitutionally incapable of looking like hell. They probably looked perfect from the moment they got out of the bed in the morning, when they'd be disheveled and—

Yeah, don't need to follow that particular train of thought just now.

Kendra put a stack of file folders on one of the two desks behind her own. Mercifully unaware of my impure thoughts about her bosses, she and Dante exchanged a few words, mostly about appointments and such for the following day. Then she picked up her jacket off her chair.

"I'm out of here," she said. "You boys behave yourselves."

Dante clicked his tongue and sighed. "Do we have to?"

Don't behave on account of me, I wanted to say.

"Yes, you do." She eyed Dante. "And would you please ask His Highness to call Mr. Vincent over at TechTron? I swear, if the man calls me one more time, I'm going to reach through the phone and choke him."

"Not in front of potential clients," Dante said in a stage whisper. He glanced at me and winked.

Kendra shot me a semi-apologetic look. To her boss, she said, "Anyway, please have Ryan call him."

"Will do. Now get out of here."

"Getting out of here." She pulled her purse out of a desk drawer and, with a sarcastic good-bye to her employers and a polite one to me, left.

"Okay, now we can get started." Dante gestured at a chair in front of Kendra's desk. "Have a seat, and I'll get all the paperwork." While I moved from the waiting area to the chair he'd indicated, he went to the third desk, the one across from the more cluttered one that had driven Ryan crazy earlier. "Now, where did..." He furrowed his brow, then called into the other room, "Angel, what did you do with the releases and quote for Jordan?"

Angel? I thought.

From the other room, Ryan said, "Bottom left drawer of my desk, under 'S', where any logical person would file it."

Dante rolled his eyes. I snickered.

He opened the drawer and flipped through a few files before pulling a folder free. He started to return to where I sat, but paused, eyeing the desk for a second. Glancing through the open door, he slid the top few folders off, knocking the small pile into a messy fan. Then he pulled a couple of pens out of a cup beside the computer and scattered them across the blotter.

I watched him, puzzled, but said nothing. He just grinned and came to Kendra's desk, dropping into her chair and laying the contents of the file folder out between us.

"Okay," he said. "Here are a couple of different quotes, depending on how much time you want for the shoot, if it'll be one or both of us, how many images you want to use for your website or ads, and if you'll be ordering prints." He slid a few more sheets across the desk. "These are model, property and hold harmless releases."

I nodded. "Yeah, familiar with those."

"Good." He tucked the forms back into the folder. "One less thing to bore you with."

"No need to worry about that." Wasn't that the truth. This may have been dull, monotonous business conversation, but he could have been reading the phone book aloud and his smooth voice would have kept me enraptured.

About that time, Ryan came back into the lobby, this time with a pair of female models in tow.

The redhead batted her eyes. "Sorry we kept you guys so long."

Ryan chuckled. "Don't worry about it. We'll give you a call sometime next week when your pictures are ready."

"Awesome. Thanks." The blonde smiled, her expression no less flirty than the other. The girls headed out, and as they did, I watched Ryan and Dante, curious to see if they'd sneak a look at either girl before they were gone.

Not even a glance.

Probably because they were professionals. They'd just finished a damned photo shoot. If they'd wanted to grab an eyeful, they'd had plenty of chances without leering at the girls on their way out the door.

Still, Ryan and Dante were guys. I was a guy. If I caught sight of someone attractive, it wasn't below me to indulge in at least a glimpse. Sort of like I'd done at every opportunity since I'd walked into this studio. Had the models been a pair of good-looking guys, I'd have thrown an over-the-shoulder glance their way before they were gone.

These two? Nothing.

Because they're professionals, idiot, I reminded myself.

While Dante and I continued going over some quotes, Ryan was constantly on the move. To the other room. Into the lobby. At the file cabinet. Back into the other room. Everywhere he went, he walked fast, the kind of quick, deliberate walk of someone who didn't like wasting time getting from point A to point B, even if it was only a few feet away. This much energy at the end of the day? Jesus, the man must have had stock in Red Bull. Just watching him made me horn—tired. Watching him made me *tired*.

At one point, he stopped in his tracks, doing a double take at the cleaner of the two desks behind Dante. Then he glared at Dante's back before rolling his eyes and shaking his head. He put the pens Dante had dropped on the blotter back into their holder, then restacked the folders neatly before he slid them into a drawer. On his way past us, he hit Dante's chair with his hip, just hard enough to make Dante stumble over his words.

They swapped playful glares; then Dante turned his attention back to me. "You'll have to excuse us. We're not terribly mature after hours."

"After hours?" Ryan laughed. "How is that different from any other time?"

"Okay, but I wasn't going to just throw that out there, you know?" Dante gave an exasperated sigh. "I like to at least try to make us look professional."

"You know I believe in truth in advertising," Ryan said.

I put my hands up. "Hey, don't worry about being professional on my account."

"See, Dante?" Ryan bumped his chair again. "Lighten up."

I started to say something, but my phone picked that precise moment to vibrate in my pocket. "Fuck, what now?" I grumbled. When I pulled it out, Laura's name flashed up on the caller ID. At least it wasn't Eli, but it probably was important. "Speaking of being professional," I said. "Do you mind if I take this?"

Dante shook his head. "Not at all."

I offered an apologetic smile, then answered. "What's up?"

"Hey, Jordan," Laura said. "Listen, I left you a note in the barn, but the boards in Bravado's paddock—"

"He knocked them down again, I know," I said. "Noreen called me about it earlier."

"Oh, okay. I reattached the middle board, but the bottom one is in three pieces."

"Guess I'm making a run to the lumberyard tomorrow, then," I said. "Anyway, just put him in his stall for the night so he doesn't impale himself on it or knock anything else down."

Dante raised an eyebrow, and I tried not to laugh. Sometimes I forgot how strange things like this sounded to people who weren't around horses all day long.

To Laura, I said, "I'm right in the middle of meeting with someone, though, so I should let you go."

"Oh, I'm sorry, I'd forgotten all about that. I'll see you tomorrow."

"See you tomorrow." I hung up and slid my phone back into my pocket. "Sorry."

Dante made a dismissive gesture. "Must have been important if you were concerned about someone getting impaled."

I laughed. "Not really. One of my stallions seems to think it's his sworn duty to break through every board in every fence on my property."

"Oh, really?"

"Yeah, if he hasn't kicked them down, he's put hoof prints in them." I made an exasperated gesture. "And the other stud has decided he's part termite and keeps gnawing on any piece of wood he can reach. They're going to bankrupt me, the fuckers."

"I never thought horses were terribly destructive creatures."

Ryan snorted as he walked past with his nose in a file folder. "Only because you haven't spent much time around them."

"You have?" I asked.

"Not for many, many years." He paused in the doorway. "But I had horses when I was a kid. 4-H, that sort of thing. Enough that I've replaced more than my fair share of boards, posts and stall doors."

I sighed. "Story of my life."

He chuckled, then went back into the other room again, leaving me alone with Dante.

"Anyway," I said, "hopefully that's it for my phone interrupting me. Just the joys of owning a business, I guess."

Smiling, he said, "I know the feeling, believe me."

"You two both own it, though, don't you?"

He nodded. "Full partners."

"So to speak," Ryan chimed in from the other room.

"Shut up." Dante laughed. He cleared his throat. "Anyway, yeah, we're business partners."

"Must be nice." I sat back, clasping my hands together on top of my belt buckle. "Believe me, there are days I really, really wish I could hand the proverbial reins off to someone else and let them deal with it for a while."

"Oh, I can imagine." Dante thumbed his chin, an unspoken thought furrowing his brow. After a moment, he shook his head and shuffled through the papers between us. "So, with all of that out of the way, let's talk about how we're going to shoot your horses."

"Appropriate way to put it," I said.

We went over some ideas for shots. I explained that I needed some headshots of both stallions, plus a few of them under saddle.

"For now, it'll just be the two stallions," I said. "But I'll probably call you back for more in the spring when this year's crop of foals are born."

"Baby horses?" Dante glanced over his shoulder, then dropped his voice to a conspiratorial whisper. "Don't say that too loudly around Ryan."

"Why not?"

"Watch this." Craning his neck, he called out, "Hey, Angel, would he have to twist your arm to do a shoot with a bunch of baby horses?"

"Baby horses?" Ryan appeared in the doorway, eyes lit up. "Really?"

"Well, not for a while yet." Dante looked at me. "Right?"

I nodded. "First foals of the season won't be for a couple of months."

"If you need pictures of them, *please* call us," Ryan said just before disappearing again.

Watching him go, Dante shook his head. To me, he said, "Told you."

"You're not into animals?" I asked.

"Oh, I love animals, but he's definitely more of a critter person than I am. He loves horses, and he'll fawn over *anything* that's cute and fluffy."

"Oh, shut up," Ryan said, reappearing with a stack of papers in his hand.

"Come on, it's true." Dante grinned up at Ryan as he walked by. "I can't let you anywhere near a puppy."

"Yeah." Ryan playfully smacked Dante's shoulder with the papers he carried. "But only because you'd be afraid of its mother."

"Hey, now."

I cocked my head. "You're afraid of dogs?"

Dante's cheeks colored. "I'm a little intimidated by big dogs."

"He's afraid of dogs."

"Shut up." Dante glared at Angel, who shot him the least convincing look of innocence I'd ever seen.

I tried not to laugh. "Good to know. I'll make sure mine's penned up when you come to the farm."

"It's okay," Dante said. "Don't worry about it."

"Trust me, it's not a big deal." I shrugged. "He's not aggressive, but if you're intimidated by big dogs, well... I'll just pen him up."

Dante smiled. "Works for me." He flipped open the receptionist's appointment book. "So, when do you want to do this shoot?"

I leaned forward, and he turned the book so I didn't have to read upside down.

"What about Wednesday?" Dante said.

"I can do Wednesday morning," I said. "That afternoon is shot, but the rest of this week and next week are flexible."

Dante turned around. "Angel, I need your input on this too. Do you have anything on your schedule that isn't in the book yet?"

Ryan came over. He put one hand on the desk beside Dante's arm, leaning on it while he rested his other hand on the back of Dante's chair. "Hmm, I think I've got something tentative on Wednesday. And didn't you have a reschedule for that day?"

"Oh, shit, that's right." Dante pursed his lips. "Thursday?"

Absently, probably not nearly as aware of it as I was, Ryan moved his hand from the back of the chair to Dante's shoulder.

"I've got two commercial clients booked that morning," he said, completely oblivious that I was watching his thumb make slow up-down arcs just above Dante's collar. "Taking traffic into consideration, I should be back here by one, and..." He paused. "How far did you say it is from here to your place?"

I jumped, forcing myself to focus on the calendar and not that down-up-down caress. I cleared my throat. "Forty-five minutes to an hour."

Ryan nodded. "Maybe we could aim for two thirty, then? That'll give us enough time, don't you think?"

"That works." Dante raised his eyebrows at me. "Work for you?"

"Yeah, that'll be fine."

"We'll mark it down, then."

Dante grabbed a pen out of the holder. He uncapped it, but Ryan put his hand over the blank on the calendar. He pulled another pen out of the holder and held it out to Dante.

"Right. Blue for appointments." Dante rolled his eyes and took the pen. "How could I forget?" As he wrote my name and the time on the calendar, I peered at the other blanks. Sure enough, there was a definite color scheme: appointments in blue, consults in red, employee days off in black.

With my appointment on the calendar—in blue, of course—Dante closed the book and extended his hand.

"Guess we'll see you on Thursday."

I shook his hand. "Looking forward to it." When I shook Ryan's hand, I tried to tell myself the warmth in his palm was his own body heat, not Dante's, but at least one part of my mind didn't want to hear it.

Once politeness, formalities and a little small talk were taken care of, I headed for the door. I surreptitiously watched their reflections in the window.

Dante looked.

So did Ryan.

I kept walking, and my heart kept thundering.

Outside, I got in my car. I turned on the engine, but before I shifted into reverse, I paused for a minute to collect my thoughts. Occasional meetings like this were part of my job, and I had never left one with blood pounding in my ears and my body damn near twitching from tension that needed to be relieved, like, *now*.

I sighed and rubbed my eyes. Yeah, they'd looked.

Damn the luck. Ryan and Dante were gorgeous, gay and together.

And I got to go home to Eli.

Fuck my life.

Chapter Three

As we pulled our camera gear out of the trunk of my car at Jordan's farm, Dante's spine stiffened. I was about to ask what was wrong, but then I heard, between deep, loud barks, gravel scattering under what must have been huge paws.

I turned, and a German shepherd loped toward us, kicking up dust and rocks. Oh, fuck. Dante and a large dog. Always a good combination. I stepped around him, figuring the dog wasn't aggressive if it was loose like this, even if there *had* been a *Beware of Dog* sign on the gate.

Then, a sharp voice came from behind us: "Sasha, *no.*"

The dog skidded to a halt, spraying gravel as it did.

I looked the other direction. Jordan was on his way up the path from the barn.

He snapped his fingers. "Sasha, come." More rocks flew as the dog scrambled to his master's side. Beside me, Dante exhaled. I put my hand on the small of his back.

Jordan scratched the dog's ears and murmured, "Good boy." To us, he said, "Sorry about that. I thought Eli put him in his kennel."

"Don't worry about it," Dante said. "I'm guessing he's...friendly?"

"Oh God, yes." Jordan looked down at the shepherd. "You'd sooner lick someone to death than bite them, wouldn't you?" The dog just panted and wagged his tail, kicking up more dust. To Dante, Jordan said, "I can put him up if you'd be more comfortable, though."

Dante shook his head. "It's okay."

"You sure?"

"Yeah, it's fine."

"Okay, well, let's go shoot some horses, then." Jordan grinned.

"Sounds like fun," I said, laughing in spite of what Jordan's expression did to my pulse.

"I bathed both of them earlier," he said, "so they'll still be clean if they know what's good for them."

"Bathed?" Dante asked, pulling his camera bag onto his shoulders. "How the hell do you bathe a horse?"

"Okay, maybe showering would be a more apt description." Jordan chuckled. "Either way, they're clean."

I closed the trunk, and we followed Jordan toward the barn. On the way down the path, I took in a long, deep breath through my nose. Just the smell of the farm took me back. Cedar bedding, alfalfa, even that familiar musty scent of dust and cobwebs. All it needed was some beauty bark to send my mind right back to my horse-show days, and I hadn't realized how much I'd missed this environment until now.

A calico cat trotted past us, eyeing the dog the same way Dante had. I stopped and knelt, holding out my hand, and the cat approached me cautiously. She sniffed my outstretched fingers, then must have decided I wasn't a threat, because she rubbed her head on the back of my hand. She couldn't have been an exclusively outdoor cat; she was much too glossy to live in the rafters, too well fed to subsist on mice.

"You have the best of both worlds, don't you?" I scratched her back, and she started purring up a storm. "Spoiled, much?"

"Hey, Dr. Doolittle." Dante's voice came from farther down the barn aisle. "We're here for the other critters. You can pet the kitty later."

"Yeah, yeah, shut up." I scratched the cat's back once more, then got up and kept walking.

About the time I'd caught up, Jordan stepped out of a stall leading one of the horses. I assumed it was a horse, anyway. From about the knees down, it was obviously equine, but aside from that, its eyes and its muzzle and the rest of its body were covered in a dusty red blanket and matching Spandex hood.

"This," Jordan said, dropping the lead rope to the cement, "is Arturo." He didn't bother tying the horse, just left the lead rope on the ground and went about undoing the straps on the blanket. He pulled off the blanket, and the dangling buckles banged and clanged as he draped it over the stall door. Then he peeled off the hood, and the horse shook himself hard enough his hooves slid on the cement.

And, wow, what a gorgeous animal. Solid bay, not a fleck of white to be seen. He was probably a good sixteen hands, maybe a little more, and quite a bit lankier than the quarter horses I'd grown up on.

I held out my hand, and the stallion sniffed it, feeling around with his upper lip in case I had any treats. "What breed?"

"Morgan." Jordan ran a soft brush over the horse's back, then patted his neck.

"Really? I didn't think they got this big."

"Some do. You should have seen his sire." Jordan smoothed a few wayward strands in Arturo's mane. "I swear to God the fucker was pushing seventeen hands."

"Damn." I stroked Arturo's face, gently nudging him away when he tried to chew my belt. "My sister had one years ago that was barely a pony."

"Yeah, that's not unusual."

I glanced at Dante. His eyebrows were up, an invisible question mark dangling over his head. We both laughed, and he shook his head. I was just as clueless whenever he talked to classic-car owners, so we were pretty much even.

"A Morgan, huh?" he said. "Shouldn't be hard for you to remember that."

I sniffed indignantly. "Like I'd forget a horse's breed even if it wasn't also my name."

"True," Dante said. "God forbid you forget such an important detail."

I glared at him but couldn't keep a straight face any more than he could.

Jordan picked up the lead rope again. "Ready?" he asked us.

"Whenever you are," Dante said.

Jordan opened his mouth as if to speak, but whatever it was he'd thought to say, he let it go. He gestured for us to follow him and led the horse toward one end of the aisle. The otherwise quiet barn came alive with the rhythmic clunk of hooves and the clatter of the dog's claws on the cement in between our footsteps.

Outside, gravel crunched beneath everyone's feet as Jordan led us past the covered arena to a larger, open-air one on the other side. Good, the lighting would be better out here. It was an overcast day, which was perfect, and we could rely on soft, diffused natural light instead of direct sun or flashes.

In the outdoor arena, Jordan stopped. Pointing toward the gate, he said to his dog, "Sasha, lay down." Immediately, the shepherd went to the gate, circled a few times and flopped down in the dirt. Jordan praised him, then nodded at the horse. "I just want to get some headshots and standing shots of this one."

"Nothing under saddle or in action?" I asked.

"Not this time." Jordan adjusted the stallion's halter. "He was limping a bit yesterday and this morning, so I don't want to push him."

"Is he okay?" I asked.

"He's fine." Jordan stroked Arturo's face. "Just an old injury that comes back to bite him once in a while, so I take it easy with him when it flares up."

"Well, whatever you want to do is fine with us," Dante said.

I took off my lens cap. "We're ready when you are."

Jordan pulled a red and white peppermint candy out of his pocket and crinkled the wrapper. Arturo's ears immediately pricked up. Jordan held it just out of the horse's reach, encouraging him to stretch his neck out a little. After a few shots like that, he patted the horse's neck, then fed him the peppermint.

"Good boy," he murmured as the horse crunched contentedly on the candy.

Photographing a horse was usually like photographing a kid or a puppy. There was about a ten-minute window before boredom set in and attention wandered. At that point, it became like pulling teeth to get the subject to look at the camera, let alone with any interest.

Not Arturo. He was a ham for the camera. Even Dante couldn't help laughing at the way Arturo showed off. I swore the stallion stopped just short of batting his eyes at us. As long as the cameras kept snapping and Jordan kept praising, the horse kept right on posing until Jordan decided it was enough.

"Okay, camera whore." Jordan patted Arturo's shoulder. "That's plenty for one day." To us, he said, "I'll go put him away and get the other. Do you guys just want to wait out here?"

"Can do," Dante said.

Jordan led the horse out of the arena with Sasha hot on his heels.

As soon as they were out of earshot, Dante turned to me. "God *damn* it, that man is hot."

"I know. Fuck." I stared at Jordan. Ever since the wedding, he hadn't been far from my mind or from conversations with Dante. Jordan intrigued both of us, what could I say? And it was probably criminal for me to think it, but watching him now, I swore his ass looked even better in dusty jeans than it had in tux pants. It would probably look even better with nothing on except my hands on his hips. Or Dante's hands on—

I shook my head and coughed behind my hand. "Anyway," I said, turning to Dante, who was clicking through some of his pictures. "How are your shots coming out?"

"So far, so good." He glanced up from the preview screen on his camera and gave me a devilish grin. "I must confess, not all of my frames have a horse in them."

I clicked my tongue. "Why am I not surprised?"

"Admit it, you did the same thing."

"Did I?"

"Oh, come on, I know you." He inclined his head. "Don't tell me you didn't."

I snorted. "Of course I did. Just like I grabbed an excessive number of candids of him at the wedding." I paused. "You know, since he was an important part of the wedding party. And...stuff."

Dante laughed. "That's what I figured."

Minutes later, hooves crunched on gravel behind us. I looked toward the barn. The horse plodding beside Jordan was a bit smaller in stature than Arturo had been, and so dark he was almost black. The lead rope was draped over his withers, and Jordan didn't even bother holding it. He focused on the horse, probably saying something to him, and I smiled to myself. At least I wasn't the only one who carried on conversations with animals.

They came into the arena, and when he stopped, the horse did too. No words, no tug at the lead rope, not even a gesture. One halted, and so did the other.

Jordan tousled the horse's forelock. "This is Bravado. You'd never guess he's Arturo's half-brother, but..."

I let Bravado sniff my hand. "Little brother, apparently."

"Three years older, if you can believe it. Just smaller." He patted the horse's shoulder. "Come on, kiddo, let's see what you've got."

Jordan set him up in the same poses he'd put Arturo through. Bravado wasn't quite as enamored of the camera as his brother, but he patiently did as he was told. He put his ears up when Jordan crinkled candy wrappers, turned his head, stretched his neck, whatever his trainer asked him to do.

"I want to get a few of this guy in action," Jordan said. "Are you guys comfortable with him being loose in here?"

I looked at Dante, eyebrows raised. He shrugged, but I didn't miss the slight bob of his Adam's apple. I tilted my head in a silent *are you sure?* He nodded.

"Yeah," I said to Jordan. "It's fine."

He unclipped Bravado's lead rope and gently tapped it against the horse's shoulder. "Go on, go play."

It didn't take much to convince him. The stallion jogged away. Once he was near the middle of the arena, he bucked a few times before he took off to the other end. There, he skidded to a halt, narrowly avoiding crashing into the fence, then turned around, and came back toward us. I knelt in the dirt to get a better angle, and snapped away as Bravado ran and played. Dante stayed back a little; we both had telephotos, so he could afford to keep a comfortable distance.

In the back of my mind, I couldn't help thinking about the way Jordan interacted with his horses. I was admittedly a little surprised to see how gentle, even affectionate, he was with them. I'd seen a lot of professionals who were cold and indifferent, sometimes even cruel, but not Jordan. He connected with them.

As if he was lacking in ways to make me weak in the knees.

After we'd gotten plenty of shots of Bravado in action, Jordan whistled. The horse spun and jogged across the arena to his master. Jordan praised him and gave him a mint. While

Bravado crunched away on the candy, Jordan clipped the lead rope back on the halter.

"Would you guys mind doing a few shots of him going over some jumps?" He gestured at three jumps set up along the far side of the arena.

"Not at all," I said. "You're writing the check, so whatever you want." Our eyes met. *Yes, Jordan. Whatever you want.*

He cleared his throat, throwing the lead rope over Bravado's neck. "He's probably warmed up enough, but let me take him around the arena a few times to make sure."

"Aren't you forgetting something?" Dante asked.

Jordan looked over his shoulder and raised his eyebrows.

Dante nodded at the horse. "A saddle?"

"Pfft. Who needs a saddle?" With that, Jordan effortlessly hoisted himself onto the horse's back. "I prefer to ride bareback." Picking up the lead rope, he grinned and gave Dante a wink. "Well, with horses, anyway."

I almost dropped my camera. Dante coughed.

Before either of us could sputter through a comeback, Jordan and the horse were gone, cantering to the opposite end of the arena.

"Did he just..." Dante gestured at Jordan. "Did he just say that?"

I nodded. "He so did."

"And here I was worried about overstepping a bound and offending him."

"Oh, I don't think we're going to offend him." I moistened my lips. "That was an invitation if ever I heard one."

"Easy, Angel," Dante said in a playfully scolding tone. "Don't scare the guy."

"Hey, if he can make comments like that, so can I."

He eyed me. "Yeah, except you're usually a bit more brazen than that."

"So?" I shrugged. "Make it brazen enough, and maybe he'll—"

"*Angel.*" He shot me a pointed look. "He was probably just kidding around. And need I remind you, he had that unsightly growth at the wedding?"

"Damn, that's right." I sighed. "Ah, well. A boy can dream."

I knelt to get a better angle and kept shooting, resting my elbow on my knee for stability as I followed horse and rider with my camera.

Bravado eased into a canter. After a couple of small circles, Jordan aimed him toward the jumps. The horse sailed over them, landing perfectly. No saddle, no bridle, and if Jordan was off-balance at any time, I sure as hell didn't see it.

Trying in vain to kneel comfortably, a task getting progressively more difficult every time Jordan fucking *breathed*, I said, "You thinking what I'm thinking?"

"If you're thinking along the lines of how strong his legs must be, then yes."

"Ooh, yeah." I paused to take a shot, waiting until the horse was in midair over a jump. "Would you be mad if I said I really, *really* want to fuck him?"

Dante's camera clicked. "As long as you're referring to Jordan, not the horse."

"Fuck you. So I suppose it would be considered"—I paused to concentrate on another shot—"unprofessional to suggest—"

"Yes, it would be."

I glanced up at him, eyebrow raised. "You don't even know what I was going to say."

"I know you."

"Admit it," I said, looking through my viewfinder again. "It would be hot."

"Never said it wouldn't be." *Click. Click. Click.* "But it *would* be unprofessional."

"Damn it."

He laughed, and we kept shooting.

Jordan brought Bravado down to a walk and guided him back in our direction. He looked at us, then past us, and furrowed his brow.

I glanced over my shoulder, and a blonde woman approached. Jordan and Bravado met her at the gate.

"Guys, this is Laura, my barn manager," Jordan said. "Laura, Dante and Ryan. They're..." He paused. "Well, the cameras probably give it away."

"Yeah, I think I can figure that out." Laura smiled at us. "Nice to meet you guys." To him, she said, "The hay company called and wants to reschedule for the end of next week, so—"

"No." Jordan put up a hand and shook his head. "We don't have nearly enough timothy *or* alfalfa to push it that far. Call them back and tell them they either deliver it by Monday, or we'll contract with Hanson's."

Laura nodded, making a note on the pad in her hand. "Also, I wanted to ask if I should give Sunny's owners a warning letter or see if they're late on next month's board."

"Give them the letter." Jordan shifted on Bravado's back, absently adjusting the lead rope he used for reins. "With people on the waiting list, we don't need to put up with late payments. Next month is on time, or they're out of here."

"What a pity," she muttered.

"Yeah, no shit." Jordan paused. "Oh, I meant to ask earlier, when you're out getting grain tomorrow, could you stop by the lumberyard and get a few more boards? Just in case this one decides to play demolition horse again?"

"Will do." She scribbled something on her notepad. "Anything else?"

"No, I think that's it. Thanks, Laura."

"Not a problem."

As she walked away, he turned to us. "Sorry about that. This shit never ends. You know how it goes."

"Yeah, we do." A mischievous grin tugged at Dante's lips. "Sounds like you don't take the orders around here, do you?"

Without missing a beat, and probably speaking without thinking, he said, "Not nearly often enough, no."

His answer sent my heart into my throat. Dante glanced at me, wide-eyed.

Jordan quickly cleared his throat. "I mean, like I said, you know how it is. Being the boss. Runs you down sometimes." He gestured at the jumps. "Want me to take him over a few more times?"

"Sure, sure," Dante said. "Go ahead."

As Jordan took Bravado to the other side of the arena again, Dante and I exchanged glances.

"You still thinking what I'm thinking?" he asked.

"Mm-hmm."

We kept snapping away until Jordan decided Bravado had had enough, but the whole time, his comments kept replaying in my mind. Were there lines here to read between? Was he really dropping hints? Perhaps subtle hints about a submissive side?

No, no, I was jumping the gun. I *wanted* him to be a sub. Dante and I hadn't had a submissive in entirely too long, so I was reading way, way too much into benign comments and body language. I had no reason to believe Jordan was a sub or would even want anything to do with our slightly-to-the-right-of-normal relationship. The only thing I knew was that whatever deities I had to appease for us to have the chance to top someone as hot as Jordan, I would.

That said, I'd been right about subs before. Like the unexplainable and undeniable chemistry between mates, there was that vibe from sub to Dom. Little tells that added up.

We'd unsettled him from the moment we'd met. I'd watched him interact confidently with people at the wedding, not to mention standing up to give a toast without a hint of nerves. He was anything but shy, but around us? He was nervous, tongue-tied, with the occasional surge of confidence in the form of a brazen remark about riding bareback or a more subtle one about taking orders.

Our last couple of subs had reacted the same way in the beginning. One was a seasoned submissive who just wasn't sure about us at first, particularly since two Doms are a wee bit more intimidating than one. The other was inexperienced, and once we'd coaxed him into admitting he was intrigued by the idea, the three of us had had a *great* time together.

Pity Jordan was tied up with that douche bag we'd met at the wedding. He'd probably have been much happier tied up with us.

Assuming, of course, I read him right and wasn't projecting what I wanted him to be. One off-the-cuff comment and some wishful thinking did not a submissive make. I tried to push those thoughts aside as I followed Jordan, Dante and Bravado back to the barn, but curiosity was a bitch to ignore. I had to know.

On the way through the barn, a crop whip hanging on the wall caught my eye. I took it down.

"Hey, Dante," I said. "Think we should get one of these?"

Just as I'd hoped, Jordan turned around, and his eyebrows shot up. Holding his gaze, I smacked my palm with the whip.

The horse barely responded. Jordan, on the other hand, stared at me with widening eyes, his lips parting.

Dante shrugged. "Sure, we can get one, but who the hell are we going to hit with it?"

Jordan gulped. I hit my hand again for good measure, the sound echoing down the aisle, and I thought he was going to faint. I put the whip back. He watched me rub my stinging palm with my other hand, and probably had no idea I caught him sweeping the tip of his tongue across his lower lip. He didn't appear in the least bit offended. A little flushed in the face and tight in the jeans, but not offended.

Then he coughed and gestured at the horse. "I'd better put him back in his stall."

As Jordan walked away with Bravado, Dante and I looked at each other.

He grinned. So did I.

Jackpot.

Chapter Four

My hands shook as I unbuckled Bravado's halter.

I'd imagined that conversation, right? Or at least its not-so-subtle implications. They were probably just joking around. I'd started it, after all, with my "bareback" comment that made me want to crawl off into a corner and die a thousand times over. Thank God Bravado could run like hell, because in that moment, I couldn't have gotten far enough away fast enough.

They didn't seem put off by it. Certainly not offended. Maybe after my lapse in verbal restraint, they'd decided I wasn't as uptight as some of their clients, and they could let their hair down a little.

A little? Something as brazen as Ryan with the crop was more than letting his hair down a little. Especially with the way he'd looked *right* at me when he did it.

Or I could have been seeing them through frustration-tinted glasses, finding interest and flirtation wherever I wanted to see it. They were a couple of professionals. Hell, they were a couple. *Keep dreaming, Steele.*

Before I left the stall, I took a deep breath and, as subtly as I could, adjusted the front of my jeans. *Come on, come on, calm down.* At least I'd held off getting turned on until after I was off the horse. Riding bareback—"Well, horses, anyway." God, what was I thinking?—was perfectly comfortable *except* when I had a hard-on. I should have known that was avoidable for only so long with them around.

And that sound, holy fuck, that sound.

Smack.

Leather on flesh.

I shivered. What I wouldn't have given...

Clearing my throat, I stepped out of the stall and hung the halter on the door. As I latched the door, I said, "Looks like that's it. Those were the two I wanted you to shoot." While I dusted my hands off on my jeans, my stomach fluttered with nerves. I couldn't breathe while they were here, but wasn't so sure I was ready for them to leave. Did I dare? I coughed again. "You're both welcome to, um, come up to the house for drinks if you're not in a hurry."

They glanced at each other. Something unspoken passed between them. Then Dante said, "Sure, why not?"

Sweet.

Oh, shit.

After they'd put their gear in their car, we walked up the gravel path from the barn to the house. In the utility room downstairs, I pointed at the dog's kennel.

"Sasha, crate."

He obediently crossed the room and lay down in his crate.

"Good boy." I looked at Dante. "He'll stay in here until you guys take off."

"Oh, don't worry about him. He's fine." Dante smiled but still sent a wary glance in Sasha's direction.

"This is where he usually chills in the evening anyway," I said. "He gets himself all worked up running around the farm, so I like to let him relax a bit. He's getting too old to run himself into the ground like that." *Why am I rambling like a nervous kid?* "Can I get either of you a beer?" *God knows I need one.*

Ryan lifted his eyebrows at Dante.

"I can drive home," Dante said. "Go ahead."

"What about you?" I asked. "Coke, water, iced tea?"

"Coke is fine."

I got a Coke for him and a couple of beers for Ryan and me, and we moved into the living room. They sat on the couch while I took a seat on the recliner, which had an old blanket thrown over it for nights like this when I didn't feel like changing clothes immediately after working.

For a little while, we talked shop, discussing how long it would take for the pictures to be edited and things like that.

While we talked, I realized this was the first time I'd ever seen Ryan sit still. Well, that wasn't entirely accurate. Though he wasn't up and moving, he certainly wasn't still. He wasn't what I'd call twitchy, just...active. Sometimes he'd run the toe of one shoe back and forth along the insole of the other. Or he'd play with the cuff of his sleeve or the hem of his shirt. One hand rested on the couch's armrest, and if his fingers weren't tapping, they idly traced the seams and patterns in the upholstery.

At one point, while the conversation meandered into one-upping each other with client horror stories, Dante put his arm around Ryan's shoulders. Ryan took a breath, released it, and was still. His foot didn't move. His fingers stopped toying with his sleeve. His other hand rested on the armrest.

Neither of them missed a beat in the conversation. I doubted they even realized it had happened.

"So how long have you been doing this?" Dante gestured out the picture window that overlooked the barn and paddocks. "Raising and training horses, I mean."

"All my life," I said. "It was a family thing, and when my parents died, I bought out my siblings so I could keep the farm."

"Seems like you've done pretty well with it," Ryan said.

I shrugged. "As well as can be when I still have to pay all the bills before I get to enjoy the profits."

They both laughed.

"We feel your pain," Dante said.

"What about you guys?" I asked. "How long have you been photographers?"

"I went pro when I was twenty," Ryan said.

"Nineteen for me," Dante said.

"And you've been working together all this time?"

"Oh, no, we both started separately," Ryan said. "Opposite sides of the country, in fact. We've been working together for, what?" He looked at Dante. "Eight years now?"

"Almost nine, I think," Dante said, his fingers moving up and down Ryan's arm, mirroring the way Ryan had caressed Dante's neck at their studio.

"Wow. Time flies." Ryan shook his head. "And we've been together..." He furrowed his brow and turned to Dante again.

Dante pursed his lips. "Twelve years, isn't it?"

Ryan whistled. "I don't usually stop and think about it, but when I do..."

"No kidding," Dante said.

"It's okay, though." Ryan shrugged. "In two years, I get to trade you in for two twenties anyway."

Dante kicked Ryan's ankle. "That's assuming you live that long, smartass."

I laughed. "You know, it always amazes me when a couple can work together. Especially for that long."

Dante combed his fingers through Ryan's hair, smiling fondly at him. "Oh, it has its ups and downs."

"I can imagine," I said.

"It helps that we keep a lot of the business separate," Ryan said. "We do plenty of work together, but there are parts we do on our own. The commercial side—product photography, stuff for catalogs, that kind of thing—is almost entirely mine."

"And I do most of the family and senior portraits," Dante said. "We both back each other up and fill in if the other can't keep up with all the bookings, but it makes it a little easier if we can at least work separately on a few things."

Ryan rested his hand on Dante's knee. "Keeps us out of each other's hair."

"Otherwise we butt heads." Dante looked right at me, eyes narrowing slightly as he added, "Since we both like to be in charge."

I wondered if I was imagining the way they both looked at me just then, like they were trying to read my reaction. I certainly wasn't imagining the way my heart skipped. I coughed into my fist. "So, did you start out doing weddings and stuff like that? Then slowly branch out or what?"

Dante shook his head. "We both started out as photojournalists. Used to travel all over the place, did some work for *National Geographic*, that kind of thing."

I nodded. "Oh, yeah, I saw that in your portfolio."

"That's actually how we met," Ryan said.

"Really?"

Dante smiled at Ryan, absently playing with Ryan's hair while he spoke. "We were both on assignment in New Delhi and ran into each other."

"Quite *literally* ran into each other." Ryan returned Dante's smile. "I was trying to get a shot of some baskets a street vendor was selling..."

"I was trying to get a wide-angle shot of the street..."

Ryan nudged Dante with his elbow. "This S.O.B. backed right into me."

Dante nudged him back. "And I almost ended up *in* one of the baskets he was shooting."

"I probably would have smacked you with one of them if I hadn't been so worried about damaging your camera."

I chuckled. "Priorities?"

"Damn right," Ryan said. "That was a nice camera. I wasn't going to fuck it up just because its owner couldn't watch where he was going."

"Not my fault someone else decided to kneel right in the middle of a busy market."

Grinning mischievously, Ryan said, "You've never complained about when and where I kneel—"

"*Angel.*" Dante's cheeks colored. To me, he said, "Sorry, this is why we usually don't let him out in public."

"He either trips you or embarrasses you?" I said.

"Basically."

"So, why did you give up the photojournalism gig?" I asked. "That sounds like a dream job."

Ryan shrugged with one shoulder. "It was a lot of fun, and we got to see some great places, but the constant traveling was getting exhausting."

"And a bit dangerous, given some of the parts of the world we ended up in," Dante said. "I decided I was done when a stray bullet went through our hotel window."

"Whoa, yeah, that would probably be it for me," I said.

"I did a few more trips alone." Ryan inched a little closer to Dante, settling against him until he could have rested his head on Dante's shoulder if he'd wanted to. "But it wasn't the same on my own, and after I had my third camera in four years stolen at gunpoint, I called it quits." He paused, glancing at Dante. "'Course, sometimes I wonder if wedding photography is just as dangerous."

Dante made a face. "No shit."

"That bad?"

Ryan laughed. "Okay, it's not really that bad."

"Usually," Dante added.

"Usually." Ryan grimaced. "Hell hath no fury like a pissed-off bride, let me tell you."

"Well, I certainly envy you for getting to travel like you did," I said. "I usually can't leave for long because of the horses, but I would kill to go to some of the places you did. Do you still travel much?"

"When it's off-peak season for weddings, hell yeah," Dante said.

"We take a lot of short trips throughout the year," Ryan said. "Skiing, hiking, that kind of thing, and we try to take at least one big trip every year."

"In fact, we finally got to Japan last year," Dante said. "Which was a blast, even after *someone* screwed up his ankle on Fuji."

Ryan shuddered. "Thank fuck we were on the way *down* the mountain at that point."

"It wasn't too bad, though." Dante moved his hand from Ryan's hair to his shoulder. "Once we got off the mountain anyway. Just meant we had to spend a couple of days in our hotel room until he could walk again."

Oh, I could think of worse things. "So, if it's not too personal," I said. "I've noticed you call him Angel. Nickname?"

Dante nodded. "I do try to remember to call him Ryan when we're working, but I'm so used to it, I forget."

Before I could ask if there was a story behind it—and knowing them, there had to be—a door opened and closed downstairs, and the hairs on the back of my neck stood on end.

I gritted my teeth. "And that would be Eli."

They both shot me puzzled looks.

Gesturing dismissively, I said, "Just the joys of living with an ex."

"An ex?" Dante's eyes widened.

I nodded. "Trust me, it's a long story."

"Hey, Jordan," Eli called from the other room, his footsteps thumping up the stairs. "Didn't I ask you to quit leaving the fucking—" He paused, lips tightening when he noticed I had company. "Oh, sorry, didn't mean to interrupt." The irritation in his voice set my teeth on edge.

"It's okay." I struggled to keep my own annoyance out of my voice. "You remember Dante and Ryan, right? From Jenny's wedding?"

He offered them a tight-lipped smile. "Right, yes, I remember."

I fought the urge to roll my eyes at the sneer in his tone.

"Did we meet you at the wedding?" Ryan cocked his head. Thumbing his chin, he glanced at Dante, then back at Eli. "Hell, we ran into so many people, it's hard to keep track of everyone. Was—" He snapped his fingers. "Right, I didn't recognize you without the tray in your hand."

Eli raised an eyebrow. "What?"

Ryan tilted his head the other direction. "You were one of the waiters, weren't you?"

Eli's voice dipped to an indignant growl. "No, I was there with—"

"He's a friend of the groom's," I said, struggling like hell not to laugh.

Eli threw me a glare, then looked at Ryan and gestured at me. "I was there with *him.*"

With what must have been the sweetest smile he could muster, Ryan said, "Well, that explains why I didn't recognize you, since I was staring at him the entire time."

Thank God I hadn't been taking a drink just then. I nearly choked on my own breath anyway, and I couldn't decide if it was because of Ryan's swipe at Eli or the implied flirtation with me. It didn't help when Dante made a casual gesture of scratching his jaw, which only served to draw my attention to his barely contained snickering.

Ryan, somehow, kept a perfectly straight face.

Eli set his jaw. "Well, I have a few things to take care of, so I'll let you all get back to your conversation." He narrowed his eyes at Ryan. "It was good seeing you two again."

"Likewise." Ryan's innocent smile was almost too much, but I managed to contain my laughter until Eli had gone downstairs and closed his bedroom door.

Dante elbowed Ryan. "You're a dick, you know that?"

"What?" Ryan batted his eyes and put his hands up. "What did I do?"

Dante tried and failed to look stern. "Sorry about him. He has no social graces."

Wiping my eyes, I said, "Don't worry about it. I'll hear about it later, but the expression on his face was fucking priceless."

"Yeah, but we don't usually make a habit of going to client's houses and ripping on their housemates." He tried to give Ryan a disapproving glare, but Ryan batted his eyes again, and all three of us cracked up.

Eventually, my ex's intrusion was forgotten, and we went back to our conversation. At some point, they had to bow out and get back to the studio to close things down, though I couldn't help noticing they were a little reluctant to leave. With a promise to call in a few days when the photos were ready— and yes, I was more than happy to come pick them up rather than have them mailed—they left.

From the living room window, I watched their taillights disappear down the driveway. A shiver ran down my spine. I swore their combined presence lingered on my tingling nerve endings.

Movement in the other room forced an aggravated breath from my lungs. Dante and Ryan may have been gone, but I certainly wasn't alone.

I went into the kitchen to find out what Eli was annoyed about earlier, before he'd realized I had guests.

"What were you asking me about?" I said. "When you came up the stairs?"

Eli paused, furrowing his brow, then shook his head. "Fuck, I don't remember."

"Guess it wasn't important, then," I said through my teeth. Obviously it was important enough to warrant getting on my case, even if he'd forgotten about it half an hour later.

"So how did the photo shoot go?" he asked.

"Good. I'll have to have them back another day to get action shots of Arturo," I said as I put the empty cans and bottles from earlier into the recycle bin. "He was still limping this morning, so I didn't want to push him."

Eli's lips thinned. "Oh, I'm sure having them come back would be *such* an imposition."

"It would be expensive," I said quietly.

"Maybe they'll give you a discount. You know, for a repeat customer." He sipped his beer. "Didn't realize you'd gotten so chummy with them."

I leaned against the counter and eyed him. "Is that a problem?"

"No, no, of course not." He eyed the living room, lip curling slightly as if he could still see Ryan sitting in there giving him hell. "They're not the friendliest in the world, are they?"

I shrugged. "I don't know; they were quite friendly with me."

Eli sniffed and, just before he took another drink, muttered, "So I noticed."

I thought about pressing the issue and admitting that yes, there had been some subtle-but-not-so-subtle flirtation going on, and yes, I wanted both of them to fuck me blind, but I wasn't in the mood to argue about it. So I changed the subject.

"Did you get a callback about that interview?"

Eli sighed. "No. And they said if they were interested, I'd hear back by tonight." He gestured dismissively, then took a drink. "Guess it's back to square one."

I fought the urge to roll my eyes. "How about sending more than one application this time?"

He shifted his weight. "Actually, I've found something that's practically guaranteed—"

"Yeah, yeah, I've heard that before," I said. "This last one was practically guaranteed, and so was the one before it."

He glared at me. "Listen, I'm doing the best I can here. The job market sucks. What do you want me to do?"

"Send more than one application at a time, for starters." I folded my arms across my chest. "And I told you, Jenny can get you in with a temp agency, and—"

"I'm not working at a temp agency," he said.

"Why the fuck not?"

"Because it's shit work? Because it's *temporary* shit work? And how the hell am I supposed to get an apartment when I'm on a temp contract?"

"Well, at least you'd have an income so you can pull your weight a bit while you're still here," I growled. "Or at the very least save some money for a security deposit on your next place." Then I put my hand up. "You know, I'm not going to argue about this anymore tonight. Just let me know when you find a fucking job." I started out of the kitchen.

"Why are you suddenly in such a hurry to kick me out, anyway?" he snapped.

I stopped and turned around. "Besides the fact that you've been dragging your feet about it for months?"

"I'm not dragging my feet."

"You're not putting in much effort to pick them up, either."

"Whatever." He slammed his beer can down on the counter hard enough to make me jump. "Well, if my presence is an inconvenience, just give me a heads up when you've got company over, and I'll make myself scarce."

I chewed the inside of my cheek. "So now I'm the bad guy because I had a couple of people over tonight? In my own house?"

"Oh, right, I forgot, it's *your* house."

I raised an eyebrow. "Isn't it?"

He exhaled hard. "Okay, it's just...it's weird... Coming home, finding..."

"Finding me talking with a couple of guys?" I growled. "Emphasis on 'couple', in case you hadn't picked up on that." *Bastards.*

He started to speak again, but I put my hand up again.

"No. No more. Not tonight." I shifted my weight. "Look, they were just here to do some promo work for the horses, but even if they had been here for something else"—*Jesus Christ, I wish*—"the fact is, I need to move on. It's over, Eli. And as long as we're still living together, things might get weird. We'll just have to deal with it."

Eli dropped his gaze to the floor between us, and my gut twisted into knots. I hoped he wouldn't turn this into another conversation like the one we'd had last week and twice the week before. We weren't getting back together. We weren't going to give it another try. There was nothing left to work out.

God, Eli, just let me go.

Finally, he pulled another beer out of the fridge and stalked out of the kitchen. I listened until his heavy footsteps faded downstairs and his bedroom door banged shut. Then I let out my breath and rubbed my eyes. Sometimes it was like living with a damned kid.

I felt bad for him, I really did. He didn't want this to be over, and I hated the fact that this whole thing hurt him this much, but it needed to happen. I just wished he'd realize it wasn't going to stop hurting until he put in the effort to move on. I'd long ago learned if I dropped the façade of indifference, even for a moment, he'd see it as a glimmer of hope, so I forced myself to stay cold and terse. Lately, that hadn't been a terribly difficult thing to do, but I still felt for him.

I rubbed the back of my neck with both hands and sighed. I glanced at the clock. It was only a little after seven, so I had plenty of time to grab a shower and get something to eat before I had to go feed the horses.

Eli's presence still knotted my neck and shoulders. Downstairs, the muffled murmur of the television and the occasional creak of hardwood beneath feet kept me aware of his continued existence. That tension and distraction merely buzzed at the edges of my awareness, though. At the forefront of my mind was the pair who'd recently walked out my front door.

They may have been mutually spoken for, but that didn't stop me from fantasizing about them. And for that matter, it hadn't stopped them from...maybe flirting wasn't the word. Being suggestive? The memory of Ryan hitting his own hand with the crop raised goose bumps under my shirt. If he only knew what that had done to me. Or maybe he did. Maybe that's why he'd looked right at me and done it again.

I couldn't work out the dynamic of their relationship. There was a presence about both of them, something that wasn't intimidating, yet somehow was. And in spite of that, or maybe because of it, I'd been drawn to them from the moment I'd laid eyes on them at the wedding. While I couldn't put my finger on just why, I couldn't shake the feeling one of them could've made me kneel with a look.

That, or it was all in my head. Wishful thinking. Projecting my own desires onto two beautiful men.

"Hey, Dante," Ryan had said. *"Think we should get one of these?"*

Smack.

Dante had shrugged. *"Sure, we can get one, but who the hell are we going to hit with it?"*

Fuck. I wasn't projecting a goddamned thing. I couldn't put my finger on exactly what their dynamic was, but there was something there. Something I couldn't define, but wanted.

I shivered. They'd been here as professionals. I was their client, for God's sake. Their paying client, and yet I couldn't shake the feeling I'd also been their prey. I hadn't missed the hint of a smirk on Dante's face when Ryan hit his hand. Or the look that passed between them when I'd said I didn't take orders nearly often enough. They'd caught the scent. Taken my bait. Or maybe I'd taken theirs? Maybe Dante had thrown that question out there for a reason.

I may have been imagining it, but I'd swear they were feeling me out the way I was feeling them out.

A man could dream, anyway.

I told myself I was getting in the shower to soothe those tense muscles and drown out the sounds of Eli being alive, and it was true. Mostly, though, I just wanted to lose myself in thoughts of them without being distracted by him.

By the time I was under the rushing water, Eli probably could have come into the bathroom and tried to strike up a conversation, and I wouldn't have known. I was hard as hell, and just like the night I'd come home from their studio, I needed to relieve this tension.

I couldn't even focus on a single fantasy. My mind may as well have been channel-surfing through an endless library of pornos starring Ryan and Dante, and the only thing moving faster than the ever-changing *click-click-click* between those imaginary movies was my hand. I closed my eyes, clenching my jaw and stroking my cock as fast as I fucking could, imagining Ryan's cool breath on the wet skin of my neck, or Dante's hand in my hair while I sucked his cock, or Ryan stroking himself while Dante forced himself deeper inside me, or—

"Oh, fuck..." I whispered into the hiss of the shower.

Jesus, the thought of both of them naked. Stroking, sucking, kissing, fucking, looking at me, looking at each other with lust in their eyes, it didn't matter; everything I pictured them doing was perfect and hot and drove me insane. My legs shook so violently I wasn't sure they'd stay under me. Didn't particularly care. I could do this on my knees if I had to. Still, I braced my equally shaky free arm against the wall and kept right on stroking, imagining, going out of my goddamned mind.

Kneeling in front of Dante, sucking his cock, looking up at those stunning blue eyes. Pinned down while Ryan fucked me hard. Dante grabbing Ryan's ink-black hair and making him beg. Both of them making *me* beg, and oh, fuck, I would.

My breath caught. My balls tightened. My rhythm fell apart, reduced to irregular strokes with a trembling hand controlled by a Dante-Ryan-overwhelmed mind in search of release.

The crop in Ryan's hand. The crop on my skin. *More, more, more.* Leather. Pleasure. Pain. *Yes, fuck, yes.* Kneeling. Begging. Pleading. *God, yes, look at me like that.* Dante. Ryan. Me.

Everything went white. Second after second of pulsing, white-hot ecstasy that felt so good it hurt, and I kept my eyes screwed shut even after the intense tremors had passed. Just needed another minute or so. A few seconds, at least. A little while longer before I let myself back into reality, alone in my bathroom instead of between Ryan and Dante.

Finally, I opened my eyes. I took a few slow, deep breaths. I couldn't remember leaning my shoulder against the wall for support, but there it was. I pushed myself off the wall and closed my eyes again, letting hot water rush over my neck and shoulders. The tingling in my cock faded, my wrist and elbow ached, and though the mental channel-surfing had slowed, it didn't stop. They were dressed now, the two photographers on my mind, but no less mouthwatering. Exchanging subtle looks. Asking loaded questions. Gazes flicking toward each other. Crop to palm.

I hoped to God I hadn't imagined any of it.

Tell me you're the hunters, and I will gladly be your prey.

Chapter Five

At a little past nine, Angel was still on his computer, clicking away at the mouse while he furrowed his brow at something on the screen. His black hair was still damp from his recent shower, and like me, he hadn't bothered putting on more than a pair of jeans.

I leaned on the office doorframe, arms folded across my bare chest. "Being a workaholic again?"

"I'm always being a workaholic." His eyes flicked up from the screen, and he grinned as he gave me a quick down-up.

"Any chance I can pry you away from your toiling to help me make something for dinner?"

"I'll be done in a few." He focused on the monitor again, absently reaching up to pet Jade, his cat. She was the one piece of clutter he could put up with, and was perched on his desk. Even she had a specified place, though. She curled up in the bed he'd bought for her, but her tail still passive-aggressively encroached on his mouse pad.

"Uh-huh." I pushed myself off the doorframe and started toward him. "I've heard that before. You'd probably starve if I didn't drag you out of here once in a while."

He laughed. "You do the same thing. I don't want to hear it."

"Okay, but you're the one doing it tonight. And it's after nine."

"Really?" He looked at the screen, then blew out a breath. "Damn. No wonder I'm getting a headache."

"Definitely time to eat something, then." I kneaded his shoulders. "Come on. The work will still be here later."

He groaned, letting his head fall forward, and I knew I was winning. Still, he said, "Just a few more pictures. I'm almost done with the Harrigan wedding."

"You need to eat."

"I need to finish." He gave a halfhearted attempt to shrug my hands away, but I pressed my thumbs in just below the base of his neck. He exhaled. "You're evil."

"No, if I was evil, I'd do this." I leaned down and kissed behind his ear. Moving down his neck to his shoulder, I whispered, "Don't make me beg, Angel."

He shivered, then reached back and slid his hand around the back of my neck. When he turned his head, I kissed him.

He licked his lips. "Keep doing this, the only place you're going to convince me to go is the bedroom."

I kissed him again, lightly this time, and released him. "We'll get there too. Now come on."

"You are such a fucking tease."

"Just giving you a little preview of what we'll be doing later." I paused. "After we've eaten something."

"Yes, Mother." His hand went back to the mouse. "Give me just a few minutes. I'll be right there."

"Uh-huh. Heard that before." I tugged at his shoulders. "Step away from the computer, Angel."

"But...just a few more..."

"I'll start moving stuff around on your desk."

He put his hands up. "Okay, okay, you win."

"That's what I thought."

He pushed his chair back and stood. Jade peered up at him and made that weird noise that was her version of a meow. Angel shrugged. "Sorry. Daddy's being mean and says I have to go eat."

Looking right at him, she kneaded the edge of her bed and purred loud enough for both of us to hear.

I hooked my hand around Angel's elbow. "She's trying to lure you back. Don't listen to her."

"But, but—"

"Kitchen. Now."

The siren's call of work and the cat were no match for his hunger and my insistence, and Angel went into the kitchen with me. This wasn't an unusual routine for us. We were workaholics, and it was a safe bet we both would have starved to death if we didn't live together. That, and Angel would have been late for work half the time because he never wanted to disturb his cat in the morning when he needed to get up and she couldn't be bothered. It was no wonder she didn't like me.

In the kitchen, we chatted while we prepped dinner, and like we always did, took advantage of any opportunity to touch each other. When he needed the pepper from the spice rack over my head, he rested his hand on my lower back while he reached above me. When I wanted something out of the drawer beside him, I made sure to stop long enough to push his hair aside and kiss the back of his neck. Lingering eye contact, a hand on an ass, a long kiss just for the hell of it. Whenever we cooked together, it was rife with verbal and tactile flirting, but there was a little more insistence in the way we made contact tonight. An undercurrent of "just wait until we get into bed".

Which is why it didn't surprise me at all that it didn't take long for the conversation to move to Jordan.

"I swear he's a sub," Angel said. "He has to be."

"That, or he wants to be."

"Too bad he's got that cunt hanging around." He smacked my hand when I reached for a piece of the cheese he was about to grate. I triumphantly held up my prize, and he threw me a playful glare before we both went back to prepping food. Angel went on, "What was that guy's name again?"

"Asshole, wasn't it?"

Angel paused, furrowing his brow. "Eli, actually."

I shrugged. "Eli, asshole, cunt. All sounds the same." I threw the bell peppers I'd just diced into the pot of sauce. "I wonder what their deal is, anyway."

He eyed the sauce but didn't say anything. He measured, I didn't, and we'd long ago agreed not to argue about it. He went back to grating cheese. "I don't know what their deal is, but they seem to like each other about as well as Eli likes us."

"Can't think why he doesn't like us." I glanced at him. "Though you probably could have been a *bit* less of a dick to him."

Angel looked at me through his lashes and the fringe of black hair falling over his eyes. "Come on, he was asking for it. And Jordan thought it was funny, so..." He shrugged.

I rolled my eyes, trying my damnedest not to crack a smile.

"Oh, honestly, Dante," Angel said. "It was funny. Admit it."

"Okay, okay, it was. But somehow I don't think it made Jordan's evening with the bastard pleasant."

"I highly doubt his evening with him was going to be pleasant anyway," he said with a flippant gesture. "At least he got a laugh out of it."

"True." I idly stirred the sauce, replaying the interactions between Jordan and Eli in my head. "Man, I'm dying of curiosity, though. About the whole thing."

"Yeah, me too. I mean, he said the douche is his ex."

"Yet they still live together?" I said, moving to the cutting board while the sauce simmered.

"It does happen." Angel put aside the grated cheese and reached down to dig a pan out of the cabinet. "I lived with Kathleen for a while even after we'd filed."

"Okay, true." I looked up from dicing tomatoes. "But a pair of broke college kids making do so they don't starve is a little different, you know? Obviously someone over there is doing fairly well financially."

"True."

"And you two didn't want to claw each other's faces off when you had to be in the same room."

"There is that." He paused. "Seems like Jordan's the one who can't stand Eli."

"Can't imagine why."

He chuckled. "No kidding."

"I wonder why they were both at the wedding," I said. "If he's that much of a punk, I'd have left his ass at home."

"Yeah, really."

We were both quiet for a few minutes, focusing on getting dinner put together. Then I broke the silence.

"Douche-bag ex or not, I would kill to find out if Jordan's really a sub. I'm telling you, he's got sub written all over him."

"You think?"

"He made those comments about wishing he could hand over control to someone else." I stirred the sauce again and glanced at Angel. "Said something about it at the studio the other night too."

"Yeah, but what business owner hasn't? Even we need a break once in a while."

"True," I said. "But how many subs have we been with who were business owners, CEOs, that sort of thing? It's practically a job requirement."

He laughed. "Aside from us, you mean?"

"Well, yeah, but since when do we ever play by the rules?"

"Good point." He carefully measured the cheese he'd grated earlier and handed it to me. As he went to the sink to wash his hands, he said, "I think you're right, though. I've been getting that vibe off him since the wedding."

"At least that means I'm not hallucinating."

"I don't know about *that*." Angel picked up a dish towel to dry his hands. "And in all seriousness, I keep wondering if I'm just seeing it because I want to see it."

"Yeah, me too. Any idea how we could broach the subject with him?"

Hanging the dishtowel back on its rack, Angel said, "Wait until he comes in to pick up his pictures, and slip 'are you kinky and can we fuck you?' into the conversation?"

"Of *course*." I pretended to smack my forehead with my palm. "Why didn't I think of such a thing?"

"Well, it's better than beating around the bush."

"There's a lot of room between beating around the bush and crashing into it with a Mack truck, setting it on fire, and nuking it for good measure."

Angel showed his palms and batted his eyes. "At least then we'd know."

"Uh-huh. Except he *is* still our client. If he was just some guy we'd met, it'd be one thing, but he's not. And he's the brother of a client too."

"True." He opened the oven and slid the pan onto the rack. Over his shoulder, he said, "I suppose Jennifer might not let us shoot her wedding if she knows we made a pass at her brother."

"Funny. You know what I meant." I shot him a playful glare when he turned around.

"Yeah, yeah, I know." Angel pursed his lips, drumming his fingers on the counter. "I'm just trying to think how we can approach him without being too forward, not to mention unprofessional."

"Well, we'll come up with something," I said as we cleaned the counter and cutting boards. "Just need to figure out how to subtly feel him out a little more."

When the kitchen was tidied to his satisfaction, Angel went to the sink to wash his hands again. "So, how do we *subtly* feel him out and see if he'll let us feel him up?"

"Or tie him up."

As he dried his hands, he said, "Think he'd go for that?"

"God, I hope so." I put my arms around Angel's waist and kissed the side of his neck. All these years together, and his skin against mine still made my breath catch. "Well, whether it's Jordan or anyone else, we *really* need another sub."

"Mm-hmm." He put his hands over mine and tilted his head to expose more of his neck.

"I know you've been missing that," I whispered. "Having someone to tie up. And take orders from you."

"God, yes." His voice edged toward a moan. "And I think someone *else* has been missing a thing or two about a sub, no?"

I shivered and drew him closer. "Maybe I have."

"Maybe?" He turned around in my arms. Trailing his fingertips up my back, he whispered, "How long has it been, anyway? Since you've gotten to be inside someone?"

I bit my lip, trying and failing not to shiver again. I didn't know how long it had been. Too long, that much I knew.

Angel bent and kissed my neck. "You'd love to fuck him, wouldn't you?"

"Damn right I would."

"Think he likes it rough?"

"God, I hope so," I said in a hoarse whisper that was almost a growl.

"I can just imagine watching you fuck him." He ran his hands up and down my sides. "Think he moans when he comes? Or roars?"

"I have no idea," I said. "But I want to find out."

"Me too." He held my face in both hands and kissed me hungrily. "I do know how *you* sound when you come, though."

"You do, don't you?"

"Mm-hmm." Another long, desperate kiss. "Think I might want to hear it again."

"Oh really?"

"Yes." His hand drifted down my neck, my chest, my sides. "Like, *now*." He hooked his fingers in my front pockets, using them to pull my hips against his own. I wrapped my arms around him, and his kiss made me weak just like it always did. After a moment, his hands left my pockets and slid up my back, my skin almost sizzling from the heat of his palms. Our kitchen was completely silent except uneven hisses of breath and the whisper of denim brushing over denim between our erect cocks.

Even when we came up for air, I couldn't catch my breath. Judging by the way his shoulders rose and fell, and the warm-cool-warm air against my lips, neither could he.

Then his eyes darted toward the window, and when they met mine again, that trademark mischievous grin materialized on his lips. "Hmm, maybe we shouldn't do this in front of the window."

"Why the hell not?" I ran my fingers through his cool, still-damp hair. "I'll kiss my boyfriend in my kitchen whenever I damn well please."

He laughed and pulled me closer. "Yeah, but Mrs. Franklin might have heart failure."

"Then she shouldn't be looking through our window, should she?"

"Hmm, good point."

I rested my hands on the back of his neck, and our lips brushed when I spoke. "We *could* find a better place to do this, though."

"Such as?"

"Somewhere with condoms and lube within easy reach."

Angel glanced over his shoulder at the oven timer. "And wouldn't you know it?" He licked his lips when our eyes met again. "We have plenty of time."

"More than enough time." I held on to the back of his neck, kissed him passionately and dragged him out of the kitchen with me.

Chapter Six

Dante pulled me from the kitchen into the hallway, but as soon as I'd regained my balance, I took over.

With my body weight against him and my hands on his hips, I shoved him up against the wall hard enough to knock the breath out of him. We both stopped, and for a moment, just stared at each other. Breathing hard, eyes narrowing, we stared at each other.

He licked his lips. I did the same.

In an instant, we were back to passionate kissing. He pulled me against him, I pushed him against the wall, and we clawed at each other. Without shirts to hold on to, we grabbed on to whatever we could—hair, hips, belt loops—and forced each other down the hall.

Once we were in the bedroom, we pulled ourselves off each other just long enough to get out of our clothes. Times like this, I didn't care if anything was tidy or cluttered or just thrown the fuck on the floor. Clothes needed to come off, and wherever they landed, oh well. Thank God neither of us had on more than a pair of jeans anyway. We hadn't even bothered with boxers or belts, and in mere seconds, my jeans were on the floor somewhere near his and I was in bed with him.

He managed to get the upper hand for a brief moment, but before the sheets beneath me had even had a chance to warm from my body heat, I had him on his back. Every kiss was more desperate and breathless than the last, and every time his cock brushed mine, I wanted him that much more.

I pinned him on his back again and didn't give him a chance to fight back before I slid my hand between us and wrapped my fingers around his cock. He exhaled, squirming beneath me.

"Like that?" I murmured, bending to kiss his neck.

"You know I do."

"God, I love it when you're this horny." I nipped his earlobe, shivering when he did. "I think *someone's* been thinking filthy thoughts tonight."

Dante bit his lip and slid his hand up into my hair, tightening his grip when I did the same to his cock.

I kissed just above his collarbone. "You've been thinking about fucking him, haven't you?"

Dante groaned softly.

"I'll bet you'd like to have him cuffed and on his knees, wouldn't you?" I squeezed him harder and stroked faster, waiting for that groan and shudder before I kissed below his ear. "Would you make him beg for your cock, Dante?"

"Fuck..."

"Exactly." I grinned against his skin. "You'd make him, wouldn't you? Just to torture him until you gave him what he wanted?"

Dante pulled in a sharp breath, shuddering against me.

I raised my head, forcing myself to keep my hand and voice steady while I watched him furrow his brow and bite his lip and look so fucking deliciously turned on. "Would you do that to him?"

"God, yes."

"While I watched?"

He whimpered, his cock twitching in my hand.

"Tell me, Dante," I murmured, pausing to kiss him, "would you cuff him, make him beg, then fuck him while he's helpless to do anything except take it?"

He shut his eyes tight and squirmed against me, like he was trying to fuck my hand.

I let my lower lip drag across his, then whispered, "Would you—"

"Fuck me."

"First, I want—"

"Angel, please," he said, almost moaning. "I want... I need...*please*..." He licked his lips and met my eyes, his wide with the most mouthwatering desperation. "Please, fuck me. Now."

God help me, I almost came right then and there. Dante didn't beg any more than I did, and when he did, fuck, it turned me on. Without another word, I leaned away and reached into my nightstand drawer for the condoms and lube. I sat on the edge of the bed and got the condom open and on as fast as my hands—*fuck, fuck, I need to be inside him, oh God, right fucking now, fuck, I want him*—could manage.

Once I had the condom and lube on, I turned back to him, as desperate to be inside him as he was to have me. I was about to tell him to get up on his knees, but he caught me off guard, grabbing me and throwing me on my back. I had just enough time to look up at him, blinking in surprise just like he had when I'd shoved him up against the wall, before he pinned my arms down and kissed me. Growling against his mouth, I tried to free my hands, my fingers clawing the air in search of his skin, his hair, his hips.

"Let me fuck you," I said.

He kissed me again. Hard, aggressive, violent, just like he knew would drive me crazy, just like I wanted to fuck him, fuck him, fuck him, *Dante, please...*

Finally, the teasing bastard sat up, then rose enough to let me guide my cock to him. With my other hand on his hip, he lowered himself onto me. A low moan escaped his lips, and he let his head fall forward as I slid deeper inside him. I rested both hands on his hips while he slowly rose and fell a few times, kept them there while he picked up speed. Jesus, he felt incredible. He made me dizzy, just like the first time and every time.

I moved my hands up to his chest and teased his nipples with my thumbs. He bit his lip, furrowing his brow and riding me harder, and my back arched under us.

Just like that, my mouth couldn't figure out how to say. *Don't stop, Dante, just like that. Oh, fuck, you're gonna make me—*

He stopped.

I groaned with frustration. "Dante, don't—"

He cut me off with a deep kiss.

"I want you to get behind me," he whispered. "And fuck me hard."

"Then you'd better turn around." I thought he might make me beg. Maybe he thought I'd make him beg. It wasn't below either of us to do just that.

Not tonight, though. We both needed this too badly to tease each other anymore.

He slowly rose off me, both of us exhaling hard as my cock slid out of him. Then he turned around, and I wasted no time getting behind him and back inside him. Someone groaned, someone shivered, and I fucked him hard, fast, thrusting with all the violent desperation a lover like him aroused in me. Muscles burned and trembled and ached, and I didn't care because I was inside Dante, deep inside Dante, fucking Dante, yes, yes, Dante.

He rocked back against me, forcing me deeper and demanding I fuck him faster. Then slower. Faster again. *Harder.* He may have been on his knees, he may have been taking it from me, but he was never, ever submissive.

I held his hips tighter, biting my lip as every stroke sent me closer to letting go.

"Oh, God..." I groaned. "Just like that, I'm almost..." A shudder rippled up my spine. Dante took over, slamming back against me, and I matched him thrust for thrust until I couldn't take another second of it. I dug my fingers into his hips. Held my breath. Threw my head back. Fucking lost it. Jesus Christ, no one could make me come like Dante, and I couldn't release the air in my lungs or draw more in until the last few aftershocks had passed. Then, and only then, I groaned and slumped over him.

We weren't done, though. If I let myself relax too long, that post-orgasmic sleepiness would set in, and Dante hadn't come yet.

Steadying myself with a hand on his hip, I pulled out. Then Dante collapsed onto his side, and I sat back on my heels. We were both sweating, both breathless, and just the sight of his hard cock made me dizzier still.

I rested my weight on one shaking arm and leaned down to kiss him lightly. "Don't go anywhere. I'll be right back."

He smiled. "I'll be right here."

After one more kiss—okay, two more, and a third for good measure—I got up and went into the bathroom to get rid of the condom. I quickly washed my hands, dried them, and when I came back to bed, Dante was waiting. He reclined against the pillow, one hand behind his head and the other slowly stroking his own cock.

I joined him in bed and gently pushed his hand out of the way. "You weren't taking care of yourself without me, were you?"

He batted his eyes. "Absolutely not. Just warming myself up for you, since you're going to suck my cock."

I raised an eyebrow. "Is that right?"

"Yes, it is."

With a hand on his shoulder, I forced him all the way onto his back. Still stroking his cock, I kissed him lightly, but kept my lips out of reach when he tried for more. "And when did I agree to do this?"

"Were you going to let me get blue balls?"

I laughed. "Of course not. But I haven't decided how I'm going to make you come yet." I squeezed him a little harder, just enough to make him suck in a breath and bite his lip. "Maybe I just want to do this, hmm?"

"Except I want you to suck me off."

"Do you?"

He opened his mouth to speak, but I stroked him faster, and all he did was groan.

I kissed him again. "I think you're enjoying this, aren't you?"

"Yes, but..." His back arched. "Oh, fuck, Angel, I want you to suck my cock." He took a breath. Licked his lips. Screwed his eyes shut. "Please, Angel..."

"Well, since you asked nicely." I released his cock and pushed myself up on my arms so I was on top of him. I kissed his neck, working my way down to his collarbone, then to his chest.

I flicked my tongue across his nipple, watching him close his eyes and gasp. He combed his trembling fingers through my hair, letting his nails drag gently across my scalp, and I shivered, exhaling against his skin as I continued working my way down to his abs. I trailed light kisses and the occasional flutter of the tip of my tongue down the center of his abs, then to his side. I deliberately let my stubble graze his skin. Blew a warm breath here, a cool one there. He squirmed and trembled, and as I drew closer to his cock, he whimpered softly.

"Fuck, Angel, you're such a tease," he growled.

"I am." I drew a circle with the tip of my tongue just inches from his cock. "And you like it, don't you?"

"It's frustrating as hell."

"Mm-hmm." I kissed my way closer to him. "Do you want me to stop?"

He released a low groan, and I laughed again when my breath on his skin made him gasp.

"No," he whispered. "Don't you dare fucking stop."

"That's what I thought."

Before he could say anything more, I flicked my tongue across the base of his cock. His whole body seized, and I was pretty sure he swore a few times before I did it again. And again. And once more just to get his teeth grinding with frustration. I ran the tip of my tongue all the way from the base of his cock to the head, just slowly enough to drive him crazy before I finally went down on him the way he wanted me to.

I took him a fraction of an inch at a time. Down a little, back up, down a little more, letting him know who was in control right then. Every time I came down, his hips moved in a subtle imitation of how mine had earlier when I'd tried to get deeper inside him. The hand in my hair didn't press down hard enough to make me choke but *just* enough to let me know he wasn't *asking* me to take more of him.

We always danced along this razor-thin line of mutual control. Neither of us gained or relinquished the upper hand for long. I'd take control, he'd take it back. He'd give me some control, I'd give it back. I led, he led, and together we'd reach our destination.

But we both craved surrender. Complete, unhesitating surrender. Total submission. And if I'd read him right, Jordan might be the one to give it to us. The very thought sent a shudder up my spine, and I stroked Dante faster, took him a little deeper, groaning softly against his cock when he arched his back and moaned.

I usually had no trouble focusing entirely on what I was doing and nothing else, but tonight, other images flickered at the corners of my consciousness: Jordan sucking Dante's cock like I did now. Jordan on his knees, pleading for the right to make one of us come, for the privilege of coming himself. Jordan pushed up against a bed, a chair, a wall, begging Dante to fuck him fast and hard the way I knew Dante ached to fuck *someone.*

I deep-throated Dante. His entire body trembled, and the quiet whimper he released sent goose bumps prickling all the way down my spine. His cock twitched against my tongue. I moved faster, gave it to him just the way I knew he loved it.

"Fuck, just...oh God..." His fingers trembled in my hair. "Jesus, Angel, fuck..." He trailed off into a groan, then sucked in a breath, tensed, and a second later, hot, salty semen hit my tongue.

I didn't stop until his grip on my hair tightened enough to keep me from moving, and when I did stop, he exhaled hard and relaxed. He put his hand over his eyes as he caught his breath.

I came up to the pillow to join him, propping myself up on one arm and trailing my fingers down the side of his face. He lifted his hand off his eyes.

"I so needed that," he slurred.

I quirked an eyebrow at him. "You *always* need a blowjob."

"And you always deliver, so we're in good shape, aren't we?"

"So we are." I lowered my head for a long, gentle kiss. He wrapped his arms around me, and I sank down to him, sliding my hands under his back. Our skin was slick with sweat, which meant we'd probably end up in the shower again before bed. Together, most likely.

When I met his eyes, the hunger was sated for now, but still alive and well. Yeah, we'd be taking another shower tonight, and it would be together. Another late night in the Morgan-James house, of that I had no doubt. Even after all this time, it was a wonder we ever left the bed, never mind the house.

Dante cocked his head. "What?"

"Hmm?"

"You looked like you were about to laugh about something."

I grinned. "Just thinking."

He lifted an eyebrow. "About?"

"About whether or not we stand a chance of getting any sleep tonight?"

Dante chuckled. "Maybe we'll just have to go to bed early, then." He combed his fingers through my hair, deliberately running the edges of his nails along my scalp until I shivered. Then he added, "You know, so we have more time to try to get to sleep."

"Yeah, because spending more time in bed is always a good way to get more sleep in this house."

He raised his head to kiss me. "Well, it looked good on paper."

"And in practice?" I said against his lips.

"Probably not so much."

"Probably? Yeah, right." I laughed and kissed him again. Though our banter had been playful as always, this was another gentle, tender kiss that went on for a long moment. We held on to each other, stroking each other's skin and just letting this go on.

When I finally convinced myself to break the kiss, I pushed myself up on one arm and ran the backs of my fingers down his cheek. He reached up to touch my face, and I kissed his palm.

"I love you," he whispered.

I smiled. "I love you too."

"Even if I tell you that yes, I have been thinking dirty thoughts about Jordan all day?"

A tingle worked its way right through me. "Especially if you tell me that."

"That's what I thought." He kissed me, just teasing my lips with his own for a long moment before he said, "And to answer your question from earlier, you're damn right I want to fuck him while you watch."

"Jesus, we could have so much fun with him if he was game." I shifted onto my side. "Think there's any way we can get his attention without betraying our flawless image of professionalism?"

Dante eyed me. "Oh, I don't think *that* part will be a problem."

"So we might as well just—"

"No." He pursed his lips. "We'll figure it out, but subtlety is the name of the game here, okay?"

I released a sigh of mock exasperation. "Fine. We'll do it *your* way."

"I knew you'd see reason." He kissed me. "Now why don't we go eat before dinner burns?"

"Good idea." I sat up. "The sooner we eat, the sooner we can get back in bed."

Chapter Seven

"Mr. Steele?"

I looked up as Kendra came back into Dante and Ryan's lobby. "Hmm?"

"This client is going to take a bit longer than they thought," she said. "But they should be out soon."

"It's okay. I'm not in any hurry."

She picked her jacket up off the chair. "It's time for me to get out of here, though, so I'll leave you in their capable hands."

I wish. I just smiled. While she gathered her things and shut down her computer, I leaned forward and looked at the portfolios on the table in front of me. I'd been through them all before, but they were something to occupy idle hands and a not-so-idle mind.

Bridal. Landscape. Commercial. Senior Portrait. 18 & Over.

Wait. Eighteen and over? I raised an eyebrow. That wasn't there before. I glanced at the closed side door, then at the leather-bound black book that just begged me to have a look. A little peek. After all, I was certainly on the "over" end of that spectrum. Curiosity finally got the best of me, so I picked up the black portfolio and sat back.

Flipping through the pages, two things were immediately clear. One, the reason for the age restriction. Though no pictures showed anything that would be deemed pornographic, they were more than a little suggestive. Models were dressed in everything from leather to strategically placed shadows. Some posed alone, some with others.

The second thing that became clear right away was that, when it came to this kind of work, Dante and Ryan were fucking *talented*. Holy hell. I didn't know much about photography, but I'd always loved erotic artwork, and these were absolutely breathtaking. I had to stare at a couple of them for a while just because the angles and shadows intrigued me as much as the eroticism and, in some cases, the visible sexual tension.

"Good night, Mr. Steele." Kendra's voice made me jump, and I hadn't even realized she'd crossed the room from her desk to the front door.

I smiled at her. "Have a good one."

"Will do." She cocked her head and furrowed her brow, eyeing the portfolio in my lap. "Oh, I didn't realize they'd left that book out. We usually keep that one put away in case someone brings their kids in."

I forced a quiet laugh. "I wondered about that."

"Well, if you don't mind, could you give it to one of the boys when they come out?" She clicked her tongue. "I tell them to put their toys away, but..." She gestured at it again.

"I'll make sure to give it to them."

"Great, thanks. Good night."

"Good night."

A moment later, the door banged shut behind her, and I was alone with the black book of beautiful risqué photos.

One in particular held my attention. It was a close-up of a hand lifting a male model's chin. Long, fine fingers, but still masculine, with a few dark hairs sprinkled across the back of his hand and wrist. Judging by the angles, the model must have been quite a bit lower than whoever was touching his face. Sitting, perhaps. Maybe kneeling. The model's eyes were so intense, gazing up with nothing short of reverence at...someone. Every detail was crystal clear, from the crisp lines of the tattooed bracelet to the dusting of stubble that nearly made me want to run my fingers over the picture in search of the coarse texture.

The book was page after page of similar work. Simple images that left a lot to the imagination, though the suggestion of what went on outside each frame was definitely there.

Ryan and Dante were obviously quite open-minded too, at least as far as what they'd shoot for their clients. For all I knew, they had a completely boring, missionary-with-the-lights-off sex life on their own, but they didn't seem to have any qualms about photographing those with somewhat more exotic tastes.

The side door opened, and I damn near jumped out of my skin. I didn't have time to conspicuously close the portfolio and put it back on the table, so when Ryan appeared, there was no pretending I hadn't been flipping through it.

"Hey, we're just about done in here, but—" Ryan paused, looking at the book I had in my lap. He grinned. "I see you found some of our more questionable work." He didn't seem surprised in the least. Certainly not put off.

I glanced down at the portfolio. "Yeah, guess I did. This is amazing work, by the way."

"Thanks," he said. "We, um, have another book of similar work, but we keep it under lock and key. I'm sure you can figure out why."

I gulped. "A bit racier than this?"

"Just a bit." Those intense, see-right-through-you eyes narrowed slightly. "I can get it out if you want to see it."

If curiosity had gotten the best of me before, it had me by the balls now. I cleared my throat. "Um, sure, yeah."

"It's, um..." He chewed his lip. "Well, if it won't make you think strangely of us." He raised his eyebrows.

"I'm assuming there aren't any pictures involving livestock?"

A laugh burst out of him. "Good God, no." He paused. "We post *those* on the Internet."

I chuckled. "I'm sure. Well, in that case, I'd love to see it."

"Don't say I didn't warn you." He pulled a set of keys from his pocket and reached for something below the receptionist's desk. A lock crunched, then clicked, and a drawer slid open. When he stood, he held a book similar to the one in my hand.

Dante's voice came from the other room. "Angel, you coming?"

"Be right there." Ryan came around the desk and handed me the book. "Enjoy."

"Will do."

Before he let it go, something on his wrist caught my eye. Something unusual about his watchband.

No, not the watchband.

The skin under the watchband, which bore the same tattoo I'd seen in that shot of the hand lifting the model's chin. I glanced up at him. He let go of the portfolio, and when he stepped away, I'll be damned if he didn't wink.

Then he was gone again, the door closing behind him with a quiet click.

Alone again with a portfolio and my heartbeat, I stared at the unassuming black leather cover of the book he'd given me. *18 & Over—By Request Only.* Just what went in here that was too much for the other book?

Finally, I flipped it open.

From the first page, my mouth watered. I'd been curious for some time about all things kink and BDSM but had kept it to myself. Eli sure as hell wouldn't have gotten involved in something so "weird" as he called it. Obviously Dante and Ryan weren't so inhibited, at least as far as their work was concerned.

I had never seen a more beautiful collection of kinky erotic art. Women meticulously, lovingly bound in ropes and chains. A naked, inked male model kneeling in front of another man clad in black leather. Welts scoring a muscular, bare back that was arched in what must have been ecstasy. That, or pain. Maybe both.

The pictures were mostly black-and-white, though a few had a single color to draw attention to one part of the image. A female model was naked, hands bound behind her back, and the only color in the photo was the bright red blindfold. Another image showed a woman's nails raking across skin, and her nails were the same shade as the previous woman's blindfold.

One particular model appeared in several photos in a row. He was fucking gorgeous—obviously divided a significant portion of his time between a gym and a tattoo shop—and he was naked in all of them except for a gag in one, a blindfold in a few others. In one, he knelt, looking up at someone off camera with that same reverent expression I'd seen in the other model's face in the previous portfolio.

I turned another page, and the next photo was the same model...and Dante.

Taking in the black-and-white image, I couldn't breathe.

Dante stood behind the model. The only clothing on either of them was the blindfold on the model. They were both shirtless, and the photo extended just far enough over their hips to imply they didn't wear anything else. The model tilted his head back and to the side, exposing more of his neck, and Dante's lips nearly touched him. The only color in the photo was Dante's vivid blue eyes, which were focused right on the camera. I swore he looked right at me, and I swore I could feel his breath on my neck like I was the blindfolded tattooed naked model in front of him.

Remembering I had to breathe to stay conscious, I turned the page. Same model, also with Dante, zoomed in closer this time. Now Dante's eyes were closed and his lips were near the model's ear, parted as if he were speaking. The way the model bit his own lip made me wonder just what Dante had said to him.

On another page, the camera zoomed in on Ryan holding what appeared to be a riding crop across the back of his neck with both hands. He inclined his head just so, looking at the camera—at Dante?—with an expression of "Yeah, you want some of this."

"Hey, Dante, think we should get one of these?"

Smack.

"Sure, we can get one, but who the hell are we going to hit with it?"

I shifted in my chair. It wasn't just the delicious suggestiveness of the images. It was *them.* It didn't surprise me at all that they both modeled. Two men with bodies like that and an eye for erotic photography; if that wasn't a natural progression, I didn't know what was.

Seeing them like this was oddly voyeuristic, as if I wasn't just seeing posed images but peeking in through their bedroom door. My heart rate would have been no higher had I stumbled across a sex tape of theirs on the Internet or walked in to see them in a compromising position. And I hadn't even seen much of them in the pictures. Just a ribbon of skin here, a glimpse of muscle there, a *look.* The raw sensuality in every photo, whether they'd taken it or featured in it, sent shivers down my spine. I already knew the two of them were attractive as fuck, but that was before I immersed myself in displays of their physical beauty, their creativity and their unashamed sexuality.

And because I liked to torment myself with tantalizing images of two gorgeous men I couldn't have, I kept turning the pages.

I reached the end of the portfolio and couldn't take my eyes off the last picture. I couldn't fucking breathe. Out of all of the images I'd seen so far, this one was hands down the most arousing.

It was Dante, partially in profile, from his bare collarbones up. His head was thrown back, lips pulled back in a grimace, eyes screwed shut, the cords standing out from his neck. A single drop of sweat glistened on his temple, and while it may have just been a trick of the light, I was sure there was a shimmer of tears just below his eyes.

The instant before release, frozen in time.

I shivered and closed the portfolio, but the images were burned into my mind, especially the last one. That one couldn't have been fake. Not unless Dante was a hell of an actor, anyway, because the about-to-break tension in that image had crackled right off the page. I set both books on the table and sat back. I closed my eyes, letting my head rest against the wall as I took a few deep breaths to calm myself down.

Yeah, right. There was only one way I was going to relieve this tension, and this wasn't exactly the time or place. *Come on, think of something. Something besides Dante on the verge of orgasm or Ryan with that glint in his eyes. Something.*

At least I always had my trusty mental bucket of cold water on standby. Since Eli and I had spent half the morning arguing again, I had something to focus on besides wondering who'd been doing what to Dante when that picture was taken. I rubbed my eyes and forced my mind back into the kitchen to replay standing on opposite sides of the island with Eli and sniping, bitching, going through the same shit we'd been through a million times before.

"What do you want me to do?" he'd growled. "Show you my applications and the confirmation e-mails when they're sent? Do you want to initial my homework every night while you're at it?"

"No, I have no desire to be your fucking parent." Oh, I'd fought to keep my temper in check, and it was harder every time. "But I need to know you're making an effort to get a damned job and an apartment."

"So you don't trust me?"

Well, no, now that you mention it. Which is why we're sleeping in separate rooms and I'm trying to move on. "Just do whatever you have to do. Get a job and get a place of your own."

And at that point, I'd walked out. By the time Bravado and I came back from a nice therapeutic trail ride, Eli's car was gone. At least he was out of my hair for the rest of the day, but somehow I doubted he'd spent his time applying for jobs. Maybe he went out and got laid. Couldn't blame him if he did. I wondered how long it would take for him to convince his next piece of ass to let him move in. Probably not as long as it was currently taking for his *last* piece of ass to get him to move *out*.

The side door opened, and...so much for my efforts to let whatshisname who lived with me distract me.

Dante appeared, and while we exchanged polite greetings, my brain went completely blank except for *that* picture. Instead of the flickering porno channel-surfing my mind had gone through when I'd fantasized about Ryan and Dante the last few nights, it was one static image. One crackling, mouthwatering image.

He said something, but I couldn't comprehend it because all I could think of was him on the verge of an orgasm. Right there. Right fucking there. Just about to let go. Right on—

"Jordan?" He raised an eyebrow.

I blinked. "Sorry, what?"

"I said, come on up and we can go over your album."

"Right, right." I stood, thanking several gods I'd had the forethought to wear an untucked shirt today. I picked up the two portfolios and brought them with me. "I assume you don't want to leave these out?"

He looked at the books in my hand, and his cheeks darkened a little. He glanced toward the side door as if shooting Ryan a glare right through the wall. "Thanks," he said quietly, taking them from me.

"That's some incredible work," I said. "I've always loved that kind of photography."

"Oh. Thanks." He smiled, though some of the extra color lingered on his face. After he'd dropped the portfolios on one of the desks, he sat across from me at Kendra's desk. He clicked the mouse a few times and entered something on the keyboard. Probably a password or something, and I didn't notice *at all* the way his long fingers moved across the keys with practiced agility.

"Did you want to look over them while you're here?" His voice made me jump. Hopefully he didn't notice, and if he did, he didn't let on.

I cleared my throat. "Oh, I can do that at home." *When I can actually concentrate.* "Don't want to take up too much of your time."

He shrugged. "Your call. You can always e-mail me if you don't like the way one's cropped or whatever. Let me just print the invoice and all of that crap." He clicked the mouse, and a printer nearby whirred to life.

As Dante got up to go to the printer, Ryan emerged from the side room, carrying on a conversation with a female model who must have been in her early twenties. He glanced at me, and the devilishness in his fleeting grin rivaled the moment he'd given me that wink earlier. I shifted in my chair. He went back to seeing his client out, and I went back to trying to keep my heart rate within safe parameters. Whether he did it on purpose or not, he knew *just* how to set my nerve endings tingling without even touching me.

Speaking of men who fucked with my head and senses just by existing, Dante came back and took a seat across from me. The papers in his hand sort of drew my attention back to business or whatever it was I was supposed to be thinking about. It wasn't like I was staring at his hand rather than the papers in it, or watching the way his lips moved rather than listening to the words coming out of them.

He slid the invoice across the desk, then flipped open a file folder and pulled out some various forms. Though we'd taken care of it the first time I came in, Dante wanted to make sure we had all the paperwork straight. We discussed the advertising agreement and web policies. We went over model releases, property releases, hold harmless releases, and *God I want to see that picture of you on the verge of rel—focus, Jordan.* I forced myself to concentrate on something that wasn't the gorgeous man sitting across from me and what he looked like right before he fucking came.

Tried to force myself, anyway. Those portfolios were like a damned Pandora's box. Now that they'd been opened, now that I'd seen everything they had to offer, I couldn't get them out of my mind. And now, so many questions, so many things they'd done on camera that I'd been curious about. But were they just posing for the pictures? Or were those slices of a life I secretly wanted to live?

Dante leaned back and turned to Ryan. "Angel, would you put a referral discount on the Steele-Dawson account?"

"On it."

"Do I get a discount if I refer someone?" I asked.

"Of course," Dante said. "Ten percent if a referral books a session."

"So what if I book a second shoot myself?" I said, chuckling. "Do I get a referral discount for myself?"

"No, but there are incentives for repeat customers." He tilted his head slightly. "Why? What else did you have in mind?"

My mouth went dry. What *had* I had in mind? The risqué images flashed through my memory. No, that wasn't what I'd been thinking. Was it?

An upward flick of Dante's eyebrow reminded me I hadn't yet spoken.

I cleared my throat and shifted.

Ryan stepped out of the other room. "I believe I was promised a chance to shoot baby horses."

Forcing a quiet laugh and silently thanking him for the save, I said, "Right, right, of course."

They glanced at each other, something unspoken passing between them.

Then Dante looked at me. "Well, just let us know when you're ready for more."

Ryan nodded. "We're always game for repeat offenders."

"Repeat *clients*, Angel."

"That's what I said."

Dante rolled his eyes. "Yeah, *anyway...*" They glanced at each other again, and I wished to God I could read their minds. I wondered if Dante was irritated with Ryan for letting me see the second book of erotic photos. Then again, maybe he wasn't. I doubted Ryan would show someone something like that if Dante wasn't comfortable with it.

I chewed my lip. If they'd offered to let me see the photos, they obviously weren't embarrassed by them. Question was, were the contents of that book something within the realm of acceptable conversation? Too personal, even if it was in a professional setting?

Curiosity was going to kill this cat yet, and before I could think twice, I blurted out, "I have a question for you."

Dante made a "go ahead" gesture.

"The, um, pictures I saw earlier. The ones with you guys in them." The heat in my cheeks didn't help me get my tongue untied. I coughed to get the air moving again. "I'm curious. Is all of that...fake?"

He cocked his head. "What do you mean?"

"I mean, were you just posing for the photos, or are you really..." I chewed my lip, searching for the words.

Leaning against his desk, Ryan inclined his head. *Oh God, just like he did in that photo, and, yes I do want some of that, Ryan.*

"Are we really into kink?" he asked.

My tongue stuck to the roof of my mouth. "Right. That."

Their eyes met briefly. Then Dante said to me, "It's not just for show. What you saw? That's us."

I gulped. "Wow. Really?"

They exchanged another look. Ryan said, "Let's put it this way: Dante is the only one who calls me 'Angel' who isn't a submissive."

Oh God. I gestured at them. "So, Dante's not a sub, then?"

Dante shook his head. "We're both Doms."

I stared at them.

Ryan stepped forward from his desk and put a hand on Dante's shoulder. "That's why we have submissives like the guys you saw in the photos. Neither of us is a sub."

"So, to answer your question, yes." Dante slid his hand over the top of Ryan's, lacing their fingers together. "What you saw in those pictures is real."

"Some of it we've done for other people or just to be artistic," Ryan said. "But the guys you saw posing with us? They were our submissives at various times. Those photos were posed but definitely real."

Including that orgasm. My heart pounded, my mind superimposing that bead of sweat onto Dante's temple.

"You weren't...offended, were you?" Dante asked.

"Oh, no, definitely not." I wet my lips. "I was just curious. They're...interesting."

Another shared look. Another silent something passing between minds I'd have sold my soul to read.

Then Dante turned to me, his expression unreadable. "Have you ever considered modeling?"

I jumped like one of them had kicked me. "I...can't say I have."

"You should," he said softly. "You're extremely photogenic."

Ryan nodded. "Between what we saw at your sister's wedding and the shoot with your horses, definitely."

Dante folded his hands on the desk. "If you're interested, we could do some shots of you by yourself. See if you like it." He gestured at the door leading into the rest of the studio. "Your call."

"You mean..." I gulped. "Right *now*?"

Dante smiled. "Why not?"

"Jump in with both feet," Ryan said. "Don't give yourself time to get nervous."

"If it's not your thing," Dante said, "we don't have to continue, and you don't have to do it again. We're not charging you for it. It's just..."

"For fun," Ryan said.

I shifted my gaze from Ryan to Dante and back again. Jump in with both feet. Don't give myself time to get nervous. Don't have to continue.

I moistened my lips, then shrugged. "Hell, why not?"

They didn't waste any time. Dante and I stood, and I followed them into the studio. It reminded me of a movie set. Tripods, lights on stands, more lights hanging from the ceiling, cords and cables taped to the floor. Around the edges of the room, dozens of meticulously labeled boxes and crates lined the walls. At the center of the whole thing was a huge, mottled grey drape hanging from a rail and covering several square feet of the floor. A muslin, I think I'd heard someone call such a thing.

Don't give myself time to get nervous. Right.

All I'd needed to get nervous was the time it took for Dante to ask if I'd ever considered modeling. Oh, yeah, I was nervous. But I was also intrigued, both with this idea and with them, so I forced the nerves back.

"So, what exactly do I do?"

Ryan adjusted a light. "Whatever we tell you to do."

"And you can say no to anything," Dante said.

That eased my nerves a little. They were in charge. All I had to do was listen to them, and there was a way out. I could leave now if I wanted to.

Dante disappeared into the shadows, then returned with an adjustable stool that had a single armrest on one side. He put it in the middle of the muslin.

"We'll have you start on that," he said. "It's usually a little easier to relax when you're sitting versus standing in the middle of a bare set."

Relax. Sure. I'll get right on that.

He gestured at it and smiled. "Have a seat."

And we're off.

I took a seat on the stool, resting my arm on the armrest. With the various bright lights around me, I could barely make out Dante and Ryan's shadows. Still, I had no trouble keeping track of them as they moved around. Their footsteps and their dark-against-darker shapes made them easy enough to track, especially when the occasional glint of light on Dante's almost-white hair distinguished his silhouette from Ryan's, but they also kept talking to me.

"Could you put your shoulders back a little? Good, just like that."

"Raise your chin a bit, just—yes, perfect."

"Turn your body about five degrees to your left. Right there, good."

Being in the middle of the set was weird. Out in the open. Exposed. Only their voices gently guiding me through where to put my hand or how to tilt my head kept me distracted from that vulnerability.

Then Ryan came out of the shadows and gestured for me to stand. "I think that's enough with the chair." He took it off the set, and Dante emerged from the darkness.

"Stand with one hip toward the front. Like this." He stood as he'd indicated, his body facing one side of the set while he looked to the front. I mirrored him, and he nodded. "Good. Just rest your weight on your left foot." When I did, he nodded again, and a moment later, he and Ryan were back behind the curtain of shadows.

He was right: without the company of a piece of furniture, I was definitely out in the open. Vulnerable, exposed, and not nearly as unnerved as I thought I'd be.

Nothing in the room was loud, but it was anything but quiet. The pop of the flash and the zing when it recycled. The snap of the shutter. My heartbeat. My own slow, uneven breathing.

Snap. Pop. Zing. Heartbeat. Heartbeat. Heartbeat. Snap. Snap. Snap. Pop. Zing.

"Hook your thumbs in your pockets," Ryan said. "Just let your arms relax." I did, wondering if he realized how far out of my vocabulary "relax" was at this point.

"Bring your left shoulder forward a little," Dante said. "Good, perfect."

Snap. Pop. Zing.

It should have been overwhelming taking commands from two people at once, but strangely enough, it wasn't. They didn't contradict each other. When one gave a suggestion, the other ran with it.

"Tilt your—" Dante stepped across the edge of the muslin. He pursed his lips, then reached for my shoulder but stopped before touching me. "May I?"

In spite of my nerves, I nodded.

Even through my shirt, the gentle contact of his fingers sent electricity down my spine. He nudged my shoulder back a little.

"Good, right there." He offered a smile, which did nothing to help me keep my balance. "Don't move."

Snap. Pop. Zing. Snap. Pop. Zing.

They kept shooting for a few minutes, offering gentle suggestions. I focused completely on their voices, letting their directions ground me. I was aware of what they told me to do, aware of whether or not I was comfortable doing it, but my body simply...did.

"Squat down and rest your elbows on your knees. Just let your hands fall between, completely relaxed."

"Turn to the left."

"Tuck your chin just slightly."

Snap. Pop. Zing. Snap. Pop. Zing.

"Stand and put your weight on your right heel."

"Don't move your head, but look up."

"Bring your chin toward your left shoulder and look straight ahead."

Snap. Pop. Zing. Snap. Pop. Zing.

Blood pounded in my ears when Ryan came up to me as Dante had done a few minutes before. And just as Dante had done, he reached for me but stopped before making contact.

"May I?" he asked, fingertips inches from my face.

I'd forgotten how to speak, so I just nodded.

He touched my face, and I closed my eyes as that warm contact pulled all the air out of my lungs. With the gentlest pressure on my jaw, he turned my head *just* a little to the right.

"You okay?" His voice was soft, and his fingers still cupped my jaw.

"Yeah." I opened my eyes.

Snap. Pop. Zing.

Ryan grimaced and blinked a few times, evidently caught off guard by Dante's flash. Then he gave me a reassuring smile, and slipped back into the dark foreground.

I continued obeying their instructions, pretending I wasn't acutely aware of the phantom warmth where Ryan had touched my skin.

After a while, Dante said, "Would you be comfortable losing your shirt?"

I took a breath. Was I? Oh, hell yes I was.

"Jordan?" Ryan said.

"Um, yeah. Yeah, I can do that." I started unbuttoning my shirt, ignoring all the fluttering in my stomach and the tingling at the base of my spine.

"Wait," Ryan said.

My hands froze, and I looked up, eyebrows raised.

"Slower," he said.

I moistened my lips, then continued unbuttoning my shirt, forcing my unsteady hands to work slowly.

Snap. Pop. Zing. Snap. Pop. Zing.

"Good, just like that," Ryan said softly. His approval sent a rush of...of something through my veins.

Snap. Pop. Zing. Snap. Pop. Zing.

"Take your shirt all the way off." Dante appeared on the set, hand outstretched.

I obeyed, shrugging off my shirt. Warm air met my skin, making me acutely aware of every inch I made visible to them. Of the fact that I no longer had my shirt to mask the front of my jeans and the effect they had on me.

Dante took my shirt but paused before returning to his place. "Tell us if you get cold, okay?"

I nodded. The lights warmed my skin anyway, but it was the heat from under my skin that was liable to make me break into a sweat. Getting cold wasn't an issue.

Snap. Pop. Zing. Heartbeat. Heartbeat. Heartbeat. Snap. Snap. Snap. Pop. Zing.

Fuck, I was half naked. Taking orders, following simple commands that were commands nonetheless. My every move was under the scrutiny of the cameras, illuminated by lights and flashes, and in full unflinching view of *them*. Dante and Ryan. Dante. Ryan. Dante, who'd made me trip over my own feet at the wedding with nothing more than eye contact. Ryan, whose subs called him Angel. Dante, who'd been *right* there; Ryan, who'd silently asked if I wanted some of this, and I did, I did, God damn it, I did.

I was dreaming. I had to be.

"Take off your belt." Dante's command was terse, bordering on sharp, and didn't invite argument. Intellectually, I knew I was free to say no, and I was free to leave if I didn't want to do this. Not that it mattered. I wanted to.

My shaking hands amplified the jingling of my belt buckle, and the metallic sound echoed in the stillness while Dante and Ryan watched. Waited.

Snap. Pop. Zing. Snap. Pop. Zing.

I imagined them zooming in for close-ups of my hands, and wondered if the camera would pick up how much my hands trembled while I tried to work the simple buckle. I wondered just how visible my hard-on was to the cameras—to them—because I sure as hell couldn't miss it. I couldn't decide if that was mortifying or exhilarating.

Then came Ryan's voice, and with four words, he tilted the scales in favor of the latter:

"Get on your knees."

I obeyed immediately. My movement was slow, but it wasn't due to any hesitation. Caution, if anything. My jeans were just a little too tight to make moving, let alone kneeling, easy when I was this hard.

Ryan came toward me, appearing from the shadows as he'd done a few times already. Every step echoed in the silence. I kept my eyes down, watching the shrinking distance between us.

He stopped. Less than a foot separated his shoes from my knees. When he ran his fingers through my hair, I shivered.

"Look at me, Jordan."

I took a deep breath and slowly raised my eyes—*oh, holy fuck, he's as hard as I am*—until I met his.

"There's one more thing I want you to do," he said, almost whispering.

I licked my dry lips. "And that is?"

"I want you to call me Angel."

Chapter Eight

My words hung in the air.

Jordan stared up at me, lips parted, eyes wide with disbelief. Though I did everything I could not to show it, nerves had my gut tied into knots. The three of us had done this little dance, testing the waters and feeling each other out, giving lines for the others to read between. Now it was out there, on the table, with no mistaking Dante's and my intentions. Someone had to make the move and cross the line, so I had. First with the strategically placed portfolio, now with this.

Where we went from here, if anywhere, was up to Jordan.

Is this what you want?

Have we been reading you right all along?

Are you as submissive as your body language says you are?

Please. Please. Please.

Jordan ran the tip of his tongue across the inside of his lower lip. He took a breath. Then, whispering so softly I barely heard him at all, he simply said, "Angel."

Relief and arousal sizzled through my veins. I smiled, running my fingers through his hair again. Before I could speak again or even think far enough ahead to decide on my next move, Jordan put his hand on my hip. The heat of his touch through the thick denim made me shiver.

I'd wanted this, I'd hoped for it, but I'd been damned sure it wouldn't actually happen. And now...was it?

He brought his other hand up, stopping just inches from my belt buckle. Unsteady hand hovering dangerously close to my very erect cock, he looked up at me and whispered, "May I?"

Yes, oh, good God, yes. Keeping my expression as neutral as I could, I nodded.

When he slid his hand over the front of my jeans, I fought to keep it together, something that was *never* a struggle for me. But there was no way in hell this was real. This wasn't really happening. Jordan Steele wasn't really kneeling at my feet with my nickname on his lips. He wasn't really unbuckling my belt, drawing my zipper down and—oh Jesus, yes, he really *was* stroking my cock like that.

His eyes met mine again. With an upward flick of his eyebrows, he asked. With a slow nod, I answered.

And with a kind of barely contained enthusiasm that made me weak in the knees, he sucked my cock. He steadied us both with the hand on my hip, stroked me with the other, and did things with his tongue that...that...

"*Fuck*, that's good," I breathed, gently stroking his hair because I needed to touch him just to anchor myself. "That's fucking amazing, Jordan..." If he was this talented with his mouth, I could only imagine what kind of kisser he was, and that thought turned me on even more.

I turned my head, and Dante met my eyes from where he watched a few feet away. His Adam's apple bobbed, and he licked his lips in the same instant Jordan swept his tongue around the head of my cock. I shuddered, sucking in a breath, and Dante grinned.

I focused on Jordan again. His eyes flicked up and met mine for a fleeting second, and if that didn't make my knees shake enough, he took care of the rest of my balance by adding a subtle twist with his hand. I moved one foot over a few inches, just to stabilize myself.

"Dante, his mouth is fucking incredible," I slurred.

"Is it?"

"Uh-huh." My fingers trembled in Jordan's hair. "My God..."

Jordan doubled his efforts, and my eyes rolled back. It wasn't usually this easy to make me come orally, but if he kept doing that...

"That's right, Jordan," I whispered, moving my hips with him, fucking his mouth while he desperately, hungrily took it. "Just like that."

Dante's hands on my sides startled me. He slid his arms around me, kissing the side of my neck. Fucking hell, Jordan's hand and mouth on my cock...and Dante's lips and stubble and warm breath on my neck...and Jordan's hand...Dante's lips...Jordan's mouth...Dante whispering something...Jordan's goddamned tongue...

"Holy *fuck*." My knees buckled. Had Dante not been behind me, I'd have collapsed, but he kept me on my feet, kept murmuring in my ear, and Jordan didn't miss a beat, just kept right on stroking, sucking and making sure I came and came and fucking came.

When I found my voice, I whispered for Jordan to stop, and he immediately obeyed, stopping so abruptly my heart skipped. I didn't move. Didn't breathe. Eventually, Dante let me go so I could stand on my own two feet. One last shiver worked its way down my spine, and reality slowly set in. We'd really done this. Jordan was—willingly, eagerly—on his knees in front of me, in my studio, wiping the corner of his mouth with the back of his hand after he'd made me come. After he'd damn near driven me to my knees with a blowjob. Holy shit.

He looked up at me through his lashes, and the disbelief was mutual. For a moment, we just stared at each other, trying to catch our breath. Then his face colored a little, and he shifted his gaze down.

"You okay?" I asked, still trying to catch my breath.

He nodded. "I've just...I've been wanting to do that for a while now."

I fucking knew it. I smiled. "Which part?"

He glanced down at his knees, then licked his lips and met my eyes again. "All of it."

"You're not the only one," I said.

While I straightened my clothes, Dante knelt behind Jordan. He put his hands on Jordan's shoulders and leaned in to kiss the side of his neck. He whispered something I couldn't hear, but the response was a shiver and a ragged release of breath. Then Jordan leaned back a little and turned his head so they could see each other.

Dante trailed his fingertips down Jordan's cheek. "I think," he whispered, "that we're going to have a *lot* of fun with you." Sliding his hand around to the back of Jordan's neck, Dante kissed him. Jordan turned a little more and put his hand on

Dante's face. I licked my lips, wondering how much it turned Dante on that his first taste of Jordan tasted like me. If I knew him as well as I should after twelve years, my boyfriend was absolutely rock hard and desperate to fuck the living hell out of Jordan.

Soon, Dante, I thought, biting my lip as I watched the two of them kiss with feverish, breathless desperation. *You'll get to fuck him soon.*

I hoped. Jordan could decide this was an impulsive mistake or just a one-afternoon stand. But I doubted it. Not with the way he'd obeyed without flinching and knelt without hesitating.

And not with the way, after they exchanged a few words I couldn't hear, Dante stood, and Jordan, still on his knees, went for Dante's belt.

Dante's eyes met mine. I grinned. So did he.

Blood pounded in my ears as I watched Jordan unbuckle and unzip, and my mouth watered as Jordan sucked my boyfriend's cock. Just as he'd done with me, he stroked with one hand, steadied himself with the other. If the movements of his jaw were any indication, along with Dante's long, delirious whimper, Jordan was doing the same with his tongue that he'd done to me.

Dante bit his lip. His shoulders rose higher and fell lower with his deepening, quickening breaths. "Oh, Christ," he moaned. "That's...oh, my God, how do you *do* that?"

Jordan moved faster now, and Dante sucked in a breath. He closed his eyes and let his head fall back. I always loved the way he looked when he neared the edge—brow furrowed, eyes screwed shut, lips pulled into a grimace—and now, knowing the magic Jordan worked with his mouth on Dante's cock, it was all I could do not to grab the camera and capture that beautiful intensity on my lover's face. But that would likely be a bit much for Jordan, so I let the camera be. No matter. What I saw was burned into my mind.

Dante cursed. Exhaled. Groaned. Then his lips parted, his eyes flew open, and a violent tremor forced a breath out of him.

"Oh fuck," he murmured. "Oh fuck, fuck, don't...oh God..." He shuddered a few times, then closed his eyes, took a deep breath and let it out slowly.

Jordan sat back on his heels, licking his lips and trying to catch his breath. I put my arm around Dante's waist, partly to touch him and partly to make sure his legs didn't collapse under him. When he looked at me with that familiar, insatiable hunger in his eyes, I pulled him to me and kissed him. He was breathless from his orgasm, and his mouth was faintly salty from mine.

Then he broke the kiss and shifted his gaze down toward Jordan. Still trying to catch his own breath, he whispered, "I don't know where the fuck you learned to do that with your mouth..." He trailed off, shaking his head.

Jordan smiled. "I aim to please."

"Well, you're getting two glowing reviews from us." I offered him a hand. He clasped my forearm, and I helped him to his feet, but he winced, faltering slightly before he was all the way up.

"You all right?" I asked.

He nodded, cheeks coloring a little. "Just spent a little too much time on my knees, I think."

I chuckled. "Kneeling on a hard floor will do that to you."

"Oh, I think I can handle it," he said.

"Good," Dante growled. He cupped both sides of Jordan's neck and moved in for a kiss. They didn't screw around with a light, gentle kiss this time; from the second their lips met, it was desperate, hungry and breathless. I couldn't decide who was more likely to either collapse or drag the other to the floor. When they broke that kiss, Dante rested his forehead against Jordan's, and they panted against each other's lips.

Jordan took a breath. "And you say I'm good with—" A gasp cut him off abruptly, and his spine straightened.

I realized after a second that Dante had slid a hand between them. He squeezed the front of Jordan's jeans, and the devilish look he shot me told me that oh, yeah, the gods had been kind to this man.

He turned his attention back to Jordan. As he unbuckled Jordan's belt, Dante whispered, "Didn't you think we'd return the favor?"

Jordan exhaled hard, then gasped again. "I...didn't... I..."

"Shh." Dante kissed him lightly, starting on Jordan's zipper. "Unless you want me to stop?"

"No, don't stop," Jordan said quickly. "Please."

"Didn't think so."

A shudder ran up Jordan's spine, and he closed his eyes, moaning as Dante stroked his cock.

"After what you just did for both of us," Dante said, pausing to let his lip brush Jordan's, "I'd say this is the very, very least we can do."

"We are gentlemen, after all." I stood behind Jordan and put my hands on his shoulders. Kissing the side of his neck, I gently drew him back so he could lean against me. "Sort of."

"Close enough to gentlemen, anyway," Dante said, "not to let you out of here without an orgasm or two."

Jordan bit his lip. "Don't let me stop you."

"You like what he's doing to you?" I murmured.

He moaned something.

"Answer me, Jordan," I whispered in his ear. "I want to know, do you like what he's doing to you?"

"Yes." It came out as little more than a soft breath. "Yes, I...oh, God..."

Dante stroked faster, his shoulder rising and falling in time with his hand, and Jordan's back arched off me. His head fell back, and when I kissed his neck, his pulse raced against my lips. My own pulse soared as he groaned, nearly whimpered. A tremor almost knocked him off-balance, and he grabbed Dante's other arm for stability.

I nuzzled Jordan's neck, making sure my five o'clock shadow grazed his skin just before my lips did. When he exhaled and shuddered, I whispered, "Don't hold back, Jordan." I kissed his neck again. "Let us feel you come." Another kiss. "And see you come." Another kiss, this time keeping my lips on his skin when I added, "Let us *hear* you come."

He pulled in a sharp breath. His entire body tensed, and when that tension broke with a long, helpless moan, goose bumps prickled the back of my neck and down my spine. I closed my eyes, imagining what it would be like to be deep inside him when he came like that, and the next shudder was mine.

"Jesus Christ, that's hot," Dante whispered. "Just like I knew it would be."

I opened my eyes and met Dante's over Jordan's shoulder. Then he leaned in and kissed Jordan, so I kissed Jordan's neck. He melted between us, gripping Dante's shoulders for support while his legs shook beneath him.

I backed off first. Then Dante broke the kiss, and we let Jordan catch his breath and regain his balance. While Dante left to clean off his arm in the bathroom, Jordan faced me.

"Wasn't what you expected when you came in tonight, was it?" I asked.

He laughed. "Not what I expected, no."

"Well, I do hope you were as pleasantly surprised as we were." I slid my hand around to the back of his neck and teased his lips apart with the tip of my tongue. When he granted me access, the saltiness of his mouth almost drew a moan out of me. That, and just as I'd suspected, his oral prowess included being a spine-tingling kisser. Even while he let me take the lead, he knew just how to drag his lower lip across mine and tantalize my tongue with the tip of his. His mouth must have been made specifically for all things sexual.

When I broke the kiss, his gaze and shoulders both dropped. I ran the backs of my fingers along his jaw, encouraging him to lift his chin. When our eyes met, I whispered, "You've never done something like this before, have you?"

"Well, I *have* sucked cock a few times," he said.

"Believe me, I can tell. What I meant," I whispered, pretending I wasn't still tongue-tied from his kiss, "was have you ever played the submissive before?"

He shook his head.

"Is it something you'd want to keep doing?" I asked.

He gave a quiet laugh. "Are you kidding?"

I smiled, then inclined my head slightly. "I'm serious. We've been looking for a compatible submissive for a long, long time, and if you're willing..." I let my raised eyebrows finish the question.

Jordan gulped and dropped his gaze. I didn't push for an answer, just let him quietly process what I'd suggested. Seconds ticked by. I was about to tell him he didn't have to come up with an answer now, that he'd be wise to sleep on it and give it some thought, but our eyes met again. The intense determination in his kept me silent.

He took a breath. "I want that more than you can possibly imagine."

Chapter Nine

Angel and I didn't talk much on the way over to Jordan's the next night. My stomach was wound up in knots, and I recognized the rapid-fire thumb-tapping on the steering wheel as an unmistakable tell of nerves on his part. I slid my hand over his thigh, and his thumbs slowed but not by much. Even when he put his hand on top of mine, his fingers twitched with the urge to tap.

I suspected he had the same concerns I did. Had we pushed Jordan too fast? Gone too quickly from strangers to something more, especially for someone as new to this as he was? We had gone fast, that much was for sure, but was it too much? Now, he'd had a full night and the better part of a day to have second thoughts. If he had them, I hoped he spoke them, but I also hoped we hadn't scared him off by coming on too strong.

Not that we'd had a hell of a lot of choice, I supposed. We had to make a move, because if he walked out of the studio last night, that would have been the end of it unless he came back. I hadn't been too sure of Angel's strategy with the erotic albums, but they'd found their mark, and though Jordan had been nervous as he progressed from looking at photos to sucking us off in the studio, he hadn't objected.

So now we just needed to sort out what had happened in the heat of the moment and what we all really wanted. Meeting at his place gave Jordan the home-field advantage. We'd be in his territory; he'd be in his own comfortable surroundings.

To some, it might have seemed a bit businesslike, sitting down like this to talk things over, but it was a necessary evil. We barely knew the guy. The chemistry was there, we'd all clicked like nobody's business, but we were still getting to know each other. That, and he'd never been with a Dom, let alone two. Rules and limitations needed to be established before this went any further, *if* it went any further.

Whether or not it did was completely up to Jordan. I just hoped we hadn't fucked this up.

Angel turned down Jordan's long driveway. Gravel crunched under the tires as we drove between the two rows of white fences toward the house that overlooked the rest of the sprawling farm. Blanketed horses dotted the grass-covered landscape, grazing in the warm light of the setting sun. It all resembled a panoramic image from a glossy coffee-table book, not a place where three men would convene to negotiate cuffs and safe words. Then again, most places where such things occurred were unassuming from the outside. Still, this was surreal. Probably because every component of this living photograph—the house, the horses, the fences, the barn— belonged to Jordan Steele.

Angel pulled up in front of the three-car garage and parked. We got out and started up the walk, and it was then that he glanced at me and spoke for the first time in I didn't know how long.

"Think he'll still want to do this?"

"I certainly hope so." I put my hand in his, and we ascended the steps to the front porch.

"One way to find out, I guess." He rang the doorbell, and we waited.

Beyond the door, muffled footsteps padded across a hard floor, and through the frosted glass, Jordan's blurred shape came into view. He opened the door, and his smile loosened some of the knots in my gut. He still seemed a little nervous, making and breaking eye contact with us while we took our shoes off, but there was no ice, no hostility.

"Sasha's in his kennel tonight," he said, "so he shouldn't bother us." His eyes darted toward me.

I realized then that I'd been so wound up about this conversation, I hadn't even thought about the dog. I swallowed. "Cool, thanks. I hope it's not too much trouble."

Jordan gestured dismissively and shook his head. "Not at all. This is his downtime anyway." He led us into the kitchen. "Can I get either of you—"

Heavy footsteps at the other end of the hall turned our heads.

Jordan released a long breath through his nose. "Fuck," he muttered.

Naturally, the asshole he lived with had to pick that moment to make an appearance.

"Someone at the door?" he called from out of sight. "I thought I heard the doorbell." He stepped into the kitchen, and scowled when our presence answered his question.

"You remember Dante and An—Ryan, don't you?" Jordan sounded like he spoke through clenched teeth.

"Oh, yeah, I remember." Eli eyed Angel, then held his hand palm up. "Would it help you recognize me if I had a tray of hors d'oeuvres?"

Angel smiled sweetly. "Oh, no, you're committed to memory now."

Jordan and I both struggled to suppress our amusement. Eli muttered something, then went to the fridge to get himself a beer.

Jordan ignored him and turned to us. "Drinks, anyone?"

"I'll take a Coke," I said.

Jordan nodded. "Angel?"

"Coke's fine."

Eli sipped his beer but furrowed his brow at us. "Angel? I thought your name was Ryan."

Jordan's cheeks reddened and he bit his lip, but Angel didn't miss a beat. "Some people call me Ryan, some people call me Angel."

"Where'd the name come from?" Eli raised an eyebrow. "I mean, is it supposed to be ironic somehow?"

Angel shrugged. "There are all kinds of angels, so interpret it how you will."

"So what kind of 'angel' are you?" The patronizing sarcasm in Eli's voice normally would have set my teeth on edge, and it certainly made Jordan fidget, but Eli knew not with whom he trifled.

Your funeral, sunshine.

"Well," Angel said, probably struggling to resist the temptation to polish his nails on the lapel of his shirt, "I'm sure as shit not the Angel of Mercy."

"Angel of Death?" I suggested.

He shook his head. "I prefer Angel of Darkness. 'Death' is a little dark, you know?"

"And 'dark' isn't?"

"Good point. Angel of Pain?"

"The Paingel?"

"Ooh." His eyes widened and he stroked his chin with his thumb and forefinger. "I like that."

Jordan snickered, shaking his head while he handed around cans of Coke. Eli just seemed irritated, which amused me. Rolling his eyes, he took a drink. Then, apparently thinking he had any chance of getting anything but a snide answer out of my darling Angel of Sarcasm, he spoke again.

"So should I call you Ryan or Angel?"

"Depends." Angel looked him right in the eye. "You willing to get on your knees and suck my cock for the right to call me Angel?"

Jordan laughed behind his Coke can. I pressed my lips together but failed miserably at keeping a straight face. God bless Angel and his ability to deadpan damn near anything.

Eli wrinkled his nose. "I think I'll pass."

Popping the tab on his soda, Angel shrugged. "Ryan it is, then."

I could almost hear Eli's teeth grinding. He took a breath and squared his shoulders. To Jordan, he said, "Well, I'm out of here for the evening. Have fun tonight."

Jordan raised his can and gave a sweet, innocent grin that must have done Angel proud. "Oh, we will, don't you worry."

Thankfully, I wasn't taking a drink just then. Angel, however, wasn't so lucky. He turned away, coughing and sputtering while Eli shot us all indignant looks. With one last eye roll and a few mumbled curses, Eli left.

I put my hand on Angel's shoulder. "You okay?"

Still coughing, he nodded and gave a thumbs-up. His throat probably wasn't yet clear enough to speak, but I was satisfied he wouldn't choke to death, so I turned back to Jordan and my own drink.

"Sorry about him." Jordan shook his head, his cheeks still a little flush with what I guessed to be a mix of embarrassment and irritation. "My animals have better manners than he does."

"It's okay." I nodded at Angel. "This one obviously keeps him in line. Even if he can be a dick about it."

Angel glared at me, still coughing.

"Oh, Eli will get over it," Jordan said.

"Good." I paused. "So, I guess we should get down to what we came to talk about."

Jordan shifted his weight. "Yeah, I suppose we should." He chewed his lip and, with some effort, met my eyes. "Listen, I've never done this before. The Dom/sub thing, being with more than one person, any of it."

"But is it something you want to do?" I asked.

Angel turned around, clearing his throat once more. "If it's not, just say no. You won't hurt our feelings."

"It's not that." Jordan rubbed the back of his neck and dropped his gaze. "Not even close. It's just...new." He stared with unfocused eyes at the floor between us. Then he took a breath. "I'm not even sure what we'd be doing."

"Well, that's why we're here." Angel's voice was low and gentle. "To make sure we all know what we're doing and we're all on the same page."

Jordan nodded. "I guess I'm following your lead, then."

I smiled. "That's why you're the sub."

He laughed quietly. "Good point."

"Though you'll actually be the one in control," Angel said.

Jordan leaned against the counter and drummed his fingers on the edge. "True, I guess I will."

"So, how much do you know about BDSM?" I asked.

"Some," he said. "I've never tried it, but I've done a lot of reading. On the Internet, that sort of thing."

"So if I mention safe words, hard limits, scenes, power exchanges, that kind of thing," Angel said, "you know what I mean?"

Jordan nodded.

"But you've never tried any of it?" I asked.

"I've been interested in BDSM for the last two years." Jordan pointed down the hall where Eli had gone. "I've been with him for three. Do the math."

I grimaced. "Point taken."

"But you still read about it?" Angel's fingernail clicked rapidly against the side of his Coke can. "Did you plan on getting involved in it with him?"

Jordan shook his head. "No, I was just curious. That, and it was something to read about when I was up late, because I was avoiding going to bed."

Angel blinked. The tapping stopped. "You mean you stayed up reading about the kind of sex you weren't having to avoid going to bed with the guy you were with?"

Jordan's cheeks colored a little, and he shrugged. "It was more fun to read about sex with people who actually cared what the other person got out of it than to have the other kind."

"Ouch," I said.

"Tell me about it."

"Still," Angel said, "that must have frustrated the hell out of you."

"What can I say?" Jordan shrugged. "I like torturing myself."

"A masochist." A grin spread across Angel's lips. "Excellent."

"You're a sadist, then?"

I laughed. "Oh God, you have *no* idea."

The devilishness in Jordan's grin almost put Angel's to shame. "Good."

Jesus. He really is one of us. Be still, my beating heart. You too, cock.

Jordan went on. "Okay, so, I get BDSM. Inexperienced as all hell, but I think I sort of know what I'm getting into there." He shifted his weight. "The one thing I'm a bit confused about is how this would work. With the three of us. How does this kind of relationship work? I mean, for lack of a better word."

"No, it's the right word," I said. "It's a relationship of sorts, just not a very traditional one." I gestured at Angel. "Particularly with the number of people involved."

"That, and it doesn't have to be a twenty-four/seven thing," Angel said. "This can be the kind of thing where we get together once in a while and play."

"Or it can be a regular thing," I said. "We've had subs we saw every few months or so, and we've had some we saw several times a week."

"It's just sex, though, right?" Jordan asked. "Not a 'relationship' in the traditional sense?"

"It's..." Angel paused, chewing the inside of his cheek and absently brushing a few strands of hair out of his eyes. Then, with a sharp intake of breath, he came back to life. "It's a little more complicated than 'just sex' or 'friends with benefits' or anything like that. What we're doing isn't going to be as casual as a one-night stand, but it won't be intimate in the same way a relationship is."

"It's not as detached as casual sex," I said. "It can't be, not with the level of trust it requires."

Jordan raised an eyebrow, his eyes flicking back and forth between us. Angel and I exchanged a brief look.

Angel tapped his nail on the side of his Coke can again. "If you're concerned about being the third wheel or the odd man out, don't be. The way we see it, our romantic relationship is its own entity, and this three-way relationship is another."

"What we have as a couple is our own thing," I said. "As a trio, a triple, a triangle, whatever the fuck you want to call this"—I gestured at the three of us—"everyone is an equal player."

Jordan nodded. "Okay, I guess that makes sense."

"Are you comfortable with the idea of playing with one of us at a time in addition to all three of us being together?" I asked.

The corner of Jordan's lips curled slightly. "Oh, I don't know if I can handle only one of you."

Angel winked. "Didn't think you'd mind."

"It's perfectly okay with us," I said. "And of course you're not committed to only us. Though it's only good manners to let us know if you're going to have an all-bareback orgy with a dozen strangers."

"No kidding," Angel said. "That way we can go too."

I closed my eyes and pinched the bridge of my nose. "I walked right into that one, didn't I?"

Jordan chuckled. "Yeah, you did."

"*Anyway.*" I glared at each of them in turn. "This isn't an exclusive arrangement, let's put it that way."

"And speaking of handling one of us at a time," Angel said. "Since you're not used to being topped, we'll start out with just one of us. Ease into being a submissive to one of us, then the other, then both."

"Where would the other be?" Jordan asked.

I shrugged. "Depends on what everyone's comfortable with. In the same room, in another room, whatever."

Angel looked at Jordan. "I assume you're okay with being watched?"

"Nope. Can't stand it. Everybody turn away." He paused. "Especially if I'm sucking someone off in a photography studio."

Angel and I exchanged glances, both lifting our eyebrows, then looked back at him.

"Why do I get the feeling we're going to have our hands full with you?" Angel asked.

"Maybe I need two Doms instead of one." Jordan kept a straight face about as well as Angel could. "You know, to keep me in line."

"There's probably some truth to that," I said, trying to sound stern.

Angel chuckled, then turned serious again. "So let's talk limits. The big one for me relates to anal sex. I never receive, only give."

Jordan nodded. "Makes sense, given that you're a Dom."

"No, it's not that. I just don't like it." Angel gestured at me. "Dante loves it, though."

"Even from a sub?" Jordan asked.

"Of course." I grinned. "Just don't think for a second that if you're fucking me, you're in control."

His eyes widened slightly, and the twitch of his shoulders suggested he was trying to mask a shiver.

"Any particular limits for you?" I asked.

He thought for a moment. "I'm still not a hundred percent sure how I'll deal with pain or bondage, so..."

"Don't worry about that part now," Angel said. "We'll get to that. Stick to the basics for now. Just us giving you simple commands, steadily taking things further than we did last night until you're ready to play with some fire." I thought the choice of words coupled with that knowing, scheming look would unnerve Jordan, but he held Angel's gaze and swept the tip of his tongue along the inside of his lower lip.

"Anything you absolutely don't like?" I asked. "Being touched any particular place or way? Anything sexual?"

Jordan fidgeted. "I really don't like my feet messed with. At all. Foot massages, tickling, anything."

Angel and I both nodded.

"Is that a boundary you'd want us to push at some point?" Angel asked. "Or just leave it alone?"

"I might change my mind later," Jordan said. "But for now, leave it alone."

"Noted," I said. "Anything else?"

"You're not opposed to sucking cock, are you?" Angel deadpanned.

"I can be blackmailed into it if you have any incriminating photos of me," Jordan shot back.

Angel and I looked at each other. *Oh, yes, we are going to have so much fun with you, Jordan.*

"Okay, smartass," I said. "Another thing: this doesn't extend beyond the bedroom. We're bedroom Doms, not full-time Doms."

"In the bedroom, you submit to us," Angel said. "Outside it, we're just three guys. So you can be mouthy and sarcastic out here—"

"Oh, great, just encourage him." I rolled my eyes.

"Trust me," Jordan said. "I don't *need* any encouragement."

"Didn't think you did," I said. "Any questions?"

He furrowed his brow. "I assume condoms are obvious?"

"Absolutely," I said. "And we use them on our own too."

"You do?" Jordan asked. "Even after all this time?"

"Yes, especially since we're not completely monogamous, and..." I put a hand on Angel's shoulder. "Just a personal preference, I guess."

"Works for me," Jordan said.

"And for safe words," Angel said. "We use 'red' and 'yellow'. Pretty basic."

"I'm familiar with how they work," Jordan said. "Red to stop, yellow to slow down."

"Good," Angel said with a nod. "And don't ever be afraid to use them. Ever."

"You'll never be punished for using a safe word," I said. "Understood?"

Something unwound in Jordan's posture. "Understood."

"It'll probably be a while before we start pushing you hard enough to warrant a safe word," Angel said.

"Starting out, it's mostly a matter of us earning your trust," I said. "Which means we figure out where you're comfortable, where *we're* comfortable, and go from there."

Angel set his Coke can down. "So basically, do you trust us enough to let us fuck you?"

I pinched the bridge of my nose again and released an exasperated sigh. Then I gestured sharply and said to Angel, "You know, one of these days, I swear to God, I *will* teach you a thing or two about subtlety."

He shrugged. "What? It was a valid question."

I rolled my eyes. "Yeah, so is 'do you want to suck my cock?', but—"

"I do, by the way," Jordan said, completely matter-of-factly and with a perfectly straight face. "Just so we're clear."

I blinked. Stared at him. At Angel. Back at Jordan. "Christ, you two really are cut from the same cloth, aren't you?"

"See?" Angel clapped my shoulder. "Subtlety is *so* overrated."

I shot him a playful glare, and he batted his eyes. Chuckling, I turned back to Jordan. "Any other concerns, limits, whatever?"

"Not offhand," he said. "I'm not quite sure what we're doing...um, whenever we...do this. Like, how far you guys are going to push things right away."

"Not very far." I set my drink down and started toward him. "Are you ready to do anything tonight?"

He took a breath. "Yeah, yeah, definitely."

"Good." I put my hand on his waist. He drew in a sharp breath but kept his eyes locked on mine as I spoke. "So now we've broken the ice, and we're all on the same page, but we'll still take things slow." I trailed my fingertips down the side of his face. "It'll take time for us to fully earn your trust and submission, but once we do..." I leaned in until our lips were nearly touching. "...something tells me you'll enjoy it."

"I have no doubt at all," he murmured and melted against me when I kissed him. When I let him go, he met my eyes, then dropped his gaze and took a deep breath. After a moment, he looked at me through his lashes. "Unless there's anything else we need to work out, should we take this someplace other than the kitchen?" He swallowed hard. "The bedroom, maybe?"

I stroked his hair and kissed him again, gentler this time. "I like the way you think. Lead the way."

Angel and I followed Jordan out of the kitchen. The stairs creaked beneath our feet as we climbed to the third floor. At the top of the steps were three doors, and Jordan reached for the center one. The slightest tremor in his hand gave me pause, and with a hand on his arm, I stopped him before he opened the door.

"Are you absolutely sure you're comfortable with this?" I asked, keeping my voice as gentle as possible.

"Yes," he said softly.

I looked down at his hand, then met his eyes again. He followed the same track my gaze had taken and pursed his lips.

Angel put his hand on Jordan's shoulder. "If you're not, just say so."

Jordan swallowed. He glanced at Angel, then at me. "No, I want to do this. Just...a little nervous."

"That's to be expected." Angel kissed the side of Jordan's neck, and Jordan shivered. Almost whispering, Angel said, "It's okay if you're nervous. Most people would be, especially with two strangers."

I drew gentle arcs on Jordan's wrist with my thumb. "We're more than willing to do this, but if you're not ready, just say so."

A cautious but unmistakable grin pulled at Jordan's lips. "If I wasn't ready"—he pushed the door open—"we'd still be downstairs."

Angel and I exchanged another fleeting moment of eye contact, then followed Jordan into the bedroom. The door clicked shut behind Angel, and I made note of the catch of Jordan's breath. Definitely nervous.

There was a chair beside the window, so Angel sat. Jordan faced me. His eyebrows lifted in an unspoken, "What do you want me to do?"

I rested a hand on his waist and the other on the back of his neck. Adopting my sharp "Dom voice", as Angel called it, I said, "Here's how this is going to work. You're going to get on your knees and suck my cock, but you're not going to make me come." I paused and couldn't help noticing the way his body relaxed a little at the sound of my voice. *God, you were born to be a sub, weren't you?* "And then I'm going to fuck you."

Jordan shivered.

I went on. "You can use a safe word at any time, or just tell me to stop. Understood?"

"Yes."

"Good." I said. "Oh, and there's one more thing."

His eyes widened, a mix of anticipation and uncertainty in his expression.

"As long as you're under his or my command," I said, "your orgasms belong to us. If you come when we haven't ordered or permitted you to, there will be consequences. Understood?"

He nodded.

I raised an eyebrow.

"Yes," he said quickly. "Consequences. Right. Understood."

"Good," I said, a little softer now. "And you're still okay with this, right?"

"Ooh, yeah."

I kissed him gently, pressing my hips against his so he could feel that I was already hard. So was he. My God, so was he.

I broke the kiss and stepped back. He dropped his gaze and sucked his lower lip into his mouth for just one more taste. Without thinking about it, I did the same.

"Unbutton your shirt." I paused. "Slowly."

Jordan closed his eyes and swept his tongue across his lip. With hands as unsteady as his breathing, he reached for his top button. He kept his eyes down. I wasn't sure if he focused on his hands or just the floor, but he didn't look at either of us. Even after the last button was open, he simply dropped his hands to his sides and waited.

"Take it off." I extended my hand. "And give it to me."

He shrugged his shirt off his shoulders, pulled his hands free and handed it to me. Our eyes met briefly, but before he'd even released the shirt to my custody, he looked down again.

I put the shirt on the bed and took a few steps back, creating a broader expanse of space between us before I said, "Take off your belt."

The buckle jingled. Leather hissed over denim. Once it was off, his belt draped over his upturned palm like a serpentine offering, he met my eyes, silently asking what to do next. I nodded toward the floor. He flipped his hand over and let the belt fall with a *clink-thud.*

"Jeans off."

He chewed his lip and hesitated, but obeyed.

Before he'd even stepped out of them, I added, "Boxers too." Tension in his shoulders slowed his movements as he stripped out of his last remaining clothes. I was well aware how unnervingly vulnerable this made him. We were fully dressed; he was completely naked. Several feet of vacant air separated us from him, and being out in the open like that often amplified the sense of exposure.

I let a few seconds tick by, which must have been an eternity for him. When at last I spoke, I kept my voice gentle and soft to avoid startling him. "Excellent. Now get on your knees."

Jordan glanced at me, at Angel, at me again. Before I could ask once more if he was still okay with this, though, he took a deep breath and knelt.

I waited a few seconds, letting the empty stillness settle its weight on his beautiful, bare shoulders. Then I moved toward him, giving him time to get used to my nearness before I stopped right in front of him. He stared at the floor between us. His fingers twitched a little on his knees. Even if my proximity unnerved and intimidated him, it likely alleviated that sense of vulnerable exposure from being naked and out in the open.

Mirroring the first contact Angel had made in the studio, I ran my fingers through Jordan's hair. He jumped at first but then exhaled, his shoulders dropping slightly.

"Look at me, Jordan," I whispered.

Slowly, he raised his chin and met my eyes. Few things in this world were hotter than submission, and kneeling at my feet, looking up at me like that, Jordan was the very picture of it.

With one hand still in his hair, I went for my own belt. Jordan held my gaze and swallowed hard. When I drew my zipper down, he bit his lip. I half expected him to close his eyes or shift them away, but my eyes hadn't given his permission.

"When we started tonight," I said, stroking my cock a few inches from him, "what did I say you were going to do?"

He swallowed again, then cleared his throat. "Suck your cock." His eyes flicked toward it, then quickly back up to me. "And then you were going to fuck me."

I nodded. "Good. You know what to do, then."

He immediately leaned forward and wrapped his fingers around my cock, and though I was silently going insane at the mere thought of what I knew his mouth could do, I stopped him just before his lips would have touched me. I put my hand over his, forbidding him from stroking, and again held his hair with the other, keeping his mouth *just* out of reach of what he wanted.

"Wait."

I couldn't tell if the way his eyebrows lifted was out of panic, confusion, or a little of both.

"Do you—" My breath caught, all of my attention suddenly drawn to his hand on my cock, where a hint of a tremor made his fingers tighten-release-tighten-release. Subtle, yes, but in my maddening state of wanting him right now, it was almost enough to throw me off-balance. I gripped his hand a little tighter, which stilled the tremor, but meant he was squeezing my cock and *God fucking damn it, I've never had a sub throw me off like you do.*

"Dante?" Angel said. "You all right?"

"Yeah, I'm good." Recovering my composure, I looked down at Jordan. "Do you want to suck my cock?"

"Yes," he said without hesitation.

"That didn't sound very enthusiastic."

Eyes locked on mine, he chewed his lip. "Yes, I want to."

"You want to what?"

"I want to suck your cock."

I raised an eyebrow. "I believe you mean you want permission to suck my cock, yes?"

He shivered. "Yes, that's what I meant."

"Then ask for it."

"Please—" He licked his lips. "Please, may I suck your cock?"

"Yes, you may." I released his hair.

My heart didn't even have time to beat before Jordan's mouth was around my cock. If I thought he was enthusiastic in the studio, that was nothing compared to now. Just a few seconds of denial, and hunger had become pure need. I thought he groaned but didn't feel the hum of his voice on my skin, and a second later, realized it had been me.

When my eyes could focus, I watched him, struggling just to breathe. I wondered if Jordan even possessed a gag reflex, so deep could he fuck me with his mouth. He deep-throated me until my breath caught. Teased the head of my cock with his lips and tongue until I shivered. Deep-throated again. His hand stroked, then steadied, then stroked. All the while, his eagerness didn't wane in the slightest. I could have let him do this all night long, and he probably would have.

But I wasn't done with him yet.

While he stroked and sucked me halfway to oblivion, I pulled off my shirt and tossed it in the general direction of his discarded clothing. Jordan glanced up at me, and though I didn't hear the sound he made, it reverberated across nerve endings that couldn't take much more.

Gently but firmly, I said, "Stop."

Without a second's hesitation, he did. He released me and rocked back on his heels.

I wet my lips. "I want to fuck you." As I stepped back and took off my jeans, I said, "Do you have lube?"

Jordan nodded. "Should I get it?"

Waiting for permission or a command. Good, Jordan. I smiled. "Yes."

Angel pulled a condom out of his back pocket and tossed it to me while Jordan got the lube out of his bedside-table drawer. Of course Angel and I had brought lube. We always came prepared. But Jordan's complete lack of hesitation when I'd brought it up signaled to me that he still wanted very much to continue. As if the enthusiastic magic he'd worked with his mouth hadn't been a clue.

Jordan returned and handed me the lube. At my command, he went back to his knees at my feet, but a wince flickered across his face.

"How are your knees?" I asked.

"They're fine." A shy, almost cautious smile tugged at the corners of his mouth. "I think I can stay on them for a while yet."

"Good." I handed him the condom. "Put it on me."

No hesitation whatsoever. He tore the wrapper with his teeth and let it flutter forgotten to the floor. Steadying my cock with one hand, he rolled the condom on with the other, and I focused on keeping my breathing slow and even. It had been so long, so fucking long, and just the familiar sensation of latex on my cock was enough to make my head spin.

When the condom was on—*fuck, yes, I want you so badly, Jordan*—I gestured at the bed. "Get on your hands and knees." He stood, and as we both got onto the bed, I added, "Facing that way so Angel has a good view."

Jordan's head snapped up, and he glanced at Angel. I wondered if he'd forgotten Angel was even here. Whether he had or not, now he was certainly aware of that presence in the corner.

"Ever been fucked while someone else watches?" I asked while I stroked some lube onto my cock.

Jordan's eyes flicked toward my cock, then my eyes. "Unfortunately, no, I haven't."

"Tonight's your lucky night, then. Turn around."

As ordered, he got up on his hands and knees while I knelt behind him. We were turned so Angel could see us in profile. So he could see just about everything.

Resting a hand on Jordan's hip, I guided my cock to him. He tensed when I touched him. I didn't pull away, just gave him a chance to relax and get used to me. *This* may not have been new to him, but I was new to him, as was Angel's presence, and submission, and everything that had transpired between the wedding and now. He wanted this, but it was uncharted territory for him, so I was patient.

And after a few seconds, I was rewarded with a long breath. Some of the tightness in his back and shoulders melted away. When I pressed against him again, I met a little resistance, but the soft moan he released told me I wasn't hurting him at all when I pushed past that resistance.

I dug my teeth into my lower lip. Watching myself slide into him, oh fucking hell, it was unreal. It had been ages, and I'd nearly forgotten just how amazing it felt to be inside someone, and just how fucking hot it looked from this vantage point.

He moaned again and let his head fall forward. A shudder rippled up his spine.

"You okay?" I asked.

He murmured something.

"I asked you a question, Jordan," I said sharply.

"Yes," he said. "Yes, I'm fine."

"Good." I ran a gentle hand up his back and down again. Some more tension melted from his shoulders, and with every slow, easy stroke I took inside him, he relaxed a little more.

My eyes flicked toward Angel. He shifted in his chair, and I didn't have to see below his belt to know he was hard.

Focusing on Jordan again, I fucked him a little harder. At the outskirts of my awareness was a quiet, staccato beat. Fingers on the armrest or windowsill probably, a rapid tempo of *Angel's here, Angel's here, Angel's here.* Knowing those blue eyes were focused on me while I moved inside Jordan, I had to force myself not to come yet.

I concentrated on Jordan. I leaned forward, resting my hands on the bed beside his, and thrust from the hips. His arms and shoulders quivered. I thought a whispered "fuck" slipped off his lips.

"Like that?" I asked.

"Yes. God, yes."

"Can you come this way?" I murmured. "Just from me fucking you?"

He gasped as a shiver rippled up his spine, and when it had passed, he nodded.

"You can?" I kissed the back of his shoulder. "All I'd have to do is keep...fucking...you..."

"Yes," he moaned.

"You can." I shifted my tone from playful to commanding. "But you won't."

Jordan whimpered, shuddering beneath me, and I guessed he was even closer to coming now that I'd denied him.

"Don't you dare come yet, Jordan," I whispered, letting my lip brush the back of his neck. "I haven't given you permission."

Another frustrated sound, and he shuddered again. "Fuck...I'm..."

"You're not going to come," I growled. "Not until I say you will."

He pulled in a deep breath and his shoulders tensed and trembled as he fought to stay in control.

"Oh God, Jordan," I whispered, deliberately exhaling across his sweaty skin. "Oh God, you feel so fucking good, I'm...oh, fuck..."

Jordan moaned. His fingers clawed at the comforter, his arms quivering beneath him, and the frustrated sounds he made were almost more than I could take.

I pushed myself upright and moaned, thrusting a little harder as my orgasm closed in fast. From the corner of my eye, movement caught my attention. I turned my head just in time to see Angel shifting in his chair again. His lips parted and his eyes were fixed on me.

On us.

Watching me fuck Jordan.

Watching me unravel.

Oh, Jesus, watching me come.

I held Jordan's hips to me, threw my head back and groaned. He moaned and shuddered, and I thought for a moment he might have come too. Even as my orgasm tapered, though, he didn't relax. He took long, deep breaths, but the tension in his quivering shoulders didn't release. I grinned to myself. He'd been close, damn close, but he'd held himself back.

I slid my hands up his back and gently kneaded his shoulders. "Good, Jordan," I whispered. "You'll get to come soon, don't worry."

I half expected a smartass retort, but he replied with little more than a vague nod. There would come a time when I'd demand quick, articulate responses, but he was still new to this. He'd obeyed a difficult order and kept his orgasm at bay. He could be forgiven, if only tonight, for an inability to speak. At this point, he was probably lucky to still be conscious.

I pulled out slowly and sat back. Jordan turned around, almost collapsing onto his back as he did.

"Fuck," he murmured, wiping sweat from his brow.

I stood, resting a hand on the bed until my legs steadied themselves beneath me. While I took the condom off, I looked at Jordan.

"You're going to make yourself come," I said. "But only when I tell you to." I gestured at the pillow. "Lie back, touch yourself. I'll be right back."

Jordan nodded. He did as ordered, lying back against the pillows. He closed his fingers around his cock, and my blood pressure skyrocketed as he stroked himself slowly.

"One thing, though, you—" I paused. "I didn't say to stop, just keep...good."

He looked at me through heavy-lidded eyes, his hand still moving, if a little slower now.

"Don't even think of stopping *or* coming while I'm out of the room," I said. "Angel will be keeping an eye on you."

The low, frustrated groan that emerged from his lips made me grin. He closed his eyes and furrowed his brow.

Angel and I exchanged winks. Then I left to get rid of the condom. When I came back, Jordan was right where I'd left him, as was Angel. I gestured to Angel, and we both joined Jordan on the bed. It was a California king, so there was plenty of room for us to give him space, but what fun was that?

We both got right up next to him. Angel flicked his tongue across Jordan's nipple. I kissed Jordan's neck, tasting the heat and sweat on his skin as his moan reverberated against my lips. I could only imagine what went through his arousal-addled mind with two men touching and teasing him while he jerked himself off but couldn't come.

I raised my head and watched him. The twin lines between his eyebrows deepened, and his back lifted off the bed when Angel teased his nipple again. Every muscle in Jordan's arm tensed and shook as he stroked his own cock, and every sound that escaped his lips was made of pure, delicious aggravation.

"Don't slow down," I whispered. "And don't come yet."

"Fuck..." His cheek rippled as he clenched his jaw. "Oh God..."

"I know you can wait," I whispered. "Just like you did while I was fucking you."

He groaned, closing his eyes even tighter.

"You'll hang on as long as I want you to, won't you?"

Jordan tried to answer, but the flick of Angel's tongue across his nipple caught him off guard. His eyes flew open and his back arched as he gasped.

"Answer me, Jordan," I said. "You'll keep going as long as I want you to, won't you? Just like you did while—"

"*Yes.*" The word came out as a half groan, half cough. "Oh, fuck, oh, fuck..."

Keeping my tone low, calm and even, I leaned closer to his ear and said, "I know we're frustrating you, Jordan. I know you want to come. You want to let go." I fought to keep my amusement out of my voice when he whimpered. "I want you to stay right there on that edge. No pulling back, no going over." Another whimper. "Not until I tell you that you can come."

"Oh God..."

Angel sat back, propping his head up on one hand. Our eyes met over Jordan, and Angel licked his lips.

I leaned down again, not quite kissing Jordan's neck, just breathing on him. His own breathing quickened. Whispered curses rolled off his lips, and even though he was going out of his ever-loving mind, his hand kept moving.

He gasped. I thought he was about to lose it, thought he was about to let go and surrender, but he held back, and I rewarded him with a single whispered word:

"Come."

In a heartbeat, his back levitated off his bed, and semen landed on his abs and chest. The helpless, throaty groan that escaped his lips was easily one of the sexiest things I'd ever heard, and when Angel fidgeted beside him, I knew he was in agreement.

Jordan's hand slowed to a trembling stop. His eyes stayed closed, his brow stayed furrowed, and he took sharp gasps of breath through his parted lips.

Finally, he opened his eyes. At first, he stared up at the ceiling. Probably letting the spinning stop. God knew I was familiar with that feeling. He blinked a few times, then looked at me.

"You've done well." I leaned in to kiss him gently. "Even if I did frustrate the hell out of you."

A soft huff of laughter warmed my lips. He took and released a deep breath. "That was...unbelievable."

"In a good way or a bad way?" Angel asked.

"Good. Definitely good."

"That's what we like to hear," I said.

Jordan looked down at his chest and his hand. "Guess I should go clean this up, shouldn't I?" He started to sit up, so Angel and I each put a hand on his back to keep him steady. I moved so he could get to his feet, and I kept a hand on his arm until we were both sure he'd stay on his feet.

With his knees more or less steady, he went into the bathroom, and I got back on the bed with Angel. As soon as I was within reach, Angel kissed me, and as his tongue slipped between my lips, he guided my hand to the front of his pants.

"Hmm," I said. "I think someone's a bit turned on."

"Damn right. I've said it before, and I'll say it again," he said, his lips almost touching mine, "watching you fuck another man is so. Fucking. Hot."

"So you'd be game for doing it again?"

"Oh, you know I will."

I kissed him lightly. "I think I might like to watch you fuck him too."

Angel shivered and pressed his cock against my hand.

A moment later, Jordan returned. "So, I assume I'm not going to leave Angel out in the cold."

Beside me, Angel squirmed with barely contained arousal.

"Depends on if you want to play with both of us tonight," I said. "If you can handle two Doms."

"Oh, I think I've got plenty left," Jordan said to Angel.

Angel nodded toward me. "I think you should ask the man in charge."

Jordan gulped and turned to me. "May I—" He cut himself off, biting his lower lip. Then he cleared his throat. "May I suck his cock?"

I smiled. "Absolutely."

"In that case." Angel stood. He pointed at the floor in front of him and looked at Jordan. "Why aren't you on your knees yet?"

Chapter Ten

Like they did every morning of my life, my eyes flew open at exactly six o'clock. This morning, I was a bit more bleary-eyed than usual, but it took my fatigue-fogged brain only a second to figure it out. The arm draped over my waist and the slow, rhythmic breathing beside me reminded me I wasn't alone. The slightly softer sound of someone else breathing reminded me *we* weren't alone.

I grinned to myself, remembering everything from last night. I'd have gladly stayed in bed a little longer, basking in the glow of the rising sun with the men responsible for the rugburns on my knees, but if I did, I'd likely fall asleep again. And if I fell asleep, I'd probably wake up to find my horses had eaten my barn. Even after a night of hot, long-overdue sex, duty called.

So, gently freeing myself from Dante's lazy grasp, I sat up. Moving as quietly as I could, I got out of bed and threw on a pair of jeans and a T-shirt, all the while resisting the urge to just stare at Angel and Dante while they slept. There was a time not long ago when I'd have said it was a crime for any man to be that fucking beautiful, but since the guilty parties were both naked and asleep in my bed, I wasn't going to complain.

Slipping out of the bedroom, I went into the kitchen and put the coffee on, then headed down to the garage to get my dog and boots.

"Ready to go?" I scratched Sasha's ears as he yawned and stretched. When I reached for my boots, he jumped and spun in circles, tags jingling and claws rattling across the linoleum.

"Okay, okay, we're going." I laughed. "Just be patient."

He whined as I went for the door, and as soon as I opened it, he tore out of the garage and loped down the path ahead of me. Most mornings, I'd jog right beside him, but every muscle in my body ached this morning, so I settled for a brisk walk.

When I caught up with him, he bounced up and down in front of the barn.

"Has anyone mentioned to you that you're a senior dog?" I said as I unlatched the door. "You're supposed to mellow with age, dummy." I slid the barn door open, and as soon as he had enough room, Sasha wriggled through and took off down the aisle in a clatter of claws on concrete.

All down the aisle, shavings rustled and horses grunted and murmured sleepy greetings. It was a little odd, stepping back into my familiar world now, going through familiar motions in a body that had gone into some very alien territory last night. Wandering up and down the aisle, distributing hay and grain over doors and into buckets, my aching body was on autopilot. My mind, however, went into overdrive.

For years, I'd wanted to try everything we'd done and everything we'd discussed. Power exchanges intrigued me, but the thought of actually handing over that power was intimidating to say the least. And yet with them, it had been...natural. My knees ached like hell this morning, but every twinge just reminded me of all the kneeling I'd done, so I didn't complain.

I'd finally had a taste of submission. *Consensual* submission. And I liked it. A lot.

Eli had been in control in our relationship, particularly where sex was concerned, but I was never his submissive. I never gave him control; he simply took it. Assumed it was his. And I'd always kept a bit from him, kept a wall between us.

With Angel and Dante, I lowered that wall. Perhaps more willingly than I should have, given that we'd just met, but they didn't rouse my usually hyperactive instinct of suspicion.

I should have felt outnumbered. Two of them, one of me. Granted, Angel sat back at the beginning and let Dante take charge, and Dante was the one giving me orders all evening, but Angel's silent authority was still there. Though he'd made little attempt to assert it, deferring most of last night to Dante, it was like we both knew if Angel gave a command, I'd have obeyed it. And I would have.

They seemed to be aware of their two-to-one advantage. They were conscious of that, of my inexperience, and of my nerves whenever they showed. All night long, they went out of their way not to overwhelm me. Of course they'd still pushed me to levels of frustration I'd never known existed, and they kept all three of my orgasms out of reach until they were damned good and ready to give them to me.

It was much too early in this strange interpretation of a relationship to tell where things would go, how this would progress, but at least where last night was concerned, it was perfect. Exactly the kind of men who could guide me into this lifestyle so I could see for myself if it was something I really wanted. And if last night was any indication, it was definitely something I wanted.

I took Arturo out of his stall and led him down to his turnout. He eyed the flake of hay under my other arm but wisely didn't reach for it. He knew better and waited patiently while I opened the gate and unclipped his lead rope. Then he jogged past me, stopped and waited for me to put the hay down before he dove into it.

I patted his neck. "Now would you kindly eat this and not the fence today, bud?"

He just sneezed.

Chuckling, I left the paddock, shut the gate and headed back into the barn.

The early feeding routine was usually enough to wake me up, particularly if it was a cool morning like this. Just walking down from the barn to the lower pasture was enough to shake me out of the grips of even a bad hangover, but this morning, I was still yawning on the way back up that path.

The car parked in front of my garage certainly did a number on my heart rate, though. Benign glass and painted steel, an inanimate object in my otherwise vacant driveway, and it screamed "last night was fucking *real*", and that thought hit my veins like a triple-shot of espresso.

I shook my head and went back into the barn to double-check I hadn't forgotten any of my various chores. It was a routine long since etched into my brain, but my mind was foggy as hell this morning thanks to the pair currently asleep in my bed. It wouldn't have surprised me if I'd forgotten to turn off a faucet on a water bucket or two or put a horse out in one of the muddy pastures without a blanket on.

All was well, though, so I started back toward the house.

"Sasha, come," I called out. He obediently ran out of a pasture and skidded to a stop right beside me. I reached down to pet him. "That's a good boy."

Together we walked back up to the house. In the garage, I dusted off my shirt and kicked off my boots. Then I grabbed a grungy towel off the washing machine so I could wipe Sasha's paws. Once he was more or less clean, I let him into the house.

Sasha trotted into the living room, and a moment later was quiet. Happily gnawing on a bone, knowing him.

I left him to his chewing and headed back up to the bedroom for a cleaner shirt. About halfway up the stairs, I paused. Crap, I needed to put Sasha outside before Dante got up.

Before I could backtrack and take Sasha into the backyard, though, Dante appeared at the top of the stairs, pulling his shirt on.

I continued up the last few steps. "Morning."

"Morning." He smiled sleepily and put a hand on my waist as he kissed me.

"I didn't wake you up, did I?" I asked.

"Nah, I'm usually up pretty early myself." He rubbed his eyes, then nodded toward the bedroom. "Just don't expect to see that one out of bed any time soon."

I chuckled. "Late sleeper?"

"God, yes. That, and your cat joined us after you left." He waved a hand at the bedroom door again. "He won't be up until she is."

"Really?"

Dante rolled his eyes. "He can't stand disturbing a sleeping cat."

"If need be, a can opener will get her out of bed quick, fast and in a hurry." I made a dismissive gesture. "Let them sleep. I'm not exactly throwing you guys out of here." I nodded down the stairs. "The dog's in the house, though. Do you want me—"

"Don't worry about it." Dante smiled, but a ripple ran down the front of his throat.

"You sure?"

"Yeah, it's fine." The smile turned to a grin. "I should probably get used to him sooner or later, don't you think?"

God, yes, they want to do this again. "I guess you should, shouldn't you?" I returned the grin. "Anyway, coffee?"

"Please."

We went downstairs to the kitchen, and I poured us some coffee. While we drank, the click of Sasha's nails on the wood floor made Dante's eyes widen a little. When my dog appeared in the doorway, I pointed at the living room, snapped my fingers and said, "Sasha, living room."

He gave Dante a curious glance, but when I snapped my fingers again, he obediently trotted out of the kitchen.

Dante watched the empty doorway warily before taking another sip of coffee.

"So, did you have a bad experience with a dog or something?" I asked. "I mean, if it's not too personal."

Dante set his coffee cup down. "I think we've gone well past the point of having to worry about getting too personal, don't you think?"

"Good point."

"To answer your question," he said quietly, "yes, I did have a bad experience with a dog. When I was really little, my dad tried to convince me a neighbor's black lab was friendlier than it was, and it snapped at us. Fortunately got his hand instead of my face, because he had to have quite a few stitches."

I blinked. "Wow, I've never known a lab to be so aggressive."

Dante shrugged, and I wondered if it was partly a shudder. "That one was, and that's my earliest memory of dogs. I've just never been comfortable around them." His eyes darted toward the empty doorway again. Then he picked up his coffee cup and took a sip.

"Are you okay with other animals, though?" I asked.

"Sure, I like animals." He gestured in the general direction of the stairs leading up to my bedroom. "Not quite as head-over-heels crazy about them as Angel, but I like them."

I smiled. "Yeah, I've noticed he's quite the critter person."

"You ain't kiddin'."

"Any pets?"

"He has a cat." He laughed softly. "She doesn't like me all that much."

"You're not mean to her or anything, are you?"

"No, no, of course not." He set his coffee down and rested his hip against the counter. "But I have no qualms about moving her if she's in the way, and I'll drag Angel out of bed even when she wants to sleep in."

"Oh, God, even I'm not that bad," I said. "He really won't disturb her?"

"God no. Whatever that little princess wants, she gets." He rolled his eyes and shook his head.

"Kind of amusing, don't you think?" I said into my coffee cup. "A Dom who's completely wrapped around a cat's paw?"

"About as appropriate as a submissive who's the alpha over his dogs and horses."

"Good point." I set my cup down. "Hadn't really thought of it that way, but yeah, I'm a total alpha with the animals. People, not so much."

"Nothing wrong with that." Dante's smile just then was seductive enough to make my knees tremble. "You just needed someone who likes to be an alpha with other people."

"An alpha without being a dick, anyway," I muttered.

He raised an eyebrow. "Ex?"

I nodded. "Long story." I chewed my lip and dropped my gaze for a second, then met his eyes. "But, I think I like the arrangement *we* have."

"Good to know, because Angel and I do too." He paused. "I have to be honest, I was a little worried when we came over last night."

"Oh?"

"Yeah, I thought we might've moved a bit fast in the studio." He shifted his weight and picked up his coffee again. "And we probably did. We just figured we needed to either put it out there or keep hoping you eventually found a reason to come back."

I finished my coffee and turned to refill it. Over my shoulder, I said, "Truth be told, I probably would have found a reason to come back."

"Also good to know. But it seemed only fair, being Doms, we should make the first move."

"I suppose that's true."

He was moving behind me. Coming closer. He waited until I'd set the coffeepot aside, then put his hands on my waist. "And by the way, last night was incredible." He kissed the back of my neck. The contradictory softness of his lips and coarse scrape of his unshaven jaw made my breath catch. He went on, "We're just getting started, but I think you are exactly the submissive we've been looking for."

I turned around to face him. Putting my arms around his neck, I said, "Well, I think you two are exactly what I've been looking for. Just, you know, two instead of one."

"Two Doms for the price of one." He traced my lower lip with his thumb. "Can't argue with that, now can you?"

"Seems like I'm getting the better end of the deal, though."

Dante held me a little closer and leaned in to kiss me. "Oh, you're not. Trust me on this one." He ran his fingers through my hair—they both did that a lot, and I so loved it—and his expression turned serious. "Just tell us if it's too much for you. I'm serious. As we get into more hardcore kink and really start pushing your limits, having two Doms might get intimidating." He touched my face. "You can always rein it back, or just play with one of us at a time."

"Somehow, I think I'll be all right."

He smiled, and the playfulness was back. "You sure?"

"Definitely."

He started to speak again, but footsteps shuffling in the hallway turned both our heads.

"I'll be damned, he's up," Dante said.

"Wonders never—" I paused, my chest tightening with preemptive annoyance. "Actually, I'd be willing to bet it's—" I let go of Dante. He instantly got the message, releasing me and taking a step back so we weren't close enough to raise more questions than his very presence inevitably would.

As if on cue, my ex-boyfriend stepped into the kitchen. He took a couple of steps toward the coffeepot, then stopped in his tracks, staring wide-eyed at Dante. A million questions put three deep creases in Eli's forehead, but he just shook his head and turned to get himself some coffee.

Dante and I quietly sipped our coffee while Eli went about making his breakfast. Everything he did had just a little more force than usual. A cabinet door banging shut harder than it needed to. A coffee cup slamming against the countertop. *Oh, goody. I'm going to hear about this later.* Knowing him, he'd take off to the living room to eat, so we'd be left in relative peace before long. I gave Dante an apologetic shrug. He smiled behind his coffee cup.

Then came more footsteps. Eli's brow furrowed, and he slowly turned his head toward the kitchen doorway.

Oh, shit.

Awkward moment in three...two...

Angel appeared wearing only a pair of jeans and my cat slung over his shoulder. His eyes immediately darted toward Eli, then Dante, then me, and the smirk that played at his lips almost made me snort with laughter. The four of us just stared at each other. The only sounds in the room were Cally purring contentedly on Angel's shoulder and the coffeepot making its usual clicking and gurgling noises.

Finally, Eli dumped his coffee in the sink, set the cup down so hard he almost broke the damned thing, and left without a word. As soon as his steps had faded down the hall, all three of us exhaled.

Angel's eyes flicked in the direction Eli had gone, then back to us. "Was it something I said?"

I let go of a laugh. "God, I am so going to hear about this later."

Dante chuckled. "We could explain it to him if—"

"No, no, that's quite all right." I shook my head. To Angel, I said, "Coffee?"

"God, yes." He set my cat on the floor while I poured him a cup.

The three of us stood around my kitchen island making small talk for a while. It took each of us two cups of coffee to finally wake up completely.

Eventually, Dante looked at the clock on the microwave and sighed. To Angel, he said, "I guess we should get going if we're going to get to work on time."

"You have to work today?" I asked.

Angel pursed his lips and nodded. "No rest for the soundly fucked, I guess."

"Apparently not," I said.

"So, do you have plans tonight?" Angel asked.

I shook my head.

"Why don't you come to our place?" Dante asked.

Angel grinned. "We'll show you some of our toys."

"I like the sound of that," I said. *Holy shit, these two are going to be the death of me.*

"Oh, just wait." The devilish sparkle in Angel's eyes made me shiver. I could only imagine being with the two of them in their natural environment with all their toys and tricks of the trade. As if they'd had any difficulty on my turf and without the aid of whatever qualified as "toys" in their world.

After everyone had dressed, we strolled out to the driveway where their car was parked.

"So we'll see you tonight?" Dante asked. "At our place?"

"Assuming the directions get me there, yes."

Angel looked at Dante. "We're going to have to work on his mouthiness, don't you think?"

Dante slid a firm hand around the back of my neck and pulled me closer to him. "I think we'll manage." Whatever mouthy remark I might have thought to give right then slipped my mind when he kissed me. It didn't matter how many times we'd kissed last night; his mouth did to me what only one other man's could do.

And that other man was standing by to do just that as soon as Dante let me go.

"If you guys keep kissing me like that," I said after Angel was done working his magic, "I'm going to end up dragging you both back upstairs."

Angel shrugged. "I could be—"

"*Angel.*" Dante raised an eyebrow.

He put his hands up. "What?"

"Work." Dante pointed at the car. "Come on, I really don't want to have to explain to Troy, Phoebe and Kendra why we're both late."

Angel clicked his tongue. "Fine. We'll do what *you* want to do."

I gave a melodramatic sigh. "I guess that means we'll just have to finish this tonight."

"Oh, don't you worry," Dante said, meeting my eyes with the most spine-tingling intensity. "We will."

After another kiss apiece, each lasting much longer than they should have if any of us thought to get any work done today, they got in the car. They drove off, kicking up a cloud of dust as they went down the long strip of gravel, and even after they'd turned at the end, I watched the empty driveway until that dust cloud dissipated. Once they were out of sight, I was almost certain every moment from last night until now had been a dream. Even the mild aches in my knees and shoulders and the twinges in my neck and lower back were barely enough to convince me it had all been real.

Oh, but it was. And tomorrow, there would be more aches like these.

For now, like Angel and Dante, I had work to do, so I went inside to get Sasha and continue my day.

In spite of my counting down the minutes until that evening, the day flew by. Such was the beauty of a demanding job: there was minimal downtime. If I wasn't showing horses to potential buyers, I was working the horses I was either training to sell or being paid to train for someone else. Then there were fences to fix, horses to turn out and bring in, boarders to appease when turnout schedules and stall assignments weren't satisfactory. One thing after another, all damned day.

I finally caught up with Laura in the afternoon as she came out of the barn office.

"Hey, Laura," I said. "Would you mind feeding late tonight and in the morning for me?"

"Yeah, sure," she said. "You going to be around tomorrow?"

"Oh, yeah, I just won't be in until a bit later in the morning."

Laura smiled. "No problem."

"You're a saint. I owe you."

"You're right, you do." She kept a serious expression for all of two seconds; then we both laughed and went in separate directions to continue with our various tasks.

Laura lived only a mile or so up the road, so I didn't feel too bad about the imposition. That, and I rarely asked. *Though I might be asking more in the foreseeable future.*

With the next two feedings squared away, I was free for the evening, so I went inside to get cleaned up and ready to go. I made a quick stop at my computer to make sure Dante had e-mailed me the directions to their house, which he had. Just his name on my list of unread e-mails made my heart race. *We're really doing this again. Holy shit.*

I printed the directions, turned off the computer, and went into the bathroom to grab a shower and change clothes. When I got out of the shower, it was a little past five, so I still had plenty of time to get to their place.

I pulled a polo shirt out of the drawer but paused.

"Unbutton your shirt." Dante's voice—and Angel's from the studio the other night—echoed in my mind. Goose bumps rose on my back and arms, and I put the polo back, reaching for a button-down instead.

Then I went back downstairs for a quick bite to eat before I took off.

And, of course, He Whose Name Made Me Roll My Eyes showed up just in time to put a damper on my good spirits.

He leaned against the counter. "Heading out?"

"Yeah. I'll probably be—" Why the hell was I explaining myself to him? "I'm going out."

He pursed his lips, and I braced myself for the barrage of questions. Or accusations. Or accusations dressed up like questions.

"So are you—"

"I'll be out late," I broke in. "Would you please make sure Sasha's in his kennel before you go to bed?"

"Whatever."

I glared at him. "Eli."

He shrugged. "Yeah, I'll make sure he's taken care of."

"Thank you."

"So, you're going out with...them?"

Pulling my jacket on, I said, "I'm going *out.*"

"I'm just asking."

"And if I answer, I'm damned if I do, damned if I don't." I picked up my wallet and keys off the counter. "If I'm going out with them, I'm rubbing it in your face that I'm moving on. If I'm—"

"So you *are* going out with them." He folded his arms across his chest and gave me that accusing glare I'd seen so fucking many times.

"I'm going out." I shoved my wallet into my back pocket. "That's all you need to know."

"Fine," he snapped.

I glared at him again. "What's the problem?"

"No problem." He showed his palms and shrugged. "You're free to do whatever you want. You *are* single, after all." The bitterness and sarcasm mingling in his tone irritated me even more.

"Glad to know I have your permission." But the words hung in empty air, his footsteps echoing down the hall. I muttered a string of profanity into that air and glared at the empty doorway.

On my way out to the car, I sighed. I didn't need this. I just didn't. I'd already spent a few years of my life playing surrogate parent to two teenagers. Now I was damn near doing the same for him, and was he *ever* playing the petulant kid.

And the man wondered why I'd called it quits with him.

Chapter Eleven

"Jordan called while you were in the shower," Dante said when I stepped out of the bedroom. "Said he's on his way. Should be here soon."

"And you're still working?"

He gave me a sheepish look over his laptop screen. "Would you believe me if I said I was playing Minesweeper?"

"Not a chance." I brushed my hair out of my eyes. "There hasn't been nearly enough swearing coming from this room."

He shrugged. "Maybe I was winning."

"Uh-huh."

"Are you mocking my Minesweeper prowess?"

"I am, actually."

He flipped me the bird.

I laughed and went around behind the couch. Leaning over him, I kissed his neck and murmured, "That doesn't look like Minesweeper to me."

"Maybe I was—"

"No more working." I kissed his cheek and rubbed the back of his neck with one hand. "The devil on your shoulder says so."

He leaned back to meet my eyes. "I thought you were the angel on my shoulder."

I kissed him lightly. "I'm whatever spiritual entity will get you off this couch to get ready before Jordan gets here."

"I *am* ready." He tilted his head to one side so his damp hair brushed my arm. "See? Showered and all."

"Mm-hmm." I leaned down to nibble his earlobe. "And if you keep working, you'll be too distracted when he shows up. Which means I'd have to take care of him all by myself."

"I don't think so."

"Then stop working." I kissed the side of his neck, closing my eyes and taking in a long breath of his familiar scent.

Dante squirmed against the back of the couch, murmuring softly as I inched down toward his collar. "Okay, I'll stop working, but please keep doing that."

"If I do, we'll be done before he even gets here." I stood. "Come on. Close the laptop, off the couch."

"Oh fine." With a dramatic sigh, he closed the laptop and set it on the coffee table but didn't get up. Instead, he leaned back and draped his arm across the back of the couch. "We have a little time to kill. You could always join me."

"Well, I'm certainly not going to pass that up." I laid back on the couch with my head in his lap and my feet over the armrest. He rested one hand on my chest and stroked my hair with the other. I put my hand over his, running my fingers back and forth across his skin. Seconds after I'd settled into place, Jade appeared on the back of the couch, then leaped onto my stomach.

I grunted. "Jesus, cat. You're heavier than you look, you know that?"

"Well, if you'd stop feeding her that expensive canned shit—"

"Yeah, yeah, yeah." We both petted the cat for a minute until she flopped down to go to sleep on my chest. Still idly petting her, I looked up at Dante. "So, do you think Jordan will stick around for a while?"

"God, I hope so." He absently wrapped and unwrapped a piece of my hair around his finger. "He seems to enjoy it so far."

"True, but we haven't exactly thrown a lot at him yet." I grinned. "Let's see how he does when I come at him with some hot wax."

Dante shuddered. "Might want to wait a little while to broach that subject, don't you think?"

"We'll see how he handles tonight," I said. "Maybe do some pain play next time, and I'll bring it up then. I have a funny feeling he'll like it."

"I guess we'll see how—"

Jade's head snapped up. Her satellite-dish-sized ears turned toward the front of the house, and her eyes reached cartoonish proportions. Normally I didn't pay attention when she did that—she'd jump if a spider tripped in the next room—but this time, I listened. Sure enough, a car door slammed outside.

I met Dante's eyes. "Ready to play?"

"You'd better believe it." He picked up the cat off my chest. "Time for you to move, lady."

I sat up and swung my legs over the side of the couch while Dante got up to let Jordan in. Excitement tingled at the base of my spine, creeping upward at the same speed as the barely audible footsteps approaching outside.

Dante opened the door before Jordan could knock, and my heart fluttered when Jordan stepped into the house. The tux he'd worn the day we met was long gone, but I was starting to wonder if it had really had anything to do with why I'd been tripping over my own feet at the wedding. His dark hair was casually arranged, like he'd given it just enough effort to make it look presentable but knew full well it would be disheveled as hell by the time we were done with him. And that ass...those jeans...

Fuck, he was hot.

And here he was. In our territory. Oh, this was going to be a fun evening.

"Jacket?" I held out my hand.

He started to shrug it off but paused. "Wait, should I be making you hang it up? You being the Dom and all?"

Dante laughed. "Under normal circumstances, yes, but Mr. Neurotic here will have a fit if it's not hung properly, so..." He gestured at me.

"Quiet, you," I said. Jordan handed me his coat, and I hung it on one of the hooks beside the door, making sure it was straight, and—

I looked at Jordan and Dante. Jordan pressed his lips together to keep a straight face. Dante didn't even try.

I clicked my tongue and rolled my eyes. "Oh, fuck you both."

They both snickered.

"Bastards," I muttered. Still snickering, they followed me down the hall. I opened the guest room door and gestured for Jordan to go in.

"Why do I feel like the lamb being led to slaughter?" Jordan asked as Dante shut the door behind us.

"Maybe you are," I deadpanned.

Jordan's eyes widened with alarm. Then he looked around the room. Dante and I didn't say anything for a moment and just let him take in his surroundings.

To the unsuspecting eye, this was a simply appointed and rarely used guest bedroom. A chest of drawers, a queen-size bed, a pair of nightstands, and a couple of lamps. There were no outward indications of all the reasons why Dante and I had to do a thorough sweep of the room any time we hosted family or other guests with whom we didn't plan to have kinky relations. "Sanitizing it," Dante always said.

It wasn't because of dust bunnies or clutter. Not in *my* house. It was just necessary to make sure my parents didn't open a drawer full of nipple clamps and ball gags, or Dante's dad didn't find several varieties of lubricant in the nightstand along with a metric ton of condoms and a bottle of peppermint oil. It was awkward enough when my sister, dropping in unexpectedly, found an ankle restraint we'd missed in our rush to sanitize the room. I'd go to my grave wondering if she opened the closet and found the rack of floggers and cat o' nine tails we'd completely neglected to stash. She'd probably go to hers before she ever admitted to seeing it. All I knew was, ever since then, she always made sure to give us ample warning before dropping in.

"What do you think?" Dante asked.

"I was expecting something a bit, I don't know, scarier," Jordan said.

"Pastels and curtains make good camouflage," Dante said.

"That, and it's a total headfuck." I made a sweeping gesture at our unassuming surroundings. "After all, what could *possibly* happen in a room like this?"

Jordan's eyes widened. He glanced at Dante. "You ought to take a picture of him like that."

Dante cocked his head, glancing at me. "What do you mean?"

"Look at him." Jordan nodded toward me. "All in black, grinning like the bastard lovechild of the devil and the Cheshire cat, surrounded by..." A sharp wave to indicate the décor. "It's like Satan himself wandered into a Pottery Barn advertisement."

Dante snorted with laughter. I raised an eyebrow and eyed Jordan, struggling to keep my own amusement contained.

I rested a hand on the back of Jordan's neck. "You know, you're awfully mouthy for a submissive who doesn't know what I have up my sleeve yet."

He gulped.

"In fact..." I ran my other thumb along his lower lip. "Just to make sure you know your place, I think Mr. Ball-gag might want to have a word with you this evening."

His eyes widened again. More when a drawer behind me opened, then closed. Keeping one hand on the back of his neck, I held out my other, and Dante placed a gag in it. Not a ball gag, of course. Neither of us ever used one on a novice sub. But it was a gag nonetheless, and Jordan regarded it uncertainly.

"Now," I said, taking a step back. "Why don't we get things started?" I verbally undressed him in the same sequence Dante had the other night. Shirt unbuttoned. Taken off. Handed to me. Belt off. Jeans and boxers off. He kept his eyes down the entire time, but I didn't miss the wary glances at the gag dangling from my still-outstretched hand.

Once he'd completely stripped, I came toward him again. I put my free hand on the back of his neck and kissed him, pressing my body against his to emphasize the fact that I was dressed and he was not, contrasting his vulnerability to my lack thereof. Just as I'd hoped, he shivered.

I broke the kiss and pulled back but didn't take my hand off him. Our eyes met.

My fingers pressed ever so gently into his neck, and my eyes flicked toward the floor, then met his again.

Without a hint of hesitation, he went to his knees.

I ran my fingers through his hair. "Look at me, Jordan."

He released a breath, his shoulders dropping. Then he lifted his chin and, after another second, his eyes. I resisted the urge to shiver. There was nothing in his expression but pure, beautiful submission, the kind of surrender that was so damned arousing, it could bring me to *my* knees. The light in the middle of the ceiling highlighted his hair, his high cheekbones, and those wide please-let-me eyes.

His forehead creased slightly, and I remembered he was waiting for me to speak.

I held up the gag. "You're going to wear this until one of us says otherwise. Understood?"

His eyes flicked back and forth a few times between the gag and me before he responded to my question with a subtle nod.

"Since you won't be able to speak," I said. "Your safe word will either be two grunts or you can put your hand up. Clear?"

He nodded again.

"It's not in your mouth yet," I said, my tone flat. "You can still speak." I raised my eyebrow.

"Yes, it's clear," he said.

"Good. Now open your mouth."

I put the gag on him, fastening the strap behind his head so it wouldn't move but wouldn't be unduly uncomfortable. I'd worn one a few times myself, since Dante and I always experimented on each other before trying things on submissives. If there was one thing that could kill the mood for me, it was a gag pinching the corners of my mouth or a strap digging into the back of my head.

With the gag in place and as close to comfortable as such a thing could be, I went around behind him. I put my foot in the middle of his back and pushed him forward onto his hands. For a moment, I kept my foot there, hard enough to let him know he wasn't moving from this position. Jordan's back tried to arch. Not to push me away, but like a cat pressing against a hand.

"Stay just like that," I said. "Don't move."

Jordan nodded.

I took my foot away, and just as ordered, he didn't move. I knelt behind him and ran my fingertips up and down his back, watching goose bumps rise in their wake.

"One of these days," I said, "I'll get to see what your back looks like when it's covered in welts from a flogger. Maybe a whip." A shudder straightened his spine. Trailing a single fingertip down the center of his back, I said, "Maybe some hot wax?"

Another shudder. More goose bumps. I looked at Dante, who leaned against the door, arms folded across his chest and feet crossed at the ankles. The grin that spread across his lips was nearly as arousing as the naked, gagged submissive in front of me.

I turned my attention back to Jordan and slid my hand up the center of his spine, the back of his neck, and into his hair. When I tightened my grasp and pulled back enough to make sure it smarted, he moaned.

"Would you want me to do that, Jordan?" I whispered. "Flog you? Maybe drop hot wax on your skin?"

He nodded as much as my grip on his hair allowed and murmured, "Mm-hmm."

"I thought you would." I released his hair. "For now, I'm going to fuck you. And you're not going to come until one of us allows it, will you?"

He shook his head and grunted something like "no".

"Good." While I got undressed myself, Jordan alternated between watching me, looking at the floor in front of him, and closing his eyes while drawing slow breaths. *Oh, Jordan, if you think you're turned on now...*

Jordan sat up as Dante handed him a condom and lube bottle. Jordan's cheek rippled. Probably clenching his teeth on the gag. He set the lube down and started to raise the condom to his mouth to, I guessed, tear the wrapper. Evidently remembering the gag, he tore the wrapper with his fingers instead.

He looked up at me, and I nodded. Once he'd put the condom and lube on me, I said, "Turn around."

Of course, he did so without hesitating, and when I nudged his back with my foot, leaned forward on his hands. I put my hand on his hip and took a deep breath. I pressed against him, giving just the head of my cock before pulling back. Then a little more. Withdrew. Still a little more. Slowly, gently, letting him relax around me and get used to me. That, and this was the first time I'd fucked him, and I intended to savor every second of it.

I held my breath and watched myself slide deeper into him. It was one thing to fuck Dante. It was always understood Dante had as much control as I did, and he exercised it. Changing speed, changing position, coming when he was damned good and ready to.

Jordan, like every submissive, had relinquished control. He'd get as much as I gave him. He'd stay in this position or change it on my whim. He'd come when I allowed it and not a moment sooner.

I'd missed this, and now I had it. I glanced up at Dante. He moistened his lips, and when he started unbuttoning his shirt, I shivered and couldn't help fucking Jordan just a *little* faster.

Jordan groaned around the gag. His fingers clawed at the floor, and his gorgeous, sculpted shoulders quivered and twitched as my strokes became thrusts. Oh, my God, I couldn't decide if he looked or felt sexier, but he and his body and his submission were fucking amazing.

Dante knelt in front of Jordan. "I'm going to take the gag off, and you're going to suck my cock. Understood?"

Jordan nodded.

Dante undid the strap and gently removed the gag. As soon as it was out of the way, Jordan was on Dante's cock, stroking and sucking vigorously. Dante closed his eyes and whimpered. Watching his face, I fucked Jordan harder. Jordan moaned softly and, judging by Dante's gasp, doubled his efforts on Dante's cock. Dante turned me on, I turned Jordan on, Jordan turned Dante on, and on and on and on, until I was sure every last one of us would lose it at the same time.

Dante threw his head back, moving his hips in time with Jordan's mouth. "Oh, fuck," he whispered. "That's...oh, fuck, that's incredible."

My legs burned and my back ached, but I didn't back off. It had to be painful for Jordan by now, but judging by the way he groaned and fucked Dante with his mouth, he loved it. He loved it, and so did I, and I couldn't take much more of it. Gritting my teeth, I screwed my eyes shut, dug my fingers in, gave Jordan everything I had, and came.

All at once, Jordan shuddered, and with a moan of helpless defeat, he came too.

Dante grabbed Jordan's hair and jerked his head up. "Did anyone say you could come yet?"

"No." Jordan paused, trying to catch his breath. "No, I'm sorry, I—"

"We might have to punish you for that," Dante said.

"I'm—" Jordan said.

I pulled out. "You going to do it again?"

"N-no."

"Damn right you're not." I leaned forward and growled in his ear. "In fact, between now and the next time we play with you..." I glanced up at Dante, who nodded. Then I went on, "...you won't come at all."

Jordan sucked in a breath.

I moistened my lips. "Clear?"

"Yes," he whispered.

"Hmm," I said. "And we won't be able to play again until Wednesday night."

"That's, what?" Dante said. "Four days? Five days?"

"Four, I think," I said.

"Five," Jordan said. "Five days."

I grinned. "Good. Plenty of time."

I nodded at Dante, then got up to take care of the condom. When I returned, I stopped to get a pair of handcuffs from the chest of drawers.

Dante still had Jordan on his knees. Like the evil bastard he was—God, I loved him—he stroked himself just inches from Jordan's mouth, and Jordan's eyes flicked back and forth from Dante's cock to his face.

"Normally, I'd let you suck me off," Dante said to Jordan. "That, or I'd fuck you. But since you came without permission..." He looked past Jordan at me and nodded. Jordan looked over his shoulder, and his gaze immediately went to the cuffs in my hand. His lips parted.

I knelt behind him and pulled one wrist around to his lower back. Before I'd even cuffed it, he offered up the other hand. I bound them together. Then I went around him to Dante.

"Since you came without permission," Dante said to Jordan, "I can't reward you by letting you do something you like, can I?"

Jordan released his breath. "No."

"But that still leaves me with a hard-on." Dante winked at me.

I put my hand on Dante's waist. "Guess I'll have to do something about that, then."

"Hmm, I guess you will."

With my other hand, I pushed Dante's out of the way and wrapped my fingers around his cock, making sure everything I did was fully visible to Jordan. Dante kissed me, I stroked his cock, and Jordan exhaled sharply.

Then I went to my knees. Looking right at Jordan, I ran my tongue along the underside of Dante's cock. The chain between the handcuffs creaked, and the frustrated sound he made was almost as arousing as Dante's moans. I glanced up at Dante, then focused on giving him an enthusiastic blowjob.

Jordan was desperate to please us both, and if I'd read him right, enjoyed sucking cock as much as I did. His mouth must have been watering, wishing his hand and mouth were around Dante's cock like this. The closer Dante got to coming, the more Jordan pulled against his cuffs, the chain protesting and clinking as he released a sharp breath through his teeth.

"Ooh, yeah," Dante moaned. "That's...fuck, just..." He whimpered, tangling his fingers in my hair as his cock pulsed against my lips. "Don't stop, Angel...don't...oh God..." His breath caught, his hips jerked slightly, and a second later, salty-sweet semen shot across my tongue.

I licked my lips and sat back. Then I stood, shared a quick kiss with my breathless, trembling Dante, and walked around behind Jordan again.

I knelt and unfastened the cuffs. "Looks like you'll have marks on your wrists tomorrow."

Jordan eyed the angry red half-moons under the heels of his hands, then shrugged. "They'll fade. I'm not too concerned."

"True, they will." I stood and offered him my hand. After I'd helped him to his feet, I put my arms around his waist. "You okay?"

He nodded, a hint of a grin curling the corners of his mouth. "You two know how to frustrate, don't you?"

I winked. "We're Doms. It's what we do." Raising an eyebrow, I added, "Especially when a sub doesn't do what he's told."

His cheeks colored, and he dropped his gaze. I lifted his chin and kissed him gently.

"You're still learning," I whispered. "Don't worry about it."

He searched my eyes, then smiled. "I really, honestly tried not to come."

"I know you did." I touched his face and grinned. "But we're still going to punish you, just because we can."

He laughed. "Evil bastards."

"Damn right we are." I kissed him again. "And even though it'll be frustrating as all hell, if you obey us and see your punishment through, it'll be worth it."

Jordan chuckled. "I think I can handle it."

"We could make it ten days," I said.

Jordan put up a hand and shook his head. "No, no, five is fine."

"That's what I thought," Dante said. "So behave yourself."

The three of us got into the guest room bed. It was much too hot for the comforter, but we pulled the sheet up over us. Even the sheet was a bit warm, but I wanted to make sure Jordan didn't get cold.

"So are you still enjoying being a submissive?" I asked.

"For the most part," Jordan said.

"For the most part?" Dante trailed a fingertip down Jordan's arm.

"Well, the punishments and frustration take a little getting used to."

"Get used to them," I said. "They'll only get worse."

"Great."

"It'll be worth it." Dante kissed Jordan's cheek. "With great frustration comes great payoff."

Jordan furrowed his brow. "I thought the quote was, with great power comes great responsibility."

"That applies to Doms," I said. "We modified it a little to fit subs."

"So I see."

"You know, as long as you're still enjoying this," I said, "I was thinking we could push a few boundaries next time. Maybe a little pain play?"

Jordan licked his lips. "I'm definitely game for that."

"Somehow I figured you would be."

"And speaking of pushing boundaries, I'm curious," Dante said. "We did that photo shoot in our studio the other night, but would you be interested in doing it again?"

Jordan shrugged. "I liked how the last shoot went, so..."

"Well, you saw the stuff in our portfolios." Dante's eyes darted toward me, then returned to Jordan. "The ones with...both of us."

"Yeah, I know which ones you mean."

"We were thinking," I said, resting my hand on Jordan's arm. "Would you want to do some like that? A bit more explicit?"

Jordan gulped. For a moment, I thought he'd pass, but then he nodded. "Yeah, I'd be game for that. I mean, I assume the photos would be..."

"Confidential?" Dante said.

"Yeah. You know, in case one of my clients ever decides to become one of your clients?"

"Don't worry," I said, running my hand along his arm. "We always keep them confidential and under wraps unless a model specifically allows it."

"I figured as much, but thought I'd check." He pursed his lips. "Seems like I ought to do something for you guys, though."

"Oh, don't worry about that." I dropped a light kiss on Jordan's bare shoulder. "You're doing more than enough for us."

Jordan laughed softly. "You know what I mean."

"And really, you're modeling for us." Dante idly ran his hand up and down Jordan's arm again. "So if anyone owes anyone..."

"Okay, point taken," Jordan said. "But I could swap, say, riding lessons or something like that."

I looked at Dante. "Hey, why don't you take him up on that?"

Dante glared at me. "Besides the part about getting on a horse?"

"Oh, go on." I smiled. "You might enjoy it."

Dante's eyes darted back and forth between us. Finally, he exhaled. "Oh hell, why not?"

"Sweet," Jordan said. "I think it'll be fun."

Chapter Twelve

Five days without an orgasm. I figured I could handle that. After all, I'd gone much longer when Eli and I were together. *Many* times.

Then again, when he and I were together, I was so stressed and depressed half the time, I didn't feel like having sex or jerking off. This was different, though. When I was under strict orders not to come, and I knew my next orgasm would be at the hands of Angel and Dante, *and* they'd promised some boundary-pushing pain play, five days was fucking *brutal*.

If ever there came a test of my resolve to obey them and see this through, it came—so to speak—on the fourth night.

Trying to think about anything except how badly I needed to do something about this ache below the belt, I'd gone downstairs to make myself something for dinner. While it cooked, I went through a stack of DVDs I'd bought but hadn't yet watched, trying to find the stupidest, goriest crapfest I owned. Preferably one with no shirtless, sweaty men.

I thought about watching *Resident Evil* but quickly shoved it back into the stack. Great. I was so spun up, I couldn't even convince myself to sit through a damned zombie movie without needing to pause it for a little "break". *God, I'm really pathetic.* In my defense, though, zombies and gore weren't nearly enough to cancel out James Purefoy in a leather jacket. Even if I wasn't this horny, I'd probably still have to pause it.

I sighed and decided to skip a movie. Just one more night, then work would distract me tomorrow, and I'd be—

No, Jordan, don't even think about tomorrow night.

My dinner was ready at that point, thankfully. I took it out of the oven, grabbed the newspaper off the counter, and sat at the kitchen table to eat, read, and not think about how horny I was.

I was two coma-inducing pages into the business section when headlights shone through the window and arced across the kitchen wall. Sasha barked, though without much enthusiasm. Out of habit, my stomach turned, but I couldn't help grinning. Eli's presence annoyed the hell out of me, which made him the perfect mood killer. For the first time in months, I welcomed his irritating, teeth-grinding presence.

I welcomed it until he walked in, anyway.

Because he wasn't alone.

Slack-jawed, I stared at them over the top of the newspaper, wondering if they were completely oblivious to me or if this was intentional. Whatever the case, they were certainly enamored of each other. I didn't think Eli even knew how to kiss that passionately. That, or I couldn't be bothered thinking back that far into our past to remember.

The newspaper in my hand crinkled, and in spite of the enthusiastic moaning and heavy breathing, Eli must have heard it, because he looked up and did a double take.

"Oh. Jordan." He blinked a few times, doing a piss poor job of appearing innocent or even surprised. "I didn't...realize you were home."

Through my teeth, I said, "My car is right next to yours."

"Oh." His face reddened, but the grin cancelled out any hint of embarrassment. He snaked an arm around his companion's waist. "This is Curt, by the way. One of the bartenders from that club downtown. Curt, this is Jordan."

Curt the Bartender and I exchanged awkward "nice to meet you" greetings. Then he and my ex went back to swapping spit and stumbling down the hall. I groaned and glared up at the ceiling, pretending I couldn't hear them even after the door closed downstairs.

A moan made it past the door, up the stairs and into the kitchen. Then another. One more, with feeling this time.

I gritted my teeth. Jesus Christ on a pogo stick. Really? Fucking *really*?

I slammed the newspaper down, then went in and put away my barely touched dinner. I took the stairs up to my bedroom two at a time, shut the door and leaned against it. Closing my eyes, I rubbed my temples, certain I could still hear Eli and

Curt the Bartender, even though there was an entire floor between us.

Then a cry did make it up to me. Holy shit. From opposite floors in a three-story house and through two closed doors, I could still hear the bastards. I groaned aloud. Eli never made that much noise in bed, and I couldn't imagine him giving his new friend any reason to. The fucker was probably trying to make me jealous. He'd succeeded, but not for the reason he believed. Damn it, everyone in this house was having orgasms except me. Well, Curt the Bartender might not have been having any either, but still. Damn it, I was horny, they were getting laid, and—

Cold shower. Need a cold shower.

I threw off my clothes, got into the shower and tried not to think of all the times I'd thought about Angel and Dante in here.

Twenty-four hours to go. I'd made it this far; I could make it that far.

The cool water poured through my hair, over my shoulders, down my abs and onto my maddeningly erect cock. God, I was going to feel like hell if I didn't do something about it, but would the guilt outlast the ache if I didn't?

I could. Right here, right now, and they'd never know.

No. No. No. They were my Doms, and they'd ordered me not to come until tomorrow night. I wouldn't be able to look them in the eye and pretend I'd obeyed, and if they knew I'd disobeyed, I could only imagine the new punishment they'd come up with.

Preemptively grimacing, I turned the shower all the way to cold. Icy water followed the same path as the tepid water before it, and I whispered every curse I could think of. I hated being cold, but it beat the alternative.

After a minute or two, it had numbed most of my skin and dulled the ache I'd intended for it to dull. I got out of the shower, dried off and went searching for the next distraction.

Finally, I put on some headphones and sat at my computer to get an early start on my taxes.

The next morning, I very carefully avoided Eli. Cleaning tack, fixing fences and working horses kept me out of the house until long after he and Curt the Bartender left. I didn't want him believing I was jealous that he was getting laid, but I was carrying around too much pent-up frustration to deal with smug gloating without hurting someone. He could assume all he wanted that I was jealous. I just hoped his new fuck buddy was thoroughly taken with him, because Eli was going to need a place to crash pretty soon.

By that evening, though, I barely even remembered I lived with anyone else, let alone the fact that he was doing his level best to give himself sex-induced laryngitis last night. All I could think of was getting cleaned up, getting in the car, and getting the hell over to Dante and Angel's place. I even spun my tires pulling out of the driveway. Hopefully none of my clients saw me, since they knew it irritated me when they did that.

Oh well. They could call me a hypocrite all they wanted. I was in a hurry tonight.

And my hurry paid off. I made it to my destination in record time, and with my nerve endings on fire with anticipation, I rang the doorbell.

Dante answered, greeting me with a light kiss. I didn't have a jacket this time—forgot to put one on for some reason, couldn't think why—so there was no need to worry about giving Angel a heart attack by hanging it incorrectly.

"Where's Angel?" I asked.

"Kitchen. Something to drink?" Dante gestured with the half-empty glass in his hand.

"No, I'm okay," I said.

"You sure?" He started toward the kitchen, nodding for me to follow him.

"I'm fine, don't worry."

In the kitchen, Angel was putting a bowl of food down for the cat. "Hey, Jordan. How's it going?"

Horny. Fucking horny. God, you guys are torturing me. I gulped. "Good, good."

"That's what we like to hear." He smiled, then went to the sink to wash his hands.

While Angel put away the cat food and Dante finished his drink, we made small talk, something I was certain they'd planned just to torment me a little longer. Even after the glass was empty and the cat food was out of sight, long after the bizarre Siamese-like cat had left, Dante and Angel leaned against the counter, and we shot the breeze like one of us wasn't dying to be paroled from five long days of complete chastity.

At one point, as if channeling my barely contained nervous energy, Angel's fingers drummed rapidly on the counter. Without even looking at him or pausing the conversation, Dante put his hand on Angel's shoulder. Angel released a long breath and his fingers slowed, slowed, slowed, stopped.

Of all the things I envied about them, that was in the top ten. With simple contact, Dante could settle Angel into stillness. The two of them probably didn't even know they were doing it. What I wouldn't have given to be with someone whose touch could calm me like that, or who calmed so quickly at the touch of my hand.

And if I could talk one of them into the touch of a hand, or a mouth, or—

You relentless, teasing bastards.

The conversation reached a natural pause, and the glance that passed between them sent my blood pressure through the roof, especially when Dante's chin dipped in the slightest of nods.

Angel came toward me, eyes narrowed. "So, did you make it through your punishment?"

Finally, thank God.

I gulped, his nearness pushing me up against the counter even though he was still an arm's length away from me when he stopped.

"Barely," I said.

He tilted his head. "Meaning?"

I licked my lips. "Meaning I think another day might have killed me."

Dante laughed. "But did you obey us for the entire five days?"

I nodded.

Angel smiled and moved a little closer, reaching up to caress my cheek. "Good. And since missteps come with punishments, naturally, obedience comes with rewards." He knocked the breath out of me with a gentle brush of his hand over my clothed erection. I could barely breathe as he unzipped my jeans and unbuckled my belt. Couldn't breathe at all when his hand wrapped around my cock. Thought I'd pass out when he whispered, "You've earned this."

He dropped to his knees right there on the kitchen floor, and I damn near came when his tongue swept around the head of my cock. *Not yet,* I told myself. *Please, God, not yet.*

As if Angel's hand and mouth weren't enough, Dante didn't just sit back and watch. He slid his hand around one side of my neck and kissed the other. I whimpered as their mouths drove me fucking crazy, gripping the counter with one hand and Dante's arm with the other.

Even with Angel on his knees at my feet, there was no denying who was in control here. I wanted to come so bad, and even with five days' worth of maddening tension built up and ready to release at the drop of a hat, I held back.

"May I—" I choked on my own voice. "Please, may—"

"Yes, of course." Dante kissed beneath my jaw. "Come for us, Jordan."

My knees buckled and my eyes rolled back. Five days, two cold showers, and oh God, for the orgasm Angel gave me, it was all worth it.

Angel stopped. Dante raised his head. One kissed me. Then the other. My lips still tingled, my vision still blurred. Straightening my clothes with unsteady hands, I'd have gladly gone through a month of frustration in exchange for this.

"I told you." Angel paused to lick his lips. "Do what we say. It'll be worth it."

I nodded. "You were right."

"Of course I was." He kissed me again. "And now that you've come once, we can *really* get started." Without another word, he gestured for me to follow him out of the kitchen. I did, and fortunately, Dante kept his arm around my waist, because my knees hadn't stopped shaking quite yet.

In the guest room, Angel faced me. "Strip."

My heart pounded. No removing clothing piece by piece, no putting me on my knees first. Right down to business tonight. Hell, yeah.

Dante released me, and I did as ordered. While I undressed, Angel opened the chest of drawers and pulled out—

Holy fuck.

The black leather-wrapped handle was probably a foot long, give or take. Angel gripped one end. From the other end dangled a dozen or so strips of leather, each about three-quarters of an inch wide. He raised it, then brought the tails down on his palm with a sharp *smack*.

I gulped.

"This," he said, holding it up, "is a flogger. Ever seen one?"

"Not up close and personal." I couldn't take my eyes off it. I'd certainly seen such things during my late-night online searches, and I'd salivated at the thought of being on the receiving end of those tails. When Angel hit his hand again, I licked my lips.

Dante chuckled. "I think he likes the idea."

Angel looked at me. "Do you, now?"

"Very much so." My voice barely rose above a hoarse whisper.

"Good." He grinned. "Get on your knees."

My knees went slack at his command rather than any conscious thought on my part. I knelt, automatically dropping my gaze to the floor.

They both approached. One ran his fingers through my hair.

"Look at us, Jordan," Dante whispered.

Shifting my gaze upward to them, I suppressed a shiver. Just this simple routine, these simple words and motions, and I was putty in their hands.

"As always," Angel said, "you're not allowed to come until we say otherwise."

I nodded. "Understood."

"Also," Dante said, "we're going to do things a little differently tonight."

I gulped. "You're flogging me, right?" *Please say yes, please say yes, please say yes.*

"That," Angel said with a slight nod, "and you'll be fucking Dante."

I blinked. "I...will?"

"Yes," Dante said. "But not yet." He turned to Angel and gestured at me. "Have fun."

"Oh, I will." Angel moistened his lips. To me, he said, "Turn around."

My heart pounded as I turned my back to him. I closed my eyes, holding my breath and bracing for the flogger. God, I'd wanted this for so long. *Yes, yes, yes.*

The first contact of leather to flesh was gentle and dull. No pain whatsoever. Another strike. Then another. Just warming my skin up, most likely, and I hoped and hoped he intended to make it hurt.

The whole time, in the back of my mind, I couldn't stop thinking about Angel's comment that I'd be fucking Dante. I was the submissive. Dante was my Dom. How would...what did...how the...

Smack. The tails hit harder this time. Still not enough to hurt, but enough to get my attention. Harder. A little harder. Just a little more and that delicious sting would come, I knew it. It was there somewhere. *Come on, come on, please, Angel...*

Finally, some of the tails bit in just enough to wake up some pain receptors. Not quite a sting, not enough to warrant even the slightest flinch, but it was there. The vague burn of a scratched itch. Another strike, more pain-that-wasn't.

He stopped. I chewed my lip. *Please, Angel...*

"Get up," he said. "Dante, he's all yours."

Aggravation tightened my jaw while arousal made me shiver. Fuck Dante? Absolutely. Wasn't going to argue. But Angel had given me a taste, just the most fleeting taste, of the pain I craved, only to take it away.

"Is there a problem?" Angel asked.

My eyes flew open, and I realized I hadn't yet obeyed him. "No, sorry." I scrambled to my feet. I looked at Dante, waiting for his command.

"You're going to get on the bed behind me, and you're going to fuck me." He paused to pull off his shirt. The more he disrobed, the more real it became, especially as he went on. "You're going to fuck me however I tell you to. As hard or as gentle, as fast or as slow, as I say." He tossed his jeans and boxers aside. "No more, no less. Understood?"

Fucking my Dom? Submitting even while being in the physical position of power? *I can get my head around this. I know I can. I know I can.*

"Jordan?" The question was sharp. "Answer me."

"Yes." I cleared my throat. "Yes, I understand."

"Good." He gestured toward the bed. Pretending my knees and hands weren't shaking, I moved onto the bed. Dante handed me a condom.

I silently begged my hands to be steady, and to my surprise, they were. Well, until I had the condom on, anyway. At least I didn't need much manual dexterity at that point, because when Dante poured some lube on his hand and stroked it onto my cock, my hands shook so bad I'd have dropped the condom if it wasn't already on. I had to close my eyes and hold my breath just to keep myself in control. The very thought of being inside him had me so turned on, I couldn't see straight, and now he was touching me, putting lube on me, ready for me, *oh God, I am not ready for this.*

Dante released my cock. When he turned around, my pulse skyrocketed. Ready or not, we were doing this. I was doing this.

I knelt behind him, resting a hand on his hip as I guided myself to him. Uncertain, I glanced at Angel, and his subtle nod of approval sent a rush of relief and arousal through me. Focusing on Dante again, I steadied myself and pressed against him, pushing in slowly. With every inch I gained, I watched, listened, and felt for any signs that I'd done anything wrong, and he gave me none.

Closing my eyes, I drew a few long, even breaths to keep myself in control. Jesus, he felt amazing. I hadn't realized how long it had been since I'd done this at all, let alone without being in a hurry. Slow, smooth strokes, in and out, just feeling him.

Then Dante rocked back slightly, and my hips immediately fell into step with his faster rhythm. When he slowed down, I slowed down. When he moved faster, I moved faster. It was surreal, being physically on top, knowing he was in total control. Surreal and so, *so* fucking hot.

Smack.

The sound startled me. When I followed the sound, my heart skipped. Angel had another flogger in his hand, stiffer than the other by the looks of it, and he'd hit it against his hand.

Smack.

Oh, fuck.

"Jordan," Dante said sharply. "I didn't tell you to slow down."

"S-sorry." I found my pace again, moving in time with him, falling into the rhythm he demanded. I tried to, anyway. Every time I managed to get in synch with Dante, Angel struck his palm with the flogger again and threw me off.

"What's wrong, Jordan?" Angel singsonged, hitting his palm again for emphasis. "Am I distracting you?"

I gritted my teeth. "Yes, you are."

"Good." *Smack.*

"Jordan." Dante's voice made me jump.

"Sorry," I whispered. Holding his hips, I forced myself to focus on everything he silently demanded. And watching us move together, watching myself thrusting into him, didn't do a damned thing to help me stay in control.

The air above my sweaty back cooled for a split second, and it drew my attention *just* before dozens of sharp stingers descended on my shoulder. My nerve endings flared with sweet, delicious pain. More stingers, this time on my other shoulder, and more pain.

"Oh, fuck..." The room spun around me. Every time Angel laid the flogger across my skin, more endorphins flooded my veins until my eyes rolled back and my entire body wanted to collapse.

Beneath me, Dante shifted, changing our cadence to a faster one. *Smack.* Slower now. *Smack.* Slower. *Smack.* Harder, faster, don't you dare stop, *smack*, faster, *smack*. My legs ached. My skin stung. I desperately wanted—needed—to come again, but held back. I wasn't allowed, not yet, not yet, not yet.

But the pain and the endorphins and my cock inside Dante...

"Oh God," I heard myself moan.

"Think we should let him come?" Angel's voice sounded miles away.

"I don't know," Dante said, his voice taut, on the verge of a moan, "I rather like what he's doing."

"Please," I breathed. Sweat trickled down the back of my neck. My whole body shook and my balls tightened with the threat of an orgasm, one I didn't know if I could hold back.

Dante rocked back against me. His body coaxed me into faster thrusts, every one of which chipped away at my ability to not come, not come, *fuck, you guys are going to kill me.*

Someone moaned, and it took a second to realize it hadn't been me.

Dante shuddered, moving a little faster, urging me to do the same. "Just like that," he whispered. "Oh God, Jordan, just like that."

Smack. Smack. Smack.

Dante let his head fall forward. His shoulders quivered, trembled, and my own shoulders burned, and I fucked him, and Angel flogged me, and Dante shuddered, and—

When Dante came, he released a throaty cry, and it was all I could do not to follow him right over that edge.

Then, from behind me, Angel whispered two simple words: "Come, Jordan."

I thrust all the way into Dante, and my balance was gone. I slumped over him, eyes screwed shut and lungs screaming for air to replace the breath my orgasm had forced out. Beneath me, Dante shook and moaned. Behind me, Angel must have set the flogger down, because gentle hands materialized on my shoulders.

Delirium kept hold of me for...a while. I knew Dante and Angel were there. I heard their voices, sensed their movement and my own.

At some point, I made it into bed between them. I'd pulled out of Dante, gotten rid of the condom, wiped some of the sweat off my tingling skin, and moved from wherever we'd been to here, but hell if I could remember. It was there somewhere in my brain; I just didn't care.

I was vaguely aware of Angel rubbing something on my back. Oil? Lotion? I didn't know.

Dante rested his arm on my shoulder, trailing a finger up and down my neck. "You okay?"

I nodded. "I thought you guys were going to kill me, though."

"Oh, come on, now," Angel said. "We wouldn't kill our shiny new plaything. We're just getting started with you."

"What about you?" I slurred. "You haven't come yet."

"I will." Angel kissed the back of my shoulder. "For now, you can catch your breath. There's plenty of time for me."

Maybe he was an angel of mercy after all, because I definitely needed to catch my breath. Settling into the bed between them, I said to Dante, "Honestly, I never thought it was possible for a Dom to be receiving and still be 'on top', so to speak."

Dante smiled, the corners of his blue eyes crinkling. "You just hadn't met me, that's all."

"Yeah," Angel said, brushing his hair out of his face. "You just hadn't met a cocky enough bastard to say, 'watch me taking it up the ass and still being in charge.'"

I laughed. Dante tried to look stern, but failed as he always did when Angel batted his eyes.

"Seriously, though," Dante said. "I just like the way it feels. Doesn't mean I'm going to give up control."

"And there's nothing in the rules that says the pitcher's always in charge," Angel said. "Anyone who says that has never seen a female Domme at work."

"I hadn't thought of it that way," I said. "Makes sense, though."

"Listen to the Angel of Wisdom," Dante said with a grin. "Well, this time. Helps to take everything else he says with a grain of salt."

"Dante," Angel said in a stage whisper. "You're not supposed to tell him that."

"Why not?" Dante shrugged. "I doubt he believes you're nearly as angelic as you appear."

"Speaking of which, I never did ask." I looked at Angel. "Where did your nickname really come from?"

"We had a sub who said we were like a devil and an angel," he said.

"And because of my name," Dante said. "He joked that the two of us were a Divine Comedy. Appropriate enough, since that's where my name came from."

"Really?" I stared at Dante. "Your parents actually named you for Dante Alighieri?"

He nodded. "My mom had a thing for the classics, and since I put her through hell..."

"Oh, that reminds me," I said. "Speaking of putting people through hell..." I shot them each a playful glare.

"What?" Angel said.

"I have to know. About this whole thing with me not having an orgasm for five days," I said. "You guys didn't get anyone else in on it, did you?"

They glanced at each other, then back at me, brows furrowed.

"No," Dante said. "What do you mean?"

I raised an eyebrow. "So neither of you had anything at all to do with my ex bringing another guy home last night?"

Angel snorted with laughter. "Are you serious?"

I nodded. "Uh-huh."

Dante pressed his lips together but couldn't keep a straight face. Angel made less of an effort to hide his amusement as he said, "So, what? He was having loud sex while you couldn't do anything?"

"That's exactly what he was doing," I growled. "I don't think he's ever been that loud in his *life*."

Angel lost it.

"I swear on everything that's holy," Dante said, unable or unwilling to contain his own laughter, "we had nothing to do with that."

Angel wiped his eyes. "That would have been brilliant, though, don't you think?"

"You guys really are evil," I said, finally allowing myself to laugh too.

"We are indeed." Angel took my hand and guided it beneath the covers. "And before you start getting too mouthy again, I think you still need to do something about *this*."

He wrapped my fingers around his hard cock, and I shivered.

Chapter Thirteen

A few nights later, Angel led Jordan into the rec room we'd converted into a studio.

"Wow," Jordan said, checking out his surroundings. "I thought you guys just did this at your other studio."

"Usually, we do," Angel said. "But we tend to keep our more..." He trailed off, pursing his lips.

"We do our racier work here," I said.

"Oh?" Jordan raised an eyebrow. "You mean like that first time I posed for you?"

"Well, that was hardly racy by our standards," Angel said. "The photography, anyway."

"And it *was* kind of impromptu," Dante said.

"True." Jordan hooked his thumbs in his front pockets. "So this is where the more premeditated stuff happens, then."

"Precisely." Angel looked at him. "No qualms about getting in front of the camera again? Even if it's in a less than professional environment?"

"After what happened last time?" Jordan grinned. "None at all."

"That's the spirit," Angel said, chuckling. His expression turned serious. "Okay, so since we don't have to break the ice and feel you out this time, we can jump right in. Still, ground rules."

"For all intents and purposes, we're both your Doms, as always," I said. "But for the most part, I'll be giving directions to both of you as the photographer, while Angel will give you instructions as your Dom."

"And if Dante and I switch, which we most likely will, the same rules apply," Angel said. "The photographer's in charge of the shoot, the Dom is in charge of the sub."

"So basically," Jordan said, "I do whatever anyone tells me to do."

Angel grinned at me. "He's a fast learner, isn't he?"

"Very." To Jordan, I said, "Safe words still apply, same as always. If you decide you're not comfortable in front of the cameras anymore, or whatever, just say the word."

"I think I'll be okay," Jordan said. "But duly noted."

"You'll probably be fine," Angel said. "The safe words are there if you need them, though."

"Tell us the safe words again," I said.

"Red to stop," Jordan said. "Yellow to back off."

I nodded. "Good. Well, with that covered, shall we?"

They went to the center of the set, under the hot lights, while I put my camera strap over my head. Then I knelt by the edge of the set and turned on the camera.

Jordan and Angel went through the usual motions: undressing Jordan, putting him on his knees, Angel running his fingers through Jordan's hair. Watching through the viewfinder, I swore a million memory cards wouldn't have held all the images the two of them created. Light and shadow playing in the groove of Jordan's spine, all the way up the curve of his back to his broad shoulders. Coppery highlights appearing in his hair between Angel's fingers as Jordan sucked Angel's cock. Jordan gazing up at Angel like he'd do anything in the world if Angel asked; Angel gazing down like Jordan could do no wrong.

The band of ink around Angel's wrist was like a curving, winding arrow drawing attention straight to Jordan's eyes, which alternated between focusing upward at Angel and closing at the same time a quiet growl of ecstasy came from one of the two men. Tension rippled across Jordan's shoulders. Angel's hair fell into his eyes as he tilted his head back and swore.

All the while, they paid no attention to me. For all I knew, they'd forgotten I was here at all in spite of the constant *snap-snap-snap* of the camera shutter and my occasional footsteps. And they may very well have. Jordan was completely wrapped up in stroking and sucking Angel's cock. I doubted Angel was aware of much of anything besides Jordan's talented hand and mouth.

I moved to another vantage point and knelt again, ignoring how increasingly difficult that was with a hard-on that didn't *want* to be ignored. Instead, I focused on them, what they did and how sexy they were.

It was easy to create an erotic image with two gorgeous men fooling around. The art was in finding everything that was easy to overlook. The details no one noticed in porn magazines and a lot of erotic art because they were too drawn to the cocks, breasts, penetration and money shots.

What I wanted were the hairs standing on end on the back of Angel's arm while he stroked Jordan's hair. Jordan's hand on Angel's hip. Angel focused on Jordan, brow furrowed and lips parted; no one who saw the image would hear Angel's whispered curses, but if I caught the image like I thought I did, the feeling would be unmistakable.

Angel's gaze shifted toward me, looking through his lashes and down the lens, right into my eyes. We could live to be a hundred and fifty years old, and that look would still give me goose bumps every time. I took the picture, then lowered the camera, and for a heartbeat, we exchanged glances without the filter of glass and plastic in between.

The moment passed. I raised the camera; Angel dropped his gaze.

Kneeling was getting progressively less comfortable, and more than once I wished I'd undressed before we'd started. Oh well, too late now. All I could do was concentrate on them, knowing I'd get my chance to take care of this hard-on very soon.

I zoomed in on Jordan's face. I wasn't after a shot of him sucking Angel's cock per se. It made a hot image, of course, but what I wanted was—

There it was.

Snap.

That upward flick of his eyes. Lust, reverence, total submission, all in a glance.

"Jesus, that's perfect," Angel whispered.

Snap. Angel's hand over Jordan's on his hip.

"Just like that...fuck..."

Snap. Fingers in Jordan's hair.

"Oh, fuck, you're...you're gonna make me..."

Snap. Angel's furrowed brow above heavy-lidded eyes.

"Oh...God...Jordan..."

Snap. The low groan he released couldn't be captured in a static, silent image, but I hoped I'd caught that perfect moment when he let go: throwing his head back, his lips apart just as his eyes flew open. Even if by chance the camera hadn't caught it, I did, and it was fucking beautiful.

I moistened my dry lips. "Angel, look at me."

Only his eyes moved, and he stared right down the camera lens, straight into me.

Snap. Shiver. Exhale.

He grinned. "Your turn."

I lowered the camera and stood. While Angel got his camera out of its case, I got out of my clothes. To Jordan, I said, "Feel like getting fucked?"

His posture straightened. The tip of his tongue swept across his lower lip, and he nodded. "Absolutely."

"Good." I pulled a condom out of my pocket and dropped my jeans on top of the rest of my clothes.

On my way past Angel, I touched his arm and whispered, "I would suggest getting every shot you can as quickly as you can."

He looked at me. "Oh?"

"Let's just say," I said with a grin, "I don't expect this to be a very long session."

Angel slid his hand over the front of my jeans and squeezed my erection hard enough to make me gasp. Our lips nearly touched as he said, "Duly noted."

I kissed him lightly, then went onto the set, where Jordan waited on his knees. He met my eyes and licked his lips. I shivered; I wasn't going to last long. No way in hell. Just watching Jordan tear the condom wrapper was enough to nearly make me come unglued. When he put it on me, I had to hold my breath. *Jesus, Jordan, if you only knew how much you turned me on.*

Once the condom was on, I gestured for him to stand.

"There's a chair over by the closet." I nodded in its direction while I put some lube on my cock. "Bring it here."

Jordan obeyed, stepping off the set and returning with the chair I'd asked for. I placed it in the middle of the set, between us and Angel, and gestured toward it.

"Put your hands on the back of it."

Jordan swallowed hard. As ordered, he put his hands on the chair's back, which required him to lean over just enough to put him in the perfect position. A shudder ran through him as I slid a lubricated finger into him. I dug my teeth into my lip, every breath he took taking *my* breath away as I moved my finger in and out of him.

"Like that?" I asked.

"Yes," he whispered, his shoulders tensing, relaxing, tensing again.

I couldn't take anymore. He was plenty ready for me, as he always was, so I withdrew my finger and guided my cock to him. Holding my breath, I pushed in slowly, and before I was all the way inside him, my vision blurred and my spine tingled.

Oh, fuck, this isn't *going to take long at all.*

I closed my eyes, biting my lip again as I moved deeper inside him. Slow, steady strokes, as much to tease him as to keep myself in control. Then, because I couldn't help myself, faster. Fuck it, I couldn't hold back when he felt this good.

Gritting my teeth and holding on to his hips for support and dear life, I fucked him *hard.*

"Now *that* is hot," Angel said.

Snap. Snap. Snap.

I kissed Jordan's neck, breathing in his scent, the heat of his skin, *him.* The chair creaked. Jordan moaned. His body shook. So did mine. Every snap of the shutter drove me insane along with every thrust I took, every tremor. Oh, fucking hell, I was inside Jordan, Angel was watching, this was perfect, perfect, fucking perfect.

Just when I couldn't hold back anymore, I whispered, "Come, Jordan."

In the same heartbeat, we both let go. I slumped over him, gasping for breath. My cock pulsed inside him, and every aftershock crackled up the length of my spine.

When it finally subsided and my vision cleared, I pulled out. Jordan's knees buckled, and he gripped the chair for balance.

I squeezed his shoulder. "You all right?"

He nodded. "Just...out of breath."

"Take a minute and catch your breath, then." I kissed the back of his neck, just below the sweaty ends of his hair. Pushing myself up, I added, "Because you're not done yet."

He looked at me over his shoulder, eyebrows arching upward.

I grinned and flicked my eyes toward Angel. Jordan followed my gaze, and the muscles in his neck tensed under my hand when Angel smacked his own palm with the tails of a leather flogger.

I leaned in and whispered in his ear, "Think you can handle a beating?"

Jordan shivered. Swallowed. Nodded.

"Good." I kissed the side of his neck. "Because I want to watch him flog you."

Another shiver.

I kissed his neck again, then took a step back. I turned to Angel. "He's all yours. Give me a minute to get cleaned up, and I'll be back with the camera."

"I still have to warm him up anyway." Angel hit his palm again. "Take your time."

I left him to get Jordan's skin warmed up, and by the time I returned, Jordan was on his knees. Angel spent a few minutes with the softer flogger before switching to a stiffer one that would give Jordan the sting he so loved.

He looked at me. "Ready?"

I raised the camera. "When you are."

The mischievousness in those beautiful blue eyes gave me pleasant chills. "I'm always ready for this," Angel said. "You know that."

I watched through the viewfinder, my mouth watering as Angel raised the flogger. He brought it down on Jordan's shoulders with a satisfying *smack*, and Jordan grunted. His expression was somewhere between a wince and total bliss, but each time Angel hit him, the scales tipped further and further in favor of the latter.

A few times, I forgot I even had a camera in my hand. Watching the two of them, I had to remind myself I was supposed to be photographing them. And what a beautiful subject to photograph.

Snap. Tails frozen in midair.

Snap. Leather tails splayed across Jordan's shoulder.

Snap. The cocktail of pain and pleasure furrowing Jordan's brow and pulling his lips into a grimace.

Eyes closed, Jordan moaned and wavered a little. He leaned forward on his hands, and his elbows and shoulders shook with the herculean effort of keeping himself upright. His skin was drenched in sweat, and he was deep in subspace now. On his knees with some post-orgasmic bliss and a rush of endorphins, he must have been in heaven.

After a while, though, Angel set the flogger down. "I think he's had about enough," he said to me as he knelt beside Jordan. I didn't argue. The last thing we needed to do was push Jordan too far, so I picked up one of the towels we'd made sure to keep handy and tossed it to Angel. He wrapped it around Jordan's shoulders and spoke so softly to him I couldn't understand what he said.

Once I'd put my camera aside and clicked off some of the lights, I joined them.

"Why don't you take him in the bedroom?" Angel said to me as he rubbed Jordan's neck. "I'll clean up in here and meet you guys in there."

"Will do." To Jordan, I said, "You okay to stand?"

He nodded. Angel and I held his arms while he rose. Once he was steady on his feet, I kept my arm around his waist and guided him down the hall to our bedroom. I helped him get into bed, then joined him and pulled the covers over us. His skin was still hot, but I didn't want to take a chance on him getting cold when the endorphins wore off.

"Water?" I asked.

"Please."

As we always did, Angel and I had left a couple of water bottles in here before we'd gotten started. I gave one to Jordan and drank heavily from the other. After a moment, he handed back the mostly empty bottle, and I set both of them aside.

Propping myself up on one arm, I caressed his face. "You okay?"

"Mm-hmm." He closed his eyes and exhaled.

"Are you hot? Cold?"

"No, this is fine."

I kissed him gently. "Lay on your stomach. You need some lotion on those welts."

He turned over and rested his head on the pillow, folding his arms beneath it. I uncapped the lotion and poured some into my hand, rubbed my hands together to warm it, then carefully rubbed it onto his back. His skin wasn't too raw, but it was definitely pink from the flogger.

"This okay?" I asked.

"Feels good," he slurred.

"Just tell me if it stings anywhere."

"Mm-hmm." His eyes were closed, and his breathing slowed. Even when I stopped rubbing his back, he didn't move.

Angel came in and sat beside us. He put his hand on Jordan's shoulder. "Not falling asleep on us, are you?"

Jordan murmured something resembling a negative.

"Don't listen to him," I said. "If you need to sleep, sleep. We're not going anywhere."

"Of course we're not." Angel slid his hand up the middle of Jordan's back. "He's in *our* bed."

Jordan's back rose with the effort of a quiet laugh.

"So that wasn't too much for you?" I asked.

"Not at all," Jordan said.

"Good."

Angel played with Jordan's hair. "Think you might want to do it again?"

"Definitely."

"Excellent," Angel said. "You have five minutes."

Jordan raised his head and gave Angel a playful glare. Then he dropped his head back onto his arms.

Angel leaned down to kiss Jordan's cheek. Jordan probably didn't even feel it, because in no time flat, he'd drifted off to sleep.

Chapter Fourteen

"Dante got hung up with a client." I stood aside to let Jordan in the house a week or two after that photo shoot. "He was just getting back to the studio when I left, so he'll be along pretty soon."

"So I'm just stuck with you, then?" He took off his jacket. "How *ever* will I cope?"

"Only one way you can cope." I held out my hand for his jacket. "By doing whatever I tell you to."

"I'm game for that." He handed me his coat, and I hung it beside the door.

"Of course you are." I winked, then led him into the living room. "That's why you're here, isn't it?"

"Damn right."

In the living room, my cat had made herself at home in the middle of the couch. It mystified me how a cat that small could expand to take up so much space, but she took up the entire center cushion, with her toes and tail creeping onto the other two.

"Baby, you have to move." I picked her up. "Sorry, kiddo."

Jordan laughed. "Glad I'm not the only one who babies animals."

My cheeks burned as I set Jade on the recliner. "Definitely guilty." I joined Jordan on the couch. "She's pretty much our kid. Well, mine. She and Dante don't get along that well. Still, she's as close as we'll ever get to a kid."

"You guys ever thought about adopting kids or anything?"

"Nah. Neither of us has ever had much of a desire to be a parent, and we're both so damned busy..." I shrugged. "That, and we tend to travel to places where I wouldn't want to take a kid."

"I thought you didn't go to all those crazy places anymore, now that you're not going for assignments."

"Oh, we still do." I smiled. "We just go for fun now." I gestured at Jade. "And unlike kids, we can leave her alone for a few weeks at a time as long as someone drops in to check on her every few days."

"She doesn't mind?" He raised an eyebrow at her as if he expected her to interject a comment or two. I wondered if he was as surprised as I was when she didn't.

"She doesn't *like* it," I said. "And she usually cold-shoulders me for a day or two when we get home, but she doesn't mind being by herself." I looked at her, then back at him. "So what about you? Ever thought about the whole kid thing?"

"No," he said. "I've already gotten a taste of parenting. That's enough for me."

"Really?"

He nodded. "I'm eight and ten years older than my siblings, and since I was an adult when our parents died, I took legal guardianship of Jenny and Jeremy until they were eighteen."

"Wow, that must have been rough."

"It was challenging. Nothing quite like going from a twenty-something kid to keeping after a couple of teenagers, making sure they get their homework done, all of that shit."

"Jesus."

"Tell me about it." He shifted, leaning on his elbow on the armrest. "It wasn't too bad, but it made me think twice about ever volunteering for it again."

"So, if you don't mind my asking," I said, "what happened to your parents?"

"Car accident." He exhaled. "On the way back from the regional championships one year. I was driving the semi with the horses; they were in the RV." He took a breath. "Interstate, logging truck, brake failure. Do the math."

I grimaced. "Sorry to hear it."

Jordan shrugged. "It was a long time ago."

"Still, I can't even imagine. Especially having to take on the care of your siblings on top of it all."

"Yeah, it was weird, I'll tell you that." He exhaled, his eyes losing focus. "Signing report cards in between taking my own classes and trying to keep the farm running. Going to parent-teacher conferences with my own teachers from a few years before." He said nothing for a moment, then shook himself back to life and met my eyes again. "I finally dropped out of college because I just couldn't keep up with everything."

"Seems like you've done pretty well with the farm, though."

"Yeah, it's done okay. It's what I've always wanted to do anyway, so it worked out. And, if there was a silver lining to the whole thing, my siblings and I are extra close now. We weren't as close before since I was so much older, but we are now."

"That's why you walked your sister down the aisle?"

He nodded, smiling. "She told me when she was sixteen that she'd have me walk her down the aisle when she eventually got married, and when the time came, she did."

"That really is great you and your siblings are so close," I said. "I'd love to be that close to mine, but..." I trailed off, shrugging.

"Well, I could think of better bonding experiences for siblings, believe me."

"I'm sure." I paused. "While I'm prying and getting too personal, I'm curious about something about your sister's wedding. And you don't have to answer."

He cocked his head, silently bidding me to continue.

"If you and Eli are done, why was he there with you?"

Jordan groaned and rolled his eyes. "For the same reason my sister decided to take her husband's name even though she would've preferred not to."

"And that is?"

"To keep the peace." He sighed. "Eli and my brother-in-law are good friends. That's how Jenny met Paul, actually. So, one way or the other, Eli was going to the wedding."

"Amazing the things we do just to avoid conflict," I muttered.

"Oh? The voice of experience?"

"God, yes." I scratched the back of my neck and blew out a breath. "We've been invited to about thirty-seven million weddings in the last twelve years, besides the ones we've been hired to photograph, and I can't tell you how many times a bride or groom has had 'that conversation' with us."

"That conversation?"

"Yeah, you know." I cleared my throat and adopted a phony, extra masculine voice. "Could you guys just, you know, don't act like you're together?"

"Oh, Jesus Christ." Jordan shook his head. "Fuck, yes, I've had that conversation a few times."

"Annoying as hell, isn't it?"

"Very much so." He chuckled. "And then I have to go to my sister's wedding and damn near pretend Eli and I *were* together just to avoid conflict."

"Can't win, can we?"

"Nope."

"And don't you love the ones where it's okay if you're 'together', just don't 'do anything'." I rolled my eyes. "What do they think we're going to do? Fuck over the buffet table or interrupt the bouquet toss with a blowjob?"

Jordan laughed aloud. "Oh, man, I'd pay to see that."

"Yeah, me too." I grinned. "People would probably shit themselves if we asked to bring our third with us."

"Oh God, I can only imagine." He paused. "So, I've never been with someone as long as you two have been together. How *do* you handle that kind of thing now? Just don't go to weddings and stuff if they tell you to pretend you're just friends?"

"Depends on who's asking and why." I shifted a little, draping my arm along the back of the couch. "If it's a close friend who happens to know her father will go postal if he so much as hears the word 'gay', then we'll go and respect her request. If it's just someone who's embarrassed to have a couple of gay guys at their wedding? Obviously we're not close enough to bother, so we decline the invite."

"Makes sense," Jordan said with a nod. "You guys ever catch hell from clients who catch on that you're gay?"

"Sometimes, but we usually just ignore it unless they get outwardly hostile." I chuckled. "We had one guy, years ago. Brother of the bride, absolutely livid that there were 'damned queers' documenting his sister's wedding for posterity." The chuckle turned to a snicker. "About three years later, he showed up asking us to photograph his commitment ceremony."

Jordan's eyes widened. "Are you serious?"

"As a heart attack. Guess a lot can change in a few years."

"Isn't that the truth." He laughed and shook his head.

"Oh, and speaking of photos, I almost forgot." I leaned forward to get my laptop off the coffee table. "We finished working on the photos from that last shoot. I assume you want to see them?"

"Hell yeah, I do." He scooted a little closer while I pulled up the folder containing his pictures. Once I'd opened it and set it to the preview window, I handed the computer to him. He rested it on his lap, and I put my arm around his shoulders.

Jordan flipped through the images, pausing on each for anywhere from a few seconds to the better part of a minute.

Even after all these years, Dante's work still blew me away. We prided ourselves on making the most erotic photos we could while showing as little as possible. Not out of prudishness, of course. We just liked the suggestiveness of understated photos. The mental images created by what *wasn't* in the frame as well as what was. There could've been a million reasons why my lips were apart and my head was thrown back. The drop of sweat suspended on the damp ends of Jordan's hair could have been from heat, from exertion, even from nerves.

Sure, Dante had made sure to get a shot of Jordan's hand around my cock in mid-stroke, but the more striking image was the other hand on my leg, holding on as much for contact as balance. Or my hand in his hair, my fingers and forearm just tense enough to suggest I was doing more than simply stroking.

Jordan stared at one photo for a long time without saying a word. It was a simple image: his bare knees in front of my booted feet. No one could have known by looking at it if he was sucking my cock just then, or if he was waiting for my next command, or if one of us was speaking. What happened outside the frame was anyone's guess, but the implication was clear. Nothing but beautiful submission.

I didn't blame him for stopping on that one. It was easily one of my favorites in the entire batch.

After a few minutes, he clicked to the next photo.

Click. Click. Click.

He stopped again. It was just a simple, straight-on shot of his face and bare shoulders. He clicked back to the one before, then forward, then back. Cocked his head a little. Clicked forward again, and back.

"Something wrong?" I asked.

Brow still furrowed, he shook his head. "No, I'm just..."

"Hmm?"

He wet his lips and gestured at the image on the screen. "There's, I can't..." He paused. "Just trying to figure out exactly what it is about some pictures, like this one, that catch my eye more than others." He clicked back to the photo, which was similar. "But this one doesn't strike me quite the same."

"Oh, right, that's because of the composition. We both swear by the rule of thirds, which is used in that shot."

"The what?"

"The rule of thirds." I gestured at the photo. "It's a principle of composition. You imagine the frame divided into horizontal and vertical thirds, and make the points of interest line up with the intersecting lines."

Jordan stared at the image.

"Here, check this out." I shifted the computer over to my lap and opened up my photo-editing software. I pulled up the picture that had caught his eye, saved it as a copy, and cropped the photo so his face was dead center rather than off to the left. Then I turned the screen toward him. "See how it isn't as dramatic and eye-catching now?"

He nodded. "Okay, I see it now."

I set the laptop on the coffee table. "It's just something that creates a more interesting composition. Adds tension, points of interest, that kind of thing."

"Obviously it works."

"Well, it's not set in stone, and we don't always follow it, as you saw, but it's a good rule of thumb."

"Rules are meant to be broken sometimes, though, right?"

"Of course." I sat back and absently draped my arm around him, not even realizing I'd done it until my palm rested lightly on his shoulder now. My hands were always drawn to Jordan. Had been since the first time he'd gone to his knees at my feet. The memory of my fingers running through his hair for the first time had them curling against his shoulder, tracing a seam of his shirt that insisted on remaining between my skin and his.

Odd, I thought. Dante was definitely the more tactile of the two of us. Always a hand on me or whatever sub we were with at a given time. Not that I had an aversion to physical contact, I just didn't seek it out the way he did.

Oh, hell, what was there to analyze? I liked touching Jordan. Who *wouldn't?* So my fingers continued their little back-and-forth dance along that seam while his body heat warmed the length of my arm, and I pretended that just that gentle contact didn't already have me shifting to try to get comfortable.

"So how did he get hung up while you managed to make a break for it?" he asked.

"Wasn't my client. Actually, I'd have stuck around and helped if I'd known what was going on, but Dante didn't call me until I was almost home." I trailed my fingers up the back of his neck. "But it worked out, because that meant one of us was here to—"

My cat flew up onto the couch, startling both of us. She glared at Jordan. If she could have, she'd probably have scowled and demanded to know just what the fuck he thought he was doing in her spot. But then he scratched her back, right above her tail, and though she made an obvious effort not to like it, she caved in and arched her back. Then the purring started, and he had her wrapped around his finger.

"She doesn't usually like someone sitting in her place." I said. "Looks like she'll let it go this time."

Jordan chuckled, still scratching her. "Oh, I don't think she minds too much."

"No, apparently not." I reached across my own lap to pet her, telling myself several times that it wasn't just an excuse to move a *little* closer to Jordan.

Of course it wasn't. Which is why he didn't notice. Or turn his head. Or meet my eyes while a playful grin worked its way across his lips.

Just like I wasn't thinking about how much I'd been craving his kiss all damned day.

My mouth watered. I leaned in a little closer, and he mirrored me, letting me decide if a move was made and when.

Dante would be along soon. There was no harm in just getting things started.

Just getting things started. Yeah, right. If I kissed him now, that would be it. Cat shoved off the couch, arms around each other, clothes landing where they fell. I wanted to wait until Dante got home, but I was horny, and Jordan's mouth was so, *so* tempting, and—

"*Fuck.*" Jordan jumped back, sucking in a sharp hiss of breath.

"What? What?"

The telltale pop of a claw coming out of denim answered my question. Jade purred extra loudly, narrowing her eyes and kneading Jordan's thigh.

"You little shit," I said.

"She's okay." Jordan laughed, scratching behind her ears. "She just startled me."

Jade, looking like the smug little mood killer she was, flopped down on Jordan's lap.

"Attention whore," I muttered.

"They always are."

"Well, she gets no shortage of attention, so it won't kill her if she doesn't get any right now." Careful to make sure she didn't claw him again, I picked her up off Jordan's lap and set her on the floor. "Sorry, baby, you're going to have to find someplace else to sleep."

"Aww, but she looked so comfortable."

"She was." I sat up and put my arm around his shoulders again. "But she was in the way." Touching his face with my free hand, I kissed him. Jordan put his arms around me, and as the kiss deepened and lingered, he sank against me. I slid my fingers into his hair, then pulled his head back just hard enough to make him grunt. When I kissed his neck, he moaned and held on to my shirt.

"Shouldn't we wait for Dante?" he whispered, making absolutely no effort to pull away.

"Of course not." I put my hand on his inner thigh and slowly drew it upward. "This way you'll be good and warmed up when he gets home."

"Don't think that'll...that'll be an issue."

When my hand made it to the front of his jeans, he wasn't kidding. I traced the outline of his cock with my fingertips, and my own erection made it almost impossible to sit comfortably like this.

I didn't care, though, because I'd found Jordan's mouth again. I slid the tip of my tongue under his, and he groaned softly into my kiss. I inhaled deeply through my nose and pulled him closer. Just the musky, masculine scent of him drove me insane. Combined with the taste of his kiss and the thick ridge beneath my hand and his jeans, I wanted him. Badly. I had to have him.

Dante and I had so many plans for tonight. Pushing some limits, teasing his senses, making him beg and plead for release. Maybe some more pain, maybe some bondage, but those plans would have to wait. Sitting here this way, making out on my couch like a couple of desperate teenagers, all I wanted to do was fuck him. Put him on his knees, hold on to his hips and *fuck him.*

I broke the kiss and tilted my head back, and Jordan immediately went for my neck. Closing my eyes, I exhaled hard as his lips found every sensitive place from my jaw to my collarbone.

"Your mouth is fucking amazing," I breathed.

"Thank you," he murmured, and gently nipped just above my collar. He dragged his lip across my skin, just the way I did to his lower lip whenever I kissed him, and I shivered. Every nerve ending in my body tingled into hyperawareness and searched for his lips, his fingers, any kind of contact, even if it was just the warmth of an *almost*-touch.

"Mmm, just like that," I whispered as he kissed his way up to my ear. He continued along my jaw, and when he raised his head, I kissed him. I gripped his hair and kissed him desperately, almost savagely, and the moan against my lips made me that much harder. Fuck, I wanted him.

My phone suddenly came to life with Dante's favorite song.

"Shit, that's Dante."

Jordan sat up to let me reach for my Bluetooth on the coffee table.

"Hopefully he's not running late." I clicked on the headset. "Hey."

"Hey, sorry about that," Dante said. "I'm on my way home now."

"About fucking time." I chuckled and put my hand on Jordan's leg. "You just leaving the studio?"

"No, I had to stop for gas. I'm about ten minutes out."

"Pity." I glanced at Jordan and winked. "Guess Jordan's stuck with me until you get here."

Dante laughed. "You're keeping him entertained, aren't you?"

A grin tugged at my lips. "I suppose I should do that, shouldn't I?"

"Well, then, I should let you go."

"No, you don't need to do that." I licked my lips. Jordan raised an eyebrow.

"What?" Dante asked. "Why not?"

"You using your hands-free?"

"Of course."

"Good. So am I." I looked at Jordan, then pointed at the floor in front of my feet. He didn't hesitate and immediately went to his knees where I'd indicated. To Dante, I said, "That means you can still talk while you're driving, right?"

"Of course I—" He paused. "Why?"

"No reason." I unzipped my jeans. Jordan gulped. I gave him a nod and said to Dante, "No reason at—oh, *Jesus.*"

"Angel, what are you doing?"

"Oh, it's not what *I'm* doing." I stroked Jordan's hair. He started slow, God bless him, teasing me with his lips and tongue instead of giving me everything he had.

"Angel..."

"Don't worry," I whispered, barely finding my voice as Jordan took my cock deeper into his mouth. "Just means we'll both be warmed up for you when—" My voice caught. "Easy, Jordan. I don't want you to make me come yet."

"You're fucking evil," Dante growled.

"*I'm* evil?" I closed my eyes and groaned. "Jesus, Dante, you know that thing he does with his tongue? That—"

As if for emphasis, Jordan did it again.

"Oh God..."

"Fuck, Angel..."

"I would, but then he'd have to stop with his mouth." I fought to find my breath. "And I am *not* stopping him."

Dante said nothing for a second. Then, "You're not joking, are you? Is he... Angel, is he really..."

"*Ooh*, yeah he is."

"Fuck. That's...oh, fuck, Angel..."

I moaned, my back lifting off the couch. "Dante, you...you need..."

"What?" He sounded almost as breathless as I was.

"Drive. Faster."

"Oh, God..." His voice was little more than a hoarse whisper, and though I couldn't be sure, I swore the engine crescendoed in the background. In a low growl, Dante said, "Tell me what he's doing."

I looked down at Jordan, struggling to focus my eyes and find the words. "That thing he does," I whispered, pausing to lick my dry lips. "With both hands at the same time."

"Tell me. Details, Angel. Come on."

I licked my lips again. Right then, Jordan met my eyes, and the need for release inched toward unbearable. The ability to speak? Gone. I grasped his hair and moaned.

"Angel," Dante whispered, and he sounded as breathless as I was. "Please..."

I forced some air into my lungs and willed myself to remember how to speak. "Both hands, up and down, one...twisting a little..." The more I described it, the more Jordan did it. I groaned, closing my eyes and letting my head fall back. "Fuck, Jordan, that's amazing."

"You're not going to come before I get there, are you?" Dante said.

"Depends." I took a breath. "How much longer are you going to be?"

"I'll be there as soon as I can," he said quickly.

"No promises, though," I said. "Because...oh God, oh God..."

"What?" In my mind's eye, Dante white-knuckled the steering wheel and put the pedal to the floor. "What? Tell me."

"He's...fuck..." I looked down at Jordan, but my eyes were watering too much to focus, so I closed them again. "God damn it, Jordan, do you even *have* a gag reflex?"

A warm huff of breath implied a quiet laugh, and both that exhalation and the subtle vibration of his voice made me even dizzier.

I dug my teeth into my lip, screwing my eyes shut and forcing myself not to come. I didn't need permission to come—Dante's or Jordan's—but I didn't want to let go until Dante was here. He heard what we were doing, knew what Jordan was doing to my cock with that incredible fucking mouth, but I wanted him to see. I wanted him to see my fingers in Jordan's hair, his head rising and falling rhythmically over my lap, and I wanted him to see my face the instant I let go, because I knew how much that would drive him insane.

The faint rumble of the garage door opening almost set me off. He was here. Dante was here. He was here, so I didn't have to hold out much longer.

"I'll be in the house in a second," he said, and the line went dead.

I didn't bother taking off my Bluetooth. I just kept my hand in Jordan's hair and closed my eyes, digging my teeth into my lip as his tongue swirled around the head of my cock this way, then that way, then this way again.

Down the hall, a door opened, and Jordan's rhythm faltered just enough to hint that he'd heard it. I gently grasped his hair. *God, don't stop, don't you dare fucking stop and look when he walks into the room.*

"Oh my God." Dante's voice, crystal clear without the static of the cellular line, raised the hairs on the back of my neck. I opened my eyes, blinking until he came into focus.

He was still for a moment. From the hallway, he just watched, jaw slack and eyes wide. Then his eyes met mine, and he was on the move again.

"This is even hotter than I pictured it," he growled, dropping onto the couch beside me. Our mouths came together in a passionate, breathless kiss. It only took a few seconds before I surrendered to both his mouth and Jordan's, and gave in to that orgasm that had been closing in on me. The world went white, and the universe concentrated itself into every pulse and shudder and *oh, my God* that surged through me.

As my orgasm subsided, Jordan released me, and I could finally catch my breath. Then, before I'd even had a chance to fix my clothes, Dante gasped. We both looked down, and Jordan met his eyes, then mine, while he unzipped Dante's pants.

He stopped suddenly. His hands froze and his spine straightened, as if he thought he'd done something wrong. He cleared his throat. "I—may I?"

Dante nodded, and Jordan's posture relaxed. He went back to undoing the zipper and buckle, and I could barely breathe as Jordan went down on Dante.

"Holy shit..." Dante groaned, resting his head on the back of the couch and closing his eyes. I slid my hand under his shirt. His abs contracted beneath my fingertips, and when I teased his nipple, he gasped and arched his back. My own skin tingled from everything Jordan had done to me, and watching him do it to Dante made me shiver.

I kissed Dante's neck, and between Jordan's mouth and mine, he squirmed and moaned. His skin was hot, his pulse racing against my lips, and every time he shivered, my own heart beat faster. I knew all too well what he felt, my nerve endings still tingling from the very same thing: the way Jordan's tongue found every sensitive place, the way he alternated between deep-throating and just teasing, even the warmth of his breath on skin. Jordan was born to suck cock, I was sure of it.

"Oh...fuck..." Dante's entire body stiffened. His breath caught, his back arched, and with a breathless moan, he came. Jordan kept going until Dante whispered for him to stop. He sat back on his heels while Dante took a few slow, deep breaths.

"Jesus Christ," he whispered. "Your mouth is amazing, Jordan."

Jordan chuckled, wiping the corner of his mouth with the back of his hand. "I try."

Dante fixed his clothes, and we moved far enough apart to let Jordan join us on the couch. Before Jordan had even settled between us, Dante grabbed the back of his neck and kissed him deeply. I put my hand over the front of Jordan's jeans, biting my lip when he shuddered against Dante. I leaned in and kissed Jordan's neck, and Dante's hand brushed mine over Jordan's cock.

"We have plenty left for you tonight," I said against the goose bumps beneath the ends of Jordan's hair. "And since we've both already come once, do you know what that means?"

He broke away from Dante's kiss just enough to murmur, "Hmm?"

"It means," Dante said, his lips barely leaving Jordan's, "that we'll both last that much longer when we put you on your knees and fuck you."

Jordan shivered.

Chapter Fifteen

What I was thinking when I agreed to take a riding lesson from Jordan, I had no idea. But I'd agreed to it, and now I was parked in front of his barn, pretending the thought of getting on a horse didn't give me vertigo. I must have seemed like a complete wimp to him and Angel, being so intimidated by anything on four legs. Dogs, I'd had a bad experience. Horses? So far, no bad experiences, but they were huge. And fast. And had a tendency to freak the fuck out if something startled them.

Oh, just do it, Dante.

Rolling my eyes at my own cowardice, I got out of the car and went into the barn. I found Jordan in a stall with a small black horse that was loosely tied and half asleep. Jordan looked up from fastening the saddle in place and smiled.

"Hey," he said. "Just about ready."

"Don't rush on account of me."

"Not rushing, don't worry."

I gestured at the horse. "So this is the beast I'll be riding today?"

Jordan laughed. "Beast? Oh, come on, now." He patted the horse's rump, a tiny cloud of dust flying up around his hand. "This is Nova. She's about the most docile creature I own."

"That's encouraging." I eyed her warily. I was really going to do this? Get on the back of a horse?

Jordan opened the stall door but didn't come out. "Come on in."

"Do I have to?"

"Yes. Get in here." He winked. I hesitated, then stepped into the stall. As I did, he leaned out the door, glancing up the aisle, then down, then up again. "We won't stay in here long." He turned to me, a hint of color emphasizing the sheepish expression. "I was just hoping for a kiss."

"Well, why didn't you say so?" I touched his face and kissed him gently, and for about three seconds, forgot all about the large animal standing next to us. Then she fidgeted, and I broke the kiss to cast her an uncertain glance.

"They really intimidate you, don't they?" he asked, his voice playful, but not condescending.

I shrugged. "Yeah. Just a city kid, not used to being around animals, I guess."

"How the hell did you and Angel travel to all those exotic places without riding once in a while?"

"By very carefully choosing places that didn't require it." I chuckled. "You should have seen me eyeballing the yaks when we were in the Himalayas."

He smiled and held out his hand, beckoning. "Give me your hand."

After a moment's hesitation, I did as he asked. He gently closed his fingers around my wrist, and drew my hand closer to the horse.

Nova sniffed my hand. Her whiskers tickled my palm, and when she ran her lip back and forth across my fingers, presumably searching for a treat, I resisted the urge to jerk my hand back. If Jordan wasn't concerned about her biting me, I told myself, then there was probably nothing to worry about. Still, having my hand that close to teeth that big was unnerving to say the least.

Jordan let go of my hand. "She won't bite, I promise." He petted her face, and nodded for me to do the same, so I did. There was certainly nothing threatening about her besides her size. If anything, she looked bored.

"This the horse you use for all your beginners?"

He shrugged. "She's one of my lesson horses. Noreen does most of the lessons, though. I train the horses, she trains the riders."

"Sounds like heaven for you, then."

"Definitely." He tousled Nova's forelock. "This one's mostly retired now, though. She spent the last couple of years leased to the therapeutic riding center, but now she's pretty much doing a lesson here and there in between playing out in the pastures."

"Retired? How old is she?"

"She'll be twenty-nine this year, if you can believe it." He smiled fondly at her. "Healthy as all hell for a horse her age, but she's earned her keep." He looked at me. "Anyway, you've never been on a horse before? In your life?"

"No," I said, still eyeballing Nova, "the idea of getting on an animal ten times my size who could run that fast just never appealed to me."

Jordan snorted. "Yet you don't have a problem hurtling down a snow-covered mountain on a couple of waxed boards with a pair of toothpicks for control?"

I laughed. "Well, when you put it like that, it almost sounds crazy."

"It is crazy." He reached out of the stall and picked up the bridle that had been hanging on a nearby hook. "Put me on the fastest, least trained horse in the world and I'll be fine. Leave me on top of a mountain with skis on? I'll still be there in the morning."

"Hey, at least my skis won't spook at something."

"No, but horses are pretty good at not crashing into trees."

"Touché."

Chuckling, Jordan put Nova's bridle on. Then we headed out of the stall, and the mare plodded between us on the way to the arena where we'd photographed Arturo and Bravado ages ago.

While we walked, I glanced over my shoulder at the thin crowd of clients congregating near the other arena.

"So, do your clients know about this?"

"What? That I give riding lessons?" He dropped his voice to a conspiratorial whisper. "Don't tell them, okay?"

I rolled my eyes. "No, I mean..."

"Us?" He shrugged. "They know I'm gay. That's all they need to know. Your clients know about you and Angel?"

"Some do," I said. "You said your sister figured it out, didn't you?"

He nodded. "Yeah, she did."

"We don't advertise it, but obviously some catch on."

"You didn't do a hell of a lot to keep it under my radar." He glanced at me, eyebrows up as a playful grin worked its way onto his lips.

"Damn right we didn't." I returned the grin. "We *wanted* you to catch on."

"Guess your evil plan worked, then, didn't it?"

"So it did."

Jordan led the mare and me into the arena, then closed the gate behind us. Sasha appeared from a nearby pasture and found a shady spot beneath a tree where he dropped into the dust, panting while he watched us. I tried not to notice him. As if I needed two animals making me nervous.

"So," Jordan said. "Since you've never done this, we'll start with the very basic stuff. Getting on and off, balancing, steering."

"Stopping?"

"Yes, stopping." He put the reins over Nova's head and laid them across her neck, just in front of the saddle. "To get on, you're going to hold a piece of her mane and your reins in your left hand, and the saddle in your right. Left foot in the stirrup, then pull yourself up and swing your other leg over." With a pointed look, he added, "Just don't drop into the saddle. Some people do that, and it drives me nuts. Let yourself down gently."

"Sounds simple enough."

"Quite simple." He stepped aside, keeping one hand on the bridle. "Go for it."

Certain this would be one of those things that was easier said than done, I stepped up to the horse. I gathered the reins and a lock of Nova's mane in one hand, put my foot in the stirrup and held the back of the saddle. Then, just as he'd told me to, I pulled myself up, swung my leg over and eased myself into the saddle.

Okay, not so difficult.

Jordan showed me how to hold the reins, how *not* to put my foot in the stirrup and all of those things that I didn't realize actually had a technique to them. With all of that out of the way, it was time to wake up Nova and make her move.

"When you want to stop," he said, "sit back in the saddle, tighten up on your reins, and say 'whoa'."

"Got it." *I think.*

"Now, when she's moving, your balance is going to come from your lower body. As the horse's center of gravity shifts, yours will too, and you want to move with her. It's tempting to hold on to the saddle, but don't. You need your hands free for the reins. You'll be using your hips and legs for balance, and while you won't be grabbing on to her with your legs if you know what's good for you, you will hold on a bit with your upper legs." He put his hand on my knee. "If your inner thighs don't hurt tomorrow, you're doing it wrong."

"That's encouraging."

He laughed. "It'll hurt less the more you do it. Just wait until I make you ride bareback." Our eyes met, and if the way he blushed was any indication, his mind had also gone right back to that comment he'd made when he was riding Bravado.

"I think I'll stick with a saddle, thanks," I said.

"Chickenshit." His eyes sparkled with a devilishness that rivaled Angel's. "Okay, let's walk. Just tap her *gently* with your feet, but don't dig your heels in."

"What would she do if I did?"

"Nova? Nothing. Any other horse? She'd be halfway across the arena, and your ass would be in the dirt."

"Oh, that's...comforting."

He chuckled. "That's why you're on Nova for now. Go on, give her a tap and let's get started."

As he suggested, I nudged her with my feet, and she lurched into motion. Jordan walked beside her head, and I tried to find my equilibrium. The shifting-swaying-shifting of the horse's gait was foreign, to say the least. As she plodded along, jarring me with every alien step, I was even more impressed with Jordan's ability. He flew over jumps with no saddle, no stirrups, but with perfect grace and balance. At this rate, I was certain if Nova stumbled or turned sharply, I'd be facedown in the dirt.

Jordan looked over his shoulder at me. "Any trouble staying on?"

"I'm still on, aren't I?"

"See? Told you it wasn't difficult. Now why don't you try steering her a bit?" He led Nova toward the middle of the arena, away from the fence. "When you want to turn, it's not just a question of pulling a rein in either direction. Turn your head and look the way you want to go. Your torso will shift, as will your lower body, and she'll respond to that." He gestured around us. "Try making some circles and figure eights."

Following his suggestion, I turned my head to the right. Sure enough, Nova responded, changing her slow, lazy course according to the direction I'd turned.

"Okay, now bring her to a stop," he said. "Remember, sit back a little, tighten up on your reins and say 'whoa.'"

Before I could, Nova stopped abruptly. I instinctively grabbed the front of the saddle to keep my balance.

Jordan laughed. "Nova, you're supposed to listen to him, not me." With a hand on her neck, he looked up at me. "Doing okay?"

"I'm still on, so I'd say so far, so good."

He smiled. "Well, now we're going to try something a bit more challenging."

"Oh, really?"

"Yeah." He gestured at the far end of the arena. "Think you can handle a few jumps?"

My heart stopped.

Jordan winked. "Just fucking with you."

"Bastard."

"Don't worry, you won't be going anywhere near a jump any time soon." He absently patted Nova's neck while he went on. "I'm going to keep leading her like this, but you're going to close your eyes."

I raised an eyebrow. "Are you still fucking with me?"

He shook his head. "Absolutely not. It forces you to pay attention to how she's moving, and adjust your body and center of gravity accordingly without relying on watching her. You have to learn to feel and respond without thinking."

"You're serious. You really want me to ride around on a half-ton animal with my eyes closed."

He nodded.

"You're insane."

"No, I'm the trainer," he said. "Honestly, I will be walking right beside her, and she's not going anywhere unless you or I tell her to."

I swallowed.

Holding my gaze, he said, "Do you trust me?"

"Of course I do." I pointed at the creature below me. "It's *her* I'm not too sure about."

Jordan laughed softly and stroked her neck. "She'll do whatever I tell her to. Just close your eyes and focus on staying balanced." His expression turned serious. "Honestly, Dante, you won't fall. You'll instinctively balance yourself more than you think, so you're just learning to trust that instinct." He paused. "You'll be fine. Just trust me."

I took a deep breath, shot him one last uncertain glance, then closed my eyes. Even like this, with the horse simply standing, I couldn't help feeling like I was on unnervingly unstable ground. She didn't move much, but just her breathing and the mere knowledge I was on her back made me nervous.

"Ready?" Jordan asked.

"I guess you could say that."

He murmured something to the horse, and she lurched into motion again.

The sway of her gait was even more pronounced now. By the time I'd shifted to accommodate a step, she took another and I was off-balance again. It was dizzying, the simultaneous side-to-side forward-back motion.

"Doing okay?" he asked.

"As well as can be expected."

"Just keep your eyes closed. You're doing fine. I'm going to turn her around now, so pay attention."

Right. Like I'd thought about anything in the last few minutes but where and how the horse moved. Denied my sight, I was more than a little disoriented when she turned. My sense of direction was all fucked up, my head spinning like she'd just gone in a dozen tight circles instead of, I guessed, making a one-eighty. The needle on my internal compass whizzed back and forth until some noise and voices from the barn behind me oriented me again.

With my sense of direction back on track, I realized Nova had been moving the whole time I'd been trying to reorient myself. Just as Jordan had predicted, I'd balanced without thinking. The more I relaxed and didn't try to second guess her motions or my responses, the less certain I was that I would fall. Eventually, her movements felt almost natural.

"That's about enough for one day," Jordan said.

I opened my eyes, squinting against the sunlight. "Damn it, just when I was getting the hang of it."

"You still want to be able to walk tomorrow, though, don't you?"

"Yeah, good point."

"Okay, bring her to a stop."

As he'd told me before, I sat back a little, gently pulled back on the reins, and said, "Whoa." Since I was expecting it this time, the halt didn't throw me quite so far off-balance.

"I assume there's a trick to getting from here to the ground in one piece?"

He shrugged. "I could undo the cinch and let you fall."

"Or, you know, if there's another technique..."

"Lucky for you, there is." He walked me through the series of simple motions, and just like getting on, it wasn't difficult. A little awkward for someone who wasn't used to it, especially when the ground turned out to be an inch or so lower than I expected it to be. I stumbled, but Jordan's hand on my back kept me from doing much more than sacrificing a few seconds of dignity.

"You'll get the hang of it," he said. I wasn't so sure, but I'd take his word for it for now.

We took Nova back to the barn and put her away. Then we strolled down the barn aisle with Sasha wandering beside us. Even while Jordan and I shot the breeze and made small talk, my eyes kept darting toward the dog. Unnoticed, I hoped.

Fat chance of that.

Jordan snapped his finger at the dog. "Sasha, lie down."

The dog immediately obeyed, dropping onto his belly at his master's feet. Jordan knelt beside him and patted his back. Sasha rolled over.

"Good boy." Then Jordan gestured at me. "Come here."

"Hmm?"

He nodded at the dog. "He's not going to hurt you."

My stomach immediately coiled itself into knots. Intellectually, I knew the dog wouldn't do a damned thing. He was on his back, showing unquestioning submission to Jordan, and didn't appear in the least bit aggressive. That, and the horse had been as docile as Jordan had said she'd be, so I had no reason to believe he'd mislead me about Sasha.

Kneeling beside Sasha, I had visions of that black lab snapping at me, and the blood on my father's hand that could have come from my face if things had gone down differently. But this wasn't some dog my dad had just met. This was Jordan's dog of God only knew how many years, so I took a breath and reached down to pet him.

I was still a little edgy, running my hand over the dog's coarse fur, but he hadn't taken my hand off yet, so maybe he was okay after all.

"See?" Jordan smiled. "He's about as docile as Nova."

I nodded. "Yeah, he didn't strike me as terribly aggressive. You know how phobias are, though."

"Yep, I do." He scratched Sasha's belly. "Sometimes just facing them down can help. I figured since you didn't have a full-on panic attack whenever he was around, you'd be okay."

"Guess you were right." I patted Sasha's side. He still made me a little nervous, but something about touching him and seeing for myself that he wasn't going to do anything relaxed me a little. It was a start.

At Jordan's command, the dog stood and shook the dust out of his coat. I held out my hand, and Sasha sniffed it, regarding me curiously at the same time.

After a moment, I pushed myself to my feet.

"On a horse and playing with the dog." Jordan grinned at me as he petted Sasha. "Angel will be most impressed."

I laughed. "That or he'll demand photographic evidence."

"That could be arranged. I have my camera phone with me."

I gave the most indignant sniff I could muster. "A camera phone? I *beg* your pardon."

He rolled his eyes. "Camera snob."

"Damn right," I said. "If it ain't Nikon, I don't want anything to do with it."

"So you'd probably have heart failure if you saw the Canon I have in the house?"

I clicked my tongue. "Well, that explains why you hired us to come take pictures."

"Good point."

With the dog plodding beside Jordan, we kept walking out to the gravel parking area. Out in the sun instead of the dim light of the barn, I glanced down at the dust and horse hair on my shirt. I brushed some of it off, but my hands weren't much cleaner, so it didn't help.

Jordan pursed his lips. "I suppose Angel will have a fit if you walk into his house like that."

"Nah." I made another futile effort to dust off my clothes. "He's been around horses. That's about the only kind of dirt he can handle."

"Still, it wouldn't be right to send you home dirty." His eyes darted toward the barn, probably making sure none of his other clients had wandered in our direction. No one had, but when he faced me again, he lowered his voice anyway. "I could, of course, assist with that."

"Could you, now?"

"If you wanted me to, yes." His eyebrows lifted slightly, a silent "please?"

"Well, when you put it like that..."

We exchanged grins, then went into the house.

In the shower, we went through all the motions of getting clean, but spent more time soaping each other than ourselves. Even that was only when we could bring ourselves to stop kissing beneath the hot water, and the longer that went on, the less we stopped for anything. We were long past the point of needing to get clean, but being naked under hot water with Jordan, I wasn't about to rush out.

Jordan lathered his hands. "Want me to get your back?"

"I most definitely do."

"Well, I live to serve."

I turned around. Jordan's soap-slicked hands slid easily over my wet skin. Up my back, down again, up and over my shoulders. He pressed the heels of his hands into my muscles, letting his fingers fan out as they followed a shiver up my spine. I had to rest an arm against the wall just to keep myself upright; my entire body wanted to melt beneath his gentle massage.

After a while, he said, "That enough? Or more?"

I could have let him do it all night, but instead, I turned around. As soon as I faced him, I grabbed the sides of his neck in both hands, kissing him passionately before he had a chance to react. He was still for a second, probably startled, but then he wrapped his arms around me, and we were once again lost in a deep kiss that was hotter than the water rushing over us. Even if his rock-hard cock wasn't pressed against mine, his arousal would have been unmistakable in the rapid, uneven breaths he took and the way his fingers clawed at my back.

I dipped my head to kiss his neck. "In any hurry to get back to work?"

"Not at all."

"Good."

It only took a hint of pressure on the back of his neck, and he went to his knees. He wrapped his fingers around my cock and looked up at me, eyes wide and eyebrows raised. I nodded.

God in heaven, I could never get tired of the way this man sucked cock. I closed my eyes, letting my head fall back while he deep-throated, teased, deep-throated, teased again. My knees shook, and my head spun. I couldn't even feel the water on my back anymore. All my senses were completely focused on Jordan's hand, Jordan's mouth, oh, God, Jordan's tongue.

As much as I wanted to, and as much as he made it nearly inevitable, I didn't want to come just yet.

I moistened my lips and opened my eyes to look down at him.

"Stand up," I said. As soon as he was on his feet, I whispered, "Go get a condom and lube."

He nodded. I kissed him lightly, and he stepped out of the shower, pausing just long enough to grab a towel before disappearing from the bathroom.

I let the water run over my neck and shoulders, rinsing away the last of the soap he'd so attentively put on my skin. My legs were feeling it from my lesson, but let a little muscle pain stop me from fucking Jordan? Not in this lifetime.

He returned, condom and lube in hand.

Stroking his cock, I whispered, "I want you to put it on me so I can fuck you."'

Before I'd even finished speaking, he had the wrapper torn and my cock in his hand. I chewed my lip, my entire body tingling and aching with the need to fuck him. The second he'd finished putting on the lube, I turned him around and shoved him up against the tile wall.

I kissed the back of his neck and released a low groan as I pushed into him. Jordan pushed back, whimpering as he took me deeper. The first few strokes I took were slow and easy as they always were, giving him a chance to get used to me. Instead of picking up speed, though, I kept moving slowly, sliding in and out of him at just the right pace to make him shiver with pleasure and curse with frustration. I continued like that, slow and gentle, until he relaxed and surrendered, no doubt accepting I'd made the decision—Dom's privilege, after all—to give him this and only this.

Then I grabbed onto his hips and slammed into him, and I fucked him hard. Kept fucking him hard. The sound he released was the most delicious cry of surprise and ecstasy, and his fingers grabbed at the wall, searching in vain for something to hold on to.

My own balance wavered, so I braced myself with a hand against the wall beside his shoulder. With my free hand, I held on to his hip, and I thrust into him like I was hell-bent on fucking him within an inch of his life.

The intensity almost forced my eyes closed, but I kept them open. I had to see him. I had to watch myself moving in and out of him. Sweat and water mingling on the back of his neck. Water droplets slipping over his shoulders, shaken loose whenever his muscles twitched and tensed and trembled. His arms shaking as he tried to keep his balance. He was so fucking beautiful.

A shudder rippled through him, and he whimpered like he was about to lose it.

"Like that?" I had to clench my teeth to keep them from chattering.

"Yes," he moaned. "Oh God, I want to come."

"Not yet." I kissed his neck. "Your orgasms belong to me. You'll come when I say you will."

He groaned and shuddered again, but held back. I fucked him harder. His shoulders bunched, and his hands clawed at the wet tile.

"Please, let me come," he moaned. "Fuck, Dante, you feel so good, please, please…"

"Not yet." *Almost, almost,* I wanted to say, but I couldn't find my breath. Forcing myself to stay in control, I shut my eyes tight and gritted my teeth. I was right there on the edge, just like he was, but I wasn't ready for this to be over quite yet. I bit my lip, taking a few more strokes, but delirium was closing in fast, and just before oblivion would have swept me under, I found enough air to whisper, "Come."

Jordan whimpered, and I let his climax carry me right into my own. I held on to him, he braced against the shower wall, and somehow we both stayed on our feet while tremor after tremor tried to knock our knees out from under us.

His orgasm tapered.

Mine tapered.

We both released our breath, and I pulled out slowly, but beyond that, we didn't move for a moment. I put my arms around him and kissed his neck.

"If this is how every lesson will go," I murmured, "do sign me up for more."

Chapter Sixteen

Dante's platinum blond hair was still damp, and as we both dried off in the bathroom, I witnessed the meticulousness with which he styled it into his customary spikes: fingers through the hair a few times, glance in the mirror, fingers through the hair once more, shrug, done.

"And here I thought you had to work at getting it to look like that," I said.

He shrugged. "Oh, I put more effort into it if I'm going out or something."

"Define 'more effort'."

He ran his fingers through it again, threw an intense scowl at the mirror, then shrugged again. Our eyes met, and we both laughed.

After we'd dried off, we got into bed and pulled the sheet up over us. Dante draped his arm over my waist, but we kept a few inches of space between us. Not that I minded being as close to him as humanly possible, but we were both still hot from the shower, so we stayed apart to stay cool.

"So do I have to pay extra for that part of the lesson?" he asked.

"I'd say we'll call it payment *for* the lesson, but I think that qualifies as prostitution."

"Hmm, yeah, good point."

"I wasn't planning to charge you for the lesson anyway," I said. "So we'll just call it even."

"Just to be sure, give me a few minutes and I'll fuck you again. *Then* we'll be even."

I shivered. Something told me he wasn't kidding.

He touched my face, then kissed me lightly. It still blew my mind how gentle he and Angel could be. Though I'd understood dominance and submission wasn't all about pain and black leather, I hadn't expected the intimacy or, if I dared describe it as such, the tenderness. They were more attentive and even affectionate than any lover I'd had before.

"What's on your mind?" he asked, drawing me back into the present.

I shrugged. "Just thinking about how this is going versus how I thought it would."

Propping himself up on one elbow, he trailed his fingertips down my cheek again. "And?"

I moistened my lips. "It's...definitely not what I expected."

"In what way? I mean, good or bad?"

"Good, good, definitely good." *I think.* "Can't quite describe it, but it's..." I furrowed my brow.

"More intimate?"

I hesitated, then nodded. "Yeah, you could say that."

He trailed the backs of his fingers down the side of my face. "Sometimes it works out this way. We've had relationships with subs that were strictly business. Get together, some flogging, some fucking, thank you and good night. With others, it's more like this." He paused. "Quite honestly, I prefer it when it's like this. Means we have a better connection with you. Not so many barriers between all of us. The closer we are to you, the more likely we are to pick up on any problems before they become problems. That kind of thing."

"Makes sense." *But how close is too close?* I cleared my throat. "I'm curious, what happened with your other subs?"

"They've come and gone over the years," he said with a half shrug. "Some were more or less one-nighters. Some found other Doms and decided to go for something more monogamous."

"Have you ever had something like this end badly?"

He was quiet for a moment, his eyes losing focus as he slowly ran the tip of his tongue across his lower lip. "A time or two, yes. We had one who fell for Angel." Dante clicked his tongue. "I mean, head-over-heels, completely in love with him."

"So, what happened?"

"We had to cut him loose." He sighed. "We have a rule about getting emotionally involved. It's not that we want to stay cold and distant, but we have to keep some distance to keep things from getting too complicated, you know?"

"That makes sense, yes."

"Most subs get that and aren't after anything more anyway." He absently combed his fingers through my hair.

"How do you guys make it work, anyway?" I asked. "With both of you being Doms?"

"Oh, it was tough at first, believe me." He watched his hand run up and down my arm. "It's probably a good thing we met when we did. We were both still figuring out we were Doms at that point. Figuring out what that means, anyway. Another couple of years down the line and we might have just passed each other by, thinking we weren't compatible."

"At least you two figured it out fairly early on." I smirked and rolled my eyes. "I made it into my mid-thirties before I even knew what a submissive really was."

Dante smiled. "Better late than never."

"True." I trailed my fingertips down the side of his neck. "On the bright side, doing so now meant I've had you guys to show me the way."

"Oh, you'd have found a decent Dom if we hadn't been around." He picked up my hand and kissed the backs of my fingers. "But of course, we're always happy to help a new sub."

"Much appreciated."

He leaned forward and kissed me gently. Then we both settled back on the pillows. "Anyway, like I was saying about me and Angel, we got together, then started figuring out how much we both needed submission. About the time he moved here to live with me, we'd realized we needed to do something as a compromise. Since neither of us is willing to submit, we decided to bring in subs."

"Seems like that's worked well for you."

"Oh, it's definitely worked." Dante smiled, though there was a distant look in his eyes. "Angel was a little worried in the beginning. He wasn't so sure he liked the idea of using someone, and in a way, that's what we were setting out to do." His eyes refocused, and he turned his head toward me. "But then we figured they needed something, we needed something, why not make a deal?"

"Interesting way to put it."

"Guess I've been around him too long. Learning to put things extra bluntly. It's true, though. We're not out to use someone like some kind of sex toy. It's supposed to be a mutual thing."

"It certainly has been with me," I said. "If you're worried I'm not getting anything out of it..."

We both laughed. He went on. "And as a bonus to this whole thing, it means I get to fuck someone once in a while."

"Angel really doesn't like it, does he?"

"No, not at all. It's just not his thing. We tried many times, and he still would if I asked him to, but..." Dante shook his head. "I don't ask him because I know he doesn't like it."

"So the only time you get to do it," I said, "is when you guys have a sub?"

He nodded.

"I think I'd go crazy."

"I make do." He smiled. "Honestly, it's been frustrating at times, but given the choice between that and being with Angel? I can live with it."

"Well, you can use me for it any time you want."

His smile faded a little, and he draped his arm over my waist. "We're not using you for anything, Jordan."

"You know what I mean."

He looked away for a second, and when our eyes met again, his were intense with something I couldn't quite identify. "As long as you're our sub, you're as much a part of this as we are. Yeah, we do this because submission is something we can't get from each other, but you're not just a sex toy for us."

I swallowed. "I know. And you guys have never made me feel like that's all I am." *Quite the contrary*, I thought with a pleasant shudder.

"Good." He lifted his head to kiss my forehead. "If we ever do make you feel like that, or like we're outnumbering you, speak up." He traced the curve of my spine with his hand. "This is as much about you as it's about us, and it should be fun for everyone."

"Nothing to worry about there."

"That's what I like to hear." He pushed himself up on one arm and pulled me closer with the other. "We want you to enjoy this as much as we do." With that, he kissed me. He and Angel were forever complimenting my oral techniques, but they could both do to me with a kiss what I did to them with a blowjob. Like Angel, Dante knew just how to send electric tingles down my spine with the gentle, deliberate way he coaxed my lips apart and drew my tongue into his mouth. He was in absolute control of the kiss, deciding how intense, how deep, how long, without ever being overbearing or unduly demanding, and I loved it.

"I could keep doing this all night," he whispered.

Please, please, please. "Don't let me stop you."

Dante kissed me gently, then sighed. "I would *so* stay if I didn't have a bunch of stupid responsible adult things to do tonight."

"We could always spend a little more time doing fun adult things." I trailed my fingers up the back of his neck. "If you wanted to, of course."

His lips curved into a grin against mine. "Oh, I absolutely want to. I'm just trying to decide between being a responsible adult and...not."

"Putting on a condom counts as being a responsible adult, doesn't it?"

"I fucking love the way you think, Steele." His palm drifted down my back and he pressed his hard-on against me. "Question is, do you want me to stay a little longer?"

"Only a little longer?"

"Okay, a while longer," he whispered and kissed me again.

A "while longer" was an understatement to say the least, but we eventually decided to return to the rest of the world. Though it required a degree of willpower I didn't think I possessed, we managed to get out of bed, into our clothes, and down to Dante's car. He didn't leave quite yet, though.

Not giving a rat's ass who saw us or what they thought about us, I put my arms around him. "So, am I going to be able to talk you into another riding lesson?"

"I don't think you'll have to twist my arm." He slid his hands into my back pockets. "Especially if the roll in the hay is included."

I laughed. "You don't even have to have the lesson to get that."

"Good to know." He kissed me, and we both let it go on longer than we probably should have.

I was out of breath when we separated. "Guess I should make sure to block out a few hours for your half-hour lessons, then."

"Or we can make do with the time we have and have a quickie now and then."

"Do you or Angel even know the meaning of the word 'quickie'?"

He made a flippant gesture with one hand. "Well, we know the *meaning*..."

"But have you ever applied it?"

"Not in recent memory, no." He inclined his head. "Unless you want us to rush things?"

"No, no, not at all. I rather like the way we're doing things."

"That's what I thought." He pulled me to him and kissed me lightly. Even when he broke that kiss, he stayed close. He kept one hand in my back pocket and brought the other up to touch my face. For the longest time, we just held each other's gazes. The only sound was Dante's thumb brushing back and forth over my cheek.

And from somewhere deep down came the certainty that there was something very, very wrong with this. A prickle of guilt started at the base of my spine and spread its tingling tentacles upward.

He shouldn't have been looking at me like that, but he was. I shouldn't have been looking at him like this, but I was. When he tilted his head and kissed me, he shouldn't have kissed me like *that*, but he did.

He touched his forehead to mine. "You're still coming over tomorrow night, right?"

Tomorrow night. Their house. *Angel.* That's what it was. Angel wasn't here. Prior to tonight, we'd played one-on-one, but always with both of them in the same room. This was the first time we'd slept together without Angel.

The prickling eased, receding back to the base of my spine but not dissipating completely. It was just something new, that's all, I told myself. I'd just had sex, an intimate conversation and a gentle kiss with someone else's boyfriend. Angel knew full well that Dante was here. If he'd come around the corner and caught us like this, he'd have sooner joined in than gotten upset.

We hadn't broken any of the agreed-upon rules, just the normal rules that most people abided by in their relationships. *All's well. Crisis of conscience averted.*

I think.

Dante touched my face again, and I jumped.

"You okay?" he asked. "You spaced out on me."

I shook my head. "Sorry. I was—" *Think, Steele, think.* "Going over tomorrow's schedule in my head. Making sure nothing had come up."

"I hope nothing has?"

"No. Barring any unforeseens, anyway."

He smiled. "Good. I can't wait."

"Neither can I."

He kissed me again, and I paid no attention to my conscience screaming at me that this was too tender and far too intimate.

"I should go," Dante finally whispered.

"I know. I need to get a few things done myself."

"Okay." He kissed me lightly, then let me go. We shared one last, long look. Then he got into his car, and I headed back down to the barn to check water, clear my head and bring a few horses in from turnout.

"Taking your work home with you?"

Noreen's voice just about made me jump out of my skin. I spun on my heel. She stood in the office doorway, arms folded across her chest and a knowing expression on her face.

"Noreen," I said. "Jesus, you startled me."

"*So* sorry." Her eyes darted in the direction of the dust cloud Dante's car had kicked up. "I know it's none of my business, but God *damn*, Jordan."

My face was on fire. "What?"

She gave an exasperated sigh. "If you're going to hook up with a hot guy, could you please not rub it in?"

"Rub it in?" I laughed. "I haven't said a word about him."

She grinned. "No, you were just letting him kiss your face off in the driveway."

"I didn't know you were watching." I made a half-assed effort to look sheepish, and she just rolled her eyes.

"I'm just messing with you." Arms still folded across her chest, she leaned against the doorframe. "Actually, it's good to see you seeing someone else." Nodding in the general direction of the house, she added, "Does this mean that dipwad will be out of here soon?"

"God, I hope so."

"We'll have an empty stall at the end of the month," she said. "You could always have him sleep there."

"I wish." I laughed. "Hopefully he'll be out of my hair before it comes down to that."

"So what about that other guy? Think you'll be moving him in here soon?"

"Noreen, Jesus," I said. "You just saw me kissing him, now you think I'm going to move in with him?"

"Well, as long as you're going to have that kind of eye candy, the least you could do is keep him around for me to ogle."

"I thought you didn't want me rubbing it in that I was with a hot guy."

"I don't." She shrugged. "Which is why you just parade him around, but don't do anything to remind me he's doing you and not me."

Clicking my tongue with mock disapproval, I rolled my eyes. "Have I mentioned lately what a lady you are?"

"Probably around the same time I mentioned that you were a gentleman."

I gestured toward the driveway. "Well, *he* says I'm pretty gentle with—"

"Oh, fuck you, Jordan."

"And to answer your question, no, I'm not planning on moving him in here."

"Damn it." She paused. "Well, when you do bring him around, would you mind keeping all that kissing and crap out of sight?"

"Homophobe."

"I am *not*," she scoffed. "I just don't want to see *you* making out with someone."

"So you don't want pictures of—"

"Fuck you." The office door banged shut behind her.

I continued down the aisle, chuckling to myself. My smile faded as I walked, though. While I brought in the last few horses for the night and topped off water buckets, I couldn't get this evening out of my mind. I'd had that momentary panic in Dante's arms that certainty we were doing something wrong, and now that he was gone, some of it resurfaced.

We were playing by the rules, I reminded myself. Nothing we'd done had been outside of what the three of us had agreed upon. Angel knew where Dante was. Even if Dante and I hadn't explicitly planned to end up in the shower or in bed together, there was no rule in place forbidding it. I imagined Angel asking Dante for every last explicit detail, both of them winding each other up before dragging each other into the bedroom.

Then why the hell was I so off-balance in the wake of that long, gentle parting kiss? So we'd shared a tender kiss? So we'd talked in bed? So we'd made—fucked? Twice? Without Angel? It was all within the rules. We'd done nothing wrong.

I sighed and ran a hand through my hair. It was just foreign territory, that was all it was. Things were getting more intimate between all three of us, so of course they'd be that way when we were one-on-one. If Angel had been the one here tonight, things would have been the same. Right down to the tenderness and the lingering looks. It was just new. That was all.

At the end of the aisle, I forced back the thoughts in my head and the butterflies in my stomach, focusing on all things work-related.

I scanned the massive whiteboard. All the horses' names were listed with their owners, lesson schedules, turnout schedules, feeding instructions, and whatever other pertinent information we needed at a glance. Today I'd had several lessons, including Dante's, but tomorrow I had none. I always tried to keep them all on the same day so I could focus on horses instead of riders during the rest of the week.

Footsteps approached behind me. Without turning around, I said, "Hey, Noreen, would you mind using Dee instead of Juliet for Heather's lesson tomorrow?"

When she didn't answer, I turned around, and immediately tightened my jaw.

"Sorry to disappoint," Eli said with a sneer.

I resisted the urge to let out a sharp, frustrated breath. I was so not in the mood for this shit. "What's up?"

He shrugged. "I was just getting ready to go out to get something to eat. Wanted to see if you wanted to go."

Going out? On whose dime? I forced out a terse, "I'll pass, thanks."

"You sure?" His expression bordered on sad-puppy-dog territory.

"I'm sure." I turned around and busied myself making some changes to my riding schedule and some turnout assignments.

"Listen, I was thinking maybe we could spend some time talking."

It was a good thing my back was turned. That way he didn't see me roll my eyes. "I've got some things to do tonight." I cringed at my own inability to just tell him to fuck off.

"Maybe tomorrow night, then?"

Tomorrow night. *Fat chance, my friend.* "Can't. I'll be out. Probably late." My tone colder, I added, "Why don't you give Curt the Bartender a call?"

Eli let out a breath. "Okay, listen, is there any time we can just sit down and talk about a few things?"

I faced him. "Depends. Does 'a few things' include you telling me where you're working and when you're moving out?"

His cheeks colored and he turned away.

"Eli—"

"I'm working on finding a job," he snapped. Then his shoulders fell and his tone softened. "I just want to talk. About...things."

I barely suppressed a groan. "We've done enough talking." I turned around to continue making adjustments to the schedule on the board. "I'm not sure what else you think we need to discuss."

"Well, you were always complaining we didn't communicate enough."

"Fixing our communication problem now would be about as effective as patching the hole in the *Titanic* after it was already at the bottom of the ocean."

His shoes scuffed on the cement. Probably fidgeting or shifting his weight. "Jordan, I'm serious, this is—"

"Hey, Jordan," Noreen called from the other end of the aisle. "Dr. Paulson's on the line. Says he needs to talk to you."

"Be right there." I capped my marker and glanced at Eli. "Sorry, I have to take that call."

"I figured," he muttered through his teeth. At least he'd learned not to argue when that particular vet called. Dr. Paulson was the vet who oversaw the farm's breeding operations, and if he needed to talk to me, that was that.

I started up the aisle, and Eli stayed right with me.

"So I suppose you'll need me to take care of the dog tomorrow night," he growled.

"If you wouldn't mind."

"I assume you'll be out with *them*." Only Eli could assign such unmistakable identity to a single pronoun just by spitting it out with so much disgust.

"Not that it's any of your business." I looked straight ahead and walked a little faster. Finally, I made it to the office door, and Noreen stepped aside to let me in.

"Have fun tomorrow night," Eli snarled and kept going, throwing over his shoulder, "I'll make sure Sasha's in."

Noreen closed the door, and I stopped, muttering a string of profanity.

Then I turned to her. "Sorry. What line is Dr. Paulson on?"

"He isn't." She leaned against the door. "Just thought you might need an escape route."

"Thanks." I blew out a breath. "I owe you big-time."

"Oh, don't worry about it." She pushed herself off the door and went to Laura's vacant desk. She dropped herself into the weathered old swivel chair. "I do hope your new man means you're one step closer to being done with that fucker."

I rubbed my forehead. "Yeah, if that one would just get out of my house."

"Kick him out."

"You make that sound so simple."

"It is simple. 'Eli, out.'" She shrugged. "What's so complicated about that?"

"I know, I know." I sat on the edge of Laura's desk. "He'll be out of here soon, one way or the other."

She shot me a skeptical look. "Jordan Steele, why are you letting this guy walk all over you?" She nudged my leg playfully. "You are not a doormat and never have been."

I shook my head. "I don't know. I guess I feel sorry for him."

"Sorry for him?" She snorted. "Why? Because you cut him loose? Sounds to me like you did him a favor."

"Gee, thanks." Under my breath, I added, "Bitch."

Grinning, she showed her palms. "Hey, I'm just calling it like I see it."

"You're as bad as my sister." I rolled my eyes. "And yes, yes, I know, I need to kick his ass out."

"Damn right. Then you can start bringing that other sexy thing around more often."

I laughed quietly. "Oh, I'm still bringing him around."

"Good. You really don't think you'll move him in, though?"

I shook my head. "Pretty sure that's out of the question."

"He's not into commitment? Or you're done with commitment for a while?"

"Uh, well." I coughed and scratched the back of my neck, avoiding her eyes. "He's definitely into commitment..."

"He's not married, is he?"

"Well, no...not..."

"Jordan, there's no 'not really' about it." The chair squeaked. "Please tell me you're not seeing a married or otherwise attached man, or so help me I will break your arms."

"Yes, he's 'attached', but—wait! Let me finish!" I put my hands up, and she sat back down, giving me a glare that said her threat to break my arms was anything but empty. "His boyfriend knows about us, and he's cool with it."

"Seriously?"

I nodded.

"So, he's such a rampant sexy bastard, he needs more than one man to satisfy him?"

My cheeks burned. "Something like that. Actually, I'm..." I trailed off. Noreen and I were such close friends, we sometimes forgot she was my employee, but how much did I really want her to know?

"You're...what?" She raised an eyebrow.

I cleared my throat. "I'm seeing both of them."

Her jaw dropped. After a moment, she let out a sharp breath. "Damn you *straight* to hell, Jordan. I swear, I want to come back as a gay man in my next life."

"What?"

"I haven't been on a date in months, and here you are nailing two gorgeous men." She clicked her tongue. "This is so unfair. And if Eli wasn't such a twat, I'd even say you were lucky to have him trying to get back together with you. He *is* a looker, after all."

"You want him?"

"Pfft." She waved the thought away and scowled. "The part about him being a twat cancels out his good looks. He's all yours."

"Gee, thanks."

"Then kick his butt out."

I hoisted myself off the desk and onto my feet. "I will, I will. We've been through this."

"And I'll keep harping on you until you do it."

I glared at her playfully. "You're such a good friend."

She grinned. "I do what I can."

"Yeah, whatever. Now get out of here."

She jumped to her feet. "Not gonna argue with that." On her way to the door, she paused. "In all seriousness, I'm glad to see you with someone else now. Even if you are being a bastard and hogging all the pretty ones."

After Noreen left, I sank into the old swivel chair she'd occupied. I couldn't argue with her about Eli. Evidently he subscribed to the philosophy that men are like driveways: lay them right the first time, walk all over them forever.

And I'd let him. I could blame him all I wanted, but the fact was, I'd let him use me as a doormat, and I was still letting him do it.

I cursed under my breath. I'd give him until the end of the month. If he didn't come up with something, then I'd put my foot down, give him an ultimatum, and kick his ass out.

Just like I promised myself I'd do *last* month.

Chapter Seventeen

Angel sat on one end of the couch. I sat on the other. My feet were on the coffee table, my laptop across my legs. Angel balanced his computer on one knee while the cat took up the rest of his lap. The only sound was the music coming from his iPod—some cover of an eighties song I couldn't quite place—and the quiet clatter of fingers on keys.

This wasn't unusual for us. We were both perfectly content spending evenings working, just being in the same room together, or even in separate rooms if one of us needed to use our desktop computers. Tonight, though, something was...off. The cushion between us seemed bigger than I remembered, pushing the ends of the couch farther apart than they'd been all these years.

It wasn't a hostile distance, just distance. A few miles of space I didn't recall being there before.

A thought occurred to me. Racking my brain, I couldn't remember the last time it had just been the two of us. We were together at work. We spent most of our spare time with Jordan. At home, we were both constantly working, and aside from cooking together and being in bed at night, we simply hadn't spent much time together lately.

I closed my laptop. "Do you want to go out tonight?"

Angel's eyed flicked up. "Anything in mind?"

"Something other than staying home and working?" *And being a million miles apart on the same couch.*

"I need to get these done." He gestured at his screen. "Client wants them by Friday."

"And you've got three hours at the studio tomorrow with nothing booked." I put my laptop on the coffee table. "Seriously, when's the last time we actually went out?"

Angel chewed his lip. Then he sighed. "God, you're right. It's been awhile." He set his computer on the end table and looked down at Jade. "You're going to have to move, baby." He picked her up and gently parked her on that ever-expanding cushion between us. She glared at him, then put her head on her paws and went back to sleep.

I stood and reached for my wallet and cell. "Whose car do you want to take?"

"How much gas do you have?"

"Full tank."

"I'm down to a quarter. Mind taking yours?"

"Not at all." I took my key off the rack, and we went out to the garage.

We'd already had dinner but both decided we could go for something sweet, so we settled on an all-night diner not far from the studio. Sitting in a fake leather and faker chrome booth in the corner, listening to a 1950s Wurlitzer playing 1980s heavy metal, we each ordered a cup of coffee. I went for the apple pie, and Angel opted for the tiramisu.

After the waitress walked away with our order in hand, I looked at Angel. "Coffee *and* tiramisu? You're going to be like a hamster on crack by the time we leave."

He winked. "Guess I'll just have to find an outlet for all that energy, won't I?"

"I guess you will."

He extended his arm across the table so his hand was in the middle, palm up. I put my hand over his.

"I definitely needed this." He rubbed his eyes with his other hand. "I was about to go cross-eyed from staring at the screen."

"Yeah, tell me about it." I ran my fingertips back and forth along the inside of his wrist, tracing the lines of his tattoo. "I think we both needed a break. And a little time with just the two of us that didn't involve work."

He smiled and laid his free hand over mine. "You were right."

About that time, the waitress arrived with our coffee and food. She paused just long enough to throw a sneer in the direction of our hands before we separated to make room for the plates and saucers, but she quickly shifted her attention to giving us our desserts. I gritted my teeth. *I do hope you know that won't bode well for a decent-sized tip, lady.*

Once she and her attitude were gone, I put some cream in my coffee while Angel, preferring it black, sipped his own.

"Ugh." He grimaced and set it down. "I thought I ordered coffee, not swamp water."

I laughed. "You know the coffee here sucks." I gestured with my cup. "Why do you think I pollute it?"

"Good idea." He reached for the creamer. "Ah, well. At least their desserts are decent."

I chuckled and sipped my coffee. He was right. Even with a liberal dose of creamer, it had about as much flavor as watered-down mud.

"So, speaking of needing a break." He absently tapped his fork on the edge of his plate. "I was thinking, we haven't even thought about where to go for our next trip."

"Hmm, good point, we haven't." I took another sip of the poor excuse for coffee. "Well, we went to Asia the last three times, so where do you think we should go this time?"

"If I can twist your arm into going to Asia again, we still haven't been to that tiger temple in Thailand."

I raised an eyebrow. "The one that turns the tigers loose with the tourists?"

"They're not loose."

"Uh-huh." The pictures of tourists sitting beside full-grown tigers, petting and scratching them like they were oversized lap cats, had made me cringe. Angel, on the other hand, had drooled all over the website and travel brochures. I was willing to do a lot of things in the name of adventure, but posing with a cat with teeth and claws that big was about as appealing as taking a dunk in a shark cage. Then again, Angel hadn't had any problem doing that either. I, on the other hand, had stayed on deck and waited to get in the water somewhere where our guides weren't throwing meat and blood over the side to attract sharks.

"Oh, come on," he said. "It would be fun. They're just big cats."

"Sure. Just big cats." I rolled my eyes. "And sharks are just big goldfish."

"Hey," he said, pointing at me with his fork, "you could at least keep an open mind. After all, I went along with *your* idea of checking out Vladivostok and Lake Baikal."

"And Vladivostok and Lake Baikal were fucking cool."

"No, they were fucking *cold*."

"Well, yeah." I sipped my coffee and shrugged. "It's Siberia. What did you expect?"

He glared at me. "We could have at least gone in, say, August."

"And you think it would have been balmy and tropical in August?"

"It might have been a bit warmer than October."

"Fair enough. But we packed for cold weather, and we stayed warm enough." I picked up a forkful of apple pie. "I'm not quite sure if dressing in layers would do us much good if a tiger got pissy."

"Oh, come on." He waved his hand. "If they were prone to biting people, the monks wouldn't let anyone in to play with them."

"Oh, all right," I said. "We can put it on the list, but no promises."

"It's on the list, that's a start," he said with a toothy, triumphant grin. "Okay, so what other options are there?"

"There's always Borneo."

Angel put his hands up and sat back, shaking his head. "No, no, I'm not going back to Borneo. Not. A. Chance."

"Not even if I beg?" I batted my eyes. "There's some gorgeous rainforest there I want to shoot."

"If we want to shoot a rainforest, I vote Brazil," he said. "Every time I set foot on that island, something bad happens."

"Honestly, Angel," I said, laughing. "Food poisoning can happen anywhere. And you've been back to Pakistan twice since you were robbed there."

"True." Ticking points off on his fingers, he said, "But Borneo's the only place I've been shot at, robbed, gotten food poisoning, *and* had the mother of all insect bites."

"Was that really any worse than that thing that bit you in Kenya?"

Angel shuddered. "Why the hell does everything bite me, anyway?" He narrowed his eyes at me. "They never bite you."

Behind my coffee cup, I grinned. "I guess you just taste better."

"Touché." He fidgeted. "Still, I'm cursed when it comes to Borneo."

"To be fair, that was on the Indonesia side, and you *were* there covering a civil uprising, right?"

He shrugged. "Okay, yeah, I was."

"So, getting shot at or robbed is kind of par for the course, don't you think?"

"That doesn't explain the bites or whatever it was I ate on the other two trips." He took a bite of his tiramisu. "I'm telling you, if I set foot there again, I'll end up as a hostage with appendicitis and a side order of leprosy."

Laughing, I picked at my apple pie with my fork. "So, what if we go but stick to the Malaysia side? Or Brunei? I've been wanting to check those out for a while."

Angel pursed his lips. "We can put it on the list. But so help me, if I get sick again, or robbed, or some little bastard bitey thing chews on me again, you're not going to hear the end of it."

"Hey now," I said, holding up a hand, "I forgave *you* for dragging me on that tornado-chasing trip."

Angel chuckled. "God, can you imagine us in an old folks' home someday? We'll still be giving each other shit for this stuff." Adopting a gravelly voice, he said, "Yeah, well, you made me climb Mount Everest when I just wanted to have a relaxing vacation in Nepal, you bastard."

In a similar voice, I said, "And you convinced me to eat a live silkworm in Shanghai just because I talked you into trying fried rat, you son of a bitch."

He snickered. "You're never going to forgive me for that, are you?"

"Abso-fucking-lutely not." I put my hand on the table as he had earlier, and he laid his over mine. Leaning a little closer, I said, "But, you did make it up to me that night, so I can't complain too much."

"Damn right you can't."

The conversation continued wandering, following our years of globetrotting while we tried to figure out where to go next. We'd long since reduced our desserts to crumbs and choked down two or three cups of swamp-water coffee when we finally asked for the check. The sneering waitress gave us a dirty look when we went to leave, but I just slipped my arm around Angel's waist and ignored her.

In no time flat, we were home, pulling in the driveway as the garage door rose in front of us. To my surprise, I couldn't help feeling a little disappointed. Though we were home together, I'd enjoyed our evening out and wasn't quite ready for it to be over yet.

I put the car in park and turned off the engine. Our seatbelts clicked, then whirred back into place, but when Angel reached for his door handle, I touched his leg.

"Wait."

Hand still on the door, he stopped. "Hmm?"

"Don't get out yet." I put my arm around his shoulders and leaned across the console. He let himself be drawn to me, and by the time my lips touched his, his hand was on the side of my face. It was a gentle kiss, the kind that happened for its own sake, not necessarily as a prelude to something else, both of us seeking just to taste and feel each other. An eternity must have passed before we even separated our lips enough to let my tongue slip into his mouth. His fingers tightened in my hair, and he inhaled deeply through his nose as we pulled each other closer.

At some point, we drew back so we could see each other. I stroked his hair. He caressed my cheek.

He swept the tip of his tongue across his lower lip. "We should do this more often."

"Make out in the garage?"

Angel laughed. "Well, okay, I won't object to that." He ran the backs of his fingers down the side of my face. "I mean, get out of the house. Just the two of us."

"You're right, we should." Pulling him closer to me, I kissed him again.

"I guess," he said between gentle kisses, "we should get back *in* the house too."

"We will." I dipped my head to kiss his neck. "Eventually." He moaned, tilting his head to the side, and I took full advantage of the exposed flesh, exploring everything from his jaw to his collarbone as if I'd never tasted him before. I loved the way his skin felt against my lips, especially the subtle vibration of his voice when he moaned. Smooth and soft here, lightly stubbled there, every inch warm, vaguely salty and unmistakably Angel.

"Have I ever told you how much I love when you do that?" he whispered.

"Mm-hmm," I murmured. "Why else would I do it?"

He started to say something else but let his voice trail off as I found that sweet spot just beneath his jaw.

It was my turn to moan when his hand drifted up my thigh to gently squeeze my erection. Angel took advantage of my distraction and nudged me with his shoulder so I'd raise my head. He kissed me, parting my lips with his tongue as he pushed me back against the driver's seat. Once he had me where he wanted me, he dipped his head to kiss my neck while his fingers drew my zipper down.

"I was thinking we could just go in the house." He paused to nibble my earlobe, pressing his teeth in hard enough to make my breath catch. "But then I thought, to hell with it. You're here." He freed my cock from my jeans and boxers. "I'm here." Stroked slowly, gently. "And I want to suck your cock."

I didn't argue, and he didn't wait for me to argue. In an instant, his mouth was around my cock. I reached back and held on to the headrest with one hand, gasping for breath every time he moved his lips, his tongue, his hand. My other hand rested on the back of his neck, and the ends of his hair tickled my skin in time with his rhythmic up-down-up movements.

"Jesus, Angel," I whimpered. "Oh, fuck...you're gonna make me..." I licked my lips. "I want you to fuck me."

He responded with a moan so soft I felt it more than heard it, and I didn't have to ask what it meant. He was going to fuck me, all right. Good and hard, as only Angel could.

But he wasn't done with me yet.

He teased the head of my cock with the tip of his tongue while he stroked with one hand. He knew exactly how I liked it. How hard to stroke, when to flick his tongue and where to flutter it, and *precisely* when to deep-throat.

"Just like that," I breathed. "Fuck, Angel, just like...just..."

Stroke. Flick. Flutter. Deep-throat. Oh God.

Soundlessly, breathlessly, gripping his hair and the headrest for dear life, I came, wondering for a fleeting second if this car could even contain the shockwave after shockwave of this powerful orgasm. When Angel stopped a heartbeat before I couldn't take anymore, I took in a few deep, desperate gulps of air.

Then Angel sat up and kissed me, and his salty kiss made me light-headed.

"Let's get in the house," I whispered, panting against his lips. "I think I owe you for that."

"I think I like that plan." He kissed me one more time before I quickly fixed my clothes. After exchanging one last glance, Angel was out of the car in about two seconds, but on my way out, I dropped my car keys.

"Shit," I muttered. I felt around on the floorboard, finally found them, and shoved them into my coat pocket as I got out.

I'd barely gotten the door closed behind me before Angel grabbed me and forced me up against the car.

"Come on," I said, panting against his lips. "The house. Bedroom. Let's—"

"No, I can't wait." He pulled my head back and kissed my neck, letting his stubble graze the side of my throat. He sounded out of breath when he whispered, "Dante, I have to fuck you. Now. I fucking have to."

"But we're—"

"You still keep that bottle of lube in your glove box?" he murmured just below my ear.

I shivered. "Of course."

"Good." He raised his head and kissed me passionately. Hungrily. Pressing his cock against mine, he whispered, "Because we need it. *Now.*"

"I don't have any condoms out here with me."

Angel patted the side of his jacket, indicating the inside pocket.

"The bedroom's right down the hall." My trembling voice betrayed me as much as my shaking knees.

Angel kissed me again, pausing just long enough to whisper, "When was the last time we did something crazy like this?"

Far, far too long ago. I didn't argue. He let me go, and I opened the door and reached for the glove box. Just as I'd hoped, I still had that small bottle we'd left in here after the last time we couldn't wait. Whenever that was.

Once I was out of the car, lube in hand, Angel was against me. His kiss was breathless and hungry like it hadn't been in recent memory, and both of our hands trembled as we struggled with my belt. Then Angel tore the condom wrapper with his teeth while I unzipped his jeans. We were both shaking now, breathing hard, and I stroked his cock a few times, enough to make him close his eyes and lose his breath.

He grabbed my wrist. "No, no, stop," he whispered. He opened his eyes and moistened his lips. "I don't want to come until I'm inside you." I let go of his cock and he nodded toward the car. "Turn around."

As soon as my back was to him, he bent me over the car with enough force that, if I gave a damn about anything besides Angel fucking me *right now*, I might have been concerned about denting the hood. While he shoved my jeans and boxers over my hips, I flattened my hands against the car, searching for some kind of handhold even though I knew I'd find none. Beneath my palms, the hood was almost completely cool, only a hint of residual engine warmth lingering. How long had we been out here? Long enough to need to fuck over the car, evidently, and Angel didn't waste any time now.

After only as much careful slowness as he needed to make sure he didn't hurt me, he thrust all the way into me. I gasped, my eyes watering from the sheer intensity, and he didn't give me a chance to remember how to breathe properly.

The shocks creaked and protested beneath us. Every breath, every groan, every thump of my hips against the frame echoed through the garage. Something about it probably hurt, being forced up against metal, fucked *that* hard, *that* fast, but if it did, I didn't notice. Let it hurt. He just felt too damned good for me to care.

A deep groan emerged from the back of his throat, and he gripped my hips tighter and fucked me just a little harder. Now it did hurt, and oh, God, it felt good. Pressing my forearms against the hood's slick metal, I pushed back as much as I could, meeting his violent thrusts.

"Holy shit, keep doing that," he moaned. "Oh, yeah, just..." He trailed off into a wordless whimper, digging his fingers into my hips so hard his nails bit my skin. Then he shuddered, forced himself as deep as he could and slumped over me. Sharp, ragged breaths cooled the side of my neck.

After a moment, he put his hands beside mine on the car and kissed just behind my ear. "We really should do this more often."

"Mm-hmm."

His lips brushed my neck, making me shiver when he spoke. "I love you, Dante."

I put my hand over his on the hood and turned just enough to be able to meet his lips. Just before he kissed me, I whispered, "I love you too, Angel."

Chapter Eighteen

"Get on your knees."

Jordan responded to Dante's command as he always did: quickly, without hesitation. Already naked from Dante's earlier orders, he knelt beside the bed in our guest room, keeping his eyes down.

Dante combed his fingers through Jordan's hair. "Look at me, Jordan."

Jordan raised his eyes. His Adam's apple bobbed once; then he released a long breath. His shoulders dropped a little. His eyes already had that blissful, almost glazed appearance. I grinned to myself before going back to stirring the melted white wax in the slow cooker. Even knowing what we had in store for him tonight—perhaps *because* of what we had planned—he slipped easily into that submissive mindset. Not quite subspace in its truest, endorphin-charged sense, but he'd be there soon.

I scooped some molten wax out with the ladle, then let it drizzle back into the cooker. Oh yes, he'd be there *very* soon.

I'd been dying to play with Jordan and hot wax for a while now. He loved pain so far, and when I'd broached the subject of wax, his eyes had lit up like I'd just offered him a small fortune. Some subs liked pain, some tolerated it and some *lived* for it. Jordan fell so hard into the third category, I was sure I was dreaming.

And now we'd see how he liked wax.

"What are your safe words?" I asked.

"Red and yellow."

"Good," Dante said. "Stand up." When Jordan was on his feet, Dante held out a black blindfold. "Put this on."

Once Jordan's blindfold was on, I looked at Dante. He met my eyes, a silent "Ready?" in his.

I nodded.

Dante guided Jordan onto a sheet we'd spread across the floor. He had Jordan lie on his stomach with a pillow under his hips and his head resting on his folded arms. While they got situated and Dante made sure Jordan was comfortable, I dipped the ladle in the wax and brought it out again. I held it a few inches above my arm and poured some wax on the inside of my wrist. It stung like a bitch, enough to make me grind my teeth and bring a few curses to the tip of my tongue but not enough to cause injury. Perfect.

"Ready?" I asked.

"He's all yours," Dante said.

Scraping the dried wax off my wrist, I grinned. "Excellent."

I couldn't help shuddering on Jordan's behalf when Angel pulled the ladle out of the wax. Any kind of pain play we did with our subs, we'd long ago tried on ourselves beforehand so we knew exactly what we were inflicting on them. Hot wax wasn't my thing, but Angel and a lot of submissives loved it.

This was Jordan's first time with wax. He loved pain, so we'd just see how he handled this particular variety.

I sat beside Jordan and ran a gentle hand up the center of his spine. His back arched a little, muscles quivering. Searching for the pain he knew was coming, I guessed. I lifted my hand away, let it hover, then touched him again. He sucked in a breath each time my fingers made contact. I waited until he didn't respond at all, until my touch didn't warrant so much as a change in his breathing.

Then I nodded to Angel. He dipped the ladle in the wax again, and I pulled my hand away.

Jordan, no doubt expecting the soft, gentle touch of my hand, nearly came up off the floor when the first drop of wax landed between his shoulders. He pulled in a sharp hiss of breath, every muscle in his body tensing while Angel drew a serpentine line of scorching wax on Jordan's back and shoulders.

I trailed my fingertips down the back of Jordan's neck, letting the ticklishness contrast with the wax stinging his back. He squirmed, gasped, moaned.

213

"Doing okay?" I asked.

He nodded but didn't speak.

"Answer him, Jordan," Angel growled.

"Yes, I'm fine," Jordan said through clenched teeth.

"Good." I stroked his hair. Angel and I exchanged glances, and he continued drizzling molten wax across Jordan's beautiful shoulders. Jordan barely made a sound besides a sharp gasp here or a profanity-laced groan there, but the breaths in between were made of pure pleasure. Just the kind of pain slut Angel had been itching for. Angel bit his lip whenever Jordan moaned. He responded to every sound Jordan made as if Jordan were giving him a blowjob, not enduring the sting of scorching rivers and lakes of wax on his skin.

The pain was unreal. It was just this side of bearable, singeing nerve endings that were unaccustomed to this kind of intense, painful heat. The more he gave me, the dizzier the endorphins made me, and the pain became some twisted coupling of ecstasy and agony, surging through me like cold fire, hot ice, something equally and impossibly contradictory.

And, oh God, it was incredible.

Instinctively, I flinched and drew away each time fresh pain came, but when the shock wore off a heartbeat later, I'd arch toward it, seeking more, only to flinch away from the next sting. I couldn't tell if the tears in my eyes were from the pain or the pleasure. Probably both.

Sometimes it all bordered on too intense. Too many nerves reeling from the heat. Wax burning a particularly sensitive area of skin. Overloaded senses. And every time I tried to find the ability to speak, to ask Angel to ease off, if only for a moment, the single word never made it past the tip of my tongue, because every time it nearly did, he backed off. Every damned time, he backed off. Even Dante's fingers stilled on my neck.

When the pain receded to something more tolerable, returning to the realms of pleasure, Dante's fingers moved again. Just gentle strokes, somewhere between a caress and a massage. And, as if he too knew, Angel waited until the exact moment when my senses were ready before he poured more liquid fire on my skin.

He stopped again, this time of his own accord. With what I assumed was his thumbnail, Angel gently removed the wax that had accumulated across my back and shoulders. Cool air touched my now-uncovered skin, and I gritted my teeth, anticipating the next barrage of delicious pain.

Before it came, though, a hand rested on my shoulder. "Get up on your hands and knees," Angel said. He kept his hand on me and steadied me while I changed position. Then he let go.

There was movement around me. Shuffling, rustling, shifting. I didn't focus too much on who was doing what or what any of the shuffling around me meant. All I could concentrate on was the lingering burning and the anticipation of more sizzling pain.

Someone's hand touched the small of my back. I gritted my teeth, my eyes screwed shut behind the blindfold, knowing what was coming. My nerve endings tingled as they searched for that burn, that sting. Where would it fall next? Where would the fire start this time?

I had only a split second to react to the unexpected cool lube against me before more liquid fire landed between my shoulder blades. I groaned, overwhelmed as Angel poured wax on my skin and Dante pushed his cock into me.

Dante slid deeper. The wax burned hotter, sending a surge of endorphins through my body. Dante's cock hit my prostate *just* right. Never in my life had I experienced this kind of ecstasy, the lines blurring between pain and pleasure until I couldn't tell one from the other. A choked sound escaped my throat as pain chased pleasure through my veins, and I couldn't draw a deep breath. As soon as I had almost a lungful of air, searing pain or a violent thrust knocked it right back out.

Angel stopped to remove the wax from my skin again, but Dante kept moving, fucking me at ever-changing speeds, never letting me get used to one. Sweat ran down my neck and my aching, trembling arms. Every muscle in my shoulders quivered and shook and threatened to forget how to hold me up.

The blindfold was moot now. There was nothing to see, because nothing existed beyond my nerve endings. Nothing in the universe except heat, pain, pleasure, and oh God, I wanted to come so fucking bad.

Heat met my arm, and I instinctively flinched, but then realized it was a soft, painless warmth. Skin. A hand.

"You all right?" Angel's voice was gentle.

I nodded. "My arms are getting tired."

Voices murmured over me. Then Dante withdrew, and I couldn't help whimpering when he pulled all the way out. No, no, I didn't want this to be over yet. *Fuck me, Dante, please, don't stop, don't stop.* But he did stop, and I didn't argue.

Angel stroked my arm with featherlight fingertips. "Let's have you get on your back."

Dante and I guided Jordan into position, making sure the pillow was still beneath his hips. Our nearly delirious submissive's arms and legs trembled. His flushed skin was drenched with sweat, and his hand shook as he reached up to wipe some of that sweat from his forehead.

We both sat back, each keeping a hand on Jordan so he knew we were still here. The unspoken question hung between us: what should we do next? Jordan had just enough hair on his chest to make wax unpleasantly painful, so that was out. I put the slow cooker off to one side. Once it was a safe distance away so no one would bump into it, I looked at Dante again.

"I've got a few more things up my sleeve," I said. "You want to keep fucking him while I torture him?"

Jordan sucked in a breath.

Dante grinned. "I like that plan." He leaned over Jordan. "Don't think we need this anymore, though." He slid the blindfold off, and Jordan blinked a few times. His eyes were wet with tears, and for a second or two, he might not have been sure where he was.

Dante stroked Jordan's cheek. "You okay?"

Jordan licked his lips and blinked a few times again. "Yeah, I'm okay."

"Good," Dante said, "because we're not done with you yet."

Jordan's eyes widened. Dante reached for the bottle of lube, and I rose to go to the chest of drawers to see what other implements we could use to make Jordan squirm. While I searched through a drawer, the sounds behind me were enough to make me unbearably hard: caught breaths, murmuring voices, flesh colliding with flesh in that unmistakable rhythm of bodies moving together. Two men in ecstasy. It just didn't get any sexier than that.

With a couple of nipple clamps in hand, I turned around, and for a moment, I just stared at them.

Watching them together was breathtaking. There were no two ways about it. Just the way Dante's body moved was beyond sexy. His arms and shoulders rippled and trembled, his powerful legs tensed and relaxed, tensed and relaxed, and it all culminated in deep, hard thrusts that made my body react as if I were the one inside Jordan. I moistened my lips and kept watching, mesmerized.

Jordan gripped Dante's upper arms with shaking hands, and Dante's expression was one of pure bliss. His lips were apart, and the slightest furrow created creases between his eyebrows. A shiver ran up my spine; I knew what he was feeling, what it was like to be deep inside Jordan like that. A twinge of guilt tried to tug at my gut, but I pushed it back.

Jordan could give Dante something I couldn't.

I flinched at my own unspoken thought and forced it out of my mind. So what if that was something I couldn't give Dante? That was one of the many reasons we had submissives in the first place.

Dante didn't quite close his eyes, instead holding Jordan's gaze. Jordan looked right back at him. They stared right into each other's eyes.

I shifted, and it wasn't just to accommodate how hard I was. Something about them, about the way they focused on each other like no one else existed, sent a chill straight to my core.

I knew that look. God damn it, I knew it, because that was how Dante looked at me.

And when Dante turned his head just then, meeting my eyes over Jordan and across the room, that was *exactly* how he looked at me. My spine tingled from the base to my neck, nearly collapsing when Dante's lip curled into the faintest of grins and he winked.

He turned his attention back to Jordan, and I crossed the room to join them in their feverish universe. Sitting beside Jordan, I held up the nipple clamp so he could see it. His eyes widened and his breath caught. When I put it on his nipple, he gasped, but it was Dante who moaned. Dante let his head fall forward and kept thrusting, screwing his eyes shut and grimacing from exertion. And ecstasy, of that I had no doubt.

I teased Jordan with the other nipple clamp, running the cool prongs over his skin, around his nipple, inching closer, backing away, inching closer again. He squirmed and his back arched, and when I finally put it on his nipple, he flinched, then whimpered.

"Fuck," Jordan said through clenched teeth. "Oh...fuck..." Eyes shut tight, he held himself back. He didn't have to be told not to come. He knew better. But the more he was told not to come, the harder it was for him to hold back, and what was a Dom if not a relentless tormentor?

"I know you want to come, Jordan." I played with the nipple clamps, moving them just enough to make sure he couldn't ignore them. "But you won't, will you?"

He growled with frustration. He knew he had to answer me, and between Dante fucking him and me manipulating the clamps, speech was probably too much to ask for. Which is exactly why I asked for it.

"Jordan, don't—"

"I won't come." The words came out fast and slurred. "I won't. I...fuck..."

"Do you want him to make you come?" I asked.

Jordan's teeth chattered, and he writhed beneath Dante. "Yes," he moaned. "*Please.*"

"Not yet," I said.

"Oh God," Dante moaned. He thrust harder. His forearms rippled and his biceps quivered, his washboard abs extra pronounced from the exertion of fucking Jordan hard and fast.

Jordan whimpered again. His back lifted off the floor. His eyes were shut tight, his jaw clenched, and I kept at it with the clamps, knowing the combined stimulation would be *this close* to too much for him to take.

Dante closed his eyes and grimaced, the cords on his neck standing out as he forced himself as deep into Jordan as he could. "Fuck, I'm gonna... I'm..."

"Don't come yet, Jordan," I whispered. "Because he's just about to, and I still want to fuck you before you do."

Jordan held his breath.

With a groan and a shudder, Dante took one last thrust into Jordan and came.

Holy fuck. The blinding, earth-shattering orgasm almost rendered my bones completely useless, but somehow, I held myself up on my shaking arms. I breathed slowly, evenly, letting the aftershocks pass.

"You all right?" Angel's voice was tinged with amusement.

"Oh, yeah. I'm good." I blinked a few times until my eyes focused. Then I leaned down to kiss Jordan, making sure to let my chest brush over the nipple clamps, and he gasped.

"What's wrong, Jordan?" I singsonged.

"N-nothing." He moaned softly. I glanced at Angel, then dropped another light kiss on Jordan's lips before I sat up and pulled out.

"I'll leave you in his hands," I said.

Jordan's eyes darted toward Angel, eyebrows lifting slightly, and I thought he held his breath.

"Looks like you're all mine, then," Angel said.

I got up, steadying myself with a hand on the bed until the room stopped whirling around me. After a moment, it did, and I bowed out to get rid of the condom.

When I came back from the bathroom, Angel was inside Jordan, and I'd never seen anything so arousing in all my life. Jordan writhed beneath Angel, and Angel leaned down to manipulate the nipple clamps with his mouth. I shivered. He'd done that to me a million times before, and it was fucking amazing. The softness of his lips and tongue contrasted so sharply with his teeth and the clamp, it was unbelievable. I couldn't *not* come to save my life when he did that, and judging by the cursing and moaning, Jordan was having a hell of a time with it too.

I knelt beside them, resisting the urge to run a hand over Angel's sweaty skin. I wanted to touch him but didn't want to screw up his rhythm.

Angel lifted his head, and he moved faster now. His brow furrowed with intense concentration, lips pulling tight over his teeth, and every breath was sharper than the one before it. His shoulders quivered, and every thrust of his powerful hips made my mouth water.

"Oh fuck," Jordan breathed.

"Not yet," I said. "Don't come yet. We're not done with you."

He groaned, digging his teeth into his lower lip. I tugged and gently twisted the nipple clamps. He screwed his eyes shut, his hands clawing at the sheet beneath him as his back arched and sweat rolled from his forehead into his hair. When I leaned down to kiss him, a helpless moan vibrated against my lips. He was losing it, there was no doubt about that, and everything we did made it harder for him to hold back.

"Oh...my God..." Angel groaned. I sat up, giving him room to lean forward, and he took it, resting his weight on his hands and giving Jordan everything he had. After a few violent thrusts, Angel's spine straightened. He threw his head back, gasped and came so hard he fell forward onto his forearms.

Jordan took advantage of the pause, keeping his eyes closed and taking slow, deep breaths. I put my hand on Angel's shoulder to get his attention. When he looked at me, I nodded toward Jordan, then gestured for him to move back.

Still trembling and panting, Angel pulled out and sat back on his heels. As soon as he was out of the way, I went down on Jordan.

He gasped. "Oh, Jesus Christ..."

"You're not going to come, are you?" Angel asked.

Jordan made a frustrated sound, probably a string of curses stopping at his lips. Then, "No, I won't."

"You're right, you won't," Angel said, his voice a combination of serious and playful. Then he got up to go dispose of the condom, and while he did, I didn't let up on Jordan at all. On and on, I stroked and sucked his cock while he went out of his damned mind. Seconds passed, maybe minutes, I couldn't tell, and he fell apart with every breath, but he held back.

"Fuck, please let me come." Jordan's voice shook. "Please, Angel—" His voice was abruptly cut off. I glanced up to see Angel kissing him deeply, passionately, just the way we both knew drove Jordan insane. Angel pulled on one of the nipple clamps, and Jordan's hand hovered in midair, opening and closing like he wanted to grab on to Angel's hair but wasn't sure if he was allowed.

Angel broke the kiss, and Jordan sounded on the verge of tears when he whispered, "Please..."

"Yes."

My entire damned world exploded.

Angel's kiss and Dante's mouth sent me into and beyond the stratosphere, and I was distantly aware of the floor dropping out from under me. I'd been riding the edge for so long, holding back for so fucking long, the release was nothing short of shattering.

Even when my orgasm had subsided, the shaking didn't stop. My back sank down to the floor, my breath found its way to my lungs, and I couldn't move. I kept a hand over my eyes, blocking out the light, and just breathed. There was movement around me. Someone came closer, someone else's footsteps faded into the background.

Someone's hand touched my shoulder. One of the nipple clamps disappeared. Then the other.

"You okay?" Dante's voice was as soft as his touch.

I nodded.

After a long moment, footsteps emerged from somewhere else, and Angel knelt beside me. Gentle fingers trailed down the side of my face.

"Think you can get up?" Angel asked.

"I think so." With both of their help, I sat up. The world shifted and lurched. I rested my elbows on my knees and closed my eyes again, taking a few deep breaths while everything spun around me. One hand stayed on my shoulder, the other went up and down my back.

"You all right?" Angel whispered.

"Dizzy."

"Take your time." He kneaded the back of my neck. "Just tell us whenever you're ready to get up."

I nodded and rubbed my temples. God only knew how long I sat like that, but they didn't rush me. When I was finally steady enough to chance it, they helped me to my feet and into the bed. I rested my head on Angel's shoulder, and with the warmth of both their bodies beside mine, the trembling gradually subsided.

Dante sat up slowly. "I'm going to grab a shower. You okay staying with him for a few?"

Stroking Jordan's hair, I nodded. "Don't think he's going anywhere."

Dante smiled. "Is he even awake?"

Jordan murmured something but didn't open his eyes.

I laughed softly. "Let him sleep if he wants to."

Dante got up and went into the bathroom. While he showered and Jordan slept, my mind wandered.

Dante and I had always fed off each other as Doms. Years of intimacy and co-dominance had given us a psychic link of sorts. We each knew the other's move before it was made, responded to thoughts that hadn't even been spoken.

We'd never developed that kind of connection with a sub, though. A connection, yes, but not like this. Jordan spoke our language, unspoken though it was. Dante and I read his subtle signs with ease, the little tells that something had become too much or that he was ready for more. The catch of his breath, when his muscles tensed more than usual and didn't relax, the exhalation just before he shook that tension out of his shoulders. Some subs were harder to read than others. When was a flinch just a flinch? When did it mean I needed to back off or stop altogether?

Of course communication between the three of us was essential, but the more we could pick up off his body language and subtle tells, the more likely we were to nip a problem in the bud rather than push him beyond what he could handle. Communication and intimacy were crucial, but now I wondered, was there such a thing as too much of both?

I hadn't missed the way Dante had looked at Jordan while they moved together. And hadn't I looked at Jordan the very same way while I was inside him? Like it was just him, me and this breathless, unbelievably intimate sex?

I didn't know what this was. What the fuck was going on? I had no clue. There was a bond between the three of us I couldn't quite define. Maybe there also existed a similar bond just between Dante and Jordan. Another between Jordan and me.

The one thing I was sure of, lying there with Jordan resting on my shoulder, was that this was unlike any Dom/sub/Dom relationship we'd ever had.

That was weird.

Hot water ran over my neck and shoulders, but I barely felt it. I was too busy feeling something else, and it had me racking my brain for answers that wouldn't come.

We'd gotten Jordan deep into subspace. Whenever he gave signs it was too much, I caught them immediately, and obviously Angel had too, since he'd backed off. Jordan had never asked us to stop or back off because he'd never needed to; everything had stopped every time before it reached that point.

This was the connection we'd hoped for with every submissive. Now that we had it, it was unsettling because it went deeper than just the connection between a submissive and his Doms. This was something more. Something that had narrowed the entire universe to the three of us.

And that was to say nothing of the sex itself. I was used to submissives turning me on, but Jordan aroused me and made me come like only Angel had before. For that matter, sex with Jordan could narrow my world to us. Just Jordan, me and the space between his eyes and mine while I moved in him.

Angel had been there. He hadn't been cropped out of the image. I'd shifted my attention to Jordan, to Angel, to Jordan, to Angel. Neither pushed the other completely out of the picture; each simply rendered the other...out of focus.

And whoever was in focus at any given time was intensely so, looking back at me like he could see straight into me. It had always been that way with Angel, but a sub?

Shit, what was going on?

Deep down, I knew. This had gone much deeper than it had ever gone with any other submissive. Much deeper than it *should* have gone. My stomach twisted with guilt while my mind reeled with confusion. I wasn't supposed to feel this way. This was against the rules. It was wrong.

But it *was*.

Lying beside Angel, it was all I could do to stay awake. I drifted in and out, not fully awake, not quite asleep.

The pain cooled. The endorphins receded. In hindsight, it all seemed so much more intense, the memory of the sensations overwhelming me now as much as the sensations had in real time. The bits I could remember, anyway. More than a few moments had melted together into a pain-blurred fog, my mind recalling only what I'd felt, not always who was where or what had happened.

That kind of half awareness might have made me nervous in the hands of someone else, but I trusted the two of them enough to let go without fear. From the beginning, it had been easy to surrender to them. With time, that surrender came easier and easier. It simply made sense to submit to them. I slipped into subspace with ease, knowing when I came back out of it I'd be safe in the arms of Dante, Angel, or both.

Something drew me out of the vague, hazy state between asleep and awake. I blinked a few times and turned to Angel.

He gave an apologetic look. "My arm's falling asleep."

"Oh, sorry." We both shifted until we were facing each other. He rolled his shoulder gingerly, then laid his arm over me.

"You okay?" I asked.

He nodded. "I'm good. You?"

"Never better." I glanced around the room, getting reacquainted with where the hell I was. "Where's Dante?"

"In the shower." His eyes flicked up, looking past me. "Actually, speak of the devil..."

I looked over my shoulder as Dante came out of the bathroom, his damp blond spikes as carefully arranged as they ever were. He got into bed beside me and draped an arm over my waist. "Doing okay?" he asked, nuzzling my neck.

"Mm-hmm."

"Mind if I go grab a shower?" Angel asked.

"Go ahead," I said. "I'll probably get one myself when I can stand."

"No rush," Dante murmured. "You can stay here as long as you want."

Angel kissed me gently, then sat up. He paused, giving Dante and me an unreadable look before he stood and left the room.

Once he was gone, Dante pulled me a little closer. With his warm breath on my shoulder and our hands clasped together against my chest, I almost drifted off again. It was only my mind that kept me awake.

This wasn't what I'd read about. The connection between the three of us was nothing like anything I'd found in my late-night searches on the Internet. Maybe it just didn't translate well into the articles and websites I'd found.

Or maybe, just maybe, this was something completely different.

Chapter Nineteen

"Ryan?"

Phoebe's voice startled me, and I looked up from...whatever I'd been staring at.

"Sorry, what?"

She started to speak but hesitated. "You okay?"

"Yeah, yeah, I'm fine." I sat back in my chair and leaned on an armrest, trying to appear casual. "What's up?"

"I said I'm done burning the DVDs for those three weddings." She pointed over her shoulder into the other room, where she and Troy shared a computer. "While I'm set up for it, did you have any others ready to go?"

I looked at my screen, blinking a few times. Hell if I could remember if I had anything ready for her. I couldn't even remember what I'd been working on just then.

"Um..." I cleared my throat. "No, no, nothing yet."

For a second, she eyed me, probably debating whether or not to question my obvious distraction. Then she just shrugged and disappeared into the studio as she said, "Okay, cool."

I pulled my sleeve back to check my watch. It was twelve thirty. Dante and Troy were at a shoot and would be back any minute.

"Actually," I called after her, "maybe we should head out to our next client pretty soon."

She leaned in the open doorway from the set. "Already? We don't have to be there until two."

I got up and took my jacket off the back of my chair. "I know, but I haven't eaten yet." I put on my jacket. "We can stop on the way. I'll buy."

"Free food?" She grinned. "Let me get my camera bag."

As promised, I bought her lunch, and we spent a half an hour or so talking shop over burgers and steak fries. She had some intriguing ideas for some engagement-portrait sessions, so I agreed to let her take over for the last twenty minutes or so of a couple of scheduled shoots, assuming the clients agreed to it.

Like our lunch conversation, the afternoon's shoot was mercifully distracting. It was a commercial client needing promotional photos of his artwork, and the eccentric artist was a relentless perfectionist. His neurotic need to control every angle, every light, every shadow, rivaled my own. Today, I welcomed that. My patience with him even outlasted Phoebe's, and she could put up with *me* on most days without breaking a sweat. As far as I was concerned, as long as he had me adjusting lights and angles down to fractions of millimeters, I wasn't thinking about anything else, so I didn't mind.

As all distractions eventually do, though, the shoot ended, and before I knew it, Phoebe and I had packed up our gear to head back to the studio. On the way, I got on the freeway, even though I knew it would be bumper-to-bumper at this hour. After taking our exit, I didn't take my usual back roads, knowing full well the main road I was on was littered with far too many stoplights and other cars.

Phoebe noticed. She didn't say a word, but the pauses in conversation and her furrowed brow in the rearview told me she was well aware of our unusual route. I was the most impatient driver on the planet and loathed sitting in traffic, and she knew it.

She didn't ask, though.

Eventually, we pulled into the studio, and my heart sank when I saw Dante's car in the parking lot. I hoped to God they'd taken Troy's car to their next shoot, but when I walked into the studio, Dante was at his desk.

I set my camera bag in my chair and shrugged off my jacket. "I thought you had something scheduled this afternoon."

He glanced up from his screen. "Fucker cancelled at the last second."

Fucker indeed. "That sucks. Did he at least reschedule?"

"Yeah, for next week." He leaned back and reached up to stretch his arms. "Which means I'll be busy as hell, since I'm booked solid all week."

"Let me know if you need me to pick up any appointments," I said. "I'm pretty light next week."

"I may be taking you up on that."

"You know where to find me."

He grinned. "Indeed I do."

I threw back a halfhearted smile, then went down the hall to our makeshift break room—a large closet into which we'd crammed a table, microwave and minifridge—and grabbed a soda. My hips and back ached when I leaned down to get the Pepsi out of the refrigerator. Wasn't like I needed any physical reminders of last night, since that had been at the forefront of my mind all damned day.

I popped open the can and leaned against the wall while I took a drink. *I should get back to work. Lots to do. I think.*

I sighed. Might as well hide in here for a little bit. I couldn't focus on anything anyway, not while my mind was stuck on last night.

Last night. Last night. Last night.

My heart had beaten that cadence into my ears all damned day like a song stuck in my head. I'd tried to ignore it, tried to focus on anything and everything else, but finally I just closed my eyes and let the song play.

Last night had left me unsettled. Truthfully, I'd had that feeling for a while now, that growing knot of uncertainty I couldn't quite explain. Like alcohol amplified whatever mood I was in when I drank, everything that had happened in that room tightened that knot. At least the liquor would have worn off by now and I'd have gone back to my regularly scheduled emotions. Now, in the light of day, out of my bed and in my clothes, that knot pulled tighter, sank deeper, and burned hotter.

Everything about last night had been amazing. Double-teaming with sex and wax. Keeping Jordan's orgasms out of his reach. Fucking each other one last time for good measure after Jordan left. Every moment was hot, and every moment was seared into my consciousness.

It was one thing to watch Dante topping another sub. There were few things in the world hotter than watching him bend someone over and fuck him good, hard and fast. But something about watching the two of them last night had me off-balance. I wanted to be jealous when I replayed the parts when Dante had fucked Jordan. Jealousy would have been easier to stomach than helplessness. Maybe that wasn't even the right word, but I couldn't think of anything else to call it. That feeling of sitting back and watching something happen that I couldn't stop.

It wasn't just the fact that Jordan let Dante fuck him or that Jordan was a submissive. He offered the power and the surrender Dante and I both craved, and I wouldn't have denied my boyfriend that submission any more than he'd have kept it from me.

What bothered me was realizing that Jordan gave Dante something more. Not just what I couldn't or wouldn't offer, but something for which Dante had always come to me and me alone. The fact was, Jordan was everything I couldn't be for Dante, and slowly but surely, if I read the two of them right, he was becoming what I had always been.

In my mind's eye, I saw that look again. That long look that meant their world had narrowed to then, there and them.

I knew that look. Dante was in love with Jordan.

I took a long drink of Pepsi, telling myself it was just the carbonation that made my eyes sting and water.

Fuck, I wanted to be furious. I wanted to be jealous. Confront him. Accuse him. Throw down the cheating card and lay into him for breaking our most sacred rule.

But I couldn't.

I set down my soda. Sighing, I closed my eyes and rubbed my temples. I'd do as well throwing any accusation I threw at Dante at the mirror instead. Ignore it, deny it, pretend it hadn't happened, but it had.

I loved Jordan too.

Not in a fleeting, butterflies-in-the-stomach, impulsive infatuation kind of way. I was in love with Jordan like I'd only ever been with one other man, never mind falling this hard.

Still rubbing my temples, I sighed. Now what?

We'd considered a permanent sub if one ever came along, but this wasn't what either of us ever had in mind. I never expected to fall in love with anyone but Dante. I'd certainly never expected both of us to fall for the same man.

I couldn't change how anyone felt, but eventually something would have to give, and I'd never imagined being this afraid of losing two men I loved this much.

I'd think of something. No idea what but something. For now, I had work to do. At least, I was pretty sure I did. The only time I'd been able to focus today had been with a client breathing down my neck, and I didn't have that luxury right now.

I'd figure it out, I supposed. Didn't have a hell of a lot of choice, did I? I drained my drink and headed back out to the lobby.

On my way, Dante and I passed each other, but he stopped me with an arm around my waist. "You okay?" he asked. "You've been kind of spacey today."

"Yeah, I'm fine." I forced a smile.

"You sure?" He narrowed his eyes like he could see right through me, and he probably could. "Even Phoebe said you've been a bit off all day."

I gestured dismissively. "Just tired. After last night."

"I can certainly understand that."

Dante, you don't have a clue. Trust me.

"A night like that's bound to take a lot out of us." His smile crinkled the corners of his eyes, and for the first time, I noticed the dark circles under them. His fatigue matched my own, reminding me yesterday really had happened. He was there. I was there. *Fuck.*

"Guess we should get back to work," I said softly.

"We should." He kissed me lightly, and the guilt and self-loathing burned a little hotter. *I'll think of something,* I told myself again.

Quitting time arrived and not a moment too soon. I still had a few things to square away at the studio and I took my sweet time, so by the time I left, Dante had already taken off. I was glad we'd taken separate cars this morning, since we both had places to be outside the studio throughout the day. I could only avoid him for so long, especially once we got home, but maybe twenty minutes or so in the car would give me a chance to gather my scattered thoughts.

It didn't help. Pulling into the garage beside Dante's car, I was no closer to working out how the hell this had all happened or what the hell to do about it.

While we made dinner, Dante tried to get our usual flirting and bantering going, but I just wasn't feeling it. He backed off and didn't ask. I knew he wouldn't. He'd long ago learned that if

229

I kept him at arm's length to just let me be; I'd come around and talk to him when I'd sorted it in my own head.

Tonight, just once, I wished he'd break that unspoken rule and ask what was on my mind, because I just didn't have the guts to bring it up. I wished he would, but he didn't.

After dinner, I worked at my desktop for a while instead of my laptop. There were a few things I could do only on this computer, so it gave me a convenient excuse to work somewhere other than the living room. Still, even with my music playing in the background, I couldn't escape the gentle click of fingers on keys in the next room, a constant reminder he was there beside my empty place on the couch.

I rested my elbow on the desk and my forehead in my hand, absently petting Jade with my other hand. None of this was going to get resolved one way or another with the two of us in separate rooms. I didn't know how much we'd solve in the same room, but this would fix exactly nothing.

Fuck it. I couldn't take it anymore. I turned off my computer and stood. Jade purred a little louder, kneading the edge of her bed. I scratched her ear, then went into the living room.

Ignoring the knot in my stomach, I leaned over the back of the couch and slid my hands over Dante's shoulders, lacing my fingers together across his chest so they wouldn't shake.

He smiled at me. "Hey you."

"Hey." I kissed him lightly.

"You sure you're okay?" he asked. "Still just tired from last night?"

"Yeah, just a little tired." I was sure he could feel my heart pounding, but hoped he bought the casualness of my one-shouldered shrug. "And a bit preoccupied, I guess."

He reached back to lay an affectionate hand on my arm. "Being a workaholic again?"

"Something like that." *Nothing like that.* I kissed him again to derail the conversation. "You staying up for a while?"

He glanced at his computer, then leaned his head back and met my eyes again. "Are you going to force me to stop working?"

I laughed. "Well, I was going to suggest going to bed and—"

He shut his laptop. I released him so he could stand, and as soon as there was no longer a couch between us, we were in each other's arms. Kissing and stumbling over each other's feet, we inched toward the bedroom.

"You're not too tired after last night?" he murmured between kisses.

I need this because of last night. "Oh, I think I can find some energy with the proper motivation."

"Hmm. Proper motivation?"

"Mm-hmm."

He groaned against my lips when I stroked his cock through his jeans.

"I was thinking," I said, my heart thundering so hard he *had* to have felt it, "tonight, I..." The words got stuck in my throat.

"Hmm?" He kissed my neck and slid his hands under my shirt. "Tonight...?"

"Would you be game for..." I swallowed and had to force my throat to cooperate. "Switching?"

Dante raised his head. "Are you serious?"

For you, anything. I nodded.

"You know I won't turn that down." He drew me closer and kissed me lightly. "Are you sure, though?"

No. I forced a smile. *No. No. No.* "Of course."

He growled something I didn't understand and kissed me again. He held me tighter, kissed me harder, and I hoped I hadn't just set us both up for disappointment. He wanted this. Had wanted it for a long time.

Please, please, let me be able to give it to him.

We quickly got out of our clothes and into bed. Dante reached for the nightstand, and never in my life had the sight of a lube bottle made me so nervous. He set a condom beside it, and I gulped.

"Since it's been so long, I'll take it slow," he whispered. "Just fingers first."

We adjusted our position so I was on my side with my back to him, and at least that meant he couldn't see me closing my eyes this tight. Part of me wanted to ask him to just get it over with, but maybe if we did take it slow, I'd be okay with it. I hoped with each slow, gentle stroke, the intensity would diminish. It wasn't painful, but it wasn't pleasant either. I chewed the inside of my cheek, breathing slowly and deeply.

I could do this. For Dante, for Dante, for Dante.

"Relax," he whispered. "Am I hurting you?"

"No, not at all." At least that much was true. It didn't hurt.

His finger slid deeper. I winced, hoping he wouldn't sense it, knowing he would.

He kissed my shoulder. "You doing okay?"

Closing my eyes, I nodded.

"You sure?"

"Yeah. Just go slow."

"I will. I am." He was. He did. Then he added a second finger, which pushed the sensation that much closer to unbearable. Fuck, how would I be able to handle his cock? Even when he found that sensitive spot and pressed his fingertips against it, the white-hot pleasure wasn't enough to tame the discomfort. I breathed, I relaxed, but I just couldn't force myself to enjoy it. I wanted to. I needed to.

I couldn't.

I exhaled. "Wait."

He stopped. "What's wrong?"

"I..."

"Angel?"

I closed my eyes. "I can't do this."

"You sure?" There was nothing but concern in his tone.

I hesitated. I wanted so badly to do this for him, but...I couldn't. I just couldn't. Finally, I nodded. "Yeah. I'm sorry, Dante, I—"

"It's okay." He kissed the back of my neck and slowly, gently, withdrew his fingers. "We've been through this. It's not for everyone."

But it's definitely for Jordan. I forced the thought to the back of my mind and turned on my other side so we faced each other.

Dante wrapped his arms around me. "Plenty of other things we can do, just like always." He kissed me, and while he did, my mind replayed what he'd said, scrutinizing every word in search of the faintest note of disappointment. I found none, but that didn't let me release my breath.

Grinning, he rested his weight on one arm and held up the condom. "We should still find something to do with this, don't you think?"

Returning the grin even though I didn't feel it, I took the condom. "Oh, I think we can manage that." I set the condom on the nightstand and gently pushed Dante onto his back. "Not yet, though." I kissed him before he could say a word, and he gasped and held me closer when I reached between us to stroke his cock.

"Oh, my God, Angel..." A long moan finished the thought.

I let go of his cock and started to move down, but he caught my arm. "No, stay here," he said. "I liked what you were doing." With a hand on my wrist, he guided my hand back to his cock and whimpered when I wrapped my fingers around him again.

"Please," he whispered, coaxing my hand into motion. I squeezed gently, biting my lip when he closed his eyes and shivered.

"Like that?" I asked.

He nodded. He released my wrist and brought his hand up, sliding it into my hair to draw me down into another long kiss. I stroked him faster, harder, squeezing and releasing just the way I knew he liked it. He moaned against my lips, and his fingers dug into my shoulders. His entire body tensed, then again, and his lips left mine in the same instant semen hit my abs and forearm. He released a cry that was almost a sob, and I kept stroking until he begged me to stop.

"Fuck me," he breathed. "Please, Angel, I want you to fuck me."

"With pleasure."

While he grabbed some tissues off his nightstand, I reached for the condom and lube on mine. He started to get up, but I put a hand on his shoulder.

"No, stay just like that."

"You sure?"

I nodded. "Yeah." *I want to see your face.*

He sank back to the bed. "I'm not going to argue with that."

"Didn't think you would." I winked and quickly rolled on the condom. Once it was in place and I'd put on enough lube, I moved over him again.

I guided my cock to him and pushed in gently. All the while, I watched his face. His lips were apart, his brow furrowing over tightly shut eyes. When I pulled out a little, then

233

slid deeper, he bit his lip and moaned. God damn it, he was gorgeous, and I realized we didn't make love this way *nearly* often enough.

Once I was all the way inside him, I found a steady, even pace; slow, but still enough to arch his back and quicken his breathing. I couldn't take my eyes off him, couldn't stop looking at him even when my vision tried to blur. Twelve years, and I never tired of watching his face while I was inside him. No matter how I felt about Jordan, no matter how Dante felt about Jordan, I couldn't imagine losing *this*.

"Look at me, Dante," I whispered, and he opened his intense blue eyes. I held his gaze until he reached up and touched my face. Drawing me down to him, he lifted his head off the pillow and kissed me. The tip of his tongue slid past my lips. I thrust deeper. His breath mingled with mine. My skin prickled with goose bumps. His nails bit into the back of my neck.

And I lost it.

He let go of my neck, and I threw my head back, a violent shudder driving me into him once, twice, a third time, before I collapsed over him. I buried my face against his neck, inhaling his scent as I caught my breath.

"Fuck, I don't know what's gotten into you tonight, but..." He blew out a breath and when I pushed myself up on my arms, he wiped sweat from his brow.

Grinning in spite of the worries on my mind that weren't yet settled, I said, "Just horny."

"Whatever it is, I like it." His humor faded, and—*yes, yes, he did*—he looked at me just like that. Eyes locked on mine, looking up at me, looking *into* me, and nothing else existed. Still breathless, words still slurred, he whispered, "I love you."

"I love you too."

And I hoped to God that was enough.

Chapter Twenty

Since Angel and Dante were getting ready for a wedding tomorrow and would be busy this evening, I made plans to grab a cup of coffee with my sister. Once my lessons for the day were done and every horse I'd needed to work had been worked, I drove down to the café we'd been going to for years. By the time I got there, she'd already snagged a table, so I ordered my coffee and joined her.

"So, how's married life?" I asked.

She shrugged. "The same as unmarried life, except I keep forgetting how to sign my own name."

I laughed. "You could have kept your maiden name, you know."

"Oh, Christ." She groaned. "Paul's parents would have had heart failure."

"All the more reason to do it."

"I know, that's what I thought." She shrugged again. "But, it really wasn't a big deal to me, and it was one less area for them to pester us."

"It's your name," I said. "Quite frankly, it's none of their damned business."

"I know, I know." She sighed. "Anyway, it's done. So are you still trying to kick Eli out?"

"Yeah." I avoided her eyes and lifted my coffee cup, stopping just short of my lips. "He's still 'working on getting' a job." I took a sip. "Don't know how much effort he's putting in, though."

"Throw him out on his ass. That'll motivate him."

I scowled. "I can't do that to him."

"Why the hell not?"

"He's broke, Jen," I said. "Where would he go?"

"How is that your problem?"

"Okay, I know, it's not my problem, but I'd still feel like a dick if I threw him out on the street."

"You *are* a dick."

"Shut up," I said, chuckling into my coffee.

She grinned. "Anyway, seriously, he's had plenty of time to find someone gullible enough to hire his sorry butt." She sat back, idly curling and uncurling the corner of her napkin. "I've offered a million times to inflict him on some of my clients, and as far as a place to live, he's got other friends, and don't his folks live around here?"

"They do, but they've already told him he's not living with them again."

Jennifer gave me a pointed look. "And that doesn't give you a monstrous clue that he's taken advantage of too many people already?"

"Yeah, it does." I sighed. "I just, I don't know. The thought of him being homeless…"

"He won't be homeless." She made a dismissive gesture. "He'll couch-surf for a while until he finds someone dumb enough to put him up in the long term."

"Gee, thanks."

"You know what I meant." She sipped her coffee and set the cup down with a delicate clink. "I'm ready to go in there and kick him out myself, to be honest with you."

"Be my guest," I said.

"I'm serious." She leaned forward, brow creased with concern. "He has no business sticking around after the way he's treated you."

"Yeah, I know."

She kicked me under the table. When I winced and cursed, she said, "You keep saying that, but you keep letting his dumb ass live in your house."

I rubbed my shin and glared at her.

Jenny sighed. "Listen, he's the only person on God's green earth who's ever been able to walk all over you, and I don't understand why you just lie back and let him."

"I did dump his ass."

"Which means, what?" She took another sip and set the cup down a little harder this time. "He's sleeping in another bedroom, but otherwise things are exactly the same?"

"Actually, you'd be pleased to know that I've been turning him down every time he asks me to go grab dinner or hang out with him or—"

"He still asks?" She made a disgusted noise and rolled her eyes. "God, I don't know which of you is thicker in the skull. Him for not getting a clue, or you for not booting him out."

"A little from column A, a little from column B," I muttered into my coffee cup.

"My point exactly." Her tone softened. "I just don't like seeing him walk all over you. That is so not you."

I nodded. "Believe me, I know."

"So throw. Him. *Out.*" She sighed. "Besides, you need to move on. You know, find some other guy to make you miserable."

"Funny you should mention that, actually."

One pencil-thin eyebrow shot up. "Oh?"

"Well, not that someone's making me miserable, but..."

She folded her arms behind her coffee cup on the table. "Do tell."

"I've kind of been seeing someone."

"Kind of?"

My face burned and I bit my lip. "Remember those photographers you had at your wedding?"

"Dante and Ryan? Of course." Her jaw dropped. "Wait, wait, wait. You scored one of those two? Oh, you lucky fucker."

I chuckled and picked up my drink.

"Funny, though," she said. "I could have sworn those two were together."

"They are."

She blinked. "Jordan Steele, you're not having an affair with one of them, are you?"

More heat rushed into my cheeks. "*One* of them? No."

Jenny shook her head slowly, staring at me in utter disbelief. "You're with...both of them?"

"Sort of." I hesitated, not quite sure how much I wanted to divulge to my little sister. "It's, um, complicated."

"Well, good, then you can put that as your relationship status on Facebook. Now define complicated."

I took a deep breath. "I don't think you need any TMI about my love life, so let's just leave it at complicated."

She wrinkled her nose. "Yeah, good call. God, you fucking bastard. Scoring both of those gorgeous men?" She made a disgusted noise, then sipped her coffee again. "So how long are you going to do the 'complicated, too gross to tell your sister' thing with them before you start thinking about chasing down a relationship?"

That gave me pause. It was just a casual relationship, of course. A sexual one, not an emotional one. Sooner or later, as these things always did, it would end. They'd ride off into the sunset. I'd go find someone for something less complicated and more permanent. In a way, I suppose I'd known that from the start, but now that I actually gave it some thought—

"Jordan?"

I shook my head. "I don't know, honestly."

She furrowed her brow. "What's wrong?"

"Hmm?"

"You were just joking and being all coy about them, and now you're all down in the dumps." She inclined her head. "Something I said?"

Exhaling, I sat back in my chair. "I hadn't really thought that far ahead, I guess," I said softly.

"Well, it's not like you'll be doing these guys forever, right?" She grinned. "Though I wouldn't blame you if you did."

I laughed, but it was forced. On some level, I guess I knew in the beginning this arrangement was temporary. Now, the thought of life without Angel and Dante didn't feel right.

Probably just because they're easier to deal with than Eli, I thought bitterly.

"Jordan." My sister's voice was sharp enough to startle me.

"Sorry, what?"

She stared at me. "You're really hung up on these guys, aren't you?"

Sighing, I shrugged. "I don't know, maybe. I think I'm just enjoying being with someone who isn't Eli."

"More like two someones who aren't Eli."

"Exactly."

"I don't know how you do it, honestly."

"What do you mean?"

She shrugged. "Being the third."

"Well..." I fought a losing battle against a laugh. "You see there's this position called—"

"Jordan, shut *up*." She closed her eyes and shuddered. "Don't. Want. To. Know."

"You started it."

With another shudder, she glared at me. "What I meant was, being their extra. Like, their toy. I don't know if I could handle being the disposable one."

Something in my gut dropped. "What do you mean?"

"How long have they been together?"

"Like twelve years, I think. Thereabouts."

"So, if things went to shit between the three of you, who do you think would be the first to go?"

I chewed the inside of my cheek and stared into my coffee cup. Of course I'd known that, but hearing it stated so bluntly and matter-of-factly engraved it into my consciousness. It was true. She was right. She was absolutely right.

I tapped my fingers on the side of the cup. "It's not exactly intended to be anything long term, though. It's not a...relationship. In the traditional sense."

She was quiet for a moment, furrowing her brow and looking down as if trying to decide whether or not to take another sip of coffee. Then she met my eyes again. "Listen, I know this is none of my business, and the baby sister isn't supposed to be giving the big brother advice, but..." She paused. "I'm worried you're setting yourself up to get hurt."

"I don't think that's going to happen."

"Sure about that?"

"We all went into this knowing it's just something—"

"No details," she said quickly.

I chuckled. "I wasn't going to give you details. I was just going to say we went into this knowing it was something casual. No commitments, nothing emotional."

My sister threw me a skeptical glance. "Uh-huh."

"What?"

"Answer me something." She looked me straight in the eye. "If they called you tonight and called the whole thing off, how would you feel?"

I chewed my lip.

"Maybe that's the wrong question." She narrowed her eyes a little and cocked her head. "Let me ask you this."

I raised my eyebrows.

She pursed her lips, folding her hands under her chin and resting her elbows on the table. "Is it really just 'too gross to talk to your sister about' stuff? Or is there a little more to it?"

I shifted in my chair. "What do you mean?"

"I mean, do you..." She trailed off, searching my eyes. Then she lowered her voice to a whisper. "Are you in love with them?"

I'd taken a pair of hooves to the chest a few years ago, and that didn't knock as much air out of me as Jenny's softly spoken question. Sitting back, I stared up at the ceiling for a moment, trying to make some sense of the fragmented thoughts she'd stirred up in my head.

This was the point when I *should* have been asking myself if I did love them. Was this more than sex? Was I in love with them? Everything that had happened since that first night in their studio flickered through my mind like black-and-white photographs: alone with Dante. Alone with Angel. All three of us. Their house, my house, their studio, anywhere. Pushing boundaries, testing limits, hot wax, hot sex.

And the intimacy. Good God, the intimacy.

I didn't ask myself if I was in love with them, though.

Of course I was.

I rubbed the bridge of my nose and sighed.

Jenny reached across the table and put her hand over my wrist. "Jordan?"

"I don't know what I feel for them." *Oh, I do. I know exactly what I feel for them.* Swallowing hard, I shook my head and lowered my hand to squeeze hers gently. "It's supposed to be just..." I forced a quiet laugh. "Just 'too gross to talk to my sister about' stuff."

She laughed too, but it was halfhearted, and the sympathy in her eyes told me I was wearing more of my feelings on my sleeve than I'd intended.

"I'm not going to pry, and you don't have to justify it to me," she said softly. "But promise me you'll be careful with this. I don't want to see you get hurt again."

I nodded. "I will. I am being careful with them, I promise."

"Good." She gestured with her coffee cup, then stood. "I'm going to get a refill. You want anything?"

"No, I'm okay, thanks."

"Wasn't going to get you any anyway."

I smacked her playfully as she walked by. Once she was gone, I closed my eyes and rubbed my forehead.

I hadn't lied to her. I'd be careful with them, and I'd been careful all along. At least, I thought I had been. Shit, how the hell did this happen? *When* did it happen? Thinking back, I couldn't remember when I started feeling this way. I couldn't remember *not* feeling this way. Not that it mattered, because I couldn't have them like that. They had each other, and I'd have sooner cut off my own arm than try to split them up.

Fuck. I hadn't gone into this to find love, but damn if love hadn't, with the worst possible timing and in the worst possible place, found me.

Chapter Twenty-One

"What the hell is Ryan's problem today?" Troy asked in a hushed voice while we changed out battery packs and memory cards.

I shoved a memory card into my camera. "Go make sure the groom's side of the family is ready to roll. I'll be out in a second."

He hesitated, probably wondering why I'd ignored his question, but rather than pressing the issue, he did as he was told. He left the room, making an obvious effort not to limp in spite of his sore feet. Still wearing uncomfortable shoes, still suffering through but wisely not choosing today to bitch to me about it. Smart kid.

I double-checked my battery pack, then pulled my tux coat over it. With a quick check in the mirror to make sure I was presentable, I left the room to join Troy and the groom's family in the gardens behind the church. The bride and groom had to be kept separated before the ceremony, so at this point, we had to take care of all of the portraits and group photos with each half of the couple. We'd already gotten family, friends, in-laws and wedding party with the bride; now she was being sequestered somewhere else in the church while we set up to do the same shots with the groom.

I caught up with Troy out in the garden. Angel already had the family members lined up and posed, and he gave directions while he and Phoebe snapped away. At least he gave the appearance of being in a pleasant mood. The last thing we needed was for a guest or client to catch on.

"He had everyone started when I came out," Troy said.

"We're on candid detail, then." I gestured around to the left side of where the family posed. "You hang around over there. I'll stay to this side." We split up, and I let Angel handle the formal portraits while I searched for those "little moments": a flower girl peering at her tiny bouquet, her brow furrowed with intense concentration. A smile passing between the matron of honor and her husband. The mothers of the bride and groom sharing a laugh.

Before long, Angel wrapped up the formal portraits. He and Phoebe picked up their gear and went in to get ready for the ceremony. Troy and I hung back for a few minutes, catching some more shots of guests milling around and socializing before we too went inside.

This particular church had a choir loft overlooking the sanctuary. Since Phoebe and Angel were situated behind the pews down below, I went up to the loft with Troy.

While Troy and I took a few quick readings with the light meters, Angel looked up at us. Even from this far away, the irritation in his expression was visible in the tightness of his lips and narrowness of his eyes. Then he turned away, shifting his attention back to whatever he and Phoebe discussed.

I gritted my teeth. Angel had his moody days like anyone else, but usually a few cups of coffee and a distraction—such as, say, a wedding to shoot—was enough to melt the ice. Today it just got worse as the day went on. I had no idea when it had started. I'd left for the studio before he was even out of bed, as I often did on wedding days, and from the moment he'd arrived, he'd given off "leave me the fuck alone" vibes. So I'd left him the fuck alone, but even that didn't seem to help.

I shook my head. Whatever. We had a job to do. The personal shit could be sorted later.

As the ceremony wound down, I sent Troy downstairs to wait for the bride and groom outside the sanctuary doors. I stayed up in the loft, shooting until the couple was about halfway up the aisle, then made a quick, discreet exit to join him. I made it with about three seconds to spare, and had my camera up and ready just when the doors flew open.

On the way out to the gardens for more group photos, Angel fell into step beside me.

"You might have mentioned you were going up to the loft," he growled, his voice low enough to keep the icy undercurrent between us.

"One of us always goes up," I snapped in an equally quiet voice. "Since you and Phoebe were already set up down below, it only made sense for me to go up."

"I figured you'd come down and touch base before you made the decision." He glared at me. "I would have sent her up with you, since she needs some experience shooting from that kind of vantage point."

"Then you should have said something to me or sent her up to trade with Troy." Before he could say anything else, I said, "Can we argue about this later? Maybe when we don't have to pretend to be professionals?"

"Fine," he snarled with the kind of venom that said I *would* hear about this later.

Christ, just what I needed. The stress of a wedding with a looming argument hanging over my head.

"*What the hell is Ryan's problem today?*" Troy asked in my head.

"Your guess is as good as mine," I muttered to myself.

We made it through the wedding without biting each other's heads off. If anyone besides our assistants had caught on to the tension between us, they hadn't let on. Pissed off or not, we were both damned good at keeping a professional façade going when there were clients around, and for the most part, we kept everything on the down-low. We maintained a pleasant, professional front around our clients and their guests. When we spoke to each other, it was behind closed doors, terse and strictly business. No pleasantries, no flirting, and no fucking clue what his problem was. Maybe he was just in a pissy mood, but the frosty shell around him seemed to pertain only to me. It was a barrier past which I was *not* invited.

All day and all evening long, everything I did raised his hackles. When I told him the portraits of the couple would be at the south end of the garden instead of the north end like before, he hadn't said a word, but his icy demeanor had just about wilted both our boutonnières. Sending Troy and Phoebe to get a few shots of the rented white Rolls Royce was a mistake for some reason. I even managed to pick the wrong time to go out to my car for a cleaner copy of the invoice and a quick gulp of water.

By the cake-cutting and bouquet toss, I was ready to throw my hands up. I probably could have gotten the punch stain out of the matron of honor's dress, repaired the damage a toddler's roving hand had done to the wedding cake, miraculously healed the bride's wheelchair-bound grandmother, and *still* been on Angel's shit list.

This wedding ran every last one of us ragged. It was nonstop, constantly on our feet, all four of us being pulled in twelve different directions. We'd all grabbed enough to eat to keep from passing out, but it wasn't nearly enough. Normally, we'd have agreed on a fast food place and stopped as a group for a late-night super-value heart attack.

Tonight, Troy and I left while Angel and Phoebe were still packing his car. We always left gigs at the same time, but I made an exception tonight. I needed to get out of this place, away from him, and some food in my system before Angel and I had it out in front of God and everyone. For the sake of everyone within a three-block radius, I got the hell out of there.

Before we went back to the studio, Troy and I stopped to eat. I was starving but could still barely finish mine. Thankfully, what little I ate was enough to dull the ache between my temples. My assistant, usually chatty to the point of annoyance, was chatty tonight to the point of merciful distraction. I listened with interest about the courses he'd enrolled in next semester, the decrepit Mustang he'd been trying to fix up for three years, and his brother's recent culinary school mishap that had resulted in twelve stitches. At least *someone* was speaking to me today.

After we'd eaten, we returned to the studio. Phoebe and Angel were unloading his car. With all the equipment still in the trunk, they must have just gotten started. They must have made a similar stop on the way back. So much for buying us some time.

No one spoke while we emptied the cars. Phoebe and Troy probably felt like two mice between two snarling cats. They swapped a few wary glances when they didn't think I noticed, which made me feel guilty as hell. I promised myself I'd apologize to them on Monday and bring peace offerings of coffee and doughnuts. For tonight, I just gave them a quick escape.

"Why don't you two call it a night?" I said. "We can put everything away."

Phoebe looked like she was about to insist on staying, but her eyes darted over my shoulder toward Angel, then returned to me. "Okay, I'll see you guys on Monday."

Troy followed suit. I didn't know if he'd caught on that now was a good time to make himself scarce, or if he was just ready to get out of his uncomfortable shoes after a long day, but he high-tailed it out of there with Phoebe.

As soon as they were gone, I turned the deadbolt on the studio's front door, and the click sounded an awful lot like the bell in a boxing ring. When I turned around, Angel was out of sight, but his tuxedo coat was draped over his desk chair, and the uncharacteristic haphazardness—one lapel tucked underneath, the opposite shoulder barely over the top of the chair—made the hairs on the back of my neck stand up.

In the other room, something slammed shut with a lot more force than was necessary.

I took a deep breath.

Let the games begin.

Chapter Twenty-Two

"So are you going to tell me why you've been so pissed at me all day?"

I looked up from putting gear away. Dante stood in the doorway, blocking my only escape, with his arms folded across his chest and *that* look in his eye.

"Let's just get all this shit put away and get out of here," I said.

Dante didn't move. "I don't really want to take this home, to be honest."

"And I don't particularly want to hash it out here."

"Well, I want to know what the fuck I was doing wrong today." Jaw set and shoulders taut, he stepped onto the set between us, into the brighter light so I could really see the fury in his features. "Every move I made was wrong. Everything I did was wrong." He up put his hands. "What the fuck?"

"Are you going to tell me why you didn't bother giving me a heads-up about anything all day?" I shot back. "Seemed like you were making all the decisions, so—"

"Well it wasn't like I was getting more than two-word answers out of you."

I focused harder than I needed to on coiling an extension cord around my hand and elbow. "You might have said something about taking the family portraits on the opposite end of the garden," I growled. "Every fucking time we shoot a wedding in that place, we do it by the fountain."

Dante shrugged. "The bride wanted it by the trellis. Or should I have asked her to hold that thought while I ran it by you?"

"All I'm saying is that a heads-up would have been nice before Phoebe and I had to drag everything back over to the other side of the damned garden."

"Take that up with the bride," he snapped. I dropped the coil of cord onto its shelf and started for the battery packs from today, which were on the opposite side of the room. Dante went on. "For that matter, you've been shooting daggers—" He paused. "Angel, stop. Just stop. Please."

I stopped and turned around, facing him across the rumpled muslin.

He took a breath. "You've been shooting daggers out your eyes at me all damned day." Dante pinched the bridge of his nose and exhaled sharply. Then he threw up his hand. "Is this even about the wedding, or are you pissed at me for something else?"

I flinched like he'd punched me, and he may as well have. Shifting my weight, I stared at the floor between us, tapping my fingers on my arm just to channel my nervous energy into something.

"Angel, you've been cold-shouldering me all day." His tone was slightly gentler, but still edged with irritation. "What did I do?"

The fury in my chest, that knot that had been tightening all day long, receded in favor of the lump rising in my throat. Guilt and worry twisted and turned in my gut.

Raising his eyebrows, Dante inclined his head enough to change his expression from interrogative to inquisitive.

I broke eye contact and ran a hand through my hair. God damn it, I'd spent all day hiding behind misplaced anger. I wasn't angry with him. I hadn't been angry with him at all, and I'd known that from the get-go. It was just easier to grind my teeth and keep my hackles up instead of letting him see everything else that was on my mind. A wall of ice and barbs seemed like the safest bet to get me through the day in one piece, but now that I faced him, that wall came down and it came down hard.

Much more of this and I'd break down with it.

"Angel?"

I cleared my throat but didn't meet his eyes. "I'd rather discuss this at home."

Before he could protest, I brushed past him. He didn't reach for me. Didn't try to stop me verbally or physically. Walking away and giving him the cold shoulder again was the last thing I wanted to do. It certainly wouldn't get us closer to resolving this. But I just needed some fucking time to get my wits about me.

I turned the deadbolt and shoved the door open. When it banged shut behind me, I half expected it to open again. Cringing, I listened for the hurried beat of dress shoes on pavement to accompany my own.

The door stayed closed. No footsteps joined mine.

I shouldn't have been surprised. Dante knew me well enough to know when I needed some time to cool down, just like he knew me well enough to know the wedding had nothing to do with why I was pissed off. I just needed a little space, a little time, then we could calmly and civilly sort it out. That's how most fights went, anyway. I wasn't sure this could be settled so easily.

I started the car and pulled out of the parking lot, mind going in a million different directions. I was a block away when I realized I hadn't put my battery packs on the charger. Three blocks when I realized I'd left my jacket on the back of my chair. A mile and a half before I remembered the check from the bride's father was still in my wallet.

I couldn't muster the energy to give a shit, though, so I just drove. Rubbing the back of my neck with one hand, I sighed. There was nothing quite like a wedding—all stress and romance—to inflame the nagging worries in my head.

While the headlight-illuminated stripes blurred past my car, my mind wandered back to a sweltering morning on the other side of the world a decade and some change ago. One second, I was kneeling in the dust, adjusting the aperture to get a more interesting depth of field on a stack of hand-woven baskets. The next, someone bumped into me, and I had half a heartbeat to be annoyed that he'd jostled my camera before I lost my balance and we both tumbled onto our asses.

Once we'd made sure our cameras were undamaged— priorities, of course—I'd stood, dusted myself off and tried to be irritated with this idiot tourist who'd broken my concentration. When I offered my hand to help him up, though, I could tell by the camera he wasn't just some idiot tourist. And when I met his eyes, I didn't care if he *was* an idiot tourist. My God, he was gorgeous. Though I didn't believe in love at first sight, in that moment I certainly believed in *lust* at first sight.

Appropriately enough, given how we'd just met, we stumbled through awkward introductions and apologies. Eventually, we reached the point where we'd been polite, laughed off our little collision, and could continue our days, assignments and lives in different directions. And we...didn't.

New Delhi hustled and bustled around us, but the world may as well have ground to a halt while we talked cameras, the assignments that had landed us there, and where we came from. At some point, we'd started walking, and we kept right on talking. The awkwardness diminished. We got the hang of interacting like we weren't bashful schoolboys, at least until we parted ways that evening. Neither of us was particularly shy by nature, but we also couldn't *quite* work up the nerve for that first kiss.

At least I'd managed to choke through a red-faced "I'd like to see you again", and the next morning, we'd met up in front of my hotel. Then he'd shown me the little rundown restaurant that would get me forever hooked on curry, and that afternoon, I'd taken him to a particular temple that had intrigued me. Sometime around sunset, he'd snapped a photo of that temple, the image that would later be his first sale to *National Geographic*.

And after the curry and the temple and the picture and the sunset, Dante had finally kissed me.

It was three days after we met before I realized I never did get that picture of the baskets. It was two days after *that* before I finally worked up the nerve to ask if he wanted to come back to my hotel room.

By the time the sun went down the fifth night, I knew. Gun-shy though I may have been after my divorce and a few failed relationships, I knew. There was no doubt in my mind as we went through the desperate if slightly awkward motions of two lovers in bed for the first time. One way or another, we were in this for the long haul.

Sure, one of us would eventually have to move to another state unless we wanted to do the long-distance thing forever. We both traveled a lot, sometimes in opposite directions. We had the earliest inklings that we were both Doms who didn't switch. All of those were bugs that could be worked out. Lying in bed in a hotel room in India, the existence of "us" was a foregone conclusion.

In the years that had come and gone since that night, we'd built a life together. We'd moved and traveled thousands upon thousands of miles. We'd bought and sold a few cars and a couple of houses in between having all the ups and downs every couple has. Submissives had come and gone.

Twelve years, a business partnership, and one particular submissive later, uncertainty found me.

I blew out a breath and tapped my fingers on the steering wheel. My feelings for Jordan made me physically ache with guilt. Dante's feelings for him scared the hell out of me. The fact was, Jordan was something Dante needed that I wasn't. Something I could never be.

Habit and muscle memory guided my car from the studio to the house. I opened the garage door, pulled in and turned off the engine, all simple, familiar movements I did without thought.

Dragging my feet, I went into the bedroom to change out of my tuxedo.

Dante would be along eventually. Knowing him, he'd kill some time at the studio. Then maybe he'd go drive around for a bit to gather his thoughts, which left me time to try to gather my own.

After I'd changed into something more comfortable, I parked on the couch with my cat and laptop. Still running on autopilot, I went through shots from a recent commercial shoot, adjusting color and contrast, cropping, watermarking, things like that. It required just enough focus to numb my mind. Work was the workaholic's anesthetic, and I dove right in.

Until the garage door opened, anyway.

The rumble was faint, but I knew the sound because my pulse was conditioned to jump a few notches whenever I heard it.

Like the chickenshit I was, I put on a pair of headphones and turned on my iPod. I kept them on when he came into the living room and sat back with his own laptop. I desperately needed to talk to him, and God, I wanted to, but I wasn't yet ready to.

I'm not being passive-aggressive, I wanted to tell him. *I just don't know how to look you in the eye and say what's on my mind.*

How much of this was my inability to find the right words and how much was nothing less than fear of the outcome, I couldn't say. The solution to this situation should have been simple. Just stick to the rule we'd put into place when we'd started bringing in submissives: if it starts becoming more than sex, break it off with the sub. We loved having submissives, craved the things only they could give us, but not if that came at the expense of our relationship.

That was the simple solution, but there were factors in place that made it complicated. I couldn't deny I was in love with Jordan. Painfully so. More than that, I had little doubt that Dante was too. And while I couldn't read Jordan as well as I could Dante, there were some strong feelings on Jordan's corner of this little triangle too.

I didn't want to lose Jordan. The very thought of breaking it off with him hurt like hell, but deep down I knew it was a necessary evil. I had to let Jordan go, because I *couldn't* lose Dante. In a perfect world, I could have had them both, but this wasn't a perfect world.

It wasn't that I felt pressured to choose between them. I knew we had to address this sooner or later, and something was going to have to give for the sake of our relationship, but I was afraid to ask Dante to give Jordan up. Whether or not he'd ever admit it, I knew it would hurt him, and I physically ached at the thought of asking him to give up the connection he had with Jordan.

Above all of that, my fear—that deep, gnawing fear that kept me awake at night and encased in ice today—was that Dante and Jordan would choose. That was why I was so fucking terrified to bring this up to Dante.

On the other side of the couch and a world away, he tapped and clicked, oblivious to me watching him from the corner of my eye. Like me, he had on headphones, and we both listened to something that wasn't each other.

It was up to me to re-establish communication. I'd been the one to cold-shoulder him and walk out. He'd tried. The ball was in my court.

I wanted to scream with frustration. We weren't like this. That was why our relationship worked so well. We talked. We talked about everything. We had this communication thing down. After all, our relationship was semi-open and we were into kink; there was no way we could function without that level of communication.

And tonight, when we needed to talk more than ever, we both froze. Well, I froze. He was probably fuming because I'd been at his throat all day for no apparent reason.

Fuck, we needed to talk. There were no two ways about it, and no matter how uncomfortable the conversation was guaranteed to be, it needed to happen. But where to start? *How* to start? I suddenly felt like I had that first evening in New Delhi, when I just couldn't quite work up the nerve to make a move.

Eventually, Dante got up, shut his laptop and went into the bedroom. A minute later, the shower turned on.

Sighing, I closed my own laptop and decided to call it a night. Maybe now wasn't the time to deal with this. We were both exhausted from the wedding. It was a safe bet he was pissed at me for sniping at him all day, and I didn't blame him.

We had tomorrow off. No clients, no plans, nowhere to be. Plenty of time to talk things over and figure out where to go from here.

All I had to do was find the words.

Chapter Twenty-Three

Though it had been a long, exhausting day, Angel was restless that night.

Not that I could sleep either, but I just stared up at the ceiling. Beside me, he tossed and turned. Even Jade got tired of it after awhile and left, dropping to the floor with a thump and wandering out of the bedroom.

We hadn't said a word to each other since he'd stormed out of the studio, leaving me with a knot in my gut and a murmured "oh shit" hanging in the otherwise empty air. I'd taken my time getting out of the studio, triple-checking things that didn't really need to be done until tomorrow. Or next week. Or...whenever. Then I'd taken the long way home. Just for good measure, I'd stopped to put gas in my half-full tank, hoping every minute I stalled would give him some time to cool off, and maybe give me some time to figure out what the hell I'd done to piss him off.

The only thing I could think of was Jordan. Maybe Angel had caught on to what I felt for Jordan. He was just waiting for me to tell him what he already knew, and my God, the guilt ate at me. I needed to tell him. I couldn't lie to him.

From the time I got home this evening, neither of us spoke to each other. Maybe he was afraid to bring it up, or maybe he was still fuming about something else. Whatever it was, we didn't touch it. I was afraid to ask if our situation with Jordan was really on his mind. Almost a decade and a half together, and this was one conversation I did *not* know how to have with him.

So we avoided each other all evening, hiding behind laptop screens and fending off conversation with headphones, and now, here we were. Lying in the place we'd made love hundreds of times. Not speaking, not sleeping.

Every time he moved, my heart sank a little deeper. Angel was always restless, always moving, but I could always settle him with a touch. And now, I couldn't. I didn't know if my touch was welcome. If I could be the cure when I was the cause.

The mattress shifted slightly, the near-silent accommodating of shifting weight filling the taut stillness. The shared sheet moved an inch or so across my chest, just another reminder we were under the same covers even if we were on other planets. I didn't have to look to know his back was to me.

And still he fidgeted. His foot moved under the sheet. Back and forth, *hiss-hiss-hiss*. That stopped. A moment later, the faint vibration of tapping fingers made it across the mattress to me. Silence. *Hiss-hiss-hiss*.

Fuck it. Not reaching for him now was killing me. Let him pull away.

Holding my breath, I turned onto my side and reached through the darkness until my fingertips found him. His foot stopped. My hand rested on his arm. His body stiffened. My heart pounded.

I made slow, gentle arcs with my thumb across his warm skin. He was still now, but tense. Barely breathing. I held my breath, waiting for the tension to tilt in favor of either "come closer" or "back off".

Then he exhaled.

And relaxed.

I inched closer until his skin warmed my chest. Dropping a light kiss on his shoulder, I moved my hand down his arm to his hand, and just as I'd hoped, he splayed his fingers to let mine slip between. Squeezing his hand gently, I kissed the back of his neck, and his sharp intake of breath gave me a little more hope that he wouldn't push me away.

I wanted to ask if he was okay. I wanted to whisper "I love you". But words didn't feel right. There was so much we needed to discuss, but at least for the moment, I just needed to know he was still here.

I gave him enough room to roll onto his back, then I was over him again. He wrapped his arms around me, and even the darkness couldn't keep my mouth from finding his. I tried a few times to break the kiss, but he held the back of my neck with *please don't go* insistence, so I didn't. I held on, let him hold on, and we just kissed in the silence.

Eventually, I shifted my weight onto one arm and let my free hand memorize him like I'd never touched him before. His hands moved too, sliding over my skin and running through my hair.

I couldn't tell if we were simply moving slower or if time itself had slowed down. All I knew was how acutely aware I was of every way we moved and every place we touched. The grooves between his muscles guiding my fingertips up his abs. The whorls of his fingerprint scuffing across my stubbled jaw with the crackle of a vinyl record between songs. The almost silent thrum of his voice against my lips. Every twitch of his fingers in my hair as they played out some internal debate between stroking and grabbing.

Our breathing fell into synch, and so did every move we made. We mirrored each other as if we could see each other. I ran my hand down his side in the same moment his palm slid over my rib cage. Coarse stubble gently abraded my fingertips as soft fingertips grazed my own cheek. His hand dipped beneath the waistband of my shorts at the same time I slid my hand into his.

And simultaneously, we separated to get boxers off. Fabric hissed over skin. My heart thundered in my chest—arousal, relief, arousal, relief—when the nightstand drawer rattled open. There was just enough light for me to make out his shadow as he sat up, presumably to put the condom on. I reached for the lube bottle, which was on the corner of the nightstand, exactly where he always put it.

I poured some lube onto my hand and joined him on the edge of the bed. While I stroked the lube onto his cock, he sought my mouth again, and time once again slowed down, this time to the speed of a long, languid kiss.

The kiss deepened. My hand coaxed time back into motion with progressively tighter, faster strokes, and Angel's breathing quickened. Then he put a hand on my wrist, a silent *stop*.

I didn't have to ask, and we didn't speak. We moved, knowing without knowing, just doing. The bed shifted and creaked beneath us, and when Angel knelt behind me, I bit my lip as a shudder of anticipation rippled up my spine.

He pressed against me, and I exhaled, willing myself to relax completely so he'd meet no resistance, and he met none. White sparks flickered around the edges of my vision as he pushed in slowly, gently, perhaps savoring this as much as I did. He withdrew, then slid deeper inside me, taking long, slow strokes. I rocked back against him, not dictating the speed, just complementing the way he moved, and oh God, he felt incredible.

Maybe the darkness would have let a less honest or less devoted lover pretend he was with someone else, but I couldn't have mistaken him for anyone if I'd wanted to. The sound of his breathing. The way he ran his hands up and down my sides while he took those deliciously long, smooth strokes. That low growl that came from the back of his throat when he moved a little faster. It was all unmistakably and perfectly Angel. My Angel. I closed my eyes. Here in the darkness of our familiar bedroom, we were back in that sun-drenched Indian hotel, making love for the first time, when I knew I'd found the man for me, and to this day, that hadn't changed.

Resting his hand on the bed beside mine, he leaned down, his chest warming my back as his other arm wrapped around me. I put my hand over his and he kissed the back of my neck. He moved from the hips, taking slow, uneven strokes, but I didn't care if he went fast or slow. He was against me and over me and inside me, and all of that mattered more to me than an orgasm.

Angel slid all the way inside me and stopped. He kissed my shoulder and the back of my neck. I turned my head, and in the darkness, his lips met mine. We kissed like that for...I couldn't say. A while. A long while. At least until my neck started to cramp, and though I didn't say a word, he must have known, because just before it would have become too uncomfortable to ignore, he broke the kiss and sat up. He withdrew, and as soon as I turned around, he put his arms around me. His kiss was gentle but passionate, confident but still somehow seeking reassurance.

Tell me you're still here.

I'm still here if you want me to be.

He pulled away again and leaned toward the nightstand. More lube, I guessed, and I was partly right. A click was my only warning before soft light met my dark-adjusted eyes. I blinked a few times.

Then our eyes met.

You're still here.

I'm still here.

We pulled each other into another long, deep kiss. With my body weight, I guided him back, and together, we sank down to the bed. More time passed us by while we just held each other and kissed, and we just let it pass. There was no hurry to do anything but be here. At some point, I even forgot we'd been having sex at all; the only thing I could think of was how much I wanted to touch and taste him and let him know that yes, yes, I was still here. It was only when he reached past me for the lube that I remembered what we were doing.

Angel put a little more lube on, then I got on top and lowered myself onto him. I rose off him, came back down, rose again, and while I did, he reached between us with one hand and gently stroked my cock. With the other, he drew me down to kiss him. Physically I couldn't have gotten any closer to him, and still it wasn't enough. Hot skin, cool breaths, the musky scent of sweat, low moans between kisses, his face whenever I could open my eyes and see through the blurry intensity. His kiss, his hands, his cock, his breath, his body, and none of it was enough.

A vague ache worked its way into my back from staying in this position so long—riding him while leaning down to kiss him—but it was nothing compared to the more powerful ache within.

God, I love you, Angel.

He stroked my cock in time with the rise and fall of my hips, and I rode him in time with his breathing and my own. With a gasp, I broke the kiss, and I touched my forehead to his as something inside me came undone, came unwound, and I struggled to keep some semblance of rhythm. I couldn't let go of enough air to tell him how good he felt, how amazing he felt, *oh God, oh God, Angel, don't stop...*

Then he made the intense more so with a long, helpless whimper, an upward thrust, and the pulse of his own orgasm deep inside me in the same instant I let go. Hot semen hit my chest and abs, most likely his too, and after a moment, we each gave one last shudder.

And it was over.

I collapsed on top of him. We didn't move. We just held on to each other and panted between gentle kisses.

Finally, I raised my head just enough to speak.

"I love you, Angel."

A ragged breath whispered across my lips, and I couldn't help thinking it felt an awful lot like a sigh of relief.

"I love you too," he murmured, and like his exhalation, his breath contained an unsettling note of relief. Before I could ask, he kissed me again, and held on a little tighter this time.

My throat ached. Fuck, the guilt.

Angel, Angel, I'm right here. I've always been here. I'm not going anywhere.

Eventually, we pulled ourselves away from each other long enough to get rid of the condom, clean up, and return to bed. The light stayed on, and for a while, we just looked at each other.

I stroked his hair and finally managed, "What's wrong?"

He avoided my eyes and released his breath.

"Angel, talk to me."

He sighed. Then he sat up, so I did too. I put a hand on his back and waited while he searched for the words in his wringing hands, the creases in the blanket, something on the other side of the room.

Finally, he drew a deep breath and met my eyes. "It's about things with Jordan."

Guilt wrapped around my spine, threatening with every breath to become visible, assuming he hadn't already seen right through me. Assuming he didn't already know. "Okay..."

Swallowing hard, he held my gaze. "We've always had the rule about not getting involved with submissives. Emotionally, I mean."

Oh, shit.

"And we've always stood by that." He paused. "I've always trusted you, you've always trusted me, and I've *always* done my damndest to not get involved like that."

Fuck. Fuck. Oh, fuck, Angel, I'm sorry...

He closed his eyes and rubbed his temples. I hoped he didn't feel the way my hand tried to shake against his back, but I was sure he did. I chewed the inside of my cheek. The accusation was coming, working its way to his lips and into the air, and when it came, I owed him only truth. No denial, no sidestepping.

"Dante, I..." He exhaled and finally forced himself to meet my eyes. "I love him."

The words shoved the breath out of my lungs. In disbelief, I stared at him. Relief had only just begun to cool the guilt in my blood when he spoke again.

"And I know you do too."

My mouth went dry. Then I took a long, deep breath and nodded slowly. "Yeah. I do."

Angel dropped his gaze, his cheek rippling and his jaw tightening.

I touched his arm. "I do, and it's been killing me, because I felt like..."

He turned back toward me and whispered, "Like you were cheating?"

Ouch. Another nod.

"Me too." He brushed a few stray strands of hair off his forehead. "I've been wanting to tell you; I just didn't know how to say it. Any of it."

"I know the feeling, believe me."

Angel exhaled hard and shifted his gaze away again. For as much as he'd been relieved to hear I loved him earlier, there was not nearly as much relief now that I'd admitted I loved Jordan just as he did. He'd known the latter, but my God, hadn't he known the former?

I put my hand over his on top of the blanket. "Angel, this doesn't take away at all from how I feel about you."

Almost imperceptibly, he flinched.

"What's wrong?" I squeezed his hand. "What aren't you telling me here?"

He bit his lip and stared at our hands for a long moment. "There's..." He paused, swallowing hard. "There are things he does for you that I don't. Things he can give you that I can't."

I lifted his chin so he looked at me. "Angel..."

He moistened his lips. "I can't be a submissive for you, and I'll never enjoy having you fuck me the way he enjoys it."

"I know."

"And he's not crazy neurotic like I am," he said. "I mean, come on, I know you get tired of that shit."

I smiled and kissed him lightly. "We both have our annoying habits. What couple doesn't?"

He avoided my eyes. "Maybe so, but when there's someone else in the picture who doesn't have those annoying habits, and also has more to offer—"

"Angel, he's not you."

With some effort, he met my eyes. "And no matter how much I'd love to be, I'm not him."

The ache in my throat intensified. I brushed the pad of my thumb across his cheekbone. "I don't want you to be him. I've been perfectly happy with you all this time. That's not going to change."

"You were happy with me before he came along." He blinked a few times, then looked me in the eye again. "But what about now that you know what it can be like with him? Now that you've experienced *him*, am I enough for you?"

"Of course you are," I said. "I wouldn't trade what we have because of a few things in the bedroom."

Angel chewed his lip. "Except things with Jordan have gone beyond just a few things in the bedroom."

"Yeah, they have." I wanted to tell him I could never love someone like I loved him, but was that a lie? Guilt gnawed at me. The way I felt for Jordan didn't detract at all from what I felt for Angel, but it wasn't something I could easily dismiss either. I was just afraid neither of them would understand that.

Angel went on. "The fact is, he's something I'm not, and I'm scared to death I might lose you because of that. What if Jordan is the best of both worlds for you? Something I can't be?"

I swallowed. I'd been so afraid he'd be hurt and angry that I felt this way for Jordan, but his fear that I'd even think of walking away from him cut to the bone and deeper.

He wasn't done. "I've been worrying about this for a while, and—" His voice cracked. "The fact is, Jordan's everything you ever wanted that I can't be."

I cupped the sides of his neck in both hands. "No. Jordan's the submissive I always wanted. And I do love him. But you're everything I've ever wanted, Angel. We knew from the beginning that we're both Doms. We knew that wouldn't make things easy. There would always be something we couldn't be for each other."

He put his hand over mine. "But we didn't know from the beginning we'd ever fall for a sub. Especially both of us."

"I know." I kissed him lightly. "Dom or sub, I couldn't be happy without you, though. No one will ever be one hundred percent perfect for each other, but you're as close as anyone ever could be. Otherwise, we never would have lasted this long."

Angel released a long breath. "So what do we do?"

"I don't know. I mean, if we cut things off with him, we all get hurt. If we keep going..." I shook my head. "Fuck, I don't know."

"I think we should talk to him." He brushed a few strands of hair out of his eyes. "One way or the other, I don't think we should play with him again until we've put this on the table. I don't think we should keep it from him, especially if we're still...involved."

"No, we shouldn't keep it from him." I hesitated. "But I don't know *how* to tell him, and I don't know where we go from here." I paused, not sure if I dared go down this road. "It's going to hurt all three of us if we let him go."

Angel nodded. "But maybe that's better in the long run. We're already in too deep, so—"

"So maybe we see how he feels, and go with it." I squeezed Angel's hand. "Maybe we can function as three instead of two."

His posture straightened and he stared at me. "Dante, are you listening to yourself?"

"Of course I am." I reached up and tucked his hair behind his ear. "Look, I don't want anything to happen to what we have. I don't want to hurt Jordan, and I don't want you to get hurt. But if we cut him loose, we're all going to get hurt."

"And if we try to make this a trio instead of a pair..."

"It may work, it may not." I rested my hand on the back of his neck. "He might not share the way we feel anyway." Even as I said the words, I didn't believe them. The kind of connection I had with Jordan wasn't one-sided, and I'd seen the way he and Angel looked at each other. I cleared my throat. "It's worth a try."

"Is it?" Angel wet his lips. "And what if it doesn't work out?"

"Then...we'll deal with that when the time comes. But I'd rather at least see how things go than preemptively cut off something that could be incredible."

"Unless we're nipping something in the bud before people get hurt more than they need to."

"Angel, you've been to the top of Mount Everest, you've walked into war zones, and you've jumped into a damned shark cage before." I managed a cautious smile. "I've never known you to be the one to take the safe, easy route if it meant passing up the chance to take a risk for some kind of cool reward."

A flicker of laughter lit up his face, but it was gone almost as quickly as it had come. "Yeah, I'm all for taking risks." He swallowed, and his expression was completely serious now. "But I don't gamble with our relationship."

"I know you don't." I kissed his forehead. "But let me ask you this: do you want to cut him loose?"

Angel winced and dropped his gaze. "I don't want to, no. I'm just not sure we have a lot of choice."

I took a breath. "Angel, I don't want to risk our relationship. I wouldn't trade what you and I have for the world. But the way we both feel about him..." I trailed off, searching for the words.

Angel touched my face. "What?"

"The thing is, the way I feel about him, and the way I can tell you feel about him..." I forced myself to look him in the eye. "I can't help thinking that if we cut him loose, we'd be missing out on something."

"Well, we'd be missing out on having Jordan as our sub."

"That's not what I mean. I mean, as a relationship. All three of us."

Angel stared at me. "You're serious."

I nodded.

"Dante, I..." He closed his eyes and shook his head. "I just don't see how we could."

We were both quiet for a long moment. Angel finally broke the silence with a barely whispered question:

"Could you be happy without him?"

That thought gave me pause, and that pause was enough to make Angel wince and turn away.

"Yes, I could be," I said. "But I won't pretend I wouldn't miss this. What we have with him."

Angel said nothing.

"What about you?" I whispered. "Answer me honestly, Angel. If we ended things with him, I know you could still be happy with me and I would be with you, but would you feel like something was missing?"

The flinch said it all. The long release of breath backed it up. And his eyes, when they met mine, left no room for doubt.

"Yes," he whispered. "I would." He swallowed hard. "I just don't see how it could work with him."

"If it could work, both of us being with him, would you want to?"

He shrugged. "If I could have you both, hell yeah. Best of both worlds."

"Then who's to say we can't make it work? Jesus, we've made a relationship work when we're both Doms, and that could have blown up in our faces a few hundred times over."

"True," he whispered.

"Listen, we've always said that, corny and cliché as it might be, we're as close to soulmates as anyone can get." I shrugged with one shoulder, hoping he didn't see how scared I was that I was somehow wording this wrong. "Who's to say we only get one?" I paused, drawing a breath. "What if you're mine, I'm yours...and he's ours?"

Angel sat back a little, his eyes losing focus and his brow furrowing slightly. "You really think something like that's possible? Making a three-way relationship work?"

"I don't think it's simple," I said. "But I see no reason to believe it's not possible. Not after the last few weeks, anyway."

"Good point," he whispered. "So what do you suggest?"

"I'll talk to him." I brushed my thumb over his cheekbone as I searched his eyes for doubts. "I'm going over there for a riding lesson tomorrow night, and it would probably be easier for him if it was just one of us. So he's not outnumbered."

"That makes sense," Angel said softly.

"We'll see what he says, and we'll figure it out from there." I tucked a few stray strands of hair behind Angel's ear. "If he doesn't feel the same way, or he isn't willing to move forward as a trio, then you and I will move on. Just us."

He nodded slowly. "We can give it a try. See what he says." He looked at me through his lashes. "I don't know what will happen with him, but the one thing I do know is that I don't want to lose you."

"You're not going to lose me, Angel." I kissed him gently. Grinning against his lips, I added, "Like it or not, you're stuck with me."

He was quiet for a second, but finally allowed himself to laugh. "Well, like it or not, you're stuck with me too."

I put my arms around him. "Oh, what a terrible thing."

"Isn't it?"

"Definitely. Now come here."

Chapter Twenty-Four

I knew as soon as Dante walked into the barn that something was wrong. The tension in his shoulders was visible from a mile away, and our eyes met for only a split second before he dropped his gaze.

"Everything okay?" I asked when I was close enough to speak without raising my voice.

Dante bit his lip. "I'd like to talk." His eyes darted around the barn aisle, which was still teeming with clients and boarders. "Someplace private."

My heart dropped into my feet. I chewed my lip, trying to think of a place where no one would overhear us. Noreen was in the office. Eli was in the house. Finally, I gestured out the door through which he'd come.

"Let's walk."

We did walk, and we did so in silence. We followed the fence to the closest to the middle of nowhere we could get on ten acres. Down by the river that divided my property from the next, in the six-foot gap between two pastures, I stopped. Out here, in the shade of the maples lining the riverbank, we were alone except for a few horses grazing nearby. There was no one around to overhear whatever he'd come to say. He hadn't said it yet, though, and the trickle of water over and around rocks emphasized the silence between us.

I leaned against the fence and rested my weight on one foot. I bent my knee and put my other boot flat against the post, hoping I appeared a little more relaxed than I felt.

"So, what's up?" I asked.

Dante leaned against the opposite fence, fixing his gaze on the tromped-down grass between us. "Angel and I have been doing some talking about a few things." He lifted his chin enough to meet my eyes. "About the three of us."

I tried to ignore the way my heart thundered against my rib cage. "Such as?"

He was quiet for a moment, once again staring into the middle distance. When he spoke again, he did so slowly, as if choosing his words carefully. "Listen, we've done this a few times over the years. Taken a submissive, that kind of thing. Quite a few times, actually. And we've always stuck to our rules about maintaining some emotional distance. There has to be some intimacy, or the trust won't happen, but still...distance."

I nodded, dread coiling in the pit of my stomach. They knew, they knew, fuck, they knew.

Dante went on. "We've had these arrangements get complicated before." He chewed his lip and ran a hand through his hair. "But...not like this."

Tighter and tighter, it coiled. *Just say it, Dante. If you know, just say it.*

He took a deep breath and set his shoulders back. "I don't quite know how to say this, Jordan, but..."

"Just say it. Whatever it is, I can handle it."

"We...we went into this because we wanted a submissive, but...we both..."

I cocked my head. Was he beating around the bush to soften the blow, or was he really having a hard time getting the words out? "You both what?"

"Angel and I...we..." Dante closed his eyes and took a deep breath. "We both love you, Jordan."

Okay, so I was wrong about being able to handle it.

I managed to find some air to pull into my lungs. I cleared my throat. "What?"

Dante looked at the ground, then at me. Quieter now, as if to keep the horses or the river from hearing, he said, "We're both in love with you."

"You're both...you...with me..." I shook my head. "You're serious."

Dante nodded slowly.

I took my foot off the post and rested it on the ground. Shifted. Put the other against the post. Still didn't feel anywhere near as relaxed as I might have appeared. "Wow. I. That wasn't what I was expecting."

Dante gave a sympathetic nod. "I know. It threw us for a loop too."

My heart sank deeper in my chest. "So, I suppose this is the part where you tell me we have to stop what we've been doing."

He looked toward the river with unfocused eyes. "No. No, this isn't that part."

"So..."

"I know this sounds crazy. It sounds crazy to us too." He shifted his gaze back to me. "But...we don't want to stop."

"And, what? Just ignore how we all feel?" My teeth snapped shut, but the truth had already slipped out. His eyebrows jumped. Trying not to notice the heat rushing into my cheeks, I coughed and said, "I mean, do we pretend this is all just physical, even if it's obviously not?"

Dante shook his head. "Quite the contrary, actually. We don't want to ignore it. We don't want to stop it."

I rubbed the back of my neck and blew out a breath. "Spell this out for me, Dante. Explain it to me like I'm stupid, because I'm having a hell of a time getting my head around it."

He pursed his lips. "We want you as more than just our friend and submissive. We want you to be part of...us."

I was too restless to stand still, so I pushed myself off the fence and paced. For a moment, the only sounds were the river behind me and the grass crushing beneath my feet.

I supposed this all should have taken some weight off my shoulders. Let me breathe a little deeper, unwind some of this guilty tension. It didn't. This was the one outcome I hadn't truly considered beyond some futile fantasizing, and now that it was reality, all I could think was *this is complicated. Seriously, seriously complicated.*

I met his eyes again. His eyebrows were raised, asking me to fill the silence that had fallen. I would have, but I had no idea how. What was I supposed to say? I didn't know what to think, what to feel; I sure as shit didn't know what to say.

Dante finally spoke. "Jordan, we're not suggesting that this is simple or that it would be an easy adjustment. We're suggesting it would be..." He frowned, pressing his lips together and, I guessed, searching for the words. I waited. After a moment, he raised his eyes again. "We're suggesting it would be worth it."

"That's easy for you to say. You only stand to lose one of us. I stand to lose both of you if this doesn't work out."

He nodded. "I know. And I know I'm throwing a lot at you."

"Oh, yeah, you could say that." I exhaled hard. "And Angel, he's, he's cool with this?"

"Yes, he is. We had a long talk last night. I came alone today because we didn't want to outnumber you."

"Well, there's a problem right there." I stopped pacing. "If I went along with this, I'd always be outnumbered."

"No, you wouldn't. The three of us would be on level ground. Equal thirds."

"On paper, maybe. I don't see how it would work in practice."

He let out a breath. "Have we ever made you feel like anything less than an equal part of this?"

"I've never been a part of your relationship, though. An equal part of this arrangement, yes. But that was something we all went into together. This...what you're suggesting...it..." I rubbed the back of my neck and cursed under my breath. "I'll always be the new kid. I could see something like this maybe working if we'd all just met, but this? How can I be an equal player when I'm this late to the game?"

"The fact that we just met you isn't something that can be helped."

"But it's a fact." I struggled to find the words. "As is the fact that I don't like the idea of being the expendable one."

Dante blinked. "What?"

I shifted my weight, jamming my hands into the pockets of my jeans. "If shit hit the fan between the three of us, and there was just no way to make this work out, say, if Angel and I decided we didn't get along anymore. What do you do, Dante?"

He dropped his gaze, but not before he flinched. Equal parts hurt and anger tugged at my gut. I didn't quite understand it, why I was angry, but I was. But then, I didn't understand a damned thing about this, so why not throw some inexplicable emotions into the churning, acidic mix?

"Jordan, it's not that simple," he said softly, and I could have sworn he sounded like my question hadn't just thrown him off but hurt him.

"Yes, it is that simple." I forced my voice to stay even, and damn it was hard. "I'm the new guy. I will always be the new guy. If something happens, I—" I stopped when my voice cracked. I cleared my throat. "I can't be someone's second choice."

There was no doubt I'd hurt him then, not when his lips tightened into a thin line and he turned away. He had to have known it was true, that there were simply factors in place that none of us could change, but that truth appeared no easier for him to swallow than it was for me.

Running a hand through his hair, he took a deep breath. "Listen, I can't help that I met Angel first. Yes, we have over a decade of history. That's only because it took us that long to find you." He paused. "That doesn't mean either of us loves you any less just because you were the last to come into the picture."

"That's easy for both of you to say now." Christ, it hurt just to say it. "I'll always be the third wheel. The one who'll be kicked to the curb if things go south. I'd either be coming between the two of you, or I'd be the odd man out."

He was quiet for a moment. Finally, barely whispering, he said, "What can I do to convince you we don't see you as the odd man out? That we would never want you to feel that way?"

"I don't think you'd want me to feel that way. I don't think you would ever set out to. It's just...the way it is." I wet my lips. "I don't think the two of you would ever intentionally hurt me, but I don't see how I could ever be on level ground with what you guys already have."

Dante said nothing.

I rubbed the back of my neck again. "I just, I can't see this not blowing up in our faces somehow."

"It's a possibility," he said with a subtle nod. "It could blow up in our faces. Or it could be something we can't even imagine now. In a good way." When I didn't respond, he went on, his tone softer. "I'm not discounting what's at stake for you or any of us, Jordan. We both know exactly what we're asking from you, and we're not approaching this lightly."

I stared out at the river and land beyond. Whether or not he intended to discount it, could he even begin to imagine what I had to lose? If I could be openly in love with them, and know what it was like for the two of them to return it in kind, but then I lost it? Being with the two of them like that would be nothing short of paradise as long as everything was okay. If things went wrong—and they always did at some point in any relationship—where did that leave me?

Dante's hands rested gently on my shoulders, and I jumped. Not because he'd startled me—though I'd only been distantly aware of it, his approach had registered at the edges of my senses. It wasn't his nearness or his touch that had startled me, but the sudden ache in my throat when I imagined this being the last time he touched me.

He put his arms around me. I released my breath, relaxing against him and laying my hands over his.

"I know this is a lot to think about," he whispered, and I thanked God he didn't kiss my neck. "You don't have to give us an answer now." He paused, and I swore he held me a little tighter when he added, "We're not going anywhere."

He loosened his embrace, and in spite of being afraid to look him in the eye, I turned around. As soon as I faced him, my arms rebelled against my better judgment and wrapped around him.

"I'm completely serious, Jordan." He touched my face. "I do love you."

"I love you too," I murmured. The words came automatically. Easily. Freely. "Dante, I love you. I love both of you. But I..." I closed my eyes to avoid the beautiful scrutiny of his. "God damn it, I—"

He kissed me.

There was nothing sexual or even seductive about it. Just gentle contact, his hands touching the sides of my face with the same tenderness as his lips moving against mine. The way I'd *always* wanted someone to kiss me. Damn it, why did everything surrounding such a simple kiss have to be so complicated?

Dante broke the kiss, but not the embrace. "The ball's in your court," he whispered. "You know where we stand."

I chewed the inside of my cheek. "I need time. To think."

Nodding, he loosened our embrace but left me to break it. I did, and didn't look at him while I took a step back to make sure I didn't pull him to me again. The kiss still tingled on my lips, and the cool air emphasized the warm ghost of his touch on my skin. We were back to distance and silence, the water rolling behind us and wind rattling through tree branches above us, but no words passing between us.

"This is...there's a lot...I..." I paused, releasing a sharp breath. "I just, I need some time. To...process all of this."

"Understandable." He chewed his lip. "Do you want me to go?"

No, no, don't go. Stay here.

But I needed some breathing room so I could think, so I told the lie with a nod, and that lie came to life with the soft crush of grass under one step, then another. The next was quieter. The one after that, quieter still. I stared at the grass between my own feet and didn't watch him leave.

When I was really and truly alone, I slumped against the fencepost again. I slid down until my elbows rested on my knees and rubbed my temples with my fingers, trying to manually work this all into my head.

"We want you as more than just our friend and submissive. We want you to be part of...us."

How could we make something like that work? How could I be sure I wouldn't be setting myself up to lose not one but two men?

I pushed myself to my feet and started back toward the barn. I needed to...to...go somewhere. Do something. Get the fuck away from here and this. I needed to think. I needed not to think. Fuck it, I didn't know what I needed to do, I just needed to *go*.

I slipped past boarders and clients in the barn, grabbed a bridle out of the tack room, and went to Bravado's stall. I took his blanket off and put the bridle on. As soon as we were out of the barn, I hoisted myself onto his back, and we couldn't get to the trail fast enough.

Down by the property line at the other corner of my land, there was an old bridge across the river. Instead of crossing the bridge, I took Bravado down to the riverbank and let him take a drink. As he always did, he pawed at the water, splashing like a little kid in a mud puddle. I just let him play, especially since the noise he made drowned out the trickling sounds around us that had been the backbeat to my conversation with Dante.

Pity it couldn't quite mask the whispers that still echoed in my ears.

"Have we ever made you feel like anything less than an equal part of this?"

"What can I do to convince you we don't see you as the odd man out? That we would never want you to feel that way?"

My conscience berated me for even throwing that point out there, but wasn't it true? There was no way I could compete with their rock-solid, decade-old relationship. I wouldn't want to. They had the kind of love most people would cut off a limb to have, and I'd never dream of stepping between them. So how the hell could I *join* them?

I was so lost in my thoughts, I almost lost my balance when something caught Bravado's attention and he threw his head up. I grabbed his mane and shifted my weight to regain my balance, my heart pounding as the *oh shit, almost fell* adrenaline rushed through me.

Ears perked up and nostrils flaring, he snorted at something in the distance. I patted his neck.

"Easy, buddy," I said softly. "There's nothing there."

He snorted again. Scanning the landscape, I finally made out the two tawny shapes against a line of trees. I rolled my eyes.

"They're just deer, stupid." I steered him away from the riverbank and we went across the bridge. He kept throwing wary looks toward the terrifying pair of horse-eating deer that grazed menacingly about fifty yards away, but he forgot all about them when I gave him a gentle nudge with my heel. Obeying my cue, he burst into a canter and tore down the packed dirt path. Holding on with my knees, I leaned over his neck, squinted against the wind and let him run. He was one of my highly trained show horses, but we both let our hair down on the trails. It was one of my secrets to keeping him from getting sour like show horses often do. And damn if it wasn't a hell of an escape for me.

Up ahead, there was a decrepit fence that blocked one side of the trail. Bravado shifted gears, gaining a little bit of speed. I could almost hear him mentally calculating the strides between here and the fence, likely focusing just as much as I was. I eased my grip on the reins and leaned a little farther forward.

Three strides away.

Two strides away.

One stride away.

Liftoff.

He sailed over the jump and landed with ease on the other side. Patting his neck, I sat back and eased him to a trot, then a walk.

"Good boy," I said. He panted and chomped the bit, fidgeting a little as he walked. No doubt he wanted to run again. There were more potential obstacles along this trail, every one of which we'd jumped a few dozen times before. But I wanted him to walk for a few minutes. No sense wearing him out, since I intended to stay out for a while.

With no need to concentrate on an upcoming jump and no rush of wind past my face to distract me from the world, the world came back into focus.

I groaned. Fuck. This just wouldn't go away.

I had never been so confused in my life. Being with Angel and Dante was as natural and right as the words "I love you" slipping off my lips. I just kept going back to that deep-seated fear that we could never make this work the way they suggested. There would always be that reality beneath the surface, pulsing under my skin beside my heartbeat, that I was the third. The new kid, the add-on, the extra. That it would always be "them" and "me", even when it was "us". There would always be that line of demarcation, seared between us by twelve years of them before there was us.

But my God, I loved them. All the trust and the intimacy, all those conversations. The way they could be so gentle and so rough. The way they'd never made me feel like the outsider I was. Commanding, never belittling. Dominating, never domineering. How could I *not* fall in love with them?

"We're both in love with you."

"We both love you, Jordan."

"We're not going anywhere."

Fuck. Fuck, fuck, fuck. It sounded so damned good, it came so damned easily, *but*. But, but, but. Always a god damned but.

I loved them as a couple, but also as individuals. I was just as in love with Angel as with Dante, and I was in love with the halves as much as the whole. I was their sub, and yet I felt their equal. We had a perfect balance. The only problem was the numbers. Three where there should have been two, and I would sooner have walked away than try to cleave them apart. And now, I had the chance to have them both the way I'd only dreamed of, but there was so much potential for disaster.

Pulling myself out of my thoughts, I looked around. The sun was getting low in the sky, so I needed to turn around and head back before it got dark. Bravado was fine for after-dark rides, but I did that only with a full moon and at least one other rider with me. That, and the bugs would be out soon.

Besides, if I rode long enough to truly clear my head, Bravado and I would both be dead of exhaustion before the end.

So, I pointed him toward the farm.

Once he was cooled down, blanketed and munching happily on his dinner in his stall, I whistled for Sasha and started up the path to the house. On my way up, another knot tightened in my gut. I desperately needed to sit for a while with a drink in my hand and my dog at my feet. Just some time to myself, staring out the window while I figured out the crap in my head.

But I didn't live alone, and the other person in my house was home. I groaned to myself and continued up the path. I may have been confused about a few dozen things right now, but one thing was for sure, and that was what I *didn't* want in my life anymore.

As I shrugged off my jacket in the garage and went into the kitchen, I thought about the three years I'd spent with Eli. I could have sworn I was in love with him at one point. Maybe in a way I still loved him. Hell, of course I did. If I didn't love him, I'd have thrown him out on his freeloading ass by now. Pity might have kept him under my roof for a couple of months, but not the better part of a year.

Comparing him to them, I couldn't imagine giving up what I had with them just because it was complicated. I didn't want to. If we could build some sort of non-traditional happily ever after with the three of us, if I could be sure my corner of this little triad was tattooed on and not just drawn in pencil, I would, I would, I would. But how the hell did we do it? Love was always a gamble. I'd lost before, as the footsteps coming down the hall reminded me, but the odds would be less than even this time.

Eli came into the kitchen. We exchanged muttered greetings.

What if I fell out of love with one of them, or both of them, like I had with Eli? What if they fell out of love with me? Or, worse, what if one of them wanted to leave the other for me? I didn't think I'd ever be able to sleep at night if I was the cause of that relationship falling apart.

"We're suggesting it would be worth it." Dante's voice echoed in my mind.

I wanted to believe him. I really did.

"Jordan?"

"Hmm?"

Eli furrowed his brow. "You all right?"

I shrugged. "Yeah. Fine. Why?"

"Because you've been staring at that bottle of Coke for the last minute or so?"

I looked at the bottle in my hand. Couldn't even remember getting it out of the refrigerator or the still-empty glass out of the cabinet. I forced a laugh and shook my head. "Just spacing out, I guess." I poured myself the drink I didn't feel like drinking, then put the bottle away.

Skepticism furrowed his brow, but he didn't press the issue.

"How goes the job hunt?" I asked.

"Oh, you know." He gave a flippant shrug and popped open a beer. "The one I was hoping for didn't pan out, so..." Another shrug, followed by a sip of beer.

I gritted my teeth. "I assume you have other applications out there?"

With a somewhat sheepish expression, he shook his head. "Nah, I really thought this one would work out." He took another gulp of beer, then set the can down. "But, remember my college buddy, Travis? He's working on this startup, and it sounds like a sweet deal. I just need a few weeks to—"

"Eli, stop." I slammed my glass down on the counter. "Just *stop.*"

His lips thinned into a bleached line, and he waited for me to go on.

"Why are you doing this?"

He cocked his head. "Doing what?"

"Making excuses. Stalling." I made a sharp, aggravated wave with one hand. "Dragging your feet."

He mirrored my gesture, but his was out of defensiveness, not frustration. "I'm not dragging my feet, I swear."

"Oh, really?" I raised an eyebrow. "All this time, you've put in an honest effort but haven't found anything?"

"The economy sucks."

"Yeah, and yet I see 'Now Hiring' signs all over the place." I tapped my fingers on the side of my glass. "You could have found *something* in all this time. Why haven't you?"

"I've been trying."

"Look me in the eye and tell me you've put in an honest effort." I set my jaw. "Look me in the eye and say it."

He dropped his gaze. "Okay, okay, I—"

"Why not?" I was *so* not in the mood for this shit. Hell, was I ever in the mood for it? "What's the problem?"

His shoulders slumped. Then he sighed. "Because I don't want to leave."

"But it's over."

"Yeah, I know."

"So, what's the point of staying?"

"Because I don't want it to be over," he said sharply. "I'm sorry, Jordan, I just...I don't want this to be over."

"It's *been* over," I said. "For months. It's a little too late, don't you think?"

He said nothing.

I took a deep breath, trying to keep myself calm. "Did you really think that hanging around and freeloading off—"

"I haven't been freeloading," he growled.

Before I could stop myself, I gave a cough of sarcastic laughter. "Really? So you've been paying rent? Putting food in the refrigerator?" I gestured at his beer. "Buying the beer you drink three times as fast as I do?"

"Oh, pardon me for not having my own business and a god damned inheritance to live off."

I raised my eyebrow again, a silent, *did you really just go there*? He knew better than to tread on the subject of my parents' money.

He sighed and rubbed his forehead. "I'm sorry. I didn't mean..." He blew out a sharp breath. "I know you work hard, Jordan."

"Yeah, you should try it sometime," I said through my teeth. "Listen, this has to stop. I need to move on, and as long as we're still living together, it's—"

"Oh, I don't think my presence has stopped you from any of *that*," he said. "You don't think I notice when *they're* here?"

"I don't think they're any of your concern." I glared at him. "Who I bring into my own home is my business."

His eyes narrowed. "Wouldn't you rather have one guy who can make you happy instead of having to resort to two?"

"Leave them out of this," I snapped, barely keeping a surge of white-hot anger beneath the surface. "You don't have the faintest clue what's going on there." *That makes two of us, at the moment.* "For that matter, if I wanted one guy who could make me happy instead of two, that would still leave you out of the equation." The words came out with more venom than I intended, and guilt tugged at my gut, especially when his jaw dropped.

"Jordan..."

I exhaled hard. "I'm sorry, I didn't mean to..." I didn't? The hell I didn't. I was miserable when we were together, and I'd tried to let him down gently for months. The time for pulling punches was over. Looking him in the eye, I said, "I need to move on. Without you."

"Seems like you've done a fine job of that," he snarled.

Forcing myself to stay calm, I said, "I want my house back. I want my life back. And I don't want to feel guilty or awkward bringing a guy or two into my own house." I took a deep breath and set my shoulders back. "Which is why you have until the end of the month to move out."

Eli blinked. "What? Jordan, I can't get a place in a—"

"Not my problem. I've given you plenty of time to get it together." I folded my arms across my chest. "Now you have till the end of the month to get out."

"I need more time. There's no way I can do that."

I shrugged, refusing to allow myself the slightest twinge of guilt at my own indifference. "I gave you time. You didn't bother to use it. Not my problem."

He shook his head, then stared at me. "You'd really kick me out like that? With no job, no money and nowhere to go?"

"Well, how long am I supposed to support you and wait for your next get-employed-quick scheme to pan out before I say enough is enough?"

He rolled his eyes. "It's not like that."

"Isn't it?" I shrugged again. "All I know is, you've been here long enough. I've given you more than enough time to get out on your own. And you just admitted you've been dragging your feet on purpose because you wanted to get back together with me."

"Okay, okay." He shifted his weight and swallowed nervously. "Just give me a little time, then. I get it, we're done, it's over. I'll—"

"You have six and a half months." I gave him just enough time to release a relieved sigh before I added, "Retroactive to the time I asked you to move out in the first place. Which leaves you about two weeks."

"Fuck, Jordan, this—"

"You've had plenty of time," I said. "This is it. I don't care if you have to couch-surf or park your ass in a cardboard box. I'm done."

He glared at me for a moment, and I didn't know if he'd argue further, blow up at me or just give up. Finally, he stormed out of the kitchen, throwing a muttered "you're an asshole" over his shoulder on the way.

I listened until the slamming door cut off his heavy footsteps. Rubbing my eyes, I took a long, deep breath. Well, that was one problem more or less resolved. There was a deadline. A cutoff. A finite end when he'd no longer be my problem and he'd be out of my hair.

Now I just had to figure out what to do about the two men I'd have sold my soul to keep.

Chapter Twenty-Five

Three days after he'd had gone to talk to Jordan, Dante's phone burst to life with Jordan's familiar ringtone. We glanced at each other. Then Dante picked up his phone off the coffee table.

"Hello?" Long pause. "I...sure." He covered the phone with his hand and turned to me. "He wants to talk. In person."

"When?"

"As soon as possible."

"Now?"

Dante nodded. "Here?"

The next nod was mine.

To Jordan, Dante said, "Do you want to meet us here or out somewhere?" Pause. "Yeah, yeah, here's fine. Okay, we'll see you then." He snapped his phone shut. "He's going to leave now, so he'll be here in half an hour or so."

I released a breath I didn't realize I'd been holding. "Guess we'll see what happens, then."

"Guess we will." He set his laptop on the coffee table and stood. "Since he won't be here for a little while, I'm going to go grab a shower."

I nodded but said nothing.

Before he left the room, Dante paused and leaned down to put his arms around me. "Whatever happens with him, we'll be okay."

"I know." I squeezed his hand. "I just want us *all* to be okay."

"Me too." He kissed my cheek. "We'll just see what happens. Not much else we can do."

After Dante had gone into the bedroom, I continued working on the photo on my screen. I told myself I was getting some work done while I had a little downtime at home, but who was I kidding? I just needed something to do while I waited. That was probably why Dante had gone to take a shower: something to do.

The faster my hands moved on the keyboard and mouse, the more I could convince myself they were steady. I wouldn't relax, though, until this was over and I knew the outcome.

Blowing out a breath, I rested my head on the back of the couch and closed my eyes. I'd been robbed at gunpoint three times while working overseas, and that was the closest feeling I could compare to this. That undeniable awareness of how much was at stake, how much I could lose in how little time.

Dante was certain we would be okay, regardless of what happened with Jordan. Either we'd go on with him, or we'd make do and move on without him, which neither of us wanted to do. Still, I was more than a little nervous about all of this.

We'd crossed an emotional line that couldn't be uncrossed, and that rattled me right to the core. Even if we went on without him, we would never again be the Angel and Dante that had never known Jordan. Our relationship was watermarked with Jordan's name. Could we be happy again without him? And if he left, how long would his shadow stretch into our future? Where did we go from here if we went there without Jordan?

The guilt burned deep in my chest. Of course I could be happy with Dante and Dante alone. I'd been happy with him all this time. But I had been before I met Dante too. If things had been different and we'd parted ways, I supposed I could have found that happiness again.

The fact was, I couldn't crave wine I'd never tasted. Couldn't miss what I'd never known. Now I'd known both Jordan and Dante. They'd known each other.

And I didn't want any of us to have to miss each other.

I finally closed my laptop and put it aside. Right about that time, Dante came out of the bedroom, barefoot and shirtless with his damp hair freshly spiked. He looked good. He *always* looked good.

"You going to put a shirt on before he gets here?" I asked with halfhearted playfulness.

"Yes, I'm going to put a shirt on." He smiled and nodded toward the garage. "I was just getting one out of the laundry room." He stopped behind the couch and leaned down to put his arms around me again. "You okay?"

I sighed. "I will be once this is over."

"Yeah, me too." He kissed my cheek. "Hopefully."

I turned my head, and he met my lips in a long, gentle kiss before he continued on to the laundry room to put on a shirt.

About fifteen minutes later, almost exactly thirty minutes after he'd called, Jordan arrived. The circles beneath his eyes suggested he'd lost as much sleep over this as we had, but he still managed a shy, uncertain smile.

I hung up his coat while Dante offered him a drink, which Jordan declined. Pretending not to notice how tense the air was with the unspoken, I followed them into the living room.

I took my usual spot on the couch. Jordan took Dante's. Dante sat in the armchair closer to Jordan. Immediately, Jade appeared on the armrest beside Jordan, then bounded across his lap and into mine.

"Sorry about her," I said, petting her as she flopped down on my leg. "She has no manners." The three of us laughed, and the mood lightened a little, but it didn't last.

Taking a breath, Jordan shifted. "Okay, we all know what I came to discuss, so there's no point in beating around the bush."

Dante cleared his throat and leaned on one armrest. "Well, you know where we stand. I assume you've given it some thought?"

Jordan nodded. He stared at the coffee table for a moment, chewing his lip, and I wondered if he had any idea how far his silence had driven up my blood pressure. *I need to know, I need to know, I need to know.*

Finally he took a breath and whispered, "I just don't know." He swallowed hard. "I...the more I think about it, the less sure I am about it."

"Which part aren't you sure about?" Dante asked quietly.

"All of it," Jordan said. "I mean, I know what I feel, but..." He sighed. "Here's the thing. I was Eli's doormat. He was in control, and I let him walk all over me. You guys have never done anything like that, but the way...this kind of..." He took a deep breath. "I need to know I'm on equal footing and am an equal part of the relationship. Not the disposable one who's added for a little spice."

Something in the pit of my stomach dropped. I fidgeted, disturbing my cat, and she left. Ignoring her, I said to Jordan, "Do you really think we'd use you like that?"

Jordan didn't look at me. "No, not..." He fell silent for a moment. Then he met my eyes. "Not intentionally."

I met Dante's eyes. Fuck, what did we say to that?

Dante swallowed. "There's nothing we can do to prove beyond a shadow of a doubt that we want you to be a part of this—an equal part—except show you over time."

"And if things don't work out?" Jordan asked.

"There's never any guarantee they will," Dante said.

I nodded. "All we can do is promise you we're going into this with every intention of doing whatever it takes to make it work."

"I understand that," Jordan said. "It's not that I distrust the two of you or question your motives or intentions. Not in the least. I just can't help feeling like the odds are stacked against me."

Dante and I looked at each other. I didn't know what to say to that. Evidently Dante didn't either.

Jordan rubbed his neck and exhaled hard. "I'm not suggesting you guys have ever made me feel like I was a lesser part of this equation. But in the long run? The fact will never change that I came in really late in this game. I don't want to be the expendable one if shit hits the fan."

I took a breath and turned to Jordan. "Can I be completely honest about something?"

His eyebrows jumped.

I moistened my lips. "You're worried about being expendable, but...you're not. The thing is, when he and I discussed this the night before he came to talk to you..." I paused, glancing at Dante before meeting Jordan's eyes. "I was scared to death he was going to choose you over me."

Dante flinched. So did Jordan.

Jordan shifted. "See, that's part of the problem too. I don't think I could ever sleep at night if I was the reason something happened to your relationship. What you guys have, most people would kill for something like that. I don't want to be what breaks that up."

"Dante and I are both well aware that making this into a triple is a risk," I said, almost whispering. "For our relationship with each other and our relationship with you. And it's not a risk either of us is taking lightly. We're willing to put our own relationship on the line because *that's* how much we want to be with you." I swallowed hard. "The reason I told you that, about my fear he'd take you over me, isn't because I'm insecure in my relationship with him. Especially now that he and I are on the same page. It's because *that's* how strongly he feels for you, and it's how strongly I feel for you. I'd just never seen him form a bond like that with anyone but me, and it threw me."

Dante nodded. "We wouldn't have suggested this if we didn't both feel strongly enough about you to take this risk."

Jordan dropped his gaze and swallowed hard. He watched his hands wringing in his lap. Finally, he said, "What about other people? Would we keep this a secret? Would you two keep me a secret?"

"Hell no," I said.

He raised an eyebrow, silently bidding me to elaborate.

I fidgeted. "Jordan, we're gay. A good chunk of the population already hates the ground we walk on. If a few more turn up their noses because we found once-in-a-lifetime love twice in a lifetime, well, fuck them. I'm not hiding it." *I'm just afraid to lose it.*

"Point taken." He looked down again, swallowing hard. "This is... It's a lot..."

"We know," Dante said. "It's a lot for all of us to get our heads around."

"And we don't have to get it all sorted this instant. It didn't happen overnight; we don't have to figure out all the answers overnight." Inwardly, I cringed. It was the truth, and I absolutely didn't want to rush this but sleep. I needed sleep. And sleep wasn't happening until this was sorted.

"Jordan, you've trusted us to be your Doms," Dante said. "Can you trust us enough to go into this knowing we do see you as an equal part of this? That we're approaching this with every intention of making it work for all three of us, not just Angel and me?"

Jordan was quiet for another long, nerve-racking moment. He didn't look at either of us, didn't say a word, barely drew a breath. Finally, his Adam's apple bobbed, and his eyes darted back and forth between us.

"Would we be able to take things a day at a time?" he asked. "Just...see how things go?"

If he only knew the relief those words, tentative as they were, sent rushing through my veins.

"Of course," Dante said. "We wouldn't expect anything else."

Jordan went silent again.

My knee bounced up and down while my fingers tapped on my other leg. Too much nervous energy. Needed to release it. Needed to relieve this tension. Needed to *know*, damn it.

Jordan's fingers tapped on the cushion between us. That was when I realized he was watching my knee. Immediately self-conscious, I slowed it down, but hell if I could stop. Not with all this pent-up energy that needed to go somewhere.

Jordan lifted his hand off the cushion, and it hovered between us, hesitation written all over his expression. Then, tentatively, he put his hand on my knee. The heat of his skin through denim sent a flood of cool relief through my veins, and my leg stopped. So did my fingers. So did my heart.

For a moment, he stared at his own hand. At my now stilled knee.

I put my hand over his. When he didn't recoil, I squeezed gently. "I promise you, Jordan, we're not going into this lightly."

"I know." His voice was barely audible.

"It's your call," Dante said. "If you want to do this, say the word."

Jordan chewed his lip, staring with unfocused eyes at the coffee table. The hand on my leg twitched, as if he couldn't decide whether to leave it there or pull it away. Or if he wasn't sure it was his decision to make.

The penny dropped. This was the wrong approach.

With my heart in my throat and whatever courage I could muster from knowing he'd been the first to make contact, I moved a little closer to him. His eyes flicked toward the shrinking space between us, and he swallowed hard, but he made no effort to move away.

I reached for his face, and when my fingers made contact with his jaw, he closed his eyes and shivered. But he still didn't pull away.

"Why don't we put it like this," I said softly. "If you want me to stop, say the word." I leaned in slowly, giving him ample time to decide if he wanted me to continue.

He didn't tell me to stop.

I moved my other hand from my lap to his neck, letting it drift up into his hair.

He didn't tell me to stop.

My lip brushed his.

He didn't tell me to stop.

I kissed him. Pulling him closer, I deepened the kiss, and when he touched my face with a trembling hand, a knot unwound in my gut.

I broke the kiss and met his eyes. My heart pounding, I whispered, "Do you want me to stop?"

He moistened his lips. "No." He ran his thumb along my cheekbone and took a deep breath. "No, I don't want you to stop."

"Then I won't." I started to move in for another kiss, but he drew back slightly, so I froze. Panic tightened my chest. "What's wrong?"

He said nothing for a moment. He held my gaze, but there was something in his, something I couldn't quite read. My heart beat faster, faster, faster.

Then relief forced the breath out of my lungs when a hint of a smile curled his lips.

"I love you," he whispered.

More relief. I smiled. "I love you too." And he let me draw him into another long, gentle kiss.

While I held Jordan, I was vaguely aware of movement nearby. Jordan pulled in a sharp breath through his nose, and when I opened my eyes, Dante was behind him, kissing the side of his neck. Jordan moaned into my kiss.

I looked past him at Dante. For a fleeting second, our eyes met, and I grinned into Jordan's kiss. The only thing between Dante and me now was Jordan.

And he didn't divide us.

Chapter Twenty-Six

Angel's mouth against mine and Dante's lips against my neck was pure heaven. I tilted my head both to let Angel deepen the kiss and give Dante more access to my skin.

Dante nipped my earlobe. "So, would we have to twist your arm to get you to stay a while tonight?"

"If you two keep kissing me like that, you'll have to twist my arm to make me leave."

Dante's breath tickled my neck. "Don't think that'll be an issue. We want you to stay."

"Then I will." *I will. Yes, I will.* This was where I wanted to stay, and coming over here tonight, there'd been no question that I wanted to. It was only a question of whether or not I would. Or should.

Should I? That remained to be seen.

Would I? Oh, fuck yes, I would.

"Bedroom?" Angel murmured.

"You two lead," I said. "I'll follow."

Dante's lips brushed just above my collar. "That's what we like to hear."

As one, the three of us stood. They led me down the hall into their bedroom.

They didn't put me on my knees this time. There was no command to take each article of clothing off one at a time. We were all too desperate for that tonight. Everything had been said. All the emotions and worries laid out on the table. The barriers had fallen, the distance was gone. For the first time, they knew, I knew, and I could let my guard down and surrender to them with nothing to hide.

Dante pushed Angel's shirt over his head and threw it aside. Someone took my shirt off. I ended up with someone's belt in my hands for a second before I tossed it on the floor and went for Dante's shirt. Buckles. Zippers. Jeans. Boxers. Everything hit the floor, and when Dante and Angel were completely naked, my knees hit the floor too.

I descended on Angel's cock and sucked him hungrily, desperately. The only thing that kept my hand from shaking was my tight grip on him, and he groaned when my hand moved in time with my mouth.

Movement beside me told me Dante was nearby, and, still stroking Angel with one hand, I turned so I could suck Dante's cock. I alternated between the two of them, stroking one, sucking the other. Someone's fingers combed through my hair. Someone moaned. Knees shook, breaths caught, and oh, God, this was what I *lived* for.

I started to switch again, this time from Angel to Dante, but Dante stopped me with a gentle hand. I looked up.

"Stand up," he whispered. As soon as I did, he cradled my face in both hands and kissed me. Barely breaking the kiss, he said, "I want you to fuck me."

My knees buckled. Speech was lost on me and my useless lungs, so I just nodded.

Angel handed me a condom. While I put it on, he and Dante exchanged a long, passionate kiss, and I had to force myself not to watch them. It wasn't jealousy. Far from it. Quite simply, there were few things in this world hotter than watching those two men kiss.

And one of those few things was being inside Dante. When he climbed onto the bed and turned his back to me while I put lube on the condom, I thought I'd come unglued.

Steadying us with a hand on his hip and the other on my cock, I guided myself to him. I pretended not to notice the way his back arched before I'd even touched him. If he wanted this anywhere near as much as I did, we'd probably set the room on fire in no time flat.

I started to push into him slowly, but Dante was having none of it. Before I'd given him an inch, he rocked back against me, forcing me all the way inside him.

"Oh God," I said. I wanted to hold him against me and give myself a moment to get my wits about me. I wanted to start out slow, pace myself, give myself a chance to keep it together.

Dante, of course, had other plans. He moved back and forth, silently urging me to follow suit. Breathing as slowly and evenly as I could, I kept up with him, willing myself not to come even though he felt so damned good. If I'd learned one thing with them, though, it was how to hold back no matter how much I didn't want to, and as I fell into Dante's ever-changing rhythm, I stayed in control.

The sharp rip of tearing foil threw me off for a split second. I glanced to one side, and realized Angel was putting a condom on. When he reached for the bottle of lube, I had to clench my jaw and look away to keep it together. And of course, that meant looking right at Dante. Looking at his beautiful shoulders, narrow hips, and my cock sliding in and out of him at the precise speed he demanded. *Fuck.*

Closing my eyes, I took a few deep breaths. *Stay in control. Stay in control. Stay in control.*

Then the bed shifted slightly behind me. A hand rested on my hip. Then the other.

Oh, fucking hell.

Dante glanced back. He rocked against me, and once I was all the way inside him, he stopped, silently commanding me to do the same.

I held his hips and held my breath, knowing what was coming. Knowing I'd be coming in no time flat if they made this any hotter.

Cool lube met my skin. Then pressure. Then...oh Jesus.

Angel's cock slid deeper. Dante started moving, pulling away, pushing back, and my hips—God damn them—followed suit, and I was fucking Dante, and Angel was fucking me, and I had never experienced anything so intense. Dante set the rhythm. My body fell into synch. Angel found a rhythm of his own, and every thrust had me inching closer to insanity. My senses were evenly divided and equally overwhelmed between being inside Dante and having Angel inside me.

Then Angel's lips brushed my neck. "You're not going to come, are you, Jordan?"

I groaned with frustration. The reminder I couldn't come made it that much harder not to.

Dante moaned, pushing back against me.

"He sounds like he's about to come, doesn't he?" Angel murmured in my ear. Then he laughed, and his breath tickled below my ear as he whispered, "Of course he's about to come. You're doing to him the same thing I'm doing to you. He feels the same thing you do. Watch him. Watch yourself fuck him like I'm fucking you." I knew looking down would just make it that much harder to stay in control, but Angel told me to, so I did, and I forced my impending orgasm back, but Angel's breath on my shoulder and his cock inside me and oh, fuck, my cock moving in and out of Dante...

I could barely breathe. *Don't come. Don't come. Fuck him faster. No, no, slower. Don't come. Don't. Fucking. Come.*

I tried to think of anything but the orgasm I couldn't have, but Angel made sure it was at the forefront of my mind.

"Don't come, Jordan," he whispered, his own voice faltering with that telltale unsteadiness. "I know how much you like being fucked, and how much you like fucking him, but don't you dare come yet."

Deep breath. Deep breath. Deep inside Dante, deep inside me, deep breath. Deep. Breath.

"Please let me come," I said, holding on to Dante's hips for dear life.

"Not yet," Dante said over his shoulder, moving his hips just fast enough to drive me insane.

"I know you want to come in him," Angel whispered. "Just like I want...like I want to come...in you." His breath caught, and I thought he cursed. Then, "I know you want to, because I know how good he feels like this." He kissed the side of my neck. "Just like you feel right now."

"Fuck..." I moaned.

Angel moved faster. So did Dante. Whether or not I wanted to, so did I.

Deep inside Dante with Angel deep inside me, I was painfully close to letting go, but I didn't. I'd learned to ride this edge and could do it almost indefinitely. An orgasm was an orgasm, but when it followed their hard-earned permission, it was pure bliss.

I couldn't say how much time passed, but I knew I'd never ridden that edge for that long. I could come almost as easily from giving or receiving, but *not* coming from both at the same time? And with Angel whispering dirt in my ear? It wasn't possible. It couldn't be. But still I gritted my teeth and forced myself to last another second, another second, another second. *Do as you're told, wait for permission, wait for them, wait...*

"Like that?"

I struggled just to draw a breath, never mind speak.

"I asked you a question, Jordan."

I shivered. "Yes, I—"

Angel slammed into me harder, interrupting my attempt at speech. "Can't hear you, Jordan."

"Yes, I like it," I said quickly. "God, yes, I love it."

"That's what I thought." Then his breathing quickened. So did his thrusts. "Fuck, I'm getting close," he moaned in my ear. His fingers dug into my hips the way mine dug into Dante's. He gasped. "God damn it, you feel good..." He was right on the edge with me. Oh fuck, how was I supposed to hold back when he moaned like that, when he forced himself deeper like that, when he hit me inside *right* there, *right there...*

I groaned, pretending I could ignore the way my body demanded release.

"Oh, fuck..." Angel shuddered. "Holy..."

The helpless, nearly breathless sound he released was more than I could take, and thank God that was the same instant Dante whispered over his shoulder, "Come, Jordan."

I managed a single gasp, then forced myself all the way inside him. He kept moving, though, just like Angel kept fucking me right through his own orgasm, his rhythm falling apart while I fell apart, and I lost it and my whole world went white, and I had never experienced an orgasm so blindingly, painfully, amazingly *intense.*

Even when it tapered, when the splintered fragments of the universe started to fall back into place, I gripped Dante's hips with trembling hands, not sure if I'd ever come all the way down from this high, least of all far enough to be able to hold myself upright again.

Angel rested a hand on my hip and wrapped his other arm around my waist. He panted against the side of my neck, his breath cooling the sweat and making me shiver.

"I hope you don't think you're done yet," he slurred.

The words made my breath catch. I closed my eyes as he pulled out. Then I pulled out of Dante, and Angel's hand on my shoulder told me I wasn't getting up.

Dante turned around. He stroked his cock as he lay back on the pillow. With a single nod and a downward flick of his eyes, he gave the command, and I immediately obeyed. I took his cock as deep into my mouth as I could, then slowly pulled back. When I made rapid figure eights on the head of his cock with my tongue, he moaned, and my pulse jumped. Every sign of approval or arousal made my heart beat faster.

"That's right," he said, almost purring. "That's perfect, Jordan. Fucking amazing."

His cock twitched in my hand. I stroked faster, flicked my tongue faster, and Dante gasped. He started to say something, but his voice abruptly cut off, and I glanced up to see Angel kissing Dante. Dante ran his fingers through Angel's hair, the same way he did whenever he kissed me, and my scalp tingled with the ghost of his touch.

I sucked his cock with even more enthusiasm now. Dante moaned, the sound barely audible since his mouth was against Angel's. His hips lifted off the bed, squirmed, twisted, then his hand thumped beside him on the mattress, and Angel's kiss muffled a deep groan just before hot semen hit my tongue.

I sat back, licking my lips. Dante released Angel and pushed himself up, sliding a hand around the back of my neck and kissing me deeply. I wrapped my arms around him.

After a moment, he broke the kiss, and our eyes met. He smiled and leaned in closer. "I love you, Jordan."

"I love you too," I whispered. He kissed me again, and for a long moment, I just held on to him.

"Hey, now, let me get in on this," Angel said.

Dante and I laughed and broke our embrace. Angel kissed him, then put his arms around me and did the same.

We cleaned up, then collapsed into bed together, breathless and sweaty. I couldn't speak for them, but amidst the post-orgasmic bliss was the most profound sense of relief. I'd been wound tight and on edge for days, since well before my conversation with Dante, and now I finally felt somewhere close to human again. Almost. Some of the tension lingered in my chest, the uncertainty tugging at my gut.

Then Angel rested his hand on my chest. His fingers twitched a little, probably with the barely contained urge to tap and fidget. I laced my fingers between his, and they settled. After a moment, Dante laid his hand over ours, and that deep-down unsettled feeling of my own quieted just as Angel's hand had beneath mine. None of us moved. Even Angel was completely still now.

I looked down at our joined hands.

There was no guarantee this arrangement would result in anything but disaster and heartbreak. The only way I could have them was to chance losing them. Whether or not the odds were in my favor, it was impossible to say.

Dante's thumb traced a soft arc along the side of my hand. I did the same to Angel's. Lying here with them, all I could think was that Dante was absolutely right: this was worth the risk. I couldn't predict the future, but I was content with the present and what I stood to gain if it worked out. Yes, this was right.

Deal the cards. I'm ready to play.

Epilogue

A little over a year later.

My eyes fluttered open. The morning sun poured in through the bedroom window, but something was out of place.

I looked to one side, then the other. Jade was curled up on Angel's pillow. Cally was sprawled on Jordan's side. Both cats were out cold, but their respective owners were nowhere to be found.

Craning my neck, I glanced at the alarm clock. It wasn't quite seven. Chuckling to myself, I rubbed my tired eyes and sat up. There was only one thing that could get Angel out of bed this side of nine o'clock, so it was a safe bet I knew exactly where they were.

I got up and threw some clothes on, then left the cats to sleep in while I headed down to the barn. At the other end of the otherwise empty aisle, Sasha lay in front of a door. He raised his head, then jumped to his feet and bounded toward me.

"Hey, buddy," I said, keeping my voice down as I scratched his ears. "Where's your dad? Where is he?" He bounced up and down, looking at me as if to say, "Who cares about them? Just pet me." I laughed and kept walking, and Sasha's claws clicked on the cement as he fell into step beside me.

Quiet voices and rustling straw drew me to the last stall on the left. Just as I knew they would be, Angel and Jordan both sat cross-legged up against the wall, watching a tiny chestnut foal get the hang of its wobbly legs. The mare, Cassidy, kept an eye on her baby but didn't seem too concerned while she munched her hay in the corner.

I let myself into the stall. Behind me, Sasha's tags jingled, and he grunted as he dropped onto the concrete to wait for us to come back out.

The foal regarded me curiously. I came down almost to its eye level and held out my hand.

"Colt or..." I paused. It was too early in the morning for all the right terms to pop into my head without a little work. "Filly?"

"Colt," Jordan said.

The baby sniffed my hand. It never ceased to amaze me how tiny they were when they were first born. If Sasha were allowed in here, he'd have dwarfed the little horse by a long shot. After a moment, the colt lost interest in my hand and resumed trying to keep his spindly legs under him.

I found a fairly clean patch of straw and sat beside Angel. I rested my hand on his thigh and leaned in to kiss him lightly. "Morning."

"Morning," he murmured, stealing one last kiss before I pulled back.

Jordan looked past Angel at me. "What? I don't get a kiss?"

"You're too far away," I said, chuckling.

"I've got you covered," Angel said, and leaned to the side to kiss Jordan.

The foal wandered toward us, dividing his attention between these strange creatures lined up against the wall and the unsteady legs that were supposed to carry him around. When the baby got close enough to us, Angel petted his neck. The grin on his face made me laugh. He'd been thrilled every time he got to be around the babies, which had been a handful of times so far this season, but he'd been especially excited about this one. This would be *his* horse. He'd adored Cassidy, but Jordan wasn't about to give up his prized broodmare, so he'd promised Angel this year's foal.

And here he was.

I was working on finding a horse for myself too. There were several on the farm that I was comfortable riding, but I wanted one of my own. One that was already trained, not a baby, thank you very much, and Jordan had gotten a few leads on some mellow, well-mannered ones for sale in the area. As for this baby, Jordan and Angel were going to train him. Angel desperately wanted to get back into competition, so I had no doubt this little guy would see the inside of a show ring in the next few years. Me, I was content just to trail ride.

The baby wandered off again. Watching him figure out his legs was comical. It was hard to believe he'd one day have all the power and grace of the other horses in the barn. With time would come balance, confidence and the ability to sail over jumps, nail a dressage test, or whatever Angel asked him to do. For now, he was just lucky to stay upright.

After making a wobbly circle around the stall, the colt stopped in front of Jordan. He seemed focused on something. If his little brow could have furrowed with concentration, it would have, and he rocked back and forth for a second before his knees buckled. Then his back legs. In a motion that was anything but dignified, he flopped onto Jordan's lap. He stretched his neck, rested his head on Angel's leg, blinked a few times and closed his eyes.

Smiling, Jordan patted the baby's shoulder. "I wondered how long it would take you to wear yourself out, kiddo."

Moving carefully to avoid disturbing his horse, Angel pulled his camera strap over his neck and handed it to me. I didn't have to ask. Slowly and quietly, I got up and took a few steps back. While I took a few shots of the two of them with the snoozing baby, hot air whooshed past the side of my neck, and I jumped before I realized Cassidy's rather large nose was right next to my face.

I stroked her neck a few times, then gently pushed her nose away so I could take some more pictures. Of course, she walked right into my frame and wandered over to her baby. He opened his eyes and lifted his head, but then put it back on Angel's leg and fell asleep again. Evidently satisfied he wasn't in harm's way—and was out of her hair—Cassidy went back to her food.

For a while, I just watched Angel and Jordan fawn over the foal, and my mind wandered back to everything leading up to this morning.

The last year had been tricky. Settling into this relationship hadn't been easy. It would have been simpler if we'd all met at the same time, if Jordan had been there on that street in New Delhi thirteen years ago, but it couldn't be helped.

With some give and take, a hell of a lot of flexibility, and plenty of long, long "are we on the same page?" conversations, we'd gotten our legs under us and made it work.

Jordan had long ago evicted his jackass of an ex-boyfriend, and after Angel and I sold our house a few months ago, we'd moved in with him. The house was big enough for each of us to have some space, and being under the same roof instead of staying divided into "his" and "ours" made it easier for all of us to get on level ground. It made Jordan feel less like an outsider.

Our lives had blended, and so too had our careers, to an extent. When Angel had time, he worked some of the horses, and we both helped around the barn. It took some of the pressure off Jordan, having two extra pairs of hands. As a bonus, I'd never imagined Angel could get any hotter, but lifting hay bales and riding horses had done things to his already glorious physique that made my mouth water just thinking about them.

Angel and I had expanded fully into equine photography. God knew we had enough opportunity to build up a portfolio. Jordan had taken a shine to modeling, at least for artistic shots. One of Angel's photos of Jordan had won a silver medal in a prestigious competition late last year, and a black-and-white shot I'd taken of Jordan's bare shoulders would be gracing the cover of a magazine this winter. Of course, we kept this little bit of moonlighting on the down-low from his clients.

Rumors flew amongst our professional circles, and we'd all laughed behind closed doors at the way people whispered about us behind their hands. There was speculation about Jordan having affairs with either of us, and we found it endlessly entertaining to hear what horrified onlookers assumed about us. Oh, if they only knew.

In between moving, working and letting the dust settle, we'd even managed a vacation together. Jordan had never been to Asia, and Angel and I both had a case of wanderlust that couldn't be ignored. Watching the two of them play with the tigers in that temple in Thailand last fall had been almost as much fun as watching them now with the newborn foal.

We'd learned to balance work and play. We'd gotten the hang of what we'd thought would be impossible, and once the growing pains had eased, here we were, up with the sun as the farm's latest addition sprawled across the laps of the two men I loved. Yeah, it had been complicated, and it would always be complicated, but I wouldn't have traded any of this for the world.

"So, any thoughts about a name?" I asked.

Angel shrugged. "I was thinking 'hey you'."

Jordan laughed. "Oh, yeah, *that'll* work."

"It's what I'll be calling him anyway, so..." Angel shrugged again.

"He still needs a halfway decent name to put on his papers," Jordan said.

Angel eyed him. "And I still need a cup of coffee before I can think about such complicated matters."

I thought for a moment. "What about Rule of Thirds?"

Jordan furrowed his brow. "Rule of Thirds?"

"Yeah, remember?" Angel idly ran his fingers through the colt's thick coat. "Dividing a composition into vertical and horizontal thirds to create more interest." His eyes flicked toward me. "To create more tension."

Jordan smiled, glancing at me, then at Angel. "Oh, yeah, I do remember."

"What do you think?" Angel asked the colt, but it didn't seem to care. Angel chuckled and kept petting his horse. To Jordan, he said, "I like it, actually."

"Me too," Jordan said.

"But," Angel said, "final approval has to wait until we've had coffee."

"That's a damned good idea," I said.

"Amen." Jordan gestured at the horse sprawled across his lap. "Um, anyone else mind going up and putting the coffee on? I seem to be...tied up."

Angel grinned. "Not right now you're not."

Jordan rolled his eyes. "Weighed down, then?"

"I'll go up and get the coffee." I handed Angel his camera. "You two, um, wait here."

"I don't think we're going anywhere," Jordan said.

I gave them one last look, then left the stall. With Sasha at my heels, I headed back up to the house to get us all some much-needed coffee.

All the while, I smiled to myself. Angel finally had his horse. We'd all finally settled into being us. Day by day, things went smoother.

It hadn't been easy. It hadn't been simple. The future wouldn't be, either, but I was content with that.

I'd known from the beginning it wouldn't be easy. I also knew it would be worth it.

And I was right.

About the Author

L. A. Witt is an erotica writer who is said to be living in Okinawa, Japan, with her husband and two incredibly spoiled cats. There is some speculation that she is once again on the run from the Polynesian Mafia in the mountains of Bhutan, but she's also been sighted recently in the jungles of Brazil, on a beach in Spain, and in a back alley in Detroit with some shifty-eyed toaster salesmen. Though her whereabouts are unknown, it is known that she also writes hetero erotic romance under the pseudonym Lauren Gallagher.

Website: http://www.loriawitt.com
Blog: http://gallagherwitt.blogspot.com
Yahoo Group:
http://groups.yahoo.com/group/gallagherwitt/
Twitter: GallagherWitt

Tattoos fade with time. Emotions never lose their edge...

A.J.'s Angel
© 2011 L.A. Witt

Luke Emerson is the last person Sebastian Wakefield expects to see strolling into his tattoo shop. But Luke's not back after four years to take up where they left off. Not even to apologize for the cheating that broke them up.

Luke wants a custom tattoo, a memorial for someone known only as "A.J." Much as Seb would love to tell Luke to take this ink and shove it, he's a professional. Plus, he's reluctant to admit, he wouldn't mind getting his hands on Luke again. Even if it's just business.

Once Luke's in the tattoo chair, though, Seb finds himself struggling with all the anger and resentment he thought he'd left behind—and those aren't the only feelings reignited. Their relationship may have been turbulent, but it was also passionate. Four years clearly hasn't been long enough for the embers of that fire to go cold.

A few subtle hints from Luke is all it takes to make Seb consider indulging in some of that physical passion. It shouldn't be that tough to keep his emotions from getting tangled up in sweaty sheets.

After all, it's not like he's in love with Luke anymore. Right?

Warning: Contains two exes who shouldn't want each other like this, steamy ex-sex they shouldn't be having, and a whole lot of ink.

Available now in ebook from Samhain Publishing.

The bigger they are, the harder they fall...in love.

Muscling Through
© 2011 JL Merrow

Cambridge art professor Larry Morton takes one, alcohol-glazed look at the huge, tattooed man looming in a dark alley and assumes he's done for. Moments later he finds himself disarmed—literally and figuratively. And, the next morning, he can't rest until he offers an apology to the man who turned out to be more gentle than giant.

Larry's intrigued to find there's more to Al Fletcher than meets the eye; he possesses a natural artistic talent that shines through untutored technique. Unfortunately, no one else seems to see the sensitive soul beneath Al's imposing, scarred, undeniably sexy exterior. Least of all Larry's class-conscious family, who would like nothing better than to split up this mismatched pair.

Is it physical? Oh, yes, it's deliciously physical, and so much more—which makes Larry's next task so daunting. Not just convincing his colleagues, friends and family that their relationship is more than skin deep. It's convincing Al.

Warning: Contains comic misunderstandings, misuse of art materials, and unexpected poignancy.

Available now in ebook from Samhain Publishing.

www.samhainpublishing.com

Green for the planet.
Great for your wallet.

It's all about the story...

Romance

HORROR

www.samhainpublishing.com

CPSIA information can be obtained at www.ICGtesting.com
Printed in the USA
BVOW042145130612

292550BV00010B/1/P